PAINE

ROSEWOOD HIGH #2

TRACY LORRAINE

Editing by My Brother's Editor

Proofread by Pinpoint Editing

Cover by Dandelion Cover Designs

Andy & Amelia

1

CAMILA

"What the hell are you doing?" I scream, running toward where Mason has Noah pinned to the floor. There's blood streaming from his nose and a split in his lip, but the most striking thing is that he's not trying to fight back. He's just taking it.

"Motherfucker," Mason growls, his voice is so low and menacing that a shiver races down my spine.

What the hell has gotten into him?

Reaching out, I place my hand on his forearm right before he's about to throw another punch into Noah's broken face.

"Stop," I shout. "Mason. Stop, please," I beg, my voice cracking.

My contact is obviously what Mason needs to bring him out of his trance. He lifts his eyes to find me. The darkness in them makes my breath catch. If I didn't know better, I'd think he wanted Noah dead. But that's not the Mason I know. Well... the Mason I knew. But it seems the boy from the end of the street is long gone these days.

"What the hell are you doing?"

He stares down at Noah a few seconds longer before allowing Jake to pull him up and away.

"I—" He looks up at me and I swear I see pain pouring from his eyes. "He was kissing that skank." His voice is low, so only I can hear as he tips his chin in the direction of Tasha, a member of the cheer squad. Her eyes are wide and she's as white as a sheet, but then so is everyone else as they stare at the scene unfolding in front of them.

"What the fuck is your problem? Not satisfied making me an outcast, now you've got to get involved and ruin my relationship too?"

"No. He was... they were in the bathroom together."

My heart pounds in my chest. He wouldn't, would he? Noah loves me, that I'm sure of. This is a joke. Mason's had too much to drink and has decided to throw his weight around, show me who's boss.

A low moan comes from Noah, and it drags me from my fog. Why am I focusing on Mason right now when my boyfriend is groaning in pain from being on the wrong end of his fists?

"Get him out of here," I bark at Jake, who immediately jumps into action. Amalie looks between the two of us, not knowing which way to go. "It's fine. Go with him. I'm just going to get Noah cleaned up and put him to bed. Everyone out," I shout, knowing that our entire class is currently watching this play out in front of their eyes.

Dropping to my knees, I place my hand on Noah's warm chest. His eyes flicker open and a small smile twitches at his lips.

Some movement to my left catches my eye, and, when I look up, I find everyone still standing there.

"Get the hell out," I scream. That, along with Alyssa

and a couple of other friends starting to usher people from the room, seems to get them moving at last.

My hands tremble as I stare down at my broken and bloodied boyfriend.

"Are you okay?" I whisper.

"Yeah, never been better," he grunts.

"Can you get up? We'll go and get you cleaned up."

"Yeah, I'm good. He didn't hit that hard."

I don't point out that the state of his face right now doesn't confirm his story.

With his arm around my waist, I lead his limp body toward the stairs as the movement of people leaving sound out around us.

No one comes to help, which kind of pisses me off, but I understand that they probably don't want to get in the middle.

"Sit," I instruct when we make it to Noah's bed. "I'll be back in a few minutes. Don't go anywhere."

I walk past his adjoining bathroom, knowing I won't find anything I need, and instead go to the main bathroom.

With a first aid box in hand, I head back toward Noah.

I come to a stop in his doorway and take him in. He's pulled his shirt off and is laid back on his bed. Blood and darkening bruises color his cheeks.

Noah's been my rock. We'd never really had much to do with each other despite being in the same classes for years, but we found each other when I was at my lowest, thanks to my inability to use a computer competently.

We were supposed to be making spreadsheets, but me and numbers aren't a match made in heaven and I was on the verge of throwing the mouse across the room when he offered his help. Grateful didn't even come close to expressing how I felt as he explained how the formulas worked in such a simple way that I couldn't not understand while our teacher focused on Mason and his gang of jocks, ignoring the rest of us.

Anger burned in my belly and I glanced over my shoulder at the special attention they got just because of their position in the school. It was just another reminder of why things turned out the way they were meant to be. Girls like me were never destined to be friends with guys like him. I guess it's just a good thing I discovered that before my heart got in even deeper. We may have been young, but I'm not naïve enough to ignore that fact that I gave part of my heart to Mason Paine long before I even knew it was a thing.

Noah's eyes flutter open like he can feel me standing there. Even with all of the swelling, I can see love in them.

Mason's lying. Noah would never do that to me. Especially not tonight.

"Babe?"

"Sorry," I say, forcing myself from my musings and walking toward him. Perching myself on the edge of his bed, I dip a washcloth into the bowl of warm water and start to clean up his face.

He winces in pain as I gently dab at the corner of his lips.

"I didn't—"

"I know."

I trust Noah with my life. He's been nothing but the perfect boyfriend since he asked me to homecoming a few weeks after that class. Another boy had consumed all my time and thoughts up until that point, and I had no idea that anyone else existed or might have been interested. He totally swept me off my feet, and I haven't had a moment of regret since.

At the beginning, I missed Mason. I was desperate to know what he thought about Noah. I was just so used to talking to him about everything, but Noah soon showed me that I didn't need Mason the way I always thought it did. I had the sweetest new boyfriend and my best friend in Alyssa. I didn't need the boy who turned his back on me when things didn't go his way.

I work in silence, cleaning up Noah's poor face.

"Where do your parents keep the painkillers?"

He tells me where to go, and, after disposing of the bloodied washcloth, I go in search of something that might help him sleep.

When I get downstairs, Alyssa, Lisa, Wyatt, and Shane are all busy tidying up the mess the rest of our class abandoned on their way out.

"Thank you so much," I say, walking into the kitchen.

"You're welcome. Is he okay?" Alyssa asks, concern shining from her eyes.

"Yeah, he'll be fine."

"What did he do to deserve that? Mason totally flew off the handle. I've never seen him like that, even on the field," Shane says. He knows Mason the best out of any of us these days, seeing as he's on the football team with the douchebags. Fuck knows why, he's nothing like any of them and actually a good guy. Things have been weird for him at school since he was accused of drugging Amalie and having the shit kicked out of him by Jake for it. He's kept his head down and avoided everyone—aside from this party, seeing as Noah's his best friend. I can still see the dark shadows that night left behind in his eyes, but he made the effort tonight. I know he's innocent, Noah too, but that doesn't mean anyone else at school agrees. Jake Thorn pinned him as guilty, so that's what he'll be unless someone's able to prove otherwise.

"Fuck knows. Mason is probably just trying to make my life harder than necessary; it seems to be his thing these days," I mutter.

"What actually happened between you two?"

"Nothing. It's nothing." It's the same excuse I've given ever since shit went down between our families. I have no desire to live through it again, and I can't see things ever going back to how they once were between us.

"You guys can get out of here if you want. I'll finish up."

"Really?" Alyssa asks, looking concerned.

"Yeah. I don't want to give him the satisfaction of ruining everyone's night. Go to Aces or something."

"As long as you're sure."

The three of them finish off what they're doing before saying goodbye and heading out.

Noah's parents wisely booked themselves into a hotel for the night, so I've got plenty of time to get the place back to normal before they get home—not that it's too bad. The party hadn't really had a chance to get going before Mason ruined it. So much for Noah's eighteenth birthday being his best ever.

I throw a few more cups into the trash before grabbing a box of Advil and going back up to Noah.

He's out cold when I walk into his bedroom. Even with just the moonlight illuminating his face, I can see that the swelling has only gotten worse and the bruising darker. He's even got a purple patch emerging on his ribs.

Mason really did a fucking number on him. My fists curl at my sides in anger. How dare he put his hands on

Noah? It's like he's intent on ruining everything about my life. I'm surprised he wasn't more onboard with pushing Amalie out of town before Jake realized he was in love with her. Getting rid of someone who's fast become my best friend is just something I can imagine he'd do to piss me off.

Placing the glass of water and painkillers on the dresser, I walk over to pull the curtain.

"Come here," Noah says, barely managing to hold his hand out for me.

"I don't want to hurt you."

"You won't."

After slipping my shoes off, I climb into his bed beside him, fully dressed. This wasn't exactly how I planned on spending his birthday night.

His arm wraps around my waist and he pulls me back against his chest. I don't miss his sharp intake of breath as he does.

"I'm so sorry, Noah."

"Hey, none of this was your fault."

His soft lips press against my shoulder before he drops his head to the pillow and falls back to sleep.

2

MASON

My entire body vibrates with anger as Jake leads me away from that motherfucker's house.

I didn't particularly want to be there in the first place, but Amalie had convinced me seeing as it was her and Jake's first appearance as an official couple. I knew I should have worked the fucking shift I was offered instead of showing my face in there.

Almost our entire class was in his house and almost every set of eyes watched as I pulled his sorry, cheating ass from the bathroom and slammed my fist into his face.

I only went for a piss. The last thing I was expecting was to find him with his tongue down Tasha's fucking throat. I expected it of her, she's one of Chelsea's little crew. But Noah? He might be a total computer nerd I'd happily never look at again, but I thought he was faithful.

If I thought I disliked him before, then I fucking hate him now.

In hindsight, I probably shouldn't have defended her. It was what she fucking deserved after everything, but still, my need to end him for betraying her got the better of me.

I flex my fingers as Ethan drives away from the scene of the crime.

"Where to, ladies?"

"Just take me fucking home. I'm done with tonight."

"But I've got the goods at my place."

"He said home," Jake barks from the backseat, managing to come up for air from devouring Amalie.

"I know you two are in love and shit, but is that necessary?"

"Wow, she really does turn you into a crazy man, huh?" Ethan muses.

"I've got plenty of fight left in me if you want a pop, Savage."

"Nah, man. I was just saying."

"Well, fucking don't."

"You'll understand when you meet her," Jake pipes up.

"Her? Who's her? Camila?"

"No, not Camila, dickwad. I mean *her*. The one."

"Fuck off. You have full permission to shoot my ass if it ever looks like I'm gonna hand my balls over to a chick. They're mine, thank you very much."

"Aw, it's not that bad. Amalie takes very good care of my— ow," he complains after the sound of a slap rings through the car. "Once you find her, my friend, everything changes. Right, Mase?"

"No fucking clue what you're talking about," I grunt, already over this fucking conversation.

"Riiight. Of course not. I forgot. You hate her."

My teeth grind. He's baiting me to admit that I've got feelings for Camila, but he's going to have to try harder than that because anything I felt for her died the moment my life fell apart.

Turning to stare at the sea as Ethan heads back to my side of town, I ignore whatever else is said. The only thing I can see and hear is that motherfucker as I pulled him away from the trailer trash and he started trying to defend himself.

I'm not sure I've ever been so fucking angry. And for what? Her?

The tension in the car is heavy. They all pretend they know how I'm feeling, but none of them have a fucking clue. Even Jake doesn't know the whole story.

I grunt some kind of a thank you before slamming the car door. My eyes catch Amalie's in the backseat now that Jake's released her, and I see a million questions in her eyes. She's desperate to fix this thing between me and Camila, but she has no idea what she's dealing with.

I once thought I'd spend my life with Camila, just like our mothers plotted from the day we were born, but the reality of the situation is very much different.

The car idles behind me. If they think I'm going to change my mind, then they've got another thing coming.

The house is silent as I walk down the hallway aside from the quiet sound coming from the TV in the living room.

"Hey, Diane. You can head off if you'd like," I say when I round the corner and find my brothers' babysitter curled into the corner of the couch.

"You're back early. Everything okay?"

I keep my aching fists behind my back. I don't need our next door neighbor prying. It's bad enough I have to rely on her to look after Charlie and Ollie so that I can attempt to have something of a normal life. "Yeah, I just wasn't really feeling it tonight."

"That's a shame. You deserve to let your hair down every now and then."

Don't I fucking know it. "There will be plenty more parties," I mutter.

"Ah, I remember it well. Senior year was the best year of my life. No commitments, no worries. Shit, sorry." She winces as she realizes her mistake.

"It is what it is. Thank you so much." I pull some money from my wallet and hand it over.

"Mason, how many times do I have to tell you. You don't need to pay me. I'm happy just to help out."

"I take up too much of your time as it is. You should be at home with your own family, not babysitting mine. Use it to take your kids out or to buy them something nice."

I could take her up on her offer of free childcare but then that would make me just as bad as my mother, and I refuse to be that person who takes everything and everyone for granted.

"Did the boys both go to bed okay?"

"Yeah. Charlie was complaining of a tummy ache, but he was acting fine."

I thank her again and see her out.

Spinning back into the home I've lived in since birth, I hate it just that little bit more.

My bloody fists catch my eye, and I head to the kitchen to clean them up and inspect the damage. Coach is going to have my balls at practice on Monday when he sees I've been fighting. Football is my only escape, and I hope it's my way into college, but I'm also very aware that it's the first thing that might have to give if things get tougher. If Mom can't find a better job, or at least more hours, then it means that I'm going to have to start picking up more of the slack, and finding a job that's flexible around school and games isn't easy to come by.

I just want to be a fucking kid and enjoy senior year while I still have a chance. Is that too much to ask?

I wince as the warm water runs over my knuckles, sending the blood spiraling down the drain. It pretty much sums up my life.

I shouldn't have hit him, I tell myself again. I should have left him there and allowed Camila to find him. She deserves a little bit of the pain I go through every day because of her fucking family.

She walks around like she doesn't have a care in the world, not giving two shits about the mess they left behind just down the street. We might still be living in this house, just, but the people who are left inside are far from the people she knew.

Turning off the water, I rest my palms down on the counter and stare out at the garden. The garden my dad used to spend his evenings and weekends maintaining when he wasn't out helping me train for my next game.

Now, it's overgrown, uncared for and totally unruly. He'd hate it—if he ever bothered to come back and see his kids, that is.

Burning anger fills my veins and I push it away, not wanting or needing the reminder of him.

Taking the stairs two at a time, I quickly check that my brothers are both sleeping soundly in their rooms before ripping off my shirt over my head and dropping it to the floor. I find a bottle of Jack I'd hidden at the back of my closet and twist the top off before falling down onto my bed. Lifting it to my lips, I shudder as it burns down my throat. I hardly ever drink, so it hits me pretty quickly. I'm usually stronger than this and focus on my responsibility, but tonight I need it gone. I need the memories and what could have been out of my head.

My room is bathed in darkness. Not even the light from the moon shines in with the curtains that are permanently closed. If I open them, all I can see is her house, into her room. It used to be great. Everything used to be great.

Darkness consumes me and images of her standing in her bedroom window fade away.

The next thing I know, my eyes flutter open and a blinding light sends a piercing pain through my head.

Motherfucker.

"Mason." A little voice filters through the alcohol haze surrounding me. "Charlie's been sick. He's really upset."

"Fuck." Sitting bolt upright in bed, my head spins and my own stomach turns over. Lifting my arm, I find my fingers still wrapped around the now empty bottle.

"Isn't Mom home?" My voice is slurred even to my own ears.

"I don't think so. Can you help me clean him up?"

"Of course, dude. Lead the way."

Case in point as to why I don't drink.

The desire to drop to my knees and crawl into Charlie's room is high, but somehow I manage to keep upright with a lot of help from the wall.

Charlie's sobbing hits my ears long before we enter his room. That along with the stench is enough to sober me up a little.

He needs me, and I need to not be a total fuck-up right now.

I dry heave as I step into the room and get a sight of the mess he's made.

"It's okay, buddy. We'll get this cleaned up and you'll be as good as new."

"I'm so sorry," he wails.

"It's not your fault. You don't need to be upset."

"You can come sleep in my bed, Charlie."

My head spins and I fight to keep the contents of my own stomach down as I begin stripping his bed, but my heart swells in my chest for these two boys. Neither of them asked for their life to be like this, to have to spend so much time looking after themselves and each other, but there's only so much I can do without totally ruining my own life and future in the process.

After throwing all of Charlie's dirty sheets into the washer, I head back up to make sure they're okay. I find them both curled up in Oliver's bed, fast asleep.

A smile twitches at my lips as I stare down at them. They might cause me more stress than most seniors are forced to endure, but I couldn't imagine my life without them. I'm pretty sure I owe them both everything, because without them, I know I could have lost myself pretty easily over the past few years.

3

CAMILA

"He said Noah was kissing Tasha?"

"Yep, apparently so," I say to Amalie over a milkshake the next morning after leaving Noah to deal with his parents.

"And you don't believe him?"

"No, not one word of it. This is Noah we're talking about. He's never been anything but totally loyal, faithful, and honest."

"I know but—"

"There are no buts, Ami. Mason hates me. It's not the first time he's done something just to hurt me for breathing the same air as him."

"Mason? Mason Paine?"

"Yes." I sigh, getting pissed off with her opinions on this situation.

"But he's always been so sweet to me."

"Yeah, well, you didn't 'ruin his life' or whatever shit he spouts at me for the reason behind his douchebagness."

"That's not a word."

I quirk an eyebrow. "Do I look like I care? I just want to forget all about this and move on. He totally fucked with my plan for last night. I need a new one."

"So, you and Noah didn't get it on after he was accused of cheating and beaten within an inch of his life?"

"Do you have to find this all so amusing?"

She does have the decency to look slightly regretful. "I'm sorry, it's just that I'm glad this kind of drama isn't directed at me. It's nice to see someone else with boy issues."

"I don't have boy issues. Noah is my boyfriend and Mason is..."

"Mason is..."

"No one. He's no one and needs to back the fuck off."

"You ever going to tell me what happened?"

"He just blames me for how his life turned out."

"That's all you're giving me?"

"Sure is. You want more, ask him."

She wraps her lips around the straw sticking up from her milkshake as she thinks. I know she's desperate to learn more about what happened, but I really just want to forget about the whole thing and that Mason Paine even exists. It's bad enough I've got to walk past his house every day and stare at his bedroom window every time I open my damn curtains. I don't need him to be the focus of my every conversation today.

"Have you even asked Noah about it?"

"Of course."

"And?"

"And he said he loves me and that I'm the only girl for him."

"Convenient."

"What do you have against Noah all of a sudden? You seem to be suggesting that he's guilty here."

"I have nothing against him, Cami. I'm just intrigued. Mason doesn't strike me as the kind of guy who starts fights for no reason."

"No offense, Amalie, but you don't really know him. You've only met the Mason who'll do anything for his best friend. To be honest, they're about as fucked up as each other." Her mouth opens in an attempt to fight for her boyfriend, but I cut her off. "Don't you even think about trying to defend him. Some of the shit he did to you should have been unforgivable."

"Can't help who you fall in love with, Camila."

"Christ, you sound like your gran," I mutter, reaching for my own milkshake. "I know that, and I'm not criticizing you for it. It's just... Mason is part of my past. Do I miss the sweet boy from down the street? Some days. But life has turned him into an asshole, and my life is better off without that kind of drama in it."

"Okay. I'll drop it." I don't believe a word of it. Her eyes are still assessing me like she can see something I'm not aware of.

"Good, because Noah's been so good to me. The perfect boyfriend. He's the one for me."

Her eyes hold so much, but thankfully she keeps her mouth shut. I don't need to spend the rest of the morning rehashing this.

"What's going on with Jake's mom? She still around?" I ask, desperately needing to change the subject.

"Sadly. Jake's refusing point-blank to talk to her, hoping that she'll up and leave again, but it doesn't seem to be working."

"You think she's serious about fixing everything she fucked up?"

"I have no idea, honestly. I think too much damage has been done. Jake's never going to give her the time of day."

"Understandable." Silence descends around us as we slurp our milkshakes. "So... how's the college search coming?"

"I'm still trying to convince Jake to come and have a look around Florida U and Maddison with me but—"

"Whoa, hold the phone. You're going to college together?"

"No decisions have been made. He just promised me he'd look into it. I found his grades stuffed at the back of one of his drawers in his bedroom. Any college would be stupid not to let him in. Plus, he's got the obvious bonus of being a fucking awesome quarterback."

"Aw, look at you getting all involved in the game. I'm so proud of you," I say with a laugh. It took enough convincing when she first got here to even see a game, let alone understand it enough to know just how talented Jake is.

"Shut up. Anyway, Maddison has potential courses for both of us, so if we did decide to go together then we could. That's still a long way off though, and I don't want to freak him out too much. He still doesn't think he has a shot at a scholarship or being accepted."

"That's crazy."

"That's what I keep saying. Plus, he could defer a year if he wants, get a job, save some money, and we could start together."

She might think the idea of going together hasn't been made yet, but the way she's talking, I think it's kinda set in stone. I'm happy for her. She had her life turned upside down but somehow, she's managed to create something pretty fantastic here, not to mention snagging Rosewood's most eligible bachelor. I never thought I'd see the day that Jake Thorn handed his balls over to a woman, but Hell must have frozen over because he is seriously whipped by my new best friend.

"What about you? Noah still want to go to Virginia?"

"Yep," I say sadly. "I still have no idea, really. I've applied for a bunch of places, but the idea of moving across the country scares the crap out of me."

"You'll figure it out."

"I guess." I shrug, feeling the pressure landing on my shoulders. Everything at the moment seems to be about college. It's all everyone is talking about, no one more so than my parents, and I don't know what to tell them. I want to go to college, of course I do, but I have no idea what I want to do with my future. English is my thing. I love reading, writing reports, that kind of stuff, but do I want to do it for a job for the rest of my life? I have no idea. The decision seems so huge and I don't feel at all prepared to make one yet.

I drop Amalie back home after our little morning rehash of the night before and our possible futures.

"Morning, sweetheart. Good night?" Mom asks as I head for the kitchen for a glass of water.

"Uh... yeah," I lie. It was entirely *not* what I was expecting, not to mention that I'd planned last night to be *the* night with Noah, and here I am, still a virgin.

"That's good. I'm glad you had fun." She gives me a kiss on the cheek as she passes and heads for her home office. Mom's job is being a social butterfly. If there's an event running in Rosewood, you can bet she's had a hand in it. Dad had a promotion a few years ago that allowed her to give up her job and focus on what she loves: party planning. It's great knowing she's enjoying herself, even if it does mean they're almost always out of the house, attending events.

"I'll be up in my room if you need me."

Pulling a packet of chips from the cupboard, I take them and my water up to my room. I turn my speakers on and stop in front of the window.

As always, his curtains are shut. It makes me sad to think that his room must always be as dark as his heart's turning out to be. He was so much fun as a kid. I have so many memories of bouncing out of bed and running down the street to find out what trouble we were going to get into that day.

But that's all it is now: memories. That Mason is long gone. In his place is someone I'd rather forget.

He's angry.

Cold.

Cruel.

4

MASON

"You've got to be fucking shitting me." Walking into school Monday morning, the first thing I see is them. Together. Like nothing fucking happened.

Noah's got her pressed up against the lockers and is staring down at her like she's the most precious thing in the world.

She looks up at him in a way I remember all too well, and it makes my blood boil.

He was kissing someone else while she was mere feet away. What the fuck is wrong with her?

"Just leave it," Jake says, noticing the tension that must be radiating off me.

"But he—"

"I thought you hated her. Why do you care if she's not dumped his cheating ass?"

"I do hate her. I'm just shocked, is all."

"Really?" he asks, a knowing twinkle in his eye.

"Yes. Now stop looking at me like that."

"Fine. Fine." He wants to say more, I can sense it, but

thankfully Amalie appears out of nowhere and cuddles into his side.

His hands immediately wrap around her waist and his lips go to hers. I'm happy for them, even happier that he's stopped being such an asshole.

I let out a sigh as I watch them. Something twists my stomach, watching how close and easy they are with each other. I haven't made a secret of the fact that I want that. The guys all think I'm crazy, although Jake should have a better understanding now he's been whipped by Amalie.

"You okay?" she mouths, placing her hand on my forearm and dragging my eyes away from the car crash happening in front of me.

"Never better," I mutter, grabbing a couple of books from my own locker and slamming the door as I head out toward our benches.

Chelsea and a few of her girls are already there. She immediately gets up when she sees me walking her way, but it's not her I'm interested in.

"Tasha," I greet, a wide fake-ass smile on my face. "Enjoy the party on Saturday night?" All the blood drains from her face.

She knows what she was doing in that bathroom. So do I, and so does Noah.

Wrapping my hand around the back of her neck, I pull until she has no choice but to stand. She shudders against me as I drop my mouth to her ear. To anyone else, it might look intimate as I dig my fingers into her waist.

"Didn't have you down as a geek lover. I thought you all only went for jocks."

"I, uh…" Her voice quivers, and I can't help the smile that tugs at my lips. "I was drunk."

"Sure you were."

When I pull back, I find exactly what I was expecting: Noah looking this way from his spot by the lockers. He's far enough away that no one around him would think anything of it. But I know.

The second our eyes meet, he looks away.

You're going down, motherfucker.

"Mason, please don't—"

"Tell anyone? Oh, Tash, you're going to regret that."

She's a good head shorter than me, and as she stares up at me with panic in her eyes, they fill with tears.

"Play with fire and you will get burned."

My hand lifts to her chin and I crash my lips to hers. I know he's watching, and I need to make this as painful for him as possible. I hold still for a second before I drop her as I step away. She stumbles backward and lands awkwardly on the bench. Her friends are too distracted by the rest of the team who've descended to notice her.

Running my eyes over each of them, I shake my head. Ethan's got Shelly on his lap, his hands tucked up the back of her tank. The other guys either have one or multiple girls' attention, and I wonder what it must be like for your only concern to be about which cheerleader you want to bang. It's no secret that I've spent private time with more than one of them in the past, but it was only to blow off steam when things got a little too much.

Backing away from the group, I look to where Noah was only a few seconds ago, but their group has dispersed, leaving only one behind.

I move toward her without really thinking about it.

"What the—" she squeaks, trying to free her wrist from my grip, but I'm stronger. Much stronger.

I drag her along with me until we reach the girls' bathroom.

"Mason, what the hell are you doing?"

"Out," I bark at a handful of students. Some I recognize and some I don't, but all scramble for the door. One benefit of being on the team and Jake Thorn's best friend is that if I say jump around here, students immediately ask how high.

Pulling Camila in front of me, I run my eyes down her body. She's hot. There's no denying that. Her curves were designed for a man, not that fucking pussy.

My fists clench as I think about him having his hands on her body. A body that should have been mine to take, if her family didn't fuck everything up.

Her chest heaves, keeping my attention on her larger than average tits. My mouth waters and I take a step toward her. She has no choice but to take a step back, making her hit the tiled wall with a thud.

Resting my forearms on either side of her head, I stare down at her, taking in her gold flecked brown eyes that plead with me to let her go.

"Mason, please," she begs.

It never used to be like this. I'd have given my life for this girl in a heartbeat. But then she had a hand in ruining my life and everything changed.

"You think Tasha begged on Saturday night?" Her eyes flash with disbelief. "How much effort do you think she had to put in to get Noah to put his lips on her?"

"Stop," she demands, her tiny hands coming up to push on my chest. Nice try. I might be one of the slimmer guys on the team, but I still have at least fifty pounds on her tiny body and a fuck load more muscle. She's got no chance in making me go anywhere.

"Do you think he used the same moves he uses on you?" She swallows as I reach out and take a lock of her dark hair between my fingers. "I've watched the two of you. This is his move, right? He grabs a piece of your hair and you melt into him. Do you think it worked on her?"

She wants to fight. Her body is practically trembling with the need to scream at me right now, but for some reason, while she's locked in my stare and surrounded by me, she's frozen.

Dropping my head slightly, I hover only a centimeter or two from her. Her increased breaths race past her parted lips.

"Looks like he's not the only one who'd willingly stray. Get your head on straight, Lopez. Do you even love him?"

Taking a step back, I put some space between us.

"Fuck you," she spits, able to speak now that she's not cornered. "You have no right to drag me in here and ask me that. You made your choice years ago and walked out of my life. You don't get to keep dropping back in when it suits you."

Her words are rushed, her eyes flitting around the room trying to figure out what to do and how to get away from me. Her uncertainty only fires me up more. That is until the door opens, and someone joins us.

"What the hell is going on?" Amalie asks, looking between the two of us.

"We were just having a little heart to heart. Nothing to worry about." With one final look at Camila, I walk out of the girls' bathroom. Principal Hartmann is right outside, but if he's at all bothered about watching me leave, he doesn't show it.

I'm late to class, but after an apology and what I've discovered is a panty melting smile, even to fully grown women, the teacher waves it off and I take my seat between Jake and Ethan at the back of the room.

"Where the hell did you go?" Ethan whisper-shouts, but I don't get a chance to reply because Camila comes rushing into class.

"A problem getting out of bed this morning, Miss Lopez?" Mrs. Peterson asks, her brows drawn together in frustration.

A smirk curls my lips. She didn't even bat an eyelid at my tardiness.

"I'm so sorry, I had to use the bathroom." Camila's cheeks flush and I sit back to enjoy the show. Her eyes briefly flick to me before she focuses back on Mrs. Peterson once again.

"What the fuck did you do?" Jake asks.

"Me?" I lift my hand to my heart as if just the suggestion that I had something to do with this wounds me.

"You might act all sweet, but I know you, Mase. I know the deal between the two of you. Back off her."

"Oh, that's rich." I laugh.

"Listen to some of your own advice. You remember telling me to leave Brit alone?"

"Different situation."

"Is it?"

"Yeah. Amalie was innocent. Camila ruined my life."

He lets out a frustrated breath but doesn't say any more. He should know it would be pointless.

5

CAMILA

His eyes burn into me as I try to defend the fact that I was late to class. I didn't really think Mrs. Peterson would be too bothered; it's not like I show up late often. I'm a good student. I do my work, keep my grades up and contribute to school life however I can. Just because I'm not part of a sports team shouldn't mean I get treated differently. If I were Chelsea, or Tasha, right now I'd already be sitting down and getting on with my work.

Eventually, Mrs. Peterson puts an end to me being the sole focus of her class and allows me to find my seat. Unfortunately, said seat is right in front of Mason. I'm always aware that he's there. His hate filled stares aren't new to me. But something's different today. There's more to his attention, and it has something tingling right under my skin.

I chalk it up to the way he made me feel as he pinned me to the wall in the bathroom. He was angry. He always is these days, so that's not exactly a surprise, but there was a heat in his eyes that I haven't witnessed before.

He was enjoying himself as he threw Tasha in my face. He can do that as much as he likes; my loyalties lie with my boyfriend, who thankfully isn't in this class. The last thing I need is a pissing contest between the two of them. I think we all know who'd win that anyway. The football god everyone loves verses the IT geek. Yeah, there's only ever one winner in that situation.

I try to focus on what we should be doing, but my mind keeps taking me back to the bathroom. The heat in his eyes keeps my temperature higher than it should be, and the memory of how close his body and lips were has butterflies fluttering in my belly.

It's so wrong.

He's gone out of his way over the past four years to prove how much he hates me. He totally ignored me to start with, and although it was excruciating at the time to go from having my best friend by my side to nothing, it was easier than what was to follow. He's put me down and belittled me at any opportunity. Yet as he lowered his head, I swear he was just a second away from kissing me.

Did I want him to?

There's the million-dollar question.

In that moment, closing my eyes and letting him sweep me away would have been so easy. My body was begging for it, my fingers pressed up against his chest and begging to grip on to the fabric of his jersey and pull him in the last little bit.

Lifting my fingers to my lips, I allow my mind to wander back to a time in my life I've tried to forget.

My first kiss.

I was fourteen. I'd missed curfew and was getting a roasting from my parents for disregarding their rules. I'd been with Mason, just hanging out in his garden, and we'd totally lost track of time before he walked me home.

He must have heard them shouting at me for being irresponsible and making them worry, because when I made it up to my room with tears streaming down my face, there he was.

I had no idea how he got in, but when he opened his arms for me all I could do was to run at him.

He was my safe place. My sanctuary when things weren't going right.

I had a good life. My parents loved me and gave me everything I needed, but as their only child, they could be a little overprotective.

Mason was my release from the pressure they put on me.

My tears soaked into the fabric of his jersey. He was tall, even then, so my head rested against his chest. I felt so safe in his arms, like nothing or nobody could touch me. Our friendship had been solid for as long as I could remember. We'd never argued or fallen out. I always thought I was so lucky when I used to see others at school falling out with their best friends. I truly believed that would never be us. When I was brave enough and lifted my head from his chest, he stared down at me with such love and adoration it made my breath catch.

"Mason," I whispered.

"Shhh." He lifted his hand and stroked the backs of his knuckles down my cheek. Right there and then was the moment I fell head over heels for my best friend.

He lowered his head and his lips pressed against mine. It was the single most perfect moment of my life.

We stayed still for a few seconds before his tongue snuck out and teased the seam of my lips. My heart was thundering in my chest. I'd talked about kissing a boy with my girlfriends time and time again. I'd imagined what it might be like, how nervous I'd be when it happened, but standing there wrapped in his arms, reaching up on my tiptoes, there were no nerves. It was just so... right.

I opened my lips and his tongue hesitantly slipped past them until he found mine. I knew this was his first time as well. We'd talked about it before, but I never expected to experience our firsts together. It was everything and more that I'd ever hoped it would be. Until it was over.

"Dinner," Mom called from the bottom of the stairs, and we jumped apart as if we'd been caught.

His chest was heaving, his eyes dark and hooded. I knew he was turned on. I knew about sex, but I was still naive enough to be shocked by it.

It was the perfect time and one I've wished to go back to many, many times over the past four years so I could ensure what happened next turned out differently.

I was still feeling out of sorts when I got down to the dinner table. My parents looked stressed, more so than they should be for me missing curfew. I would soon discover why, but I never could have imagined how it was going to change my life.

The next time I saw Mason, everything had changed. Gone was the sweet, caring boy I'd fallen so hard for, and in his place was a cold and callous teenager who hated the world and everyone around him.

———

"Earth calling Camila." When I look up, I find the concerned stares of Noah, Alyssa, and Shane all staring back at me.

"I'm sorry," I whisper.

"Where'd you go? Anywhere good?" Alyssa asks, elbowing me in the ribs.

"Nah, just planning an assignment I was given this morning." The lie rolls off my tongue a little too easily, and I hate myself for it.

In truth, I can't get that memory of Mason and me in my bedroom four years ago out of my head. I have no idea if that's what he was trying to achieve this morning, to get under my skin, but shit if he hasn't succeeded.

"You sure you're okay?" Noah asks, as perceptive as ever. His hand squeezes mine under the table.

"Yeah, promise." Lifting my free hand, I gently run my thumb over the cut on his lip. "Does it still hurt?"

"Not enough to stop me from doing this." His lips brush over mine and I lose myself in his kiss, only in my head it's not him I'm kissing.

Damn him and his games.

6

MASON

Fuck this shit.

Getting up from my seat, I swipe my tray from the table and deposit what's left into the trash on the way out.

Fire burns through me as I think about finding him on Friday night with Tasha pushed up against the bathroom wall. I fucking hate cheaters, even if the person they're cheating on is someone I don't care about.

That's not true, a little voice says in my head, but I push it down.

"Mason, where you going, man?" Ethan shouts as he passes me on his way into the cafeteria.

I ignore him. I'm not in the mood to have a heart to heart right now. Instead, I head to the gym. I need a distraction, and short of spending next period inside a cheerleader, this is my only option.

There are a few freshmen working out when I walk in, but they mostly keep their heads down and ignore me. I can only imagine it's the murderous look on my face that ensures that happens.

Heading over to the bench, I load up some weights and lie down. My whole football career I've had grief about my size. I've spent the past few years working tirelessly on building myself up so I don't look like the weed of the team. It's worked to a point—I'm bigger than I've ever been, but I've also managed to find something to keep me focused along with football. When I have the time.

I push my arms until my muscles burn. I love the pain. It makes me feel alive and like one day I might be able to leave this bullshit life I'm forced to live.

If he was still here, everything would have been different, only *they* sent him away. Thoughts of the hand that the Lopezes had in my dad's absence from my life spurs me on.

By the time I drop the weight back onto the stand, I'm alone in the gym. I find my phone from the bottom of my bag, shove in some earbuds and turn it up as loud as I can stand.

Memories that I managed to shut down years ago have started to threaten to bubble back up to the surface. I might have wished that karma would come and bite her in the ass, but witnessing it with my own eyes has stirred something within me. My need to protect her is slipping back in. It's a feeling I remember all too well, seeing as when we were kids it was my one and only focus. She was the most precious thing in my life, and I'd have done anything to keep her safe. I'd have happily taken her pain as my own in the hope to save her from it.

Then everything changed and my need to protect her soon turned into a need for revenge. But even that started to wane as time went on and I realized that I didn't really have it in me to hurt her. I wanted her to suffer, sure. She needed to know what they'd done to me, to my life. Will exposing her scumbag boyfriend settle that little need for revenge that still lingers inside me or, like earlier, will it get me too close to her once again?

I turn the speed up on the treadmill as the image of her large, dark eyes as she stared up at me earlier fill my mind. I haven't looked at her like that for years, or more so, she hasn't looked at me like that for years. The want, need, adoration that I remember all too well was right there in her eyes, or maybe I was imagining it because after the way I've treated her over the past four years, she'd be right to hate me.

When I first discovered the truth about what happened, I ignored her. I was too angry to even be able to mutter a word to her. I could see how much it hurt her, I could see her devastation as she looked at me from across the classroom or cafeteria, her need for me to wrap my arms around her and tell her everything was okay. But it wasn't okay, because my world was on a downward spiral that would only get worse. It hurt when she stopped searching me out in the crowd, supporting me at games and finding any excuse she could to try to talk to me. That's when things changed. She started to look happy; all the while I was continuing to fall apart.

I never wanted to humiliate her, not in the public way that Jake did to Amalie, but my need to make her suffer just a little bit of the pain I'd experienced was too much to ignore. I'd do pathetic stuff, stuff I'm even embarrassed to admit, but mostly belittling comments that I knew would eat at her. Having my best friend turn into my enemy meant I knew exactly what to say to get a rise out of her. I knew that calling her out in class, in front of a crowd, would piss her off, so I did it. I knew how much she hated being the center of attention, so I forced her into it any chance I got. The redness of her face and the hardness of her eyes as everyone looked at her made it so worth it. It helped to squash down my memories of just how important she once was to me.

"You been in here all afternoon?" Jake asks when he sticks his head into the room. I wasn't supposed to be in his last class, but there's no doubt Amalie's already filled him in on what happened with Camila earlier, so he was probably worried I'd gone to do something stupid, like shove Noah's smarmy face down one of the toilets for disrespecting her.

"Yeah, I needed to escape."

He narrows his eyes at me but doesn't say anything. "You'd better not be too exhausted for practice or Coach will be pissed."

"I'm good," I say, although in reality, my muscles feel like jelly as I follow him out to the locker room. He's yet to see my fucked up knuckles, so that should distract him if I'm a little sluggish.

Our practice session is grueling. Coach doesn't let up for even a second, but knowing our away game against Penshore is approaching, I can't blame him. The Chargers are the ones who ended our season before it even really began last year and ruined any chance of us getting to the playoffs. Thankfully he takes one look at my scabbed up hands, tuts and shakes his head.

I can barely put one leg in front of the other by the time he lets us leave the field. In hindsight, my hours in the gym might not have been my best move.

"Fuck, man. If he keeps that shit up we'll all be dead by Friday night."

"He knows what he's doing," Jake grunts, slapping Ethan on the shoulder.

"I know, but fuck, it hurts."

"Growing a pussy or something, Ethan?"

"Nah, just worried about my stamina for the girls tonight."

"You're so full of shit," I mutter, following both into the locker room and then into the showers.

"Aces?" Jake asks. "I told Brit I'd meet her there."

The thought of sitting and watching the two paw all over each other doesn't sound like my idea of fun, even if I could. "Nah, got plans tonight."

"Okay, well... I'll see you tomorrow then."

Jake knows exactly what I mean by 'plans,' and being the loyal friend that he is, he never outs me.

Slinging my bag over my shoulder, I head out to the parking lot on shaky legs. I desperately want to just go home and fall into my bed, but that won't be happening for a few hours yet.

"Evenin', Mason," Heather sings when I walk through the entrance to the store I work in, now fully dressed in my yellow and green Price Chop uniform.

"Sorry, I'm a few minutes late. Practice ran over."

"No problem, sweetie."

I dump my bag in back before heading toward the checkout to find out my list of jobs for the night.

I should be at home starting the homework assignments I was given today, but instead I'm here making sure we've got enough money to feed the boys. It shouldn't be my concern, but sadly this is my reality.

Thankfully it's fairly busy for a Monday night and time passes quickly. That is, until my entire world grinds to a halt and three girls enter.

I look around for Heather but she's out back on break, leaving me to keep an eye on the small store alone. Normally that wouldn't be an issue, but then on any other day no one I know walks through the front door. There's a very good reason why I found a job as far out of Rosewood as possible.

Turning my back, I make it look like I'm busy stacking stuff behind the checkout as they pass, praying they don't find what they came looking for and leave just as fast as they entered.

7

CAMILA

"Aces?" Amalie asks when she finds me after school.

"And here I was thinking you hated the place?"

"I did, when I hated Jake. Things change." She shrugs. Yep, they sure do. And in the blink of an eye if you're really unlucky. "I told him I'd meet him there after practice. Where's Noah?" She looks around as if she's expecting him to be following me.

"He's got his computer club thing this afternoon."

"Just the girls it is, then," she says when Alyssa joins us.

"You still okay coming to that art shop with me later?" Alyssa asks me.

"Yeah, of course." I plaster a smile on my face. In reality, I'd totally forgotten.

"Oh, art place?" Amalie asks, and the two of them start chatting away. Leaving them to it, I head toward my car and wait for them to join me.

"As long as Jake doesn't have plans for me, I'll come too."

"Of course Jake will have plans for you," I say with a wink in my rearview mirror as she settles in the back of my car after Alyssa calls shotgun. "When the trailer's a rockin'." Her cheeks flame red but her eyes widen in horror and my stomach drops.

"Trailer?" Alyssa asks, and I immediately feel awful. Amalie trusted me with that bit of information about Jake's life that he keeps close to his chest.

"Yeah, it's their little love shack. All sorts of unmentionable things go on in there."

"Every Rosewood girl's dream, time in a trailer alone with our star quarterback," Alyssa swoons.

"I thought you were more of a basketball fan?"

"I am. Those guys are banging, but you can't say you'd turn down one of the football team if you had half a chance."

My mind wanders back to the bathroom earlier. Did I have half a chance? What would have happened if I closed that tiny amount of space between us?

"Hey, you okay?" Amalie asks, poking her head between the front seats. "You've turned as white as a sheet."

"Yeah, I'm good." She eyes me curiously. "You both know I've got more of a thing for the geeky guys. At least they've got a better reputation."

"Do they?" Amalie whispers, sitting back and thankfully shutting the hell up. I don't need everyone else judging Noah after Mason's false accusations.

"You find out what the hell went down between Noah and Mason Saturday night?" Alyssa asks as if she can read my mind.

"It was just Mason being a dick," I mutter, hoping she'll change the subject and soon.

"Really? It didn't look like he was playing around."

"Who the hell knows with Mason these days. His mood changes with the wind."

Alyssa accepts my comment and starts talking about some gossip she heard earlier. Thankful that the heat is off me, I focus on where I'm going and try to banish thoughts of Mason from my mind.

Alyssa and Amalie chat away, but I hear none of it. My mind is still in the girls' bathroom with Mason's dark eyes staring down at me. Taunting me.

Our usual table is free, and the second we're seated the waitress comes over to take our order.

"These are on me," Amalie announces. "I never really thanked you both for taking me in on my first day and not allowing me to be an outcast."

"It was nothing," I say, waving her off. "We should be thanking you. Our lives were pretty boring until you turned up."

"I'm sure there are people who say otherwise." Amalie turns toward the entrance where Chelsea and Tasha are walking through the doors, Tasha holding it open for her hobbling captain.

"Shouldn't they be out on the field trying not to fall from the top of their pyramid?" Alyssa mutters, taking in their scantily clad bodies.

"Ignore her," Amalie mutters when she notices me follow Tasha across the diner. "If you're so adamant that Mason's lying, there's no need to drag her into the drama."

Just before they get to their usual table, Tasha looks up and directly at me. If she's surprised by my attention then she doesn't show it. She gives me a wicked, fake smile and continues to their booth.

"What the hell's her problem?" Alyssa spits.

"No idea," Amalie responds, but she doesn't take her eyes off me. The fact she doesn't share the confidence I have in my boyfriend pisses me off. I'm just going to have to prove somehow that he's only got eyes for me.

Three strawberry milkshakes are placed on our table and all conversation halts while we enjoy the creamy treat. I don't care how old I get, I'm pretty sure I'll always feel like a little girl while drinking one.

I relax with a full belly and enjoy some girl time. We chat about school, homework, last week's Homecoming and upcoming parties.

"You're coming to the game Friday night, right?" Amalie asks.

"Um..."

"Oh come on, Cami. You can't let him stop you from enjoying yourself. You love football games."

It's not the game I enjoy so much as it is the atmosphere and knowing that I'm part of something. I've never really been one for group activities or sports, so I've never really got involved in any other way than supporting those who do.

"I'll think about it," I mutter, much to Amalie's disappointment.

Of course I want to go. I love the buzz of game nights and I love supporting our team. Minus a certain number eleven, of course.

"Oh, here they come."

Silence descends on Aces as most of the team comes barreling through the front doors. The Rosewood Bears are like royalty in this place. They all head in the direction

Chelsea and Tasha went earlier and fill the diner with loud chatter and banter. It's weird, but the place doesn't feel right unless they're here.

My eyes scan each of them as they walk past our table, giving us little to no attention until Jake and Ethan follow behind the rest of the team. But it's just the two of them. Mason's nowhere to be seen.

Unlike the others, they stop at our table. Jake drags Amalie from the booth and pulls her into his arms, his lips immediately seeking hers out. Ethan rolls his eyes at the pair of them before glancing at me and then turning his sights on Alyssa.

"Whatcha say, sweetcheeks." He wiggles his eyebrows, much to Alyssa's horror.

"I say no thanks, hotshot."

"Aw come on, you know you want a piece of this." He lifts his shirt, showing off his chiseled six pack, a smug grin on his face.

"Please tell me that move doesn't work on the likes of them?" She flicks her eyes toward the huddle of cheerleaders, a disgusted scowl on her face.

"Them? Nah. One look in their direction and they're begging for a ride."

"Jesus," Alyssa mutters, clearly unimpressed by both Ethan and the cheerleading team's slutty ways. "And this is just one reason why I prefer basketball."

Ethan's hand comes up to cover his heart. "Ouch, you wound me. Actually wound me."

"Oh, get over yourself. You ready to go?" she asks, turning to me.

"Sure. Can't wait." Alyssa rolls her eyes at me but doesn't let me off the little trip I agreed to.

"You coming, or are you too busy sucking Jake's face

off?" she says with a laugh as she squeezes past the loved up couple.

"I'm coming. Just give me two minutes."

"We'll be in the car," I call over my shoulder.

It takes almost ten minutes for Amalie to remove herself from Jake's hold. We've just about given up on her when she appears through the doors.

"You're just as bad as her with Noah, you know that right?" Alyssa says to Amalie when she gets into the car.

"You're just jealous," I call back.

"Yeah, and...?"

"Maybe you should have taken Ethan up on his offer. Bet he'd show you a good time."

"After he's already showed most of the female population at school one too? No thanks. Where was Shane? I expected him to show his face."

He always used to. It was fairly standard that he wouldn't arrive with the rest of the team, seeing as he makes no secret of the fact they're not his friends, just teammates. But ever since Jake accused him of spiking Amalie's drink, he's kept his distance. Although, I'm with Amalie on this one; I've known Shane since we were little kids, and spiking someone's drink isn't really his style although I must admit that not showing his face does make him appear a little guilty.

I back out of the space as Alyssa puts the address into the GPS.

"You didn't say we were going west."

"I didn't think it would matter. It's not like we're staying."

"True," I mutter. I just hate going to the west side of town. I know it's probably stereotypical of me, but I feel like I'm going to be offered drugs or get mugged every time I go there.

Before I know it, I'm pulling my car to a stop in a dark and dingy looking parking lot behind a row of shops. I might offer to stay with it to ensure I keep all my wheels, but that would mean I'd have to stay here alone and there's no way in hell that's happening.

I rush to get out when the others do and double check I've locked it before walking away.

"You think you're being a little paranoid?" Amalie asks.

"Have you heard any of the local news recently? This place is a ghetto."

"Really?" she asks, one eyebrow raised in question. "It wasn't that bad when Jake brought me here for breakfast."

"I'm sure everything is a little less scary with Jake Thorn on your arm." Alyssa laughs.

"Yeah... that could be it." Amalie gets this far off, wistful look on her face which makes me want to puke. I'm starting to understand why she always used to complain about mine and Noah's PDAs.

"This is it. You're going to love it, it's like Aladdin's cave," Alyssa says to Amalie as I follow behind, clutching my purse tighter to my body than necessary.

An hour. I'm dragged around a damn art shop for a whole hour while Alyssa and Amalie fill their baskets. The only good thing about the experience is that they had quite an extensive notebook section and I was able to feed my addiction.

"Can we run into the store? I promised Mom that I'd pick up a few things for her."

We follow Alyssa across the road and around the discount food store while she selects what she needs. I don't pay all that much attention to my surroundings until we head toward the checkout and Amalie elbows me in the ribs.

"What?" I snap, rubbing the sore spot.

She nods her head toward the register. I'm about to ask what the issue is when my legs stop working.

Standing behind the register dressed in a hideous yellow and green polo shirt is Mason.

"What the fuck is he doing here?" I whisper.

"Working, by the look of it," Amalie adds helpfully, as if his uniform wasn't a dead giveaway.

"Fuck, Alyssa's..." I don't finish my sentence. I don't need to as both Amalie and I watch her walk up to him, much to his horror, and place her basket on the counter.

He's frozen as he stares down at the items in front of him, but eventually, he must realize that no one else is going to ring it all up.

Blowing out a long breath, he reaches out and scans each item before dropping them into a bag. At no point does he look up and register that Amalie and I are standing here, but I have no doubt that he's aware that Alyssa's not alone.

Mason takes the cash for her purchases and all but shoves the change back at her before turning around and attempting to look busy. Unfortunately for him, it's obvious to all of us that he's not actually doing anything.

Alyssa looks over her shoulder at us, her brows drawn together in confusion, and together we follow her from the store.

No one says anything until we're safely back inside my car, and even then it takes a few seconds for Amalie to break the silence.

"Well... that was weird."

"Right?"

"Did you know he had a job over here?" Amalie asks, once again poking her head between the seats and looking at me.

"Me? Why the fuck would I know. He hasn't spoken to me like a human being in four years." I slam my lips shut, aware that I've said too much.

"Four years?"

"It's nothing," I say, trying not to make a big deal out of it.

"It's really not, Cami. You were best friends. How do you go from that to nothing for four years?"

"Shit happens. You of all people should understand that. Things happen for a reason. I'm sure it's better this way."

"You really believe that?" Amalie's voice is full of disbelief, and I can't say I blame her.

I shrug. "What else is there to think?"

"He really didn't want us to see him tonight, did he?" Alyssa chips in. "He looked seriously pissed to have been spotted."

"Yeah. Probably best we keep this to ourselves."

"And now you're protecting him?" I should have known that Amalie would call me out on my bullshit.

"I don't want any more drama than necessary. He's clearly got a job on this side of town for a reason, so let's just let it be."

"Okay, whatever you want." She sits back and thankfully ends the conversation.

It's not until we're approaching a burger place that Alyssa breaks the silence, suggesting we go and get something to eat. I can't really say I'm feeling all that hungry after seeing Mason, but when Amalie agrees, I don't have a lot of choice.

It's later than I was expecting to be home when I let myself in through the front door. Kicking off my shoes, I walk through to the kitchen to grab a drink before heading up to do some homework. My parents are sitting at the dining table in silence, both looking stressed as they turn to me.

"Sorry I'm late. I went to an art shop with Alyssa and Amalie and then for food. Are you both okay?" I ask hesitantly, taking in their deep frown lines.

"Uh... yeah. We were just hoping you'd have been home before now. We need to discuss something with you."

"Is it urgent? Because I really need to complete my English assignment for tomorrow."

They both glance at each other before Dad nods and turns to me. "Not at all, sweetheart. You do what you need to do and we'll all have dinner together tomorrow night. How does that sound?"

"Sounds great." I grab a bottle of water from the refrigerator and head for the stairs.

"Why did you put it off?" I hear Mom snap.

"School's more important."

Mom scoffs. Now I'm desperate to know what's going on but equally afraid to find out. It didn't look like they had happy news.

8

MASON

A ngry doesn't even begin to describe how I feel as I watch the three of them walk out of the store. I got a job in this part of town for a very good reason, so the fact they've just found me pisses me off more than I'm willing to admit. My life is one big series of fuck ups and the fact I even need to be working this shitty job is just another one, but it's the only place I could find that would be flexible enough for me to work around school and football games.

It's almost midnight when I eventually pull up at home. The lights are all out aside from the living room, where I'm assuming tonight's babysitter is currently hanging out, waiting for either Mom or I to appear. But to my surprise when I get there to let them off for the night, the person I find laid out on the sofa with a bottle of vodka in their hand is none other than my mother. She shouldn't be here yet. Her shift at the bar doesn't finish until two AM.

"Mom," I shout, louder than necessary seeing as she's asleep. I have no qualms about waking her. She sleeps most of the day and does whatever the fuck she likes whenever she feels like it.

"Shit, fuck. Yeah, what is it?" she asks in a panic, sitting up and pulling the bottle to her chest protectively.

"It's all right, I'm not going to fucking steal it. Shouldn't you be at work?"

"I... uh... got laid off."

"I'm sorry, you fucking what?" Red hot fury explodes through my body. She only works a handful of shifts each week as it is. She needs to be picking up more hours to support her kids, not losing her fucking job.

"It's a total misunderstanding. I didn't steal anything."

Rolling my eyes, I take a step from the room. "You're a fucking joke," I spit over my shoulder. "How about you lay off that bottle so you're sober enough to find a new job in the morning, eh?"

I take the stairs two at a time as I head for the safety of my room. Of course, I stop to make sure my brothers are sleeping soundly before I shut myself away. I'd put money on the fact *she* didn't do the same when she got home. The only thing she wants to ensure is okay is her fucking vodka.

I crack my knuckles as I walk through my bedroom door in an attempt to release some of the frustration that's pulling at my muscles. It does fuck all to help, but the sound is somewhat soothing. I could really do with hurting someone right about now. I picture the terror on Noah's face as I drove my fist into it on Saturday night and something inside me settles just a little bit. That is until the image of who I was misguidedly doing it for pops into my mind.

"Fuck." Rubbing my hand down my face, I scratch at my rough jaw as I think back to her finding me in Price

Chop earlier. I've gone out of my way to hide my reality since the day my dad walked out and I was forced to step up to the plate.

Without thinking, I rip my curtains open and stare down the street. Her curtains might be closed, but there's an obvious light shining behind them. She's awake. That's all the invitation I need.

Turning on my heels, I race from the house and down the street. I don't bother knocking on her front door, it'll only alert her parents. They know full well that things went south between us, so there's no way they'd allow me inside at this time of night, even if they are up.

Instead, I walk around the side of the house and across the grass. I'd always wanted to try climbing up here, but there was only one time I actually attempted it. I'm fairly sure after the kiss it led to that if things didn't play out the way they did, I'd have done it time and again if it meant I got another taste of her.

Memories of that night threaten to bubble up, but I do my best to swallow them down. I don't need to remember the sad look in her eyes as she stared up at me that evening. I felt terrible. It was totally my fault that she was late home and ended up in trouble. I was being selfish and didn't want to let her go. It broke my heart to hear her getting laid into by her parents for breaking curfew. When her first sob sounded out through the barrier of the front door, I knew I couldn't leave her. I made my way around to this trellis, I gave it a tug, much like I do right now to ensure it's secure, and I pulled myself all the way to the top so I was able to climb into her open window. A window that was always damn open. I'd warned her about it before, knowing how badly I wanted to climb up meant others would too, but she never shut the fucking thing. It was almost as if she was inviting me to join her. That's what my fourteen-year-old hormone filled body imagined, anyway.

Opening her window wider, I throw my leg over like I've done this a million times and silently slip into her room.

The only sound I can hear is that of my heavy breathing, and it's not until I poke my head out from behind the curtain what I realize why. She's scared of sleeping alone in the dark. My heart threatens to pound out of my chest as I run my eyes up the bump in her sheets until I find her dark hair that's fanned out on her pillow.

Walking over, I allow myself a second or two to look at her peaceful, sleeping face and imagine things weren't so fucked up. That the last time I was in this room was the beginning of something incredible, when in reality it was the end of everything I'd known. The events of the weeks following that night will forever be burned into my mind as the worst weeks of my life, and although Camila didn't personally have a hand in it, it was the actions of her dad that threw both mine and my little brothers' lives into meltdown. Charlie was only a baby, Oliver not much more; neither of them deserved to lose not only their father but practically their mother as well.

Thoughts of that time ignites a fire in my belly and reminds me why I'm here.

Finding a glass of water sitting beside her bed, I pick it up and raise it above her head.

My hand trembles slightly as I tip it, but the sight of the small stream of water pouring over the edge mesmerizes me enough to continue.

"Argh, what the fu—Mason?" Her eyes are wide as she

sits up and pushes my arm away with so much force that the glass and the remainder of the contents crash to the floor. "What the fuck is your fucking problem?" She scrambles from the bed, wiping at her wet face, and stands tall in front of me. I want to laugh at her attempt to square up to me—like she'd be able to win anything with her tiny size. My eyes drop from the fire lighting her usually dark ones in favor of her body, and the moment I do, any amusement falls from my lips.

Fuck. She's standing before me in a ruby red satin cami and tiny short set. The top is twisted around her body, her left breast all but falling from behind the fabric.

My eyes lock on to that smooth, porcelain bit of skin. How easy would it be to reach out and expose the rest, to be able to get just one look at the body that's featured in so many of my dirty teenage dreams? My temperature soars and my cock begins to swell inside my pants at the thought of how perfect her pink nipple is bound to be. I wonder if it tastes as sweet as I always hoped, or sour like I'd be tasting a rotten piece of fruit?

"Why the fuck are you here?" She tries again, her hands going to her hips, sadly dislodging the fabric and allowing it to fall back into place.

"I'm..." Standing in front of her dressed as she is seems to have zapped my brain. I fight to remember why the hell I'm here, but I come up short. My only thoughts are of her and how quickly I could get that satin on her bedroom floor.

No. You can't have her.

My sudden realization drags tonight's events to the forefront of my mind and reminds me why the hell I am here.

I take a step forward. "You look like you were

expecting company, dressed in this sexy little outfit." Lifting my hand, I run my fingers along the soft scrap of fabric resting on her shoulder. Her shoulders tense at my contact, but I don't miss how her nipples pebble behind the satin. "Did he stand you up? He's probably got better company. I hear Tasha is a stellar lay."

Her arm flies out, but before her palm connects with my cheek, I wrap my fingers around her wrist. I trained my entire life to catch that vital ball, I'm not going to miss her arm.

Her eyes harden and her teeth grind.

"Get out of my fucking bedroom."

"Why? Don't you want to give him a taste of his own medicine? He seems to be more than happy playing away. Maybe you should see what the fuss is all about." I tug her arm. She tries to fight, but she's no match for me and I get my way. Her soft breasts press against my chest and I all but moan out loud at the sensation it causes within my body.

Dropping my head, I brush my lips against her ear. "We could even send him some evidence if you like. Really hit him where it hurts."

"Fuck you." Her knee lifts, but I'm expecting it and jump back before she makes any contact.

"You're going to regret that."

"Am I?" She rolls her eyes before reaching for the hoodie that's hanging over the back of her chair and wrapping it around herself. I'm not ashamed to admit that it's a damn shame to hide that banging little body away.

"Are you always this clueless? Your boyfriend's banging a cheerslut and here you are, letting him get away with it."

"He's not. Fuck." She shoves her hands into her hair,

pulling it away from her face and allowing the hoodie to fall open. My eyes have a mind of their own and once again drop in favor of her curves. "I'm not talking about this with you. It's none of your fucking business. You gave up any right to have an opinion on my life years ago. Now do me a fucking favor and get the hell out." She gestures toward the window with her outstretched arm and widens her eyes in impatience.

"Don't I fucking know it."

"What's that supposed to mean?"

"Nothing. Listen, what you saw tonight. I need you to keep it locked."

She laughs, actually laughs in my face. "Hang on, let me get this right. You've broken into my bedroom, thrown water over me, harassed me, told me I'm an idiot, and all because you need a favor. Fuck you, Mason. Fuck. You."

"First, it's not breaking in if the window is open." Her eyebrow quirks, but I don't give her a chance to argue. "Second, I'm only telling the truth. Not my fault if you choose not to believe me."

"And third?"

"Third. I just... I just... I need it kept quiet. No one else needs to know about my life."

"You've got a job, so what? You're not the only one out earning a bit of their own cash."

"It's..." Her eyes bore into mine as if she's trying to read my mind, and for a second I'm worried she might just be able to. We were always on the same wavelength. We'd finish each other's sentences, blurt out the same ridiculous idea simultaneously. It only makes sense that she can see right through my bullshit. "You're right. No biggie. I just wanted to sneak in to try my luck. I mean, if your boyfriend's out getting his dick wet then there's no harm in me doing the same."

Her face damn near turns purple with anger. "Get the hell out of my room, Mason, before I scream for my parents."

It's an empty threat. I'm pretty sure she wouldn't bring that kind of drama down on either of us, but just in case I'm wrong, I take a step toward the window.

"I'll see you soon, Cami-bear. And if you're still dressed like that, then even better." I wink, allow myself one last trip around her body despite the fact she's now pulled the hoodie around herself as tight as it'll go, and climb from the window.

I let go when I'm halfway down the trellis and jump to the grass. Her burning stare tingles down my spine as I make the short walk back to my house, but I refuse to turn around. That is, until I know I'm about to disappear from her sight. Then I turn and face her window. Just as I suspected, her face is tucked between the curtains, watching me. Once she realizes I've caught her and the fabric falls in front of her face, ending our connection. I can't help laughing as I let myself back inside.

I might not have got what I went over there for, but I left with much more. If this morning in the girls' bathroom wasn't evidence enough, then tonight was: if I were to so much as drop my lips while I was touching her then she'd cave to me.

9

CAMILA

After securing the window and changing my pillow for a dry one, I have the worst night's sleep I've had in a long time. I know that shutting the window doesn't change the size of my room, but the second I pull it closed, I can't help feeling claustrophobic and like the walls are closing in on me. It's crazy, I know, but I guess it's true what they say: fears are irrational. I feel like I can't breathe without that small amount of fresh air flowing in, and I hate him for it.

When I do manage to fall asleep, it's only two hours before I need to be up for school, and when my alarm goes off, I'm in a bitch of a mood.

The second I push through the doors into school, I see him. He's standing at his locker, which is unfortunately directly opposite mine, as Chelsea and a couple of her sluts surround him. One of them runs their fingers down his arm while Chelsea presses her palm against his chest, laughing at whatever he just said. I throw up a little in my mouth at the sight.

I don't take two steps when my skin starts tingling with

awareness. I don't want to look up at him. I want to ignore him and show him that I'm indifferent to his attention. Sadly for me, but although my brain might want this, it seems my body has other ideas because as I come to a stop in front of my own locker, my head twists and I find myself locked in his dark stare. His blonde hair is falling over his face where he's bent down attempting to look interested in what the girls are saying, but they don't have his eyes. They're firmly burning into me.

Even with the distance between us I can see how incredibly dark they are. A shudder runs down my spine as I'm transported back to last night when he stared down at me with such intensity. I couldn't help but think he was about to devour me, and in that moment, just for a second, part of me wished he would.

"Good morning, beautiful," Noah sings, coming to a stop beside me and wrapping his arm around my waist. I freeze and he notices. "You okay?"

My eyes betray me and flick over to Mason, who I find staring daggers at the back of Noah's head. His words from last night slam into me.

"Are you always this clueless? Your boyfriend's banging a cheerslut and here you are letting him get away with it."

Looking back into Noah's kind eyes, he smiles at me, clearly concerned with where my head's at this morning. Reaching out, his fingers twist around a lock of my loose hair and he leans in toward me.

"Missed you last night," he murmurs against my lips before pressing them against mine.

I don't kiss him back immediately like I usually would, and he soon notices. He pulls away, and I panic. Lifting my hand, I wrap it around the back of his neck and pull him down to me. The last thing I need is him questioning my resistance. It's not his fault that Mason's lies are on repeat in my head. Because that's what they are... lies, right?

Fuck, I hate this. I trust Noah one hundred percent, and that asshole is making me question everything. If he'd told me these things about a boyfriend four years ago, I'd have dropped them like a stone, but Mason's been nothing but a pain in my ass all this time, trying to ruin my life for something I had zero control over. So why I'm giving his accusations head space I have no idea.

When Noah's tongue slips between my lips, I move mine to join it. His kiss is the same as always, but I can't help but feel something's changed.

When he eventually lets me up for air, his eyes are heated, his eyelids slightly lowered, and an excited smile plays on his lips.

My stomach drops. I never told him about my plans to lose my virginity on his birthday night, but I had told him that it would happen soon. He's been the perfect gentleman waiting for me. I know many teenage boys who wouldn't have been so patient, but I also feel like it's starting to wear thin. We've done... stuff. Or more so, I've done stuff. He hasn't got past the odd hand roam with me. I knew that once things started getting too serious, it was likely to go from zero to one hundred in the blink of an eye. I don't know why I've been holding off, it's not like everyone around us isn't doing it. But, I don't know. Something just hasn't felt quite right.

I stare off over his shoulder as my mind races with all these crazy thoughts, but I'm soon pulled from my misery when I lock with that pair of brown eyes. Only it's different this time. The girls have gone, leaving Mason standing alone, and the way he's staring at me, he looks kind of vulnerable. It's unnerving and not a look I've seen on him for a very, very long time.

"You coming to my house after school?" Noah asks, pulling my attention back to him.

"I'm sorry, I can't tonight. I promised my parents that I'd be home. They've got some drama they need to talk to me about."

"Is everything okay?" he asks, genuinely concerned.

"I have no idea. They looked a little stressed last night, but I didn't have time to chat. I still hadn't finished that English assignment."

"Still? I thought you were planning on finishing it over the weekend?"

Yeah, I was, but then Mason beat the shit out of you and I was left with my head spinning out of control. I don't want to admit that though. Instead I go with, "I ran out of time."

"That sucks. Maybe tomorrow then?"

"Yeah maybe." Turning away from him, I open my locker and switch out some books from my bag, ready for the day.

Noah seems to get the idea that we're done, and after a quick kiss on the cheek and an 'I'll see you later,' he turns and heads off in the direction of his own locker.

I let out a breath I didn't know I was holding and stare at the picture that's pinned to the back of my locker. It's of Noah, Shane, Amalie and me at Dash earlier in the year. Noah's standing behind me with his arms around my waist, a huge smile on his face as he stares down at me and not at the camera like everyone else. A smile twitches at my lips, but it's not enough to put to rest the confusion swirling around my head.

I give myself a talking to and swing the door shut.

What I'm not expecting when I turn and take a step in the direction of my first class is to find Mason still watching me from his side of the hallway.

Anger surges through me and I turn toward him.

"What? What is your fucking problem? Breaking and entering and scaring the shit out of me not enough? You've got to be a creepy stalker too?"

His lips thin and his jaw ticks with frustration. "Just watching you fuck your life up."

"Don't you have your own life to lead? Why are you so interested in mine all of a sudden?"

I didn't think it was possible, but his features harden even more at my words.

"Don't worry, I've got enough of my own bullshit without adding yours to it."

I'm silent for a few seconds, trying to figure out if there's some secret message I'm supposed to pick up in those few words, before I decide to be the adult in the situation and walk away.

"That's it, run away from what's right in front of you."

My spine stiffens as his parting words settle into my body, and I fight myself not to react further. He doesn't need to know his words affect me.

I only get a few minutes of relief because it feels like only moments after having sat in my seat and pulled my books out that he joins me in our chemistry class. I keep my eyes down, but that doesn't mean I don't feel his stare burning into the top of my head as he passes to take his seat at the back of the room.

By the time it gets to my AP English class before lunch, I'm starving and can barely keep my eyes open. I hand my assignment in that I finished sometime before midnight last night, only to be handed another.

"The title of the piece is to be *Against All Odds.*" Miss Phillips points to where she's written it on the board before fully explaining that she wants a piece of creative writing in any form we wish to convey that title.

I'm so tired that my mind fails to come up with a single idea and I panic that he's going to have ruined my creativity as well as my night's sleep.

Writing the task in my diary, I pray the clock will tick around so that I can eat.

If I had the energy, I might cheer with delight when the lunchtime bell rings out through the school. I rush to pack up my stuff and leave the room as fast as my legs will carry me, hoping to get a spot at the front of the line.

I practically inhale my burger and fries once I've placed them on our usual table. I'm over half done before I sense someone coming to join me. Glancing over my shoulder, I find Shane making his way over.

"Hey stranger. How's it going?" I mumble around a mouthful of fries.

"It's... going." He lowers his tray and himself to the bench opposite me, blowing out a huge breath.

"You still moping about what happened at your party? We all know it wasn't you, you don't need to sweat it."

"You might, but does everyone else?" he asks sadly, glancing around at the students now filling the cafeteria. "I keep getting these accusatory, disappointed looks from everyone. That's not me, Cam. I wouldn't ever do that, especially to someone I—" He cuts himself off, pain and regret filling his eyes. We all know he liked Amalie, he made no secret of that fact. I think he was hopeful that she'd warm to him, but unfortunately for Shane she fell head over heels for the captain of his football team instead. I'm pretty sure that outcome didn't feature in his plans whatsoever.

"Those who matter know it wasn't you."

"I feel like an outcast. No one wants me around anymore in case I'm a threat."

My heart bleeds for him. Although he has a spot on the football team, Shane is one of us. He's fought for years to be accepted by both parts of his world, but whoever it was that spiked Amalie's drink and framed Shane has managed to shatter both in one fell swoop. I feel for the guy, I really do, but I'm not sure what to say other than to wait for someone else to do something that'll take the heat off him, because this is high school: gossip only lasts for so long before someone trumps you and steals the limelight.

"They think I drugged her. That's not going to go away easily. I'll never be invited to a party again."

"It'll pass. Just focus on showing everyone how kind and caring you are and everyone will soon realize that you're not capable."

"Shane, my man. How's it hanging?" Noah says, dropping down beside me. He doesn't bother waiting for Shane's response. Instead he pulls me into his side and slides his fingers into my hair so he can drag my lips to his. His kiss is over the top and excitable, and it puts me off even more than I was this morning when he kissed me.

"What's up with you today? PMSing or something?"

"Yeah, something," I mutter, turning back to my fries.

He nudges me in the arm. "Hey, I was only messing. Are you okay?" he whispers a little more softly, his hand sneaking around my back to wrap around my waist.

"I'm—" I don't get to make my excuses because Shane cuts me off.

"I should go." His voice is broken and defeated at best.

When I look up, I find him staring over my shoulder with sad eyes. Following his gaze, I find Amalie and Jake walking in, hand in hand. The entire room seems to fall silent for a second or two as their king and his queen arrives.

Jake Thorn was always Rosewood's bad boy, but as I watch him pick up two trays, one for himself and another for Amalie, I wonder if we all hadn't gotten him very wrong. He's so sweet with her, like a totally different person to the Jake we've all seen over the past few years. They stand in line, their trays resting on the rail, and he wraps his arm around her waist, pulls her to him and kisses the top of her head. He lingers for a beat too long and I swear my heart nearly explodes on the spot. He's fallen so hard for her, it really is a sight to behold. I also know from how she talks about him that he's it for her. There's absolutely no doubt in her mind.

Everyone's chatter seems to start again, and I turn back to Shane who's just about to push up from the bench he's sitting on.

"Please stay."

"No one wants me here, Camila. *They* don't want me here." He flicks his eyes to where the couple are waiting for their food.

"She knows it wasn't you."

"Doesn't stop him wanting to take my teeth out... again," he mutters.

"He had his pop at you. He's moved on to other, more satisfying, things," Noah helpfully adds while Shane visibly pales at the thought of what the girl he wanted is now up to.

"I'll see you guys later." Before we can argue, he's gone, lost in the crowd.

I turn my eyes back to Amalie, who gives me a smile before returning to concentrate on whatever her boyfriend is saying.

Something twists uncomfortably inside me. Is that... jealousy? Why would I be jealous of Amalie and Jake? I'm sitting here with my boyfriend. I've got what they have, I've had it for quite a while now. *Have you?* a little voice in my head asks, but I push her away and turn to Noah. I smile at him, but it doesn't reach my eyes. I fear Mason's words might be making more of an impact than I want them to, and every time I look into Noah's eyes, I wonder more and more if he is indeed hiding something.

———

The last thing I want to do when I get home is to have a heart to heart with my parents, but it seems I don't get any reprieve because when I walk into the kitchen, they're already sitting at the table waiting for me. The fact that my dad should be at work doesn't even really register as I drop my bag and get myself a drink.

The atmosphere in the room is heavy as I make my way over to join them. The morose looks on their faces don't help the ball of dread that's sitting heavy in my stomach. Are they about to tell me they're splitting up? No, surely not. They're happy, right?

My mind runs a mile a minute as I wait for one of them to put me out of my misery.

"Darling, we need to discuss something with you," Mom starts.

My heart pounds as I wait for her to ask me who I

want to live with, as if I'd have that answer easily to hand, but when my dad takes over, it's very different words that fall from his lips.

"Our office is closing."

"Oh my god," I gasp. I'm equally shocked and happy that they're not separating. "I'm so sorry. You can get another job though, right?"

"That's what we need to discuss."

"Okaaaay."

"The company is relocating everything to their main office in New York. So I've still got a job if I want it, it's just—"

"In New York," I say, guessing where this is going.

"Yeah."

Anger burns within me that they've already made this decision. "So this isn't a discussion, this is you telling me that we're moving?" I snap, pushing the chair out behind me in frustration.

I'm in my senior year, they can't just tell me they're going to drag me halfway across the country and think I'll be okay with it. And it's not only school. What about my friends? What about Noah? *What about Mason?* a little voice adds, but I ignore her because I don't give a fuck about him.

"Sit down please, Camila. That's not what this is." I look between the two of them. Both have encouraging expressions on their faces and I slowly lower myself back down, hoping they really have thought this through.

"We're not expecting you to up and move to New York, sweetheart. Unless of course, that's what you want. Your dad has been given a very generous offer for him to work four days a week and to commute, but before any decisions are made, we wanted to discuss it with you. We know this won't affect your life like moving would, but we're both very aware that it will disrupt your senior year and our priority, as ever, is your happiness and success."

"Right, okay." I sit back and let that sink in for a few seconds. "So, what happens if you turn down this offer?"

"Honestly," Dad says with a sigh, "I have no idea. There's nowhere close that does what I do. So right now I'm faced with the decision of travelling or changing my career."

"Neither is an issue. We've got investments that we're in the process of liquidating so that we have money should be need it. Money isn't really the issue here, it's more our happiness and our quality of life as a family."

I nod, understanding where they're coming from before I turn to look at my dad. "What do you want? Like, really want?" I know how much he loves his job. He's a total IT geek and lives for everything computers.

"If I'm being really honest, and probably selfish then... I'd love to take their offer. Working in New York has always been a dream of mine and it will give me a lot more opportunities to climb the ladder. But the most important thing here is my girls. I need both of you to be happy no matter what."

I hate to say it, but I refuse to be the one to hold either of my parents back, especially because in less than a year I'll be off at college somewhere. The thought has a ball of dread forming in my stomach because I'm still none the wiser as to what I want to study or where, but time is closing in on my decision. "Then you should do it."

"But that would mean Dad wouldn't be here most of the time, and if I'm also being honest, I don't want to always be left behind. I'd really like to experience city life too."

"I'm nearly eighteen. I'll be at college soon without you both. I'm sure I can cope."

Mom and Dad look between each other, a silent conversation happening in front of my eyes, but I have no idea what they're saying.

Eventually Dad nods and they both turn to me. "We trust you, Camila, and we know that you're more than capable of being alone sometimes. I won't go all of the time, but I wanted you to be aware from the outset that I might not always be here like I have been."

I bite down on the inside of my cheek to stop from saying that she's not here all that often as it is. All the social events that she organizes have her out more than she's in. I can't remember the last Saturday night we all spent as a family.

"It'll be fine. I want you guys to be happy. I'll be too focused on school to notice."

"Nice," Dad says with a laugh. "Seriously though, I'm so proud of you, Camila."

"Thanks. Are we done? It's just, I've got homework to do."

"We are. I need to pop out for a bit but then I'll sort dinner when I get home, okay?" Mom says.

"Sure thing."

After grabbing a fresh drink, I make my way up to my room and pull my books from my bag.

I stare down at the assignment I got from Miss Phillips and think about what I'd like to do.

10

MASON

All day I waited for someone to walk up to me and mention my job, but by the time the bell rang signaling the end of the day, no one had. After everything that I've done to Camila, I really thought she'd tell the entire school my little secret the first chance she got. I'm amazed that she hasn't spilled.

She was angry with me this morning after what I did last night. Her dark eyes had a fire burning in them that I've never seen before as she stood in front of me with her hands on her hips. I can't deny that her temper didn't fire me up a little too. I remember all too well from when we were kids that she could have a temper if she wanted to. It wasn't directed at me all that often, but when it was, I knew about it.

"What are you smiling about?" Jake asks when I join him in the locker room ready for practice.

"Oh, nothing."

"You get a hand job during history or something?" Ethan adds. He really does have a one-track fucking mind.

"No, sadly not." His words make me realize how long

it's been since I did receive that kind of attention. "Chance would be a fine thing."

"You're shitting me. You've seen the girls who drool after every step we take, right? Just look at one of them the right way and they'll drop to their knees."

"I'm well aware. But it's not one of them I really want."

"Oooh, does Mason have a little crush?" Ethan's eyebrows wiggle in delight that he might be about to discover a secret.

"No. I just don't want a cheerslut who's already sucked on yours."

"Why not? I'm clean."

Rolling my eyes at him, I pull my locker open and start getting ready for practice. Truth is that just a few months ago I wasn't really all that bothered about who was on the other end of my cock as long as they made me come at the end of it. They were the perfect distraction from my bullshit life. But as time goes on, I've realized that those experiences were pretty meaningless. It might make me sound like a pussy, at least it does in Ethan's eyes, but I want more than a quick, dirty fuck with a girl who's already done at least one lap of the team. I want... I want what Jake's found with Amalie. I want someone who's going to stand by my side despite what my life is, despite what my family situation is. I want someone I can rely on when times get hard, not just someone who turns up when they want something.

Practice is fucking killer. I swear we'll all be broken by the time Friday night's game comes around if Coach keeps up with this level of craziness.

I probably should have seen if I could snag an extra shift tonight, but knowing that I need to speak to Mom meant I didn't pick up the phone and beg for extra hours.

It's coming though. I just know that Mom's not going to be proactive as she should be about finding another job.

I'm proved correct when I pull up outside our house not long later to find her car parked in the driveway and then her sitting in front of the TV with a tub of ice cream in her lap. At least it's an improvement on the vodka from last night.

"I see you're busy looking for a way to pay the bills," I mutter as I pass her heading to the kitchen. "We need to talk."

A few months ago, when Mom's hours were cut, I forced her to sit down with me so we could write down a list of all our expenses and the day each bill needed to be paid. It's now pinned to the front of the refrigerator in the hope that seeing it might spur her into action. Clearly that was wishful thinking, seeing as she has no job whatsoever now.

I pull it from its clip and sit down at the breakfast bar with that and a can of soda praying I can figure out a way around all of this. I have a little bit of money in savings ready for college, but it's nowhere near enough to keep us afloat until Mom gets off her ass and brings in some money.

"What are you doing now?" she mutters, eventually joining me in the kitchen.

"Trying to figure out a way to ensure we're not evicted and forced to live on the streets."

She lets out an amused sigh which only adds to my irritation levels. "That's not going to happen."

"Why not? We've got no way of paying all of this." I wave the piece of paper in her face. "So why wouldn't we be kicked out?"

"Just trust me, okay?"

"You're fucking joking, right?"

She narrows her eyes at me before pulling the refrigerator open and reaching for a bottle of wine.

"So I'm assuming you haven't got another job yet?"

"It's only been a day, Mase. Calm down."

"Calm down? Calm down? Am I the only one who cares about those two boys playing upstairs? Have you even fed them since they got home from school?" Guilt twists her face and I get my answer. "You're meant to be our fucking mother. You should be the one worrying about paying the bills, about whether we all eat correctly or not. It is not my job to be their father," I call when she decides she'd rather spend her evening alone with her bottle of wine. "Fucking waste of space," I mutter, staring back down at the list of numbers.

Pinning it back up where I found it, I set about making dinner for myself and my brothers. If she doesn't care enough to do it, then she can fend for herself. I'm not making her life even easier for her.

After making sure Charlie and Ollie have a bath, I leave them in their rooms with the understanding that they can play for another thirty minutes before they must be in bed. Thankfully, Ollie is a pretty responsible kid and I'm confident that when the time comes, he'll ensure Charlie does as I said and climbs into bed. My blood boils that my seven-year-old little brother has to take on that kind of responsibility. But I can't do everything myself. I need to keep my grades up if I have any hope of graduating and going to college. I also need to be out on that football field, but I fear that might have to go by the wayside if I need to pick up more hours to keep this roof over our heads.

Thankfully, it seems to have gone quiet down the hall.

I get up to go and check on them but at the same time, there's a knock at the front door. I turn to go and answer it but soon realize that I don't need to, seeing as Mom's footsteps sound out before female voices fill the air. The other woman's is one I recognize well. I've almost heard it as much as my own mother's.

I should head back to my room and leave them to it, but my need for another drink gets the better of me and thank fuck it does because if I don't overhear what I do, then fuck knows when Mom would ever have told me the truth.

"I'm really sorry to have to do this, Nicky, but we're selling the house," Mrs. Lopez says.

My spine immediately stiffens, but I stay out of sight. *Sell the house? Why does she need to apologize for selling their house?*

"What does that mean for us?"

"I don't know, Nic. Do you have enough to rent somewhere else? I'm sure you could get something a little smaller that you could afford on your salary."

Wait... what?

As I storm around the corner, both of them look up at me. Shock covers both of their faces that they've been caught.

"Oh, hello Mason. I didn't realize you were home."

Bullshit, seeing as my car's parked in the drive.

"Cut the crap. What were you both just talking about?"

"It's nothing, baby. Just go back to your homework."

I'm already fighting the fury that's filling my veins. The last thing I need is her patronizing tone, talking to me like a goddamn child.

"No, I think I need to hear this, seeing as I'm the only one bringing money into this house right now."

Mrs. Lopez's mouth drops open as she looks between the two of us.

"What happened to your job, Nic?"

"They let me go."

Mrs. Lopez lets out an exasperated sigh. I've always wondered why these two are still friends. They're polar opposites in every way, but even after everything that happened that ripped our family in two, they're still as close as ever.

"Why didn't you tell me that just then when we were discussing..." She trails off.

"Yeah, about that. Who owns this house, Mom?" She visibly pales before looking down at her feet. "Mom. Who owns this fucking house?"

"They do." It's so quiet that I almost miss it, but I already knew the answer. Her opening her lips was only to confirm it.

"Motherfucker."

"Language, Mason."

When her eyes find mine, they're hard and disappointed. She's disappointed in me? That's fucking rich.

"So the mortgage I've been busting my ass to help pay isn't our mortgage. It's just rent, and rent to *them*." I don't even try to cover the disdain in my voice. Everyone in this room knows exactly how I feel about the Lopez family and how they ruined my life, I'm not going to start sugar coating that shit now.

"You don't pay any rent," Mrs. Lopez admits before my mom fires a few daggers at her and she promptly slams her lips shut.

"Fucking hell." Lifting my hands, I run them through my hair and tug. This is not fucking happening. So not only did the Lopezes ruin my life by running my dad out of town, but they basically own my life.

"We'd like to do some renovation before we put it on the market. So I'm sorry to ask, but we really need you to move out as soon as possible."

I stand stock still and watch the panic start to cover Mom's face. So it appears being on the verge of homelessness is what it takes to make her realize what a dire situation this is.

"But... but we have no money," she whispers.

"What happened to all the money I thought you were paying the mortgage with?" I ask and watch her pale even more.

"It's gone."

"Gone? That would have been thousands of dollars. How can it just be gone?"

"I spent it."

"On what?"

"Stuff. Nights out."

My fingers tug at my hair impossibly hard until I think I'm going to start pulling it from my scalp.

"So what you're saying is that unless by some miracle you find a seriously well-paying job in the next few days, we're homeless. Well, isn't that just fucking great." A cold laugh falls from my lips because, really, why didn't I see something like this coming?

"Nic?" Mrs. Lopez questions. When I look back at Mom, at least she has the decency to look upset by this. Tears fill her eyes, and fair play to her because her bottom lip actually trembles a little.

"So come on. You must have a plan. When you decided to spend every penny we had, you must have had a backup plan. You're our mother, after all. You're supposed to have our best interests at heart. You can't possibly be standing here and telling me that you're about to make us all homeless because of your stupidity." My words might be cruel, and just a tiny bit of regret hits me when she starts to sob, but fuck it, she deserves everything I can throw at her right now.

She shakes her head as she cries. Mrs. Lopez is clearly softer than I am, because as I stand there with my arms crossed across my chest waiting for her to fill me in on her big plan, she pulls Mom into her arms and rubs her back.

"I know it's been hard since he left," she soothes in her ear.

"Fuck that. It's been four years. She's an adult. She's supposed to be a mother," I seethe.

"She's ill, Mason. Give her a break."

"Ill?" I ask, an unamused laugh falling from my lips. "Don't make excuses for her."

She opens her mouth to respond but clearly thinks better of it, not wanting to get into an argument with the person who somehow manages to keep this family barely above water.

"Come and move in with us—"

"No, Gabriella, we can't—" Mom tries to weakly argue, lifting her head from Mrs. Lopez's shoulder.

"You can and you will. Just until you get yourselves sorted. Clint and I won't be there all that much while we get him settled in New York."

"No, no, we—"

"No," I state, my heart slamming against my chest. I can't live in their fucking house. I can't live with Camila. Fuck. If it weren't for the Lopezes then my dad would still be here, and we wouldn't be in this fucking mess.

"Mason. We have no other option." There's hope

shining in Mom's eyes, but I'm not stupid. I know it's because she just got offered an easy way out. Having a roof over our heads means she can fuck about for a while longer. She doesn't care that that roof might be the last place in the world I want to be. I think I'd actually rather be homeless. The image of me living in a cardboard box pops in my mind and I realize I'm being a little dramatic, but I really don't want to have to move into that fucking house.

"I'll stay with Ethan or something," I mutter, turning to leave them to it, unable to listen to any more of this bullshit. I have no idea if the Savages will put me up, but seeing as he lives in a huge house and his parents are almost never there, I doubt anyone will even notice.

"Think about your brothers, Mase. They'll need you."

Spinning, I pin my mother with a searing look.

"Think about my brothers. Are you fucking joking? All I do is think about them. I'm risking my future, my career, my everything for them right now, not that you have any fucking clue what I do *for them.*"

She balks, but not as much as Mrs. Lopez who looks like she wants to take a swing at me. I guess that's the benefit of me avoiding her and her only spending time with my manipulative mother: she doesn't really know the whole truth about what plays out inside this house.

Storming away from both of them, I poke my head into the boys' room to make sure they're sleeping peacefully before silently making them both a promise. *I won't allow her bad choices to ruin your lives. I swear it.*

The second I close my bedroom door behind me, I pull my phone out and call work. If we're going to get through this and get out of the Lopezes' before I do something stupid then I'm going to need money, and to get that money I need more hours.

Heather's hesitant to agree to my plans, but I know she's struggling for other options seeing as two members of staff have quit recently. That seems to be the only thing about my life that's falling into place right now.

Tomorrow I'm going to have to make some concessions for my new work schedule. My stomach is already in knots knowing what I'm going to have to give up, but I'll do anything for those two little boys, to ensure they grow up with at least one person looking out for them.

Picking my phone back up, I message both Jake and Ethan.

I need a drink. You free?

Almost immediately three little bouncing dots appear and replies start filling my screen.

Ethan: Fuck yes. Get your asses over here. Free house.

Jake: Sure thing. Mase, pick me up?

I reply telling Jake that I'll be twenty minutes before jumping into the shower and trying to ignore everything that happened downstairs.

Tomorrow everything's going to change, but tonight I can enjoy spending time with my friends. I have no idea when I'll get the chance again, so I need to make the most of it.

11

CAMILA

I stayed up too late working, and when my alarm first goes off the next morning, I turn it off and roll over. Bad idea.

When reality comes crashing down, I sit bolt upright in bed and realize that I've only got thirty minutes to get to class.

"Fuck." I jump from bed, drag some clothes on and pull my hair up into a messy bun. I'm still brushing my teeth as I run for my car and throw it into reverse.

The hallways are empty as I run toward my physics class.

Everyone turns to look at me as I crash through the door, and I want the ground to swallow me up. I look terrible, I'm well aware of that. That last thing I want is everyone judging me for it.

"Good morning, Camila. How nice of you to join us."

"I'm so sorry, sir. Problem with my alarm."

"You haven't missed much, go and take your seat."

I breathe a sigh of relief that he's not going to roast me for it and do as I'm told. All sets of eyes in the room follow my journey. Well, all but one. The set of eyes I expected to torment me, or to be filled with joy that I'm once again in trouble, stay locked down on the desk in front of him.

Don't get me wrong, it's not that I wanted to look into Mason's dark, hate filled eyes after the morning I've had, I just find it bizarre after the interactions I've had with him the last few days.

Ignoring whatever it is that twists at my insides, I drop down into my seat at the desk next to his and pull my books out.

I'm just reading through the information on the board, hoping I can catch up, when I feel his stare.

Glancing at him out of the corner of my eye, my breath catches at the look on his face. He looks exhausted. His eyes are dark, the shadows around them even darker, and his mouth is turned down at the edges. It's so weird seeing that look on his usual cheerful, if not tormenting, face.

The sudden urge to ask if he's okay is all-consuming, but I force my lips to stay firmly shut for two reasons. One, I don't want to be caught talking after already being late, and two, I shouldn't care.

His eyes bore into mine as our connection holds, and I can't help but wonder what he sees staring back at him. I fear it's just the girl he hates who he thinks ruined his life. He's not stupid, he must know I had nothing to do with that. I guess it's just my connection to the man who had a hand in everything.

I let out a sigh and turn back toward the board. I don't want to fall even more behind than I already am.

I don't see Mason for the rest of the day, but when I catch up with Amalie outside her locker at the end of school, I learn the reason for the look on Mason's face. It seems that he, Ethan, and Jake had one too many last night.

"They're all hanging out of their arses," she says in her British accent that always makes me smile.

"On a school night? I thought they were more sensible than that. Did something happen?"

"Not that I'm aware of. Coach has been pushing them hard for Friday's game. I think they just needed to blow off some steam. They're all regretting it today though."

If I had any sympathy for how Mason looked this morning, then it's gone the second Amalie told me it was a hangover. Fucking idiots.

"Have you decided if you're coming Friday night?"

"No, I—"

"Come on, Cami. Don't miss something you love because Mason's being a dick."

"It's not him, it's..." I wrack my brain for a reason before the conversation with my parents last night comes back to me. "My dad's kinda lost his job."

"Oh shit, I'm so sorry," she says genuinely as we make her way to my car.

"It's not quite that dramatic, I don't think."

"Oh?"

I wait until we're in my car until I explain about New York.

"Woohoo, house party at Camila's," she says with a laugh. "You must be buzzing about getting some time to yourself."

Truth is, I am. My parents can be a little overbearing, but as it is, they're hardly home when I am. I doubt I'm going to see much of a difference aside from them not stumbling their way into the house in the early hours of

Sunday morning after whatever event they've attended has come to an end.

"It'll be good. I'll be able to focus on homework and graduating."

"Plus, you can have me there whenever the hell you like."

"As if you have time, you're always with Jake."

She's silent for a few moments, forcing me to look over to make sure she's okay.

"What is it?"

"I've been thinking about something recently, but I can't help thinking it's crazy."

"Go on, I like a bit of crazy."

"I've had all my parents' inheritance come through, and I want to invest some of it."

"Invest it how?" If she's about to ask me for stocks and shares advice, then she's going to be bitterly disappointed.

"In property."

"You want to buy a house?"

"Yeah. I figure that I'm eighteen and don't have to live with Gran, and Jake, well, he doesn't exactly have the world's greatest home, so I thought—"

"Hold the fucking phone. You're not talking about investing in a rental here, are you? You're suggesting buying a house for you and Jake to... live in?" The idea sounds so absurd coming from my mouth, but I realize that as I say the words, it's also actually kind of perfect.

"You think I'm insane, don't you?"

"If I didn't know you both then I'd say hands down yes. But actually, for the two of you, it could be incredible. So long as you don't fall out."

"We won't," she says with every confidence in her boyfriend. My stomach drops a little because it's the kind of confidence that I used to have in Noah, but seeing as he blew me off for his friends this afternoon after we agreed to spend time together, I'm starting to get more and more suspicious after everything that's happened.

"Does Jake know about this?"

"No, I haven't said anything yet."

"What about college?"

"That's what we need to figure out, but I'm pretty set on staying close so I can be here for Gran. There's a lot to consider."

"It all sounds very grown up."

"If I was still in London, I'd be living on my own right now at university. I don't really see it as any different, and Jake's basically been living on his own for years, so not much will change for him." Every time she mentions Jake's hidden life, my heart aches for him a little. Much like everyone else at school, I just thought he was a cold asshole. I had no idea what had been happening to him behind the scenes. Almost everyone still thinks that about him, there's only a select few of us that now know the truth about his life, and I can't help thinking that a stable life in his own home with Amalie will be incredible for him. Being abandoned in your uncle and aunt's damp trailer at the bottom of their garden is no way to live.

"You meeting Noah tonight?"

"Apparently not. He's busy."

"Oh right. Have you spoken to him properly about what happened at the party?"

I'm not sure what she means by properly, but no, I haven't brought it up again, or my growing suspicions that something isn't right with him.

"Nothing to talk about."

"If you say so. Fancy a milkshake before we're forced to do more schoolwork?"

"I don't think I can say no to that."

I chuckle as I make the next right and head toward Aces. The boys are at practice, so I know I've got my best friend to myself for the next couple of hours and I intend on making the most of it.

We end up going back to her possible house purchase and find ourselves searching for houses on the outskirts of town so that it would be a reasonable distance to both Rosewood High and Maddison if they do end up going there. It's crazy that I'm not even eighteen yet and I'm sitting looking at houses. I thought this kind of thing was meant to happen way in the future. I guess it is for 'normal' kids, but with everything Amalie has been through and the amount of money sitting in her bank account, I guess she's anything but 'normal.'

By the time I get home, I know that I need to start on my homework if I've got any chance of getting a full night's sleep tonight.

I don't bother going to the kitchen and risk being distracted by whoever is crashing around in there and instead head straight for my room.

I'm not a nerd. Well, I don't think I am, but I'm also not one of those students who leaves everything to the last minute and hope that it's going to be okay. I pride myself on being organized, on doing my homework the night it's assigned then sitting back knowing that I'm sorted and can enjoy my weekends. Alyssa is the former, which is one of the reasons we started to grow apart even before Amalie arrived in town. She wanted to hang out every night of the week and then would spend all weekend trying to catch up. I hated it. So when Amalie appeared and turned out to be on my wavelength, I couldn't be happier. It's just a shame she was forced to start at Rosewood as a junior. If she were a senior, I think we'd have been great study partners.

My mind wanders back to when Mason and I first started at Rosewood. We'd hop off the bus and head for one of our houses so that we could do our homework together. My strength has always been English whereas his leaned toward math. We were a match made in heaven as we helped each other out and studied for tests together.

I let out a sad sigh. I miss those times. When I allow myself to think about it, I miss a lot of things that used to involve Mason.

Pushing my thoughts aside, I look down at my calendar to see what I'm going to do first when a knock sounds out from my bedroom door.

"Yeah," I call seconds before Mom pokes her head inside.

"Hey, sweetie. Good day at school?"

"Yeah, not bad. You had a good day?"

She lets out a sigh that tells me all I need to know and falls down onto my bed. "Sorting out your dad's stuff. It kind of feels like he's moving out. I hate it."

I walk over to the bed and wrap my arm around her shoulders. "I thought you were okay with this?" She seemed so set on the idea when we all spoke yesterday.

"I am. I think it's a fantastic opportunity for your dad. I'm so proud of him. I just want to be a part of all his new experiences."

"He'll make sure you are. Plus, you can go with him and experience it firsthand as often as you like."

"I don't want to abandon you."

"Mom," I start but pause to consider my words. I

don't want to hurt her; it appears she's already having a hard enough day. "Please don't take this the wrong way, but you're not here all that much now. You spend evenings and weekends either planning or attending events, and Dad's been working more late nights than ever."

"You're right," she breathes, regret filling her voice. "We haven't been here enough for you."

"No, that's not what I'm saying." And exactly why I wanted to choose my words carefully. "You're both incredible parents. I'm lucky to have you." That's been proven so much more obvious as I've learned of Amalie and Jake's reality. I really am lucky to have two supportive parents who just want the best for me.

"Aw, Cami-bear." My heart twists at the nickname Mason made up for me back in the day that my mom picked up somewhere along the way. "Anyway, you're not going to be totally alone while we're gone." She glances at me nervously and I lift a brow at her, waiting for her to spill the beans, although from the glint in her eye, I don't think I'm going to like it. "It's just temporary, but the Paines are moving in. Just until they get themselves sorted," she rushes to add.

"No, no, no," I say, getting up from the bed and pacing in front of her. "I can't live with them... with *him*."

"Camila, I know it's not ideal but we're having to sell their house and I kind of sprung it on them, so it's only fair we help out where we can."

"Wait, *you're* selling *their* house?" Confusion mixes with my anger and I come to a stop in front of her.

"We bought it as an investment property when things got tough for Nicky when David left."

"Wow," I breathe. I really didn't see this coming. "So

why can't they just go and rent somewhere else?" I spit, not wanting to have to deal with Mason on a daily basis.

Mom's face drops and I fear there's a lot more to this than she's letting on, or that she even knows. The image of Mason in his Price Chop uniform floats back into my mind. He was mortified at being discovered. I guess their issues run deeper than being abandoned by David after he lost his job. Suddenly his school night drinking session last night makes a little more sense. Is that how he decided to deal with this?

I shouldn't feel any sympathy for him. I don't want him here... I think. But knowing that his family is falling apart does tug at my heartstrings a little.

"They don't have anything, sweetheart. I'm pretty sure I speak for Nicky when I say that they'd rather not move into our house. But sometimes life just gets too tough and we all need to do things that we'd rather not."

"I get that, Mom. I do. And I'm all for helping out in their time of need but—"

"Mason," she finishes for me. "I can assure you that he wasn't all that thrilled by the idea either. That boy is so different to the sweet one we used to know. I don't expect him to cause you any issues, he wants to be here even less than you want him here."

"Not sure that's possible," I mumble. Falling down on the edge of my bed, my head falls back as I try to process all of this.

"Who knows," she says, staring off into space. "You might even find a way to rekindle your friendship."

"Yeah, maybe." Really un-fucking-likely, but I refrain from telling her that when she's got that twinkle of hope in her eye.

"You two were so sweet as kids. I really thought he'd end up being my son-in-law one day."

Me and you both.

"When are they moving in?"

"They're going to move stuff over the next few days with the intention of being in completely over the weekend. We've got builders starting renovations next week."

"Does it need a lot of work?" I ask. My memories of the place are that it wasn't all that different from this house. Warm, cozy, welcoming. But I guess that was a while ago.

"It just needs a little TLC. We'll have it on the market in no time and the money should help if your dad's job doesn't go as he's hoping."

I nod, because what else can I do? This decision has already been made, and me kicking up a fuss right now isn't going to change anything. They're probably all over there now packing up all their stuff ready for the big move.

A large ball of dread sits in the pit of my stomach. It's hard enough seeing Mason at school every day and wondering what the hell's going to come out of his mouth every time I pass him in the hall. What's it going to be like with him down the hall in my home?

Disaster.

It's the only thing it can be.

"I'm sorry to spring this on you. I know it's less than ideal, but everything will work out." She taps my thigh and stands. "Dinner will be about thirty minutes, sweetie. Do you need help with anything?" She glances at my books spread out across my desk.

"No, I'm good. I've got a report to start."

"Okay." She gets up and walks to the door, leaving me standing like a lost sheep in the middle of my room. "Everything will work out for the best, Cami. Everything happens for a reason, right?"

That's her little motto. And I must say that I'm usually happy to go along with it. But right now, I can see absolutely no good reason for Mason and me living under the same roof. It's got disaster and pain written all over it.

She closes the door behind her, and after blowing out a very long, frustrated breath I fall down onto my chair. I stare at my diary but no thoughts of what I might write fill my mind. I'm too lost to my memories.

We were nine, maybe ten. My parents had gone away for the weekend to celebrate their wedding anniversary. The Paines had agreed that they'd look after me so they could have an adults only weekend. I was buzzing as I packed my small bag and tucked my pillow and teddy bear under my arm, ready to walk down to their house. It wasn't the first time Mason and I had had a sleepover, but it was the first time we were allowed to be left alone for a few hours and to order in our dinner. It felt so grown up and my innocent mind wanted to pretend we were practicing for the future when we might have a house of our own and order takeout every night of the week.

His mom and dad were just going out for dinner. I think they were testing us to see if we could actually be left behind, but neither of us cared. We had the whole house to ourselves, free rein on the takeout menus and a stack of DVDs to get through.

There had been a storm warning all week, but we have yet to see any of it, and it was looking like it was starting to veer away from us, so no one thought any of it. We'd eaten our body weight in Chinese takeout and downed enough soda to rot every single one of our teeth, but we were on top of the freaking world as we ran around the house, dancing to music louder than we were usually allowed and just generally being crazy kids. It was incredible.

Until that storm hit.

Mason's parents were still out as the wind started roaring through the trees outside, some of the branches hitting the windows, making harrowing noises. The rain lashed down and from our seats on his couch we watched as it bounced off the ground outside. It was fine. We were in the house. We were safe and we were together. Then the lights went out.

I hate the dark. I always have. But being in the dark during a storm is so much worse. My heart was racing, my palms were sweating as I sat trembling beside Mason, who was vaguely aware of my fear seeing as he knew that I slept with a night light, but he had no idea the severity of it. The wind blew stronger, and noises that I was unable to identify sounded around us. We had no idea if the house was about to collapse on us or if some madman was about to crash through the front door and tear us limb from limb. I knew the thoughts were irrational, but the second darkness falls around me, even now, I'm frozen with fear as all these crazy images about what could happen to me fill my mind.

"I can't find the flashlight," Mason admitted after a quick search of the usual places.

"Candles?" I whimpered. I needed anything to cast a little light in the house, anything that could stop me falling headfirst into a debilitating panic attack.

"I don't know where the matches are."

"I'm scared," I admitted in a soft voice.

The next second, there he was, his body pressed up against mine, his arm around my shoulder.

"It'll be okay, Cami-bear. I'll keep you safe. I'll always keep you safe."

He held me until the lights eventually flickered back on. I have no idea how long we were in darkness for but thankfully the storm passed and his parents were able to make it home. The house didn't crumble around us and no one tried to kill us, but even to this day, being in the dark terrifies me. Those exact thoughts still haunt me. But that night, he made it all better. He distracted me with his warmth, kind words, and endless support.

I wonder what happened to that boy? I think as I stare out the window at his—my parents'—house. Is he still in there or has he been banished for good? His curtains are shut like always. It'll be weird to see them open again when someone else moves in.

"Dinner," Mom calls and I'm forced to abandon my pathetic attempt at starting my homework in favor of her tacos. It's no secret that they're my favorite and I wonder if she's done them tonight to soften the blow of the news about our new lodgers.

12

MASON

Mom's weirdly organized for this move. I wish she was as proactive about getting a fucking job, but as I arrive home from work late that night there seem to be boxes everywhere. This is the only house I've ever known. It's going to be weird walking away. I've got so many memories here, although not all of them good. Maybe a fresh start wouldn't be a bad thing. There's still evidence of my dad in the fabric of this building; maybe being away from that will have a positive influence on Mom. It's a long shot, but I can only hope. I worry that the reason she's so excited to move down the street is that she's expecting to have a few more babysitters for the kids she should be looking after. She's going to be seriously pissed off because it sounds like Gabriella and Clint are going to be spending most of their time in New York. I hope that doesn't mean she's going to expect Camila to pick up the slack in her childcare. I don't really want my brothers getting too attached to her.

"Can you make a start on your bedroom please,

Mase?" Mom says when she sees me standing in the kitchen doorway watching her box up plates.

"Sure. What are you doing with all that?"

"Clint said we could store this kind of stuff and any furniture we want to keep in their garage."

"That was nice of him," I mutter, but she still hears it.

"Can you promise me something?"

"That all depends on what it is." Pulling the refrigerator open, I find a bottle of water and twist the top.

"Can you please be nice to them? They're doing us a huge favor... they've done us a huge favor. If they didn't buy this place after your dad walked out, then I have no idea what we'd have done."

"They only did it out of guilt."

"No, they didn't. They did it because they are nice, honest people. Mason," she says on a sigh, placing a bowl down and turning toward me. My breath catches because she looks more like the mom I remember than I've seen in years. "You need to stop blaming them for what happened. It was your dad who fucked up. He deserved to be caught and to be laid off."

"I don't disagree, Mom. It was just the way it was done. They went behind his back. That didn't need to happen. If they were more considerate about it all then he might still be here. This might not be happening right now." I wave my arm around at all the boxes.

"We're better off without him. He'd have ruined us no matter what."

"You really believe that?" She makes it out like it was all his fault. She seems to forget that the final nail in the coffin for Dad firmly rests on her shoulders.

"I do. Your childhood memories of him aren't the man he was."

I don't believe a word she says. My dad was a good man until everything went to shit. Okay, so he didn't have to leave, but Mom didn't give him much choice in the end.

When I allow myself to think of him, I see afternoons on a football field as he supported me either from the sidelines, out in the garden as he helped me practice plays, or on the computer as he taught me how to play games and baffled me with his tech knowledge that I didn't have a chance in hell of understanding, but it was what made him tick.

Leaving Mom behind with a couple of flat boxes in my hand, I head to my room. My entire childhood—my life—is in this one room. The thought of packing it all into the boxes propped up against the wall fills me with dread, although not as much dread as the prospect of where we're going to be moving to.

Falling down on my bed, I make the mistake of closing my eyes.

The next thing I know, the sun's pouring in around the edges of my curtains and my alarm is blaring loudly next to me.

Sitting up, I realize that I'm still in my Price Chop uniform and the boxes I left by the door are still there waiting to be filled.

"Fuck," I shout, dropping my head into my hands and scrubbing them down my face.

I'm fucking exhausted, but I can't see it getting better anytime soon. Heather was reluctant, but she agreed to let me pick up shifts at the store every day after school until closing. I promised her it was going to be a short term thing until I could get enough cash together to at least give us a deposit on a place. I refuse to allow my brothers to live in someone else's house because their parents are fuck-ups for too long.

Coach was less than pleased when I went to his office yesterday morning to explain that I was having to step down from the team. He was rightly concerned. He knows as well as I do that my only shot at college next year is a football scholarship, but what choice do I have? My family has to come first. I can always go to college in the future, but my brothers will never get a second chance at their childhood.

Ignoring the boxes, I drag my weary body toward the shower and start getting ready for another long ass day where I've not done the homework that's going to be expected of me and I work in a shitty discount store until I can't put one foot in front of the other.

Mom's nowhere to be seen when I eventually get downstairs with both Charlie and Ollie in tow. Thankfully, Ollie has a friend in the next street whose Mom picks them both up to take them to school. I have no idea how I'd cope if I had to do more than get them up and dressed.

"Good morning, my gorgeous boys."

"Mom? What are you doing up?"

"Don't looked so shocked, Mase. I am capable of getting up and making my boys breakfast."

"Really?"

Her eyebrows almost hit her hairline, although I have no idea why she's surprised. I can't remember the last time I saw her this side of midday. I know she worked late, but I'm sure there are other parents out there who do nights and still manage to be a parent.

"I thought I'd take my little men to school today."

A look passes between Ollie and Charlie. They look anything but pleased. What I wouldn't give to know what they're thinking right now.

"It's okay, Mrs. Richmond can take us."

Mom pales. "Oh, okay. Well, I'd like to pick you up."

Ollie blows out a frustrated breath, but he doesn't refuse.

I have no idea what she's up to, but quite frankly I don't have the time to sit around to find out. "Well, if you're making these guys breakfast, I'm going to head out."

Playing happy families was not on my to do list today. If I can get into school early, maybe I can hit the library and attempt to do some of the homework most other kids will manage while I'm working my ass off.

———

"What the fuck's going on?" Jake demands when he falls down into his seat in History later that morning. Our teacher is standing at the front of the class ready to start, but in true Jake Thorn style, he doesn't give a shit and stares me down until he gets the answers he wants.

"Not now," I mutter, knowing we're going to have people listening around us.

"Yes. Right fucking now. Let's go."

He's up and out of his chair with his bag over his shoulder waiting for me while Miss White's face turns beet red in frustration.

"Mason and I have another engagement," he barks as he all but pushes me through the doorway and away from our bewildered teacher.

"We can't just walk out."

"Why the fuck not? You can't tell me you actually wanted to be sitting in there." I open my mouth to respond, but I don't really have an argument. Where I really want to be is in bed sleeping, but knowing my luck, it's probably already been moved into the Lopezes' garage.

Silence hangs heavy between us as we walk out toward the field. The stadium's deserted and I realize that was Jake's plan. To get me alone and get the truth out of me.

"Coach said you'd bailed on the team. What the fuck don't I know, Mase? I know I've been spending more time with Brit but fuck, man. If you need me, you know where I am."

I blow out a long breath, turning away from his assessing blue eyes and stare across the field.

"Everything's fucked up. Mom's lost her job. The Lopezes own our house and are selling it, and with no other fucking option we're all moving in with them."

Jake doesn't respond immediately, and when I turn to him, he's sitting with his mouth agape as if he can't find the right words.

"I've had to increase my hours at the store in an attempt to do something. I can't fucking stay under the same roof as them."

"You mean as her?"

"Yes. No. I don't fucking know." I stand and shove my hands into my hair. "I don't know anything right now other than I've had to give up the one thing that keeps me going in order to bail my fucking mother out again. This is my senior year. It shouldn't be like this."

"I know, man. Trust me, I know."

I turn to look at my best friend with frown lines

marring his forehead. I know that out of everyone, he understands, but his sympathy isn't going to help me right now.

"How much do you need? Maybe you could ask Bri—"

"No. No fucking way am I asking your girlfriend for a handout. I'm not a fucking charity case."

"I know that, and it would only be a loan until you get yourself sorted."

"And how exactly would I pay it back? We need every penny I can earn for rent, bills and food."

He blows out a breath. "I just need you on the field."

"I know. I need to be there too, but something's got to give."

"This is bullshit."

I fall back down beside him as the silence stretches out as we contemplate the lives we've been dealt, even though Jake's is very much looking up these days.

"How long do you think it'll be before you fuck her?"

"What?" I blanch. "I'm not going to fuck her. Kill her maybe," I muse.

"Whatever. Getting a bit of action might help chill you out a little though." I give him a side eye and he just shrugs. "You coming to Ethan's party Friday night? Maybe you could pull and blow off some steam."

"I'll be working."

"Come after. You know it'll be an all nighter if Ethan has anything to do with it."

The thought of going and having fun with our class and watching them all down drink after drink and act like they've got no cares in the world doesn't thrill me with joy, but what's my alternative? A night in the Lopezes' guest room?

The next thing I know, it's Friday night, my stuff is all packed into boxes in my room ready to be moved up the street, and I'm standing behind the checkout in Price Chop when I should be on the field with my team trying to kick Penshore's asses.

Amalie keeps messaging me and I keep checking my cell to see the score even though it kills me to know what they're achieving without me. Seeing that they're winning is bittersweet. Of course I want them to win. I want them to walk all over the Chargers after they knocked us out last year, but I hate that they don't need me. Being a Rosewood Bear gave me something to belong to when my life has felt like it's spiraling out of control, and I don't want to be disposable to them much like I am to some of the people in my life.

Yes, my mother relies on me, but it's not me she needs, she just needs someone. Camila doesn't need me. She moved on with her life pretty fast after I gave her the cold shoulder. My brothers need me, but that's only because our parents are fuck-ups. What they really need is a decent Mom and Dad.

A couple of customers walk up to me and I'm forced out of my depressing thoughts so I can scan their items.

My cell vibrates in my pocket again with another update, and my fingers twitch to pull it out midway through checking, but the last thing I need is to be caught and fired.

I end up with a line, and by the time I get to pull my cell out again, it's vibrated at least six times and the game's long over. Shame my shift isn't.

A smile curls at the corners of my lips when I look

down at Amalie's penultimate message telling me that we smashed it. My chest swells with pride for the team, who for all intents and purposes are my family, but sadness that I'm not a part of their elation right now sits heavy in my stomach.

Amalie: We'll see you at Ethan's, yeah?

I stare down at her message. I'm tempted, but I'm pretty sure it's the prospect of drinking my body weight in alcohol that makes Ethan's party seem appealing more than spending time with my classmates who'll probably spend the night asking where I was tonight.

The rest of my shift drags on until eventually the clock hits midnight and at least I'm able to help Heather close up for the night and head home.

My eyes are heavy as I drive from the west side of town toward our street. The only house I've ever called home looks different as I pull up in the drive. We haven't even moved out and yet it feels like it should belong to someone else already. The connection I've always felt to the place, to my dad, has already been broken. That feeling is only strengthened when I step into my sparse bedroom. The only thing that remains is my bed; everything else is gone. Mom told me that Clint and a few friends were coming today to clear the place, but I didn't want to believe it. I wanted to believe that this was all one big joke and I'd come home to Mom laughing about it while telling me about her new job. Sadly, that's not the case. After poking my head into my brothers' room, I find that totally empty along with Mom's, and I know they've already moved out.

I stand surrounded by nothing but old memories and

realize I have two options: I stay here alone and miserable, or I find alcohol and a distraction or two. The second option wins out.

13

CAMILA

It takes all of about five seconds after the Bears hit the field to notice something—or someone—is missing.

"Where's Mason?" I ask, turning toward Amalie who's shouting and screaming along with the crowd. It a far cry from the girl I dragged along to the first few games of the series.

"He uh..." A conflicted look crosses her face. "He wasn't able to play tonight." I narrow my eyes at her but don't press the issue. It's obvious she knows more than she's letting on but has promised Jake she'll keep Mason's secrets. I should respect that she's being loyal, but mostly it just pisses me off.

Mason's not one to miss a game. It took everything we all had to stop him playing with a broken collarbone back when we were friends. Nothing short of a disaster would keep him from the field.

I briefly wonder if his reaction to having to move in with us is enough to do it, but I can't imagine he's anything but thrilled that he gets to torment me under my own roof for the foreseeable future.

The game is incredible. Our Bears are all over their Chargers, and Jake is on fire as he leads our team to an outstanding win. Amalie screams beside me for her man until her throat must be hoarse. He's in for a good night once she gets her hands on him, that's for sure. Jealousy stirs within me knowing that neither of them are going to be able to keep their hands off each other whereas my boyfriend didn't bother traveling for this away game. I know it's out of town, but I was driving no matter what, he could have at least showed his face. He's been irritating me more and more this week, and I hate that it's Mason's words that ring out in my head every time I even think about him.

We usually hang out quite often, but I feel like I've hardly seen Noah this week. I know I've had stuff going on and some of that's on me, but still, I haven't seen him long enough to even begin to explain about Mason moving in, and I need to because he needs to hear from me that his presence in my house isn't going to affect us. Noah's never been the kind of guy to get jealous. Our relationship's been so steady and easy that neither of us has needed to. But equally, neither of us has had to live with our ex-best friends who could quite easily have been more, either. If he finds out from someone else and assumes that I've been lying to him then it's really not going to look good.

When I asked him if he was going to Ethan's after we all get back later, he just mumbled a maybe. Not exactly the kind of response I was looking for.

"Come on, we need to meet the guys."

"You mean you need to shove your tongue down Jake's throat the second he appears."

"Yeah, that." She doesn't even attempt to apologize, instead just grabs my hand and drags me from the stands. Penshore clearly has more money than Rosewood does. Its football stadium is seriously impressive and huge in comparison to ours, and while it would take us barely five minutes to find where the guys will exit at home, here it's almost fifteen.

Much to Amalie's delight, we're just in time and the guys come barreling out all fresh from their showers with wide smiles on their faces as they laugh and joke with each other, celebrating their win.

Jake takes one look at his girl heading his way and takes off running until he scoops her up in his arms and spins her around while she squeals.

I smile as I watch them, but it doesn't get rid of the heavy feeling in my stomach.

Because Jake is a law unto himself, he manages to get both himself and Ethan excused from traveling home in the school bus with the rest of the team. I soon discover why, because I haven't pulled out of Penshore's parking lot before he's got Amalie pinned to the backseat.

"Really?" I bark.

"What? I'm celebrating our win. You watched, it was fucking epic. I deserve this."

"I'm not denying that, but maybe you do deserve it in private later."

Jake flips me off over his shoulder and I blow out a long, frustrated breath.

"You jealous? I'm sure we could solve that, baby." Ethan's hand stretches between the console between us as if he's going for my thigh. I slap it away like it's a wild animal.

"Ow," he complains, rubbing the back of his hand.

"You only had to say no." He sulks while the lip smacking behind continues.

"No," I state. "Not in a million years." I glance over at him, ensuring disgust fills my eyes.

"So where's your *lovely* boyfriend tonight? Too busy to escort you to the game?"

"Busy with friends."

"Well at least we know he wasn't with a certain cheerleader, seeing as she was shaking her pom poms for a crowd with us."

A loud slap rings out around the car before Ethan complains once again.

"Shut the fuck up, man," Jake says between his heavy breathing.

"What? I was just saying what we were all thinking."

My stomach turns over to the point I think I might puke in my lap. Is that what everyone thinks of me? Am I that girl who just turns a blind eye to my boyfriend's actions because I'm stupid and trust him?

"He's just being a dick, Cam. Ignore him." Amalie's hand lands on my shoulder in support. Although from the things she's said about the situation, I suspect she's on Ethan's side.

"You all think I'm stupid, don't you?"

"Only you know the real situation and the real Noah," Amalie soothes. "If you say he's trustworthy, then we support you, one-hundred percent. Right, guys?"

"Right," Jake agrees. Not that he has much choice. He's more clever than to go against Amalie and end up with blue balls until the end of time.

"Sure. But if it all goes south, hit me up. I can make you feel so good about it all, baby."

My lips curl in disgust. "You're a dog."

Conversation turns to tonight's game and I mostly zone everyone out as I stew on my current situation. That on top of not knowing where Mason was tonight is enough to have the beginnings of a headache throbbing at my temples. I want to ask about him, I'm desperate to, but I know how it'll look to the guys, so as much as it pains me, I keep my lips sealed.

"Pizza. I need pizza," Ethan suddenly chirps when we head toward a restaurant.

"Don't you need to be back to let people into your house?"

"Nah, they all know what they're doing. Come on, you guys must be hungry."

Sounds of agreement ring out around the car, and I find myself pulling into the parking lot so we can feed the beast.

I try to allow their excitement over their win to filter into me, but the truth is that Ethan's words about Noah are on repeat in my head. We know he wasn't with her, but where was he tonight? Where's he been all week?

I fucking hate questioning him. He told me he was meeting friends to do some homework. Never before would I have questioned him. He's got a plan for next year and he needs the grades, I've always appreciated that, but now, after what Mason did and accused him of, I just don't know anymore. Everything's festering inside me and it's making what I feel for my boyfriend turn sour, which is ridiculous because he's not done anything wrong. Or has he?

"Mason would have fucking loved tonight. I hate that he's not here." Those few words from Ethan are enough to drag me back to the present.

"I know, but he's got to do his thing. Hopefully he'll be

back," Jake says sadly, but from the tightness of his features I'm not sure I believe him.

"What the fuck's he got going on? Banging some hot chick we don't know about who's more important than us?"

My spine stiffens and Amalie doesn't miss it. I shouldn't give a shit. Just like Ethan, it's no secret that Mason's made his way around the cheer squad and half the female population at Rosewood. Hearing this isn't unusual, but why do I suddenly care so much?

"Ha, nothing like that, man. Just family shit, you know how it is."

If I wasn't watching Ethan quite so closely for his response then I might miss the brief darkening of his eyes and the way his muscles tense for the slightest moment. He shakes himself out of whatever it is quickly before saying, "Yeah. I get that. Sucks though."

"What family shit have you got to worry about? Your dad's filled your bank account and leaves you a mansion of a house to party in most weekends?" Jake says it lightheartedly but Ethan pales nonetheless.

"It's not all about money."

"Don't I know it."

The atmosphere around our table suddenly takes a depressing turn. I glance at Amalie, who shrugs a shoulder at me.

"So... one step closer to the playoffs then. You think you guys can hit top spot in the division this year?"

It takes a few minutes, but eventually, with the subject back on football, the air lightens and their previous excitement wins out.

With my belly bloated with pizza and soda, we head back to the car, ready to hit Ethan's house to party.

I'll admit that I've never really thought about him and his home situation that much. He's always living it up with his lavish parties and throwing money around, but hearing him talk about his parents' absence, it suddenly makes me realize how lonely his life must be aside from the wild parties. It makes me wonder how much of the real Ethan we all actually see. He's the joker, the one who gives zero fucks about everything; is he hiding his reality just as much as Jake was?

His mammoth house appears before us as the gravel of his driveway crunches under my tires. There are already people everywhere, and all the lights in the house are glowing from the windows. It looks like they've started without us.

I park my car, blocking in about five others when Ethan tells me just to stop in favor of jumping out.

"I can't just leave—"

"It's fine. None of these people will be leaving until morning," Jake says, also getting out and dragging Amalie with him.

This might be my first time attending one of Ethan's parties, but I'm not naive as to what they're like. Stories fly around for days after one of his blow outs. I can't say that I haven't been curious about experiencing one for myself, but being in the wrong friendship group as well as staying as far away from Mason as possible meant that I've never stepped foot inside Ethan's house before.

"You coming?" Amalie shouts back, making Jake pause halfway to the house.

Dragging my eyes away from the building that must be at least four times the size of my parents' house, I pull the keys from the ignition and step out.

Kids loiter around the outside of the house, some just

chatting to friends, others clearly already so drunk they can hardly stand up straight. *How long has this party been going on for exactly?* I wonder as we walk past everyone and follow behind Ethan, who throws the door open and holds his arms out in a 'the king is home' stance.

People look our way immediately, as if they can feel both his and Jake's presence, and cheers erupt.

Even from behind, I watch as Ethan's chest puffs out in pride while Jake pulls Amalie into his side and they duck off to the right. Not wanting to be part of the 'Ethan show,' I trail behind them until they come to a stop by a keg and Jake gets us all a drink.

"So this is an Ethan Savage party then?" I look around the room as the pounding music rattles my bones.

Scantily clad women fill the vast space, some hanging off guys, others dancing and drinking together. When I find Ethan again, he's in the middle of a group of girls wearing only bikinis. They all rub themselves up against him and he eagerly kisses one. My eyes widen. I know he's got a reputation, everyone at Rosewood knows that, but to see it with my own eyes is a bit of a shock. It seems I may have lived a somewhat sheltered life with my group of friends.

A red Solo cup is thrust in my hand, and in only a few minutes, I find it's empty. Turning back to Jake and Amalie, I find them tongue tied again, so after getting myself two more cups of beer, I head off on my own to explore the place in the hope I find some other friends who aren't going to spend the night sucking each other's faces off.

As I make my way through the house, I find I recognize about fifty percent of the people here. Fuck knows where the others have come from. I can only assume they're from the west side and living it up east style.

I don't find any of my friends, and even after the rest of the team appears, it soon becomes clear that Shane's also swerved this party.

The beer goes down a little too well, and by the time I find Amalie again in the kitchen she's watching Jake and a couple of other members of the team lining up shots of tequila.

"Hey, beautiful. How's it going?" Zayn, our wide receiver, slurs, wrapping his arm around my waist.

"Fine," I reply, my spine stiffening as I try to remove his hands from my body.

His hold tightens and I find myself pressed up against his body. "I haven't seen you here before."

"No, but you're in my math class and I've got a boyfriend."

"That won't stop him," someone calls from behind me.

"Well, it matters to me." I finally manage to escape his hold and move to the other side of Amalie.

Reaching out, I grab one of the shots in front of her before downing it and going for another. I hope like hell that the alcohol helps me find the fun in this party, because right now I can't think of anything that could make this evening worse.

I just knock back the second shot when silence falls over the room.

"Mason, my man! We missed you tonight."

Every muscle in my body locks up tight just hearing his name. I haven't been this close to him since the morning after the night he found his way into my bedroom. Yeah, I've seen him around school and in classes, but he's mostly kept his head down. I can only assume that's got something to do with his new living accommodation. I can't forget about the fact that in only hours, he's going to be moving into my house.

His eyes find mine and a shudder runs down my spine. How the hell are we going to survive each other living under the same roof?

"Yeah well, I couldn't let you fuckers party without me as well. Who's got the good stuff?" Prying his eyes away from mine, he glances around the room.

I spin on the spot, reaching for another shot and downing it instantly. I don't even feel the burn like I did with the previous two.

My head spins but I welcome the distraction. The sensible thing to do right now would be to call an Uber and leave, but something tells me to stay. Some fucked up part of me wants to experience this party and all it has to offer. I tell myself that's got nothing to do with the guy who's just entered, but I'm not so sure that's true. I'm desperate to know why he bailed on tonight's game but is seemingly okay to turn up here ready to drink.

A shiver runs down my spine seconds before his scent fills my nose. I suck in a deep breath and hold it, not knowing what's about to happen.

"Why the fuck are you wasting this stuff on the likes of her?" Disdain drips from his words, making Amalie's mouth drop open and the muscle in Jake's neck pulsate.

"Play nice," Jake barks. "Hopefully this will chill you the fuck out." He hands Mason a shot.

He lifts it in the air as if he's going to make some big speech, but when he doesn't say anything, I stupidly look over my shoulder. His eyes find mine and they hold for a second too long, his dark ones becoming almost black as something unpleasant crackles between us.

Every dread I had about what we've got to come once he moves in quadruples in those few seconds before he drags his eyes away and downs his shot. The muscles in his neck ripple as he swallows, and I hate myself for not being able to look away.

"I need more than that."

Jake sets about fulfilling Mason's request to get steaming drunk as the song booming from the speakers in the other room changes.

"Come on, let's dance." Amalie grabs my hand and drags me away to where we can see a makeshift dance floor.

"Did someone say dance?" Zayn calls. I look back to see him bouncing toward us like an overexcited puppy, but the heated stare coming from behind him that burns into me soon catches my attention.

I knew coming here was a bad idea. It's a real shame that I'm already too drunk to really care or do anything about it.

Amalie drags me in front of her, and, with our hands locked together, we start moving to the music. Zayn comes up behind me, places his hands on my hips and joins in. I should push him away. I should be thinking about Noah, but in that moment, all I think about and feel is the beat of the music pounding through me and the way my body moves.

One song blurs into another. Zayn continues to grind behind me, and eventually I feel Amalie move away from me. When I drag my eyes open I understand why when

Jake pulls her back into him and they move smoothly together.

My heart aches as I stare at them so in sync, so connected, so in love. Whereas I'm here dancing with a guy I barely like and no idea where my actual boyfriend is.

The thought is sobering at best, and after detaching myself from Zayn, I head back to where the alcohol was. The tequila bottle is laying empty on the counter, so I'm forced to take a beer when someone offers it to me.

"Careful who you take drinks from. You don't know who's been here before." I look up to find a junior with a smirk on his face. "Oh, that's right. Shane's not here."

"Shane didn't do that," I seethe. "He's not like that."

"Facts speak for themselves though, don't you think."

"Fuck you."

The guy's eyes widen slightly but he doesn't respond, instead grabbing two cups of his own and stalking from the kitchen.

With two cups in hand, I lean against the wall and watch the bodies dancing and gyrating against each other. Some of the scantily clad girls from outside seem to have appeared and are hanging off most of the football team, hoping to get lucky. Seeing all the bare skin makes me realize that the cheer team are nowhere to be seen. I can't believe they'd miss one of Ethan's parties.

Someone walking through one of the many doors that leads to the garden catches my eyes.

"Noah?" I ask, even though he's too far away and the music's too loud for him to hear me. My brows draw together as he sways his way toward me, looking three sheets to the wind already. So much for him not coming, it seems he's been partying for quite some time.

He doesn't say anything as he steps up to me. Instead he wraps his hand around the back of my neck and pulls my lips to his. He's forceful in a way I've never experienced before, but I put it down to the alcohol and allow myself to melt into him.

His other hand grips my hip as his tongue delves into my mouth. The taste of strong alcohol explodes on my taste buds, and that's saying something because I've had enough now to make the world spin around me.

I must have somehow managed to get the cups I was holding onto the table beside me, because the next thing I know, I'm back on the dance floor moving against Noah. My body follows orders but for some reason my brain screams that I shouldn't be doing this.

Why isn't it as fun as when I was dancing with Zayn?

I look up to find Noah's kind eyes in the hope it'll settle whatever is going on in my head, but I don't make it that far. Instead my gaze falls on Chelsea and her team's grand entrance. I stifle a giggle because she can only be so grand while hobbling along on two crutches. The image of Jake pushing her from the stage at Homecoming fills my mind, and my previous laugh falls from my lips. It really was a fall from grace for our queen bitch.

Flanking her sides is Tasha and Shelly followed by the rest of the team. Everyone but Chelsea is only dressed in their bikinis, and water droplets from the pool glisten under the spotlights.

There's a lull in the noise level as they enter, exactly as Chelsea would want it, and almost every set of eyes turn their way. Breasts get pushed out and hair is flipped over shoulders. It's really quite a sight to behold, and it only makes me glad I never pursued wanting to be a member of the team. When I was seven or eight, I thought it would be a great idea, especially because it would keep me close to Mason, but it wasn't long before I discovered that I wasn't the kind of girl that belonged on the squad. I don't care all that much about my appearance and I certainly have no intention of sleeping my way around the entire class, evidenced by my intact virginity. I wonder briefly if that's what Noah's intensity tonight is about. Is he hoping that I'll get drunk tonight and give it up? Well, if that's the case, he can think again. I've got too many questions running around my head about him to do that. Until I can get Mason's warning from repeating in my mind that most definitely isn't happening. I don't care how blue his balls are.

I follow the squad's progress as they make their way through the room. A couple drop off to find their boyfriends or the guys they're dating, but Chelsea seems to have a destination in mind because she doesn't stop hopping until she reaches it.

Oh fuck.

Mason.

He's standing at the edge of the room watching everyone, much like I was a few moments ago, but the crowd hid him from me.

Chelsea somehow manages to maneuver herself so she's pressed right up against him while Shelly takes his other side. It leaves Tasha standing somewhat awkwardly in front of the trio. She hovers for a few seconds in her skimpy red bikini before looking over her shoulder and directly behind me. Noah noticeably tenses as their eyes meet. Mine narrow at her but at no point does she look at me before she flicks her hair over her shoulder and saunters off.

I should say something. I should accuse him after

letting him off so easily at his birthday, and with the alcohol fueling my thoughts I'm just about to—that is until Chelsea frees one of her hands and threads it into Mason's hair. His body stills for a beat like he's not really all that happy about her attention. He glances up and our eyes collide. I shouldn't be watching this car crash, and that one look he gives me really shouldn't hit like a baseball bat to the chest, but I'm powerless to pull my eyes away as an evil smirk appears on his lips before he lowers his head and gives Chelsea exactly what she wants.

My stomach turns over, threatening to expel the alcohol sloshing around in it as even from here I watch his tongue slide in her mouth.

Suddenly I'm fourteen again and I'm watching my best friend, the boy who gave me my first kiss, flaunting how much he hates me in public. Anger bubbles within me, my veins turning red as lava fills them, and I spin in Noah's arms.

Concern twists his features. He watched every moment of what happened just like I did, but also unlike me, he's not questioning any of it. *It's because he's covering something up*, a voice screams in my head, but at this moment, I ignore her.

Reaching up on my tiptoes, I find his lips and kiss him as eagerly as I was just subjected to watch Chelsea kiss Mason.

My heart pounds, my temperature increases, but it's got nothing to do with Noah and everything to do with *him* and what he may or not be doing behind me.

I'm still kissing Noah when I drag my eyes open, and to my shock I find his wide and staring over my shoulder.

Is he watching us?

Breaking away, I drag some much needed air into my

lungs. I wait what I think is a suitable amount of time, but in reality, I'm drunk as fuck and it could be immediately that I look over my shoulder to find what, or who, has his interest.

There's no one there.

I scan the room, but I can't see Mason, Chelsea, Shelly or Tasha anywhere.

Noah's phone vibrates in his pocket between us. I look back to him as he pulls it out. His eyes are swimming with desire, but there's also something else in their depths that I'm too far gone to decipher.

"It's one of the guys wanting to know where I am. I'll be back. Get us a drink, yeah?"

Then as quick as he appeared, he's gone, disappeared into the crowd, leaving me standing alone with my chest heaving and my head spinning with confusion and anger.

What the hell just happened?

Not wanting to stand like a loner, I walk toward the drinks and grab myself another beer—not that I need it. My previous drinks are swirling around my stomach and making my head spin pretty bad. I've been drunk before, but I don't remember my surroundings moving quite this much.

I drink the beer faster than I intended as I try to find someone I actually like, but I come up short. The only person I spot that I know and would possibly talk to is Ethan, but he's otherwise engaged with the three—yes three—girls he's dancing with and molesting. They're lapping up his attention as they practically strip him naked on the couch.

He must realize he's got another's attention because he looks up and finds me staring.

"Always room for another, Cam-Cam." He opens his

arms wide as if trying to prove his point, but all it achieves is making my feet move faster.

With my need for the toilet starting to get the better of me, I go in search of a bathroom. I find a huge line for the one in this floor, but knowing just how big this house is I know there's more.

I just about manage to put one foot in front of the other to climb the stairs, and with the help of the gold handrail I eventually stumble into the second floor hallway.

"Jesus," I mutter as I stare down the long hall that's lined with doors.

There are a few people up here, most kissing and stumbling toward what they're hoping are empty bedrooms.

Ignoring them, I set out on my quest. Avoiding any doors that are shut, fearing what I might find behind them, I go for the open ones. I get an eyeful when I poke my head into a couple that I was not expecting, and even the ginormous family bathroom has a couple going at it on the tiled floor, but eventually, right at the end I find an empty bedroom with what looks like an en suite.

Breathing a sigh of relief, I stumble into the room, managing to catch my toe on the corner of the bed and face planting the floor.

"Ow," I complain, trying to grab my toe to inspect the damage but not managing to find it.

Giving up, I crawl to the door at the other end of the room.

My fingers don't want to follow instruction and it takes me about a year to pop the button on my jeans and shimmy them down my legs. But eventually I manage to do my business. I have no idea how long I sit there for, but when a noise sounds in the bedroom I just came through, I can't be sure I didn't fall asleep a little bit.

I manage to get my jeans up without making friends with the floor and step from the room when the two people that crashed inside become clear.

"Mason?"

14

MASON

I know the second I walk into Ethan's back garden that this is a bad idea. The cheer team are slutting it up in the pool—well, all but Chelsea, who's sulking with a drink on a lounger seeing as she can't get her cast wet.

They all shout for me to join them as well as questions about where I was tonight. Ignoring them in favor of drinking everything about my life away, I go in search of the alcohol. I know Ethan's house well, and if something doesn't get placed in my hand the second I walk into the kitchen then I'll go and find my own. His dad might think his office is secure, but the three of us know differently.

She's the only person I see when I walk into that kitchen, and damn her because the second I look into her eyes and see just how drunk she is, my need to get obliterated is overtaken by my stupid need to protect her. It's been four years. At what point can I actually stop caring?

I take the shot that Jake hands me, but after we watch both Amalie and Camila leave the room, I refuse any more. Jake doesn't question it. He knows I like to stay sober in case my brothers need me.

The whole night is a waste of fucking time, but it only gets worse when I stumble across Camila with her fucking boyfriend. Their hips grind together in time with the music like I'm sure they've done a million times before. My fingers twitch to rip her away from him for ever getting to touch her like that. They've been together for years now, I'm sure he's well acquainted with her body. My lips curl in disgust that someone else has been able to explore what should have been mine.

Because my life isn't already bad enough, I stay exactly where I am, leaning against the wall watching them. It's fucking torture but no less than I deserve.

The second the noise level dips and the sea of people in front of me part, I know I'm in trouble. Chelsea's eyes lock onto mine, and like a lion stalking her prey, she hops over to me.

Something burns down my spine as she gets closer, and a glance over her shoulder confirms that I've managed to get Camila's attention.

Happy to flaunt your cheating boyfriend in my face? I can do better.

Chelsea's a slut, almost all the cheer squad are, but she's one I've only had a few 'moments' with seeing as prior to Amalie's appearance, she only had eyes for Jake. Since he's now quite obviously taken, she seems to have set her sights on me. I, however, have no intention of receiving anything from her aside from the odd blow job if she really insists because damn, she's fucking good at them. Must be all the practice she's had.

I'm not proud of my actions, but with Camila's stare burning into me, I slam my lips down on Chelsea's. I regret it the second her sickly sweet perfume fills my nose and her fake ass nails dig into my skin.

It's worth it for all of a second when I see the mortified look on Camila's face. But that second is soon over because she firmly plants her lips on that motherfucker's, and I'm forced to watch him kiss her while he stares longingly across the room at Tasha.

Anger has my body trembling. My need to go and rip him from her and rearrange his face again is strong. But she chose not to believe me the last time, so why should I waste the energy in trying to show her what he really is?

Instead, I rip myself away from both Chelsea and Shelly, who's now joining in and rubbing my cock through my jeans, and storm from the room. I leave Chelsea sulking behind me but Shelly must decide it's her turn for a bit of one on one time because she follows me.

I need a drink, but the last thing I want is to not be aware of what I'm doing right now. I've made plenty of bad decisions in my life, but I don't want tonight to be one of them.

I walk around the house hoping to find Jake and Amalie while Shelly follows me like a lost fucking puppy. It's sad, really fucking sad, but I allow her to trail me thinking that I might be able to make use of her.

The moment I see Camila attempting to climb the stairs, I realize that she could be about to come in very handy.

"You wanna head upstairs?" Shelly's eyes light up like I've just offered her my lottery win, but I don't feel bad about using her weakness. I'm probably saving her from one of the assholes down here who'll really use her if she gives them half the chance.

Taking her hand, I pull her up the stairs, making sure I

stop to find an empty room, but I know the one I want. Ethan's is right at the end of the hall and everyone knows it's off limits. Everyone aside from the person I've just seen disappear inside.

"Mase, we can't, that's Eth—" Case in point about his room being off limits.

"I'm his best friend. The rules don't apply, baby." My stomach turns with saying those words to her, and to make my point, I tilt her head up and kiss her as I back her into the room. She soon sags against me, willing to give me everything I want.

I worry about Chelsea and her squad of hussies. They're going to get themselves into some serious trouble one day if they continue being so free and easy.

I slam her back against the door to make our appearance known, and it works like a fucking charm because only a few seconds later, Camila appears in the doorway.

"Mason?"

I glance at her, my lips still attached to Shelly's, and I don't miss how her face pales at finding us together.

"Perfect," I drawl when I pull away from a panting Shelly. "You fancy adding another to our party, Shell?"

"The more the merrier."

With my arm around her waist, I pull her over to where Camila's frozen on the spot. I reach for her but stop the second she looks like she's about to throw up, and thank fuck I didn't grab her because she bolts to the bathroom and heaves into the toilet.

"Ew," Shelly complains, backing up toward the door. Clearly I wasn't all that important if she's going to run before she's even got any action.

I let her go—I didn't even want her here, really—before stepping inside the bathroom to check on Camila.

She's slumped next to the toilet, her eyes are closed and her head lolled to the side. She's out of it.

"Camila?" I flush the toilet before bending down in front of her. "Cami-bear?"

She moans as if she can hear me but doesn't respond.

"Where's your useless cunt of a boyfriend? He should be looking after you right now."

"I dunno," she slurs. "Gone."

"Motherfucker." I slam my palm down on the tiles behind her and she doesn't even flinch. "When are you going to realize what a waste of fucking space he is, huh?"

She doesn't respond other than to snore lightly.

I should leave her here. After everything, it's what I should do, but that's not who I am. I can act like I hate her, like she single-handedly ruined my life, but even I know that it's a lie. And telling myself that I stopped caring about her after her family ran my dad out of town and sent my life into a spirally mess is an even bigger lie I tell myself most days. Underneath all my hate and frustration at the world is still the little boy who would do anything for his girl.

Forgetting about my need for revenge and my mission to hurt her, I scoop her up in my arms and walk from the room.

"Where we going? Noah, need Noah."

Just hearing his name falling from her lips when the fuck-up is probably balls deep in Tasha as we speak pisses me off beyond belief and almost has me dumping her on Ethan's bed for him to deal with later. But when I glance down at her conflicted sleeping face, something bigger tugs at my heart and I find myself walking from his house and laying her across the seats in the back of my car to get her home.

Thankfully, knowing Ethan's house as I do, I take her out the back and only a handful of people spot us.

It's long past midnight when I pull up outside her house. Seeing my mother's car parked in her driveway brings reality crashing back down on me. This isn't just her home now, it's mine too for the foreseeable future.

How am I supposed to look at her every day? How am I supposed to deal with her fucking boyfriend coming around and playing nice with her parents, which I'm sure he does? He's just that kind of smarmy fucker.

Knowing everyone will be fast asleep by now, I pull the key out that my mom gave me and let us in. The house is in darkness as I carry her up the stairs. She stirs, telling me that she's not completely comatose, but she's still had way too fucking much to drink. Where the fuck was *he*? It's his job to ensure she's safe. He must have known how much she'd had to drink when he was dancing with her. This right now, it's not my fucking job.

I kick her bedroom door open and step inside, managing to flick the light on without dropping her. I'm immediately hit with memories I'd rather disintegrated with our friendship. The walls are the same shade of soft pink they always were, and everything's in exactly the same place.

I remember sitting at her desk, working on homework. Lying on the floor, playing with our toys. Snuggling under her duvet watching films that were too old for us. My heart aches for what we once had and what we could have been if it weren't for me and my need for revenge.

This girl was my everything and I ruined that. The realization is startling. That first kiss we shared in this room, it could have led to something incredible. Or did everything work out as it should? Would we have always ended up hating each other in the end?

She stirs in my arms and I'm reminded of why I'm standing here right now, wondering what if.

"Mason," she moans. I have no idea if she's realized it's me holding her or if she's dreaming, but the sound of my name falling from her lips does something to me. My veins fill with fire and my cock swells. "Mase, please." There's heat in her words, a heat I don't need to hear, ever.

"Fuck," I grunt, placing her on the bed and backing up to the door.

I have one more night where I'm able to put space between us, so instead of heading to my new room, I leave the house and go home for my last and lonely night in the only home I've ever known.

15

CAMILA

When I come to, I soon realize that I'm lying in a puddle of my own drool and that my head is fucking pounding.

What the— "Oh fuck," I whisper into the silence of my room as hazy images from last night start to hit me.

Shots of tequila.

Noah.

Mason.

Bathroom.

Mason and Shelly.

Fuck. My stomach churns and I prepare to puke over the side of whoever's bed I'm currently sleeping in.

I remember being carried and being laid out on a comfortable bed, but I don't have the fucking slightest of clues as to who did that. Noah, maybe? Jake? Did Amalie find me and look after me?

My head spins as I try to make sense of anything other than the fact that I drank way too much. I went to that party wanting to forget, but before I've even opened my eyes, I'm regretting the stupid decision.

I suck in a few deep breaths through my nose, and once the swirling of my stomach has subsided, I crack my eyes open.

What the—

I'm in my bedroom. I blink a few times, thinking I must be still asleep, or my alcohol fuzzed brain is making me see things. But I really am in my bedroom. Looking down, I find that I'm still in my Rosewood Bears t-shirt and my jeans that I pulled on before last night's game, although they now have puke on them. Gross.

Whoever it was who got me back here last night certainly did not see me at my best.

I prop my pillows up against my headboard and lie back. My usual glass of water is sitting on my nightstand, but unusually there's a packet of Advil sitting next to it. The sight makes me smile, but it doesn't help me figure out how I got here.

A thought hits me and my head snaps to the side, expecting to find I have a bed partner, but that part of the bed definitely hasn't been slept in.

Reaching for the tablets, I pop two out while thanking whoever was thoughtful enough to leave them and wash them down with the water.

Slinking back down under the covers, I will them to kick in soon so I can get up without worrying that I might puke on my feet.

I lie there wondering how much of a fool I made of myself last night as the sounds of people moving around and chatter downstairs filters up to me.

Fuck. Today's the Paines' official moving in day. Groaning, I roll over and somehow the pounding in my head subsides enough for me to fall back to sleep.

Eventually banging from the other side of the wall

wakes me back up. Thankfully, the pounding inside my head has lessened and I don't want to puke the moment I sit up, so I take that as a positive. Looking at my alarm, I blanch when I see it's almost lunchtime. I love sleeping, but I'm not one to sleep in this late.

Swinging my legs from the bed, I grab a change of clothes and head for the bathroom.

I feel like a new woman once I've brushed my teeth. It's almost like the simple task washes away my hangover. I turn the shower on nice and hot, strip out of yesterday's clothes, and step under the spray, hoping it'll wash away the memories as well as the stench of alcohol that seems to be clinging to me.

With my dark hair freshly blow dried and straightened, and a fresh white tank with a simple pair of sweats where my dirty old clothes once were, I pull the door open and step into the hallway.

The banging I could hear had totally passed me by in my need to get clean, but the second I round the corner I almost crash into reality.

There in front of me, topless and showing off what seems like miles of rippling muscles, is Mason attempting to single-handedly maneuver a double bed into the bedroom next to mine.

I'm powerless but to stand and watch as he tries to twist it this way and that to successfully get it into the room that used to be my dad's home office. It had been emptied a few days ago for our new tenants. I'd hoped that maybe his mom or brothers would be allocated that room, but apparently the universe wants to torture me some more by making him my neighbor.

His muscles ripple and stretch as he continues to fight with the huge wooden base.

What I should do is sneak back into the bathroom before he sees me, seeing as I need to pass him in order to get to my bedroom. But obviously that isn't what happens. I move, but it's not to hide. Instead I lean against the doorframe and watch, too fascinated to drag my eyes away from his body.

A guy's body isn't an alien thing to me, but seeing as Noah's more of a computer geek than a jock, it's safe to say that I'm not used to the kind of definition my eyes are feasting on right now.

I have no idea if I make a noise, there's a very good chance as he bends to try to lift the bed over the doorjamb that I moan or something else equally embarrassing, because he does have one fine ass. Even if the guy attached to it isn't all that pleasant. There's got to be something good that comes out of this arrangement, and if it's that I get a bit of regular eye candy then I guess I can live with that.

His head pops up and he immediately finds me watching him. Even with the distance between us, I see his eyes darken and drop as they take in my scantily clad body. I immediately regret not putting a bra on under my tank when I feel my nipples beginning to pebble under his intense stare.

"You just gonna stand there staring or are you going to fucking help?"

"Oh... uh... yeah, sure." I drop the dirty clothes I'm holding on a pile on the floor and race over.

"Can you squeeze through that gap and pull from inside?" He nods toward the tiny space between the bed frame and the door, but he must realize it's probably impossible when his eyes drop to my breasts once again. They definitely aren't getting through that gap.

"How about you squeeze through. That way if it falls, it'll only fall on you." His eyes widen in shock, although I swear I see a little pride in there too.

Over the past four years I haven't made all that effort to stand my ground with him. I figured there wasn't much of a point. He was going to hate me whether I bit back or not. I just preferred it to be over quicker so I could attempt to move on with my life. Things have changed over the past couple of weeks though, especially with him now moving in here. I'm not going to sit back and accept whatever shit he wants to throw at me. This is my house, and if he thinks he can walk all over me, then he's got another think coming.

"Sounds good. I always prefer the girl on top anyway."

The image of him with his hands and lips all over Shelly last night hits me out of nowhere, and I sway slightly with the sheer force of it.

"What?" he asks when he notices a change in me.

"Bet Shelly fucking loved that last night. She's probably spent all morning bragging to her pathetic friends about riding number eleven." I don't realize my mistake until I say his number. He didn't play.

He blanches but covers it quickly. "She fucking better be. I rocked her fucking world."

"'Course you did, hotshot."

His eyes narrow. "You're just jealous because you'll never get to find out."

"Ha, yeah. Jealous. How'd you figure me out?" I roll my eyes so hard they actually hurt, but the way my blood heats beneath my skin makes me wonder how true his words might actually be. Seeing him with both Chelsea and Shelly last night did something to me. Shaking my thoughts from my mind, I find that Mason's slipped through the gap. "We doing this or just stroking your already fucking massive ego?"

"It's not my massive ego you should be thinking about, Cami-bear."

"Fuck you, Mase. Do you want my help or not?"

"Fine, but only so I can have a bed tonight."

"For sleeping," I add. "I refuse to listen to you banging your conquests on the other side of the wall from where I sleep."

He tugs the frame and the whole thing moves forward. I hold it but barely, allowing him to do all the work and get it into place. He gently lowers it to the carpet, and I stand back to watch, still too fascinated by his body than I should be. Nothing's said between us. My last statement hangs heavy in the air. Until he turns and pins me with his dark stare.

He takes a step toward me and I take a huge one back. He looks like he's a lion stalking his prey, and I get the feeling he's about to have me for lunch.

"You'll fucking love it, lying there listening to the moans I drag out of them. Imagining it's you beneath me. Imagining it's my hands bringing you more pleasure than you've ever experienced before."

My back hits the wall, but he keeps coming. I glance over his shoulder but I have no hope of ducking him and getting to the door.

"We both know that I'd be more capable than that waste of fucking space boyfriend of yours. I would say I bet he hardly knows where to put it, but we both know that's not true because he's sticking it to Tasha pretty well, so I hear."

"Fuck you." My arm flies out to slap him, but just like

the last time I tried this move he catches it before it makes contact and pins it to the wall above my head.

The move makes my back arch, my breasts thrusting forward. He closes the space between us, his heat burning through my thin clothing.

"If only you stopped resisting." My head spins for a few seconds, trying to figure out what the fuck I said, but the moment I realize, my cheeks heat and I fight to get away.

"Yeah, because you're an asshole," I spit. "Now get your fucking hands off me." I push from the wall, but all it achieves is for us to press closer together. My skin tingles and something explodes low down in my stomach.

His manly scent fills my nose, and I'm powerless to stop the hitch in my breathing as he stares down at me.

"You fucking love me being an asshole. That's why your heart's racing, why your nipples are fucking begging me to suck on them, and I bet you're wet as fuck for me right now." His free hand lifts and he trails one fingertip along the edge of my tank.

Sure as shit, my nipples tighten almost painfully as goosebumps skate across my skin. He hooks his finger in the fabric at my cleavage and pulls. My breath catches that he's about to expose me, but his eyes don't leave mine. He releases the fabric in favor of running the same finger around the waistband of my sweats.

"Shall we find out if I'm right? I bet you're wetter for me than you ever are for him. What do you think?"

"Mason." I wanted his name to be a warning, but fuck if it doesn't just sound needy.

My pussy throbs for attention and I'm almost at the point of demanding he does something about it when he removes all contact from me and stands back.

An evil smirk tugs at his lips. "Wow, Cami-bear. I thought you'd at least put up a bit of a fight. Seems you and your boyfriend deserve each other if you'd give yourself over to me that easily. Now get the fuck out of my bedroom."

I push from the wall and all but run to the door.

"And Cami-bear?" I shouldn't turn around but fuck if it's not what my head does the second I hear him say my name. "I don't want to hear you strumming one out next door now that you're all hot and bothered."

"Fuck. You." I don't hang around long enough to hear his response. Instead I run to my room and slam the door.

Why doesn't this door have a fucking lock on it?

16

MASON

I'm equally amused as I am fucking horny after watching Camila run from my new bedroom. It was true what I said, I was shocked she allowed that to go as far as it did and fuck if I wasn't about two seconds from sliding my hand into her fucking hideous sweatpants to find out what she really thinks of me. She was begging for it, that much was obvious. It makes me hate her fucking boyfriend that much more for not taking care of her as he should be and putting all his efforts into his cheerslut.

I think back to last night and the state she was in. Where the hell was he? He was at the party, I'd already seen Camila sucking his fucking face off. What guy in their right mind disappears on a girl who's all over them like she was him?

"Fucking idiot," I mutter as I throw my mattress on top of my bedframe and fall down onto it. My chest heaves from the exertion it took to get the fucking thing over here. Mom had help from Clint and his friends to move all her shit. It seems no one cares how I move in. In fact, they've already settled in so well that they've all gone for a fun family day out. I wasn't even invited.

Dragging my cell from my pocket, I pull up my recent messages and find our group chat.

Me: Workout?

It's probably the last thing the guys want to do after the game last night, but I'm agitated and storming into Camila's room and finishing what we started up against my bedroom wall isn't really an option, so I go for the next best thing.

Ethan: Fuck that, man. Still got two chicks in bed.

I shake my head at my best friend. I want to be disgusted with his ways, but right now even I can admit that I'm jealous as fuck. I didn't want to fuck Shelly last night, but damn, that doesn't mean I don't need to. My balls are so fucking blue right now they're almost fucking ice.

Jake: I'm in. If Ethan's busy you'll have to put up with my gym though.

By his gym, he means his little set up behind his trailer. We both kinda rely on Ethan to get us into his decent gym, seeing as neither of us has the money for the membership that he does.

Me: Perfect. Give me twenty.

I'm not fussy. I don't need a fancy weight bench or an

all singing, all dancing crosstrainer. A tree branch and the rusty bike Jake pulled from a skip a few months ago is all I need to burn off a little steam and try to get the idea of how fucking up for it Camila was just a few moments ago from my head.

Despite the fact that I'm going to work out, I head for the shower first before pulling on my own pair of sweatpants and a fresh t-shirt. My hair's still wet as I walk into the Lopezes' kitchen to fill up my water bottle.

I'm expecting it to be empty, so I startle a little when I turn the corner and find Camila bent over the oven, her ass on full display.

"Now you're just starting to look as bad as *them*, trying to flaunt it and rub it in my face."

She jumps up and backs away from me.

"How long is it you're staying exactly, because it's been a few hours at the most and I'm already sick of the sight of you." The way the gold flecks in her eyes sparkle, I know this isn't entirely true.

"Fuck knows. You'd be better off asking my mother how long before she pulls her head out of her ass and does her fucking job." I don't mean for so much to pour from my lips. It seems that even being around Camila this long is dragging the old Mason out who used to tell her everything once again.

She opens her mouth to respond. I shouldn't really need to worry about spilling too much, because with us all living in one happy house, everything I've been trying to cover up is going to be out in the open in mere days.

"Just forget I said anything. We'll be gone as soon as I can do something about it."

"It's not your job to do anything about it." Her voice is

softer than it was a moment ago. "That's why you didn't play last night, wasn't it? You were working."

"It doesn't fucking matter why I didn't play. And you need to keep your nose out. You've already done enough damage to my life."

"Fucking hell, Mase. How long is it going to take you to realize that none of that is on me? I had nothing to do with what happened with your dad. Why are you still punishing me for that?"

My chest heaves as she takes me back to the day my dad walked out. My mom was sobbing behind me where I stood in the doorway, watching him head to his car with just one suitcase of belongings to his name.

"Blame your dad, blame my dad, blame your mom. Who the fuck ever but me. I was as innocent in all of that as you were. They might have been the ones to push your dad to leave and for your mom to fall apart, but *you* are the only one to blame for ruining this." She gestures between us. "*You* single-handedly ruined the friendship we'd built for years. *You*, Mason."

Her index finger jabs me hard in the chest, and when she looks up and meets my eyes, hers are full of tears. "You weren't the only one who lost something, Mason. Okay, so it might have been worse for you, but you weren't the only one to have your life turned upside down, and that's something I don't think I'll ever be able to forgive you for. Now get out of my fucking way."

I can't move. I'm frozen to the spot as the words she just said to me filter into my brain.

"Move," she demands, her voice cracking on that one word alone. Keeping my eyes on the tiled floor, too afraid to see the emotion on her face, I stand aside and allow her to pass with her lunch.

"Fuck." My hands lift to my hair. I should follow her. I should attempt to fix something, but as I look around her perfect family home, I'm reminded of everything she still has. She lost me, so what? I lost everything.

I get to Jake's trailer in record time in my need to get the fuck away from that house and everything it represents.

I know he's here waiting for me, so I pull the door open and step inside. If I wasn't so lost in my own head, I'd probably be able to predict the scene I walk in on. At least they're fully fucking clothed, I guess.

"Ever heard of knocking, asshole?" Jake mutters, pushing himself up from Amalie and none too discreetly rearranging himself in his pants.

Jealousy burns through me faster than I'm able to control. I fall down on the opposite couch, rest my head back against the wall and wait for them to sort themselves out.

"What the fuck's eating you?" Apparently my torment is obvious to my best friend.

"I moved in this morning."

"Moved in where?" Amalie asks. Her soft, innocent voice makes me look up at her.

"You don't know?"

She glances over at Jake with narrowed eyes, but I know she's not pissed he kept my secret.

"Into the Lopezs' house."

Her brows are drawn together in confusion when she looks back at me.

"The Lopezs' house? As in, Camila's house?"

"The one and only."

"Why?"

With a sigh, I give her the basics so she understands just a bit of the disaster that is my life.

"That might explain why she's been ignoring my calls all morning. She just disappeared on us last night. I assume Noah got her home safe."

"Not exactly," I admit but regret it instantly when their intrigued eyes turn on me. With a sigh, I resign myself to explaining. "He disappeared too. I found her drunk off her ass in Ethan's bathroom."

"Where the hell did Noah go?"

"You took her home, didn't you?"

Jake and Amalie ask at the same time.

"I have no idea," I say to Amalie to address the issue of Noah. "Balls deep in Tasha, probably. And yes, I took her home. She doesn't know it was me, though, and I'd appreciate if you didn't tell her." I turn my stare back on Amalie.

"Why? She might go a little easier on you if she knows you looked after her."

"She just doesn't need to know," I snap, not really wanting to dissect the issues between Camila and me. It's bad enough that I can't get her and her practically see-through tank out of my head.

"Right, well. If you two are heading to work out, I'm going to go and see Camila and make sure she's okay. Maybe see if I can convince her to dump Noah's arse."

"She won't listen," I mutter.

"She'll figure it out eventually."

"Come on then, let's attempt to get her out of your system," Jake says after giving Amalie a kiss goodbye with a smug as fuck smile, as if he knows exactly what he's talking about.

17

CAMILA

"How's the hangover?" Amalie asks when she strolls into my bedroom later that afternoon.

"Fine," I mutter. "Don't ever let me drink tequila again."

"Yeah, because you'd have listened to me last night if I'd told you to stop."

I shrug at her because we both know she's right.

"So..." she starts, falling down onto my bed behind where I'm sitting at my desk, attempting to make a start on my 'Against All Odds' paper. "Were you planning on telling me about your new housemate?"

"I was hoping that if I didn't acknowledge it, then it wouldn't happen."

"How'd that work out?"

"Fantastic. He moved his stuff in the room on the other side of that wall this morning." A smile that she tries to fight tugs at her lips, her eyes shining with delight. "Do you need to enjoy this quite so much?"

"I'm sorry, but it is quite entertaining. He was wound as tight as a spring when he turned up at Jake's earlier."

"You've seen him?"

"How did you think I found out he'd moved in, seeing as you didn't want to tell me?"

"Jake. What did he say?"

"Not a lot. Why? Has something happened in the short few hours he's been here?"

"No." She raises an eyebrow. "I just helped him move his bed in and he was an ass. He keeps going on about Noah, accusing me of being dumb."

"Can you blame him?"

"Noah's not cheating." Even I can admit that the argument is weak at best.

"Right, so what happened to him last night then?"

"He brought me home when I was too drunk to keep my eyes open."

"Did he?"

I open my mouth to tell her that it was him, but her cell ringing cuts me off.

"Shit, sorry, it's Gran. I promised her I'd be home to help with something this afternoon. We will be continuing this conversation though."

"Fantastic. Can't wait." She gets up and heads for the door. "Wait. If it wasn't Noah then... was it you and Jake?"

She laughs, and it makes my blood boil. "What do you think, Cami?" Her head tilts to the side like she's talking to a cute little kid and then she's gone, leaving me even more confused about what's going on than I was before she arrived.

Pushing thoughts of last night's party and my new neighbor aside, I focus on the task at hand.

Against All Odds. The only person who I can think right now who's done anything even close to the title is

Jake. The hard to crack, ultimate player, bad boy, finally reformed, against all odds, by my new best friend.

Tapping my pen against my chin, I consider how I might play this.

In the end, I turn what is a very real story into a somewhat fictional newspaper article set in the future about an NFL player overcoming his adversities and making it despite his early years.

By the time I hit print and shut the document down, I'm proud of what I've achieved. My back's stiff from sitting in the same position for so long, and my shoulders ache.

The sun's long set, and as I sit back and stretch, I realize that I'm starving.

The house is still quiet. My parents told me yesterday that they intended on taking Mason's mom and brothers out for the day in the hope that the boys will be distracted from having to move from their family home. I like their positive thinking, but I'm not sure how much it's going to help in the long run. I might not know them all that well —they were only babies when I used to spend most of my time around them, but just from hearing Mom talk about them over the years, I know they're perceptive kids. There's no doubt, even at their age, that they don't know what's going on with their lives right now.

I find myself some dinner before settling on my bed for an evening of binge watching some trashy TV. Mason has not reappeared since our interaction in the kitchen earlier today, and I couldn't be happier. The last thing I need is for him to turn back up, demanding we continue where we left off. Whether that's from his bedroom or the kitchen, neither fills me with joy. Okay, that might be a bit of a lie. Something is still tingling just beneath my skin after he backed me up against the wall earlier, even though I know I should have forgotten all about it already.

I'm just losing myself in the latest episode of *The Bachelor* when my phone buzzes on the side. I assume it'll be Noah, seeing as I haven't seen nor heard from him since last night despite sending a couple of messages to him this afternoon to try to dig into what actually happened. I snatch it from the side and look down at the screen. But instead of my boyfriend's name staring back at me, it's an unknown number.

555-617-9764: Are you ready to learn the truth?

My finger hovers over the reply button, but in the end I think better of it. Whoever this is is just using me for some cheap entertainment.

I'm just putting it back on the nightstand when it vibrates in my hand once again.

555-617-9764: Shane's house. First bedroom on the right. Now!

My hand trembles that this might be something serious, or at least the answer to the question that's been spinning around in my mind since I watched Mason slam his fists into Noah's face about this time last week.

My hands tremble as I get off the bed. I still. This could be one big joke and I could find Mason at the other end, laughing his ass off. But why would he be at Shane's? They've never got along, even less so after the whole spiked drink situation at Shane's last party.

I decide that I need to find out for myself, knowing

that if I sit here thinking 'what if' then it's going to eat me until I do shift my ass, and by then it could be too late.

Pulling a zip up hoodie on over the top of my tank top, I slip my feet into the first pair of shoes I find and go to leave the house.

Just as my foot hits the bottom step, the front door opens and Mason walks through. As if he knows I'm there, he looks up and finds my eyes immediately. Amusement fills them, especially after he's taken in my outfit.

"If that's what Noah asks you to dress in for a booty call, then he's even weirder than I thought."

"I don't have time for this bullshit," I mutter, storming past him and snatching my keys from the sideboard as I pass.

"Have a good night. Don't do anything I wouldn't do."

Flipping him off over my shoulder, I slam the door behind me and head for my car.

Thankfully it starts the first time, and in seconds I'm on the road heading for Shane's house to find out what awaits me.

By the time I pull up on his street, my hands are shaking uncontrollably and my stomach is knotted so tight I fear I might not be able to stand straight. It's clear there's a party going on inside, but I don't register the fact that my friends are partying without me. I just need to know what I'm going to find in that bedroom. Mason's at home, or at least I assume that's where he stayed, so I'm pretty confident this isn't a prank he's organized.

Turning off the engine, I suck in a deep breath and step from the car.

The walk to his house feels like the slowest of my life, but all too soon, I'm pushing down the door handle and stepping inside.

There's no music like I was expecting, and the house isn't full to the brim like the cars lining the street led me to believe.

Laughter filters down from where I know Shane's den to be, and I can only assume it's a boy's night and they're all down there watching whatever sport's on the TV.

Ignoring them, I take a step for the stairs.

With each step I take, I tell myself that this is just a joke. Noah is probably waiting for me, expecting me to hand myself over to him. Why is it that the thought of that being about to happen makes me more anxious than any other alternative?

The dread that's sitting heavy in my stomach tells me that whatever I'm about to find behind that door is going to turn my world upside down, but I'm powerless not to keep moving toward it.

I lift my hand to the doorknob, my heart racing, my head spinning as I consider that Mason is about to be proved right.

I twist it as slowly and as quietly as I can. I have no idea what I might find, and I haven't decided if I want my presence to be known.

I push the door open just a crack and squeeze my eyes closed tightly as I pray that I'm not about to witness what I think I am.

A loud moan has my eyes flying open, and when I look up, I find exactly what I feared. My boyfriend thrusting as hard as he can into a cheerleader.

I gasp but quickly cover my mouth with my hand, not wanting to be caught standing here staring.

Noah's head is tipped back in pleasure as his fingers grip onto Tasha's hips, who's on all fours in front of him.

"Fuck, fuck," he grunts, and I start to back away from

the car crash in front of me. Tears burn my eyes, but initially it's not for what he's doing or even what I've lost, it's for the fact that I didn't trust the one person who I'd have given my life for not all that long ago.

Mason told me what is happening almost right in front of my eyes, and I chose to ignore him. To call him a liar, time and time again.

A sob rips from my lips as I fly back down the stairs, my stomach clenching and my mouth watering like I'm about to lose the contents of it any moment.

I can't get to the front door quick enough, but a throat clearing as me halting my retreat and turning around.

Standing in the far corner of the room is Shane. His eyes are soft and full of sympathy. My fists clench with my need to run over and slam them into him. If he knew about this and didn't tell me, I'll never forgive him.

He opens his mouth, but knowing I'm not going to be able to deal with whatever he's about to say, I turn back and race from the house. The front door slams behind me. I'd like to think it might alert the couple upstairs that something might not be right, but I doubt it.

I don't remember the drive home. I have no idea if I run any lights or cut off any other drivers. With my tears threatening to spill over, my only focus is locking myself inside my bedroom so I can fall apart in the safety of my own space.

I race through the house and up the stairs, praying that I don't run into my parents on the way, wanting to know what's wrong. The last thing I want to do is explain what I just witnessed.

18

MASON

It seems that the Lopezes could be a good influence on Mom, because I was expecting her to bail the second they all got back this evening, but to my total shock she bathed them both and put them to bed. The relief I felt knowing that I didn't need to worry was huge and just showed how much pressure I'd been under over the past few years, not only looking after myself and trying to keep the house running, but playing dad to my brothers. It was exhausting. I didn't pick up any shifts this weekend seeing as we were moving, and I had no idea how that was going to go. If it went as badly as I was anticipating, then I fully expected to need to escape to Ethan's to get drunk and high instead of running to work. As it is, it hasn't been too bad. I mean, I can hardly say that my encounter with Camila this morning was a bad one. Much the opposite with the way she longingly stared at me, practically begging me to put my hands on her. The way her breasts swelled in her tank. Fuck, I'm getting hard just thinking about it.

Sitting up on my bed, I look around the room. It's

nowhere near the space I left behind up the street. Gone are my navy blue walls and the wonky shelves my dad had put up badly when I was a kid that held my football trophies from over the years. Instead, they're in boxes, stacked with a load of other stuff in the corner. I've only unpacked the necessary stuff in the hope that if I don't move in completely, it means we're not staying all that long. It might be wishful thinking.

This room's been Clint's office for as long as I can remember. It was always off bounds to us as kids. We made it our top priority to break in and find out why on many occasions. We assumed, the naive kids that we were, that there was something worth finding. We were disappointed every time we snuck in here to only find a bookcase of boring IT books, a huge computer with more monitors that I'm sure any one person actually needs, and old coffee cups that had been there so long they were growing things.

The last time was the only time we found something to make the risk of sneaking in worthwhile. There was a bottle of half empty whiskey sitting on the desk next to Clint's keyboard.

"You ever wondered what that stuff tastes like?" Camila asked.

We were probably twelve or thirteen at the time, both of us had had the odd sip of wine that our parents had allowed with our dinner and both of us at that point had turned our noses up, not understanding why our parents were so fascinated with it.

Hard liquor though, the amber liquid that our dads drank when they got together for an evening. Not a drop of that stuff had passed my lips and I'd be lying to say I wasn't curious.

Giggling like the naughty kid she was, Camila wrapped her slim fingers around the neck of the bottle and twisted the top.

Both of us kept an eye on the door the entire time. We were alone in the house, but we had no idea how long it would stay that way.

I watched as she lifted the bottle to her lips and poured a generous amount into her mouth. The second she swallowed, she started sputtering, her eyes going wide as it burned down her throat.

"Oh my god. That's..." She coughed, her eyes watering. "Awful. Here."

I laughed at the fact I had to join in even though she so obviously regretted drinking it. I was a little more hesitant when I lifted the bottle and only took a small sip. Honestly, I didn't think it was so bad, but when I looked up to find Camila staring at the bottle in my hands like it actually offended her, I followed her lead. "Yuck."

I lowered the bottle as something flashed in Camila's eyes.

"It couldn't have been that bad, maybe I had too much." She waved her hand out for the bottle and took another sip.

Thirty minutes later and we were both drunk, although we had no idea at the time. Life was great as we laughed and messed about in Clint's office before we were caught.

To this day, I remember the look on Camila's face as Clint and Gabriella took me by the arms and marched me back down the street for my own parents to reprimand me, not only for breaking and entering but stealing and getting drunk. She looked at me like her parents were taking her right arm from her. Her eyes dropped and her bottom lip trembled. She didn't care we'd been caught, she just wanted us to serve our punishment out together, but our parents all knew that the best way to punish us was to keep us apart.

Pushing my memories back down, I swing my legs from the bed to take a shower and head to Ethan's. He might have only had a party last night, but seeing the messages that have come through in the past hour, it seems he's at it again. Twice in a weekend is unusual for him, but I may as well go and see what the hell's going on.

I pull the door open and step into the quiet hallway, ready to head for the bathroom when something, or someone, slams into me.

"Fuck," I grunt, the force of the collision making my breath catch.

Her sob hits my ears before I get a chance to look down, my arms instinctively wrapping around her, and I hold her against me for a beat. The feeling is too fucking good but when she starts fighting I don't resist. It shouldn't feel that good.

"Get the fuck off me," she wails, loud enough to wake my brothers. I want to tell her to be quiet, but the look on her face as she takes a step back steals my words.

"What's wrong? What's happened?" She has tears streaming down her face and her eyes are red. This hasn't just started.

She sucks in a few shaky breaths as she stares down at the carpet beneath our feet.

"Don't make me say it," she whispers so quietly that I have to lean in toward her to hear. Her strawberry scent fills my nose, and that mixed with her state tugs at my chest in a way I'm not all that happy about.

"Say what?" My brows draw together as I stare at her,

trying to figure out how I should know what's going on right now.

"Oh don't look at me like that." She lifts her hands and wipes her cheeks with the back of each. "Like you're concerned. You've been waiting for this to happen."

"Waiting for what?" I ask hesitantly, slowly putting two and two together in my head.

She huffs out a frustrated breath. "You were right, okay? Does that make you feel better? Make you feel like the winner? You were right, I was an idiot and look where it got me. You happy seeing my world fall apart?"

"What happened?" I seethe, ignoring all her other comments and needing to know exactly what I'm dealing with.

"Noah," she sobs, her bottom lip starting to tremble again as her memories of whatever's happened hit her. "He's fucking her."

"Motherfucker," rumbles up my throat. My fists clench with my need to lay into him again for ever hurting her.

"Why are you so fucking angry? You wanted this."

My mouth drops as a humorless laugh falls from my lips. "I didn't fucking want this." I wave my hand around in front of her but keeping it far enough away from her that I won't be tempted to pull her into my arms once again. "I warned you. I told you what he was up to but you chose not to believe me."

She stares at me, her eyes turning hard, argument forming, but it never leaves her mouth.

"I'm so fucking stupid."

She drops her head into her hands and cries. "Excuse me," she mumbles into her palms and goes to move past me. But she doesn't get to take a step before my arms shoot out to stop her.

I push her back against the wall when she tries to run from me. "Mason, don't. I don't need—"

My hand cups her cheek and forces her to look up at me. The sadness swimming in her eyes guts me. No one else should have the power to hurt her like this. Noah's a worthless motherfucker, and I'm so fucking glad she's learned the truth.

"Mason?" My name is almost a plea on her lips as she stares up at me. There're only inches between us, our increased breaths mingling as the silence stretches out around us.

"You need to forget him. He doesn't deserve your tears."

"I—"

The sound of footsteps on the stairs beneath us filters up and I panic. Gripping Camila's arms, I pull her into my room and shut the door behind us.

I push her back against the wall and step into her. My foot lands between hers and my arm rests on the wall beside her head. Her eyes, although still sad, hold a fire that wasn't there before.

"He shouldn't be the only one enjoying himself, Cami-bear."

My fingers lift and find the zipper that runs the length of her hoodie. I pinch it between my thumb and forefinger and pull. The sound of the metal separating is the only sound filling the room besides her increased breathing.

"How did you find out?"

She tenses as I get to the bottom of her hoodie and it falls open, exposing her tank covered breasts. Pushing my hand inside, I wrap it around her hip.

"I... I saw them."

My jaw pops at her admission. *Motherfucker.*

19

CAMILA

Mason stares down at me, his dark eyes wild as he tried to control his anger. If the situation were different, I might be scared. He's directed almost all his anger at me for four years over how his life turned out, but right now I'm not even on his radar, not for his anger at least.

His fingers tighten on my hip to the point that he'll probably leave bruises, but the way he's looking at me right now, I really don't care.

There's a promise in his eyes. A promise that he can make me forget even if just for a few moments.

The image of Noah's bare ass as he plowed into Tasha is burned into my eyes. I'll do just about anything now to remove it. So when his hand releases me to run his fingertips along the bare sliver of skin between my sweats and tank, I don't stop him. Instead, I stupidly allow my head to fall back against the wall as tingles erupt throughout my body. My thighs clench and my core throbs as anticipation races through me.

Surely, he's not going to...

I shouldn't even let him.

I should run. Run and lock my door—if it had one—but that image that's on repeat in my head and the prospect of it happening is too much.

His eyes stay locked on mine as his fingers slip just slightly under the waistband of my sweats. The skin around them crinkles slightly as he narrows them, giving me an out, but it's only for the briefest of seconds because no sooner have I registered the warning than his hand is sliding lower and into my panties.

I gasp when his fingers part me and press against my most sensitive place.

"Oh...oh..." I moan when he puts more pressure on my clit and starts to circle. "Oh..." Heat floods my entire body as a knot tightens in my lower stomach.

His breath hits the skin of my neck, and goosebumps break out across my body. His eyes stray from mine to my lips when my tongue sneaks out to lick across the bottom one, but at no point does he make a move to kiss me.

The realization of what this is hits me harder than the sight of them on that bed tonight. Mason doesn't want me. He's merely taking something from Noah in his need to punish him for what he did to me. I'm under no illusion that Mason's about to step in and take his place.

My fingers wrap around his wrist, ready to push him away. I don't want this because of some fucked up male rivalry that he can use against Noah. I should only want this with someone who wants it with me, someone who's going to treat me with the respect and love I deserve, but just as I go to push him away, he reaches lower, a finger circling my entrance and slipping inside.

My grip loosens at the sensation and my hand falls away in favor of what he's doing to me. It feels so fucking good. My head goes fuzzy, all the thoughts, the devastation of tonight melting away as my chest burns for more air and my body gets ready to tip over the edge of the pleasure he's holding me on the cusp of.

His head leans in closer to my ear and I shudder. I can't see his mouth but I know he's smiling at the reaction I'm having to him.

"Come for *me*, Camila." His fingers thrust deeper and my body snaps. My hips jolt forward, allowing him to get even deeper which only strengthens the explosion racing through my veins.

My nails scratch against the wall at my back, my knees threatening to buckle beneath me.

The high fades almost as fast as it hits, and I'm left with my chest heaving as Mason slips his hand free of my clothing. He pulls back and stares at me once again. Only this time, instead of the concern for me that was there before, his eyes are full of achievement.

Heat stirs in my belly, but it's not lust this time. It's anger.

"Fuck you, Mason." I slam my hands down on his chest and force him to back up. Surprisingly, he does allow me to push from the wall to make my escape. I'm mortified that I just allowed him to put his hands on me like that but fucking furious for his reasons for doing it.

Reaching out, my fingers wrap around the handle ready to drag it open and leave him behind. But the sound of my name falling from his lips behind me has me stalling. My brain screams at me to run, but my body betrays it. It seems to naturally respond to the deep timbre of his demand, and I fucking hate it.

Unable to stop myself, I look back over my shoulder.

"I bet he never made you come that hard."

My eyes narrow. I'm desperate for a quick comeback, but the second he lifts the fingers that were just inside me and sucks them into his mouth, his eyes fluttering closed, all words vanish. My chin drops, my cheeks heat and all thoughts leave my head. My breathing catches once again, but it's not until he pulls his eyes open that I find it in me to run. And I run as fast as my shaky legs will allow.

————

I barely leave my room, only sneaking out for the necessities like the bathroom and stealing chips and ice cream from the kitchen when I'm confident I won't be caught. I know he's in the room next door—the beat of his music has been quietly filtering through the wall all morning—but I've yet to see anyone. I know I'm on borrowed time though.

It can't be thirty minutes after that thought when a soft knock sounds from my bedroom door. I look down at the pajamas that I'm still wearing despite the fact it's long after lunch. I don't bother getting out of bed or trying to make myself look anything but the mess that I currently am when I call out for them to enter.

As expected, Mom slips inside my still darkened room. She takes one look at me and the closed curtains and a deep frown mars her usually smooth face.

"Camila? What's wrong?"

All morning I've fought my tears, but one look at my mom's concerned face and they spill over. Whether they're for Noah or just my stupidity for what happened with Mason last night, I have no idea. At this point, my turmoil has just mixed into one. She rushes to me and pulls me into her arms.

"It's okay, baby." I cry like I should have when I got home last night, only I was distracted.

When I eventually pull back, Mom's shoulder is soaked with my tears.

Her face is still full of concern when she takes my cheeks in her hands and wipes away the tears with her thumbs.

"N-Noah..." My words get stuck in my throat. "He...He..." I shake my head, not able to vocalize the words, especially to Mom. "It's over."

"Oh, baby." She pulls me back into her arms but it seems that I've run out of tears—for now, at least. "I remember it well," she says on a sigh. "I know it feels like the end of the world right now, but I promise you, it'll get better." She rubs my back as she tries to console me, but it only makes me realize something. Although I'd been adamantly defending him for the past week since his birthday party, I think on some level I knew because as much as last night was a shock, it's not hurting as much as I think it probably should right now. What's hurting more is knowing I allowed Mason to take advantage of my emotional state. I should have been stronger. I should have pushed him away. Told him no. But I did none of those things. I actually fear that I may have even encouraged him.

Now he's got ammunition, something he can use against me, and I have no doubt he will.

"Don't move," Mom instructs before rushing from the room, leaving the door ajar.

I have no idea where she disappears to but I don't put much thought into it, especially when the music next door stops and the sound of his door opening has me on full alert.

When he starts walking and his footsteps only get louder, my breath catches. It's ridiculous because the bathroom's right there and he's probably just going to use that, but my fucked up brain's convinced he's coming here.

The footsteps slow and my heart threatens to beat out of my chest as I wait for him to appear in the gap.

I blink and he's there. I may only be able to see a couple of inches, but every muscle in my body clenches at the sight of him in his black shirt and light ripped jeans. His hair's flopping down in front of his face so I only get to look into one eye as he finds me sitting cross-legged on my bed. His eye drops as he leisurely takes in what I'm wearing—or not, as the case may be. My body heats under his scrutiny, my nipples pebbling and my core clenching as memories of how easily he played me last night slam into me.

His attention eventually comes back up to my face and his mouth opens like he's about to say something, but lighter footsteps sound before my mom's voice has Mason turning away, allowing me to suck in a much needed breath.

"You heading out, sweetie?"

"Yeah, party at Ethan's." Mason's deep voice rumbles through me, reminding me of when he whispered in my ear last night.

Another party, and on a Sunday night? I know Ethan likes to enjoy his freedom, but shit.

"Well, I won't get in your way. You deserve to go out and enjoy yourself."

"T-thank you." With the briefest of glances back at me, he's gone. His footsteps thunder down the stairs.

"Here we go," Mom announces, pushing the door open wider and revealing her carrying a tray loaded with freshly made nachos, a bottle of what looks like mojito, and a couple of glasses.

Now this is something I can get on board with. My resolution to never drink again after Friday night's disaster goes flying out the window. I'm with my mom, she won't allow me to get trashed.

"Oh my god, I need this," I say, my stomach grumbling as the aroma of melted cheese fills the room.

I scoot over in bed to allow her space, and, once she's comfortable, I pull up *Mean Girls* on the TV and we sit back and enjoy a little girl time.

Mom suggests calling Amalie and Alyssa to join in, but as much as I love spending time with them, this right now is perfect. She's going to be off next week to help Dad set up his apartment in New York, so this might be the last time we get to spend some quality time together in a while. Anyway, I have no idea about Alyssa, but I could pretty much put money on Amalie being otherwise engaged right now with a certain star quarterback.

"What's that look for?" I didn't realize thinking about how happy Amalie is caused my face to change, but apparently it did.

"Nothing. Just thinking that Amalie will be with Jake. You haven't seem them together yet, but..." I sigh, trying to find the right words. "You know when you just look at two people and know it's it. That's them. They're just so... connected. It's weird."

"I know exactly what you mean, baby. I was one of the last of my friends to meet the man who was to become your dad. I know how it feels to think you're being left behind."

"No, that's not it. I know I've got plenty of time. I'm not even eighteen yet. I don't know, it's hard to explain." Or hard to admit just how jealous I am of them when I once thought I had exactly the same with the boy next door.

"Speaking of your eighteenth, young lady. The table is all booked for Friday night. Are you sure you just want it to be just the three of us? You're more than welcome to invite some friends or—"

I cut her off before she suggests the Paines. It's bad enough living under the same roof, I'm not dealing with anything else. "No, just us. I'll be seeing the girls all day Saturday, so it's fine."

She eyes me curiously. When she first brought up my birthday a few weeks ago, I think she was expecting me to want a big party like Noah and invite my entire class, but honestly, I couldn't think of anything worse than spending the night worrying about someone damaging the house or throwing up god knows where. A nice quiet weekend with my favorite people is all I need.

One chick flick soon leads onto another, and before we know it, Dad has to come to find where his wife's disappeared to. He makes a joke about her sneaking out of the living room to cheat on him. My stomach clenches, and although I never said the words to her, Mom reaches over and squeezes my hand in support.

Once she's disappeared off with Dad, I make the most of knowing Mason is out and head for the bathroom for a shower before bed. All my homework's done, so I can hopefully get an early night so I'm ready for whatever drama is sure to come my way this week.

The thought of having to see Noah and Tasha has my stomach turning, but not as much as having to be in the same room as Mason. My need to hurt him might just get the better of me.

I end up tossing and turning for what feels like forever

before I give up and turn my TV back on. I never had issues sleeping until all of this kicked off last weekend; now every time I close my eyes, all I can see is Mason staring at me as he told me how stupid I was, Noah as he nailed Tasha, and imagining everyone's looks of sympathy when the truth comes out. I put my cell on silent before I made the journey home from Shane's yesterday and I've stopped myself looking at it ever since. I'm pretty sure he'll have texted, but I have no idea if he's aware he's been caught or if he still believes he's getting away with it. Either way, he's not concerned enough by my radio silence to turn up here looking for me. I take that as a sign that this is probably for the best.

It's sometime after midnight when my world falls into darkness. I was watching some late night chat show with some reality star I'd never heard of when there's a click and everything goes out—the TV, the ceiling light, my night light, and the hall light. Everything.

My chest immediately constricts as I stare into nothingness. There's not even any moonlight filtering through the curtains.

My hands tremble and my heart races as I sit in the middle of my bed, wrapped in my sheets, and rock, praying that everything will come back on any second.

The seconds stretch into minutes and my panic begins to get the better of me. Realizing that sitting here in the dark is more terrifying than seeing what Noah has to say for himself, I find myself leaning over the side of my bed to find my purse. Digging around blindly inside, I wrap my fingers around my cell and pull it out, only when I go to wake it up, nothing happens. I press the power button and the only thing I get out of it is the little red flashing battery telling me that it's dead and absolutely no help whatsoever. I did have a flashlight in my top drawer, but I took it to Dash and I can't remember what happened to it.

My fear increases, my breaths coming out scarily fast, but I don't seem to drag any air back inside. Everyone else must be sleeping, and even in my panicked state, I feel ridiculous for even considering waking them. I'm almost eighteen for fuck's sake. It's just a little power outage, nothing's going to ha—

The front door slams shut and my heart jumps into my throat. I sit perfectly still, trying to hear what's happening. I feel my pulse in every inch of my body as I wait.

There are a few bangs before feet hit the stairs. With each step, my body flinches. I grip the sheets tightly to my chest, my nails digging into my palms despite the fabric between them.

My door's shut, but I still see the flash of light that appears underneath. I'm torn between running out there and confronting whatever it is that's making light or hiding under my bed in case it's a man who's come to murder me under the cover of darkness.

I'm still trying to convince myself to stay on the rational side of my imagination when it's gone. The light goes out but there's no noise. That is, until the click of my door has me scooting up the bed in an attempt to get away.

The sheets raise to my mouth. Only my eyes would be showing if anyone could actually see me as I sit trembling in fear.

The sound of another person's breathing fills the room and I bite down on the inside of my cheeks to stop me from screaming.

If he's here to kill me, I hope he makes it quick, I think as footsteps get closer.

"M-Mason, is that you?" I whisper so quietly that even if it is him, the chance of him hearing me is slim.

Whoever it is doesn't respond as they make their way around the bed. It's not lost on me that they must know my room, seeing as it's pitch black and they haven't bumped into anything.

"Mason?" I snap a little louder, my fear getting the better of me.

Oh my god, oh my god, I chant to myself when the bed dips.

His familiar scent fills my nose as he gets closer, but I don't release the breath I'm holding. Nor do I relax. I'm still frozen in fear and waiting to see what he's going to do.

His hot breath sweeps over my face. The faint scent of whiskey fills my nose, but it's not enough for him to be drunk, I don't think. A shiver runs down my spine when his lips brush against my ear. Then softly he whispers words that take me back to another night when we were cloaked in darkness.

"I'll keep you safe. I'll always keep you safe."

A whimper falls from my lips. I hate to admit it, but having him here with me allows me to breathe since the lights went out.

He sits up and I hear rustling before the sheets are tugged from around me.

"M-Mason, w-what are you doing?"

"Shhhh."

My heart races, but suddenly it's for an entirely different reason as I'm pulled down the bed so I'm lying on my back in only my silk cami and short set. Mason pushes my thighs apart with his hand, and the second they part, he settles himself between. The roughness of his jeans brushes the sensitive skin inside my thighs and my core tightens at the sensation.

What the hell is he doing?

The mattress dips again as he falls on top of me, his hands resting on either side of my shoulders. My breathing is incredibly loud in the silence of my bedroom, and it gives away everything that I'm feeling right now.

Everything about this moment is so wrong, but being here in the dark with him hovering above me, I can't help but want everything from him. Everything that was ripped away from us all those years ago.

I. Want. It. All.

He dips down, his lips brushing against the soft skin of my neck. My back arches at the contact, and my thighs pin him in place.

This is wrong, a little voice screams in my head, but I push her aside and focus on the electricity racing around my body. I flex my fingers, feeling it all the way to the tips as he continues to kiss me.

"Mason," I moan when the heat of his tongue runs across my collarbone.

Lifting my hands to find him, they connect with the hot skin of his back. I guess that explains the rustling of fabric before he climbed between my legs.

I run my palms up his bare skin and don't miss his entire body freeze and his breath catch at my contact. It's nice to know he's as affected by this as I am.

He comes back to himself barely a second later, his lips descending toward the lace that lines my cami. My nipples pebble at the thought of him revealing them, and my cheeks heat. It doesn't matter that it's totally dark and he can probably only just make out the outlines of my body like I can him. The thought of being exposed to him still has butterflies erupting in my belly.

"Mason... w-what—" His finger slips one strap from my shoulder and he pulls it low enough that the soft fabric skims over my nipple. I can't help but arch a little at the sensation, my body begging for more.

"Stop overthinking. Just feel. Just forget."

"Oh god," I whimper, powerless to do anything but what he just instructed as the scorching heat of his tongue licks around my breast before zeroing in on my sensitive peak and sucking it deep into his mouth. A bolt of lust shoots straight down between my legs, and I fight to squeeze them together to get some friction.

"All in good time."

My other strap follows the same path as the first, and he's soon giving my other breast the same treatment. I writhe beneath him, desperate for more, for everything.

Crazy thoughts start filling my head, despite my attempt to do as he said and forget.

Am I willing to give myself over to the boy who's hated me for the past four years?

Is this the reason I held off with Noah?

Was it always meant to be Mason despite what's happened between us?

By the time he starts kissing down my belly, I only just about hold myself back from pushing him lower. I may not have done this before, but I know damn well what I need, and if last night against his bedroom wall taught me anything, it's that I need him between my legs right fucking now.

Not even a second later, his fingers wrap around the waistband of my shorts and he tugs them and my wet panties down my thighs.

Instead of telling him no, like I probably should, I lift my hips to assist him with his mission.

My cheeks burn so much that I feel it on my neck as he crawls down the bed, lying on his front so he's in line with my core.

Holy shit, this is happening.

He blows a stream of air across me and I damn near fall apart from that alone. I moan, rolling my hips, needing some kind of friction to put an end to this delicious torture. Of all the horrible things he's done to me over the past few years, holding out on me right now might be the worst. If he were to stop and walk out right now, I'm not sure I could be held accountable for my actions.

Just as I start to believe that's actually going to happen, his fingertips dig into my thighs as he reaches forward and runs his tongue up the length of me. He moans like I'm the most delicious thing he's ever tasted before moving closer and flattening his tongue against my clit.

I cry out, totally forgetting where we are and who I could wake up. Grabbing the pillow beside me, I cover my mouth as he starts to increase the tempo. He licks, sucks, bites, and teases my entrance with both his tongue and fingers. He builds me up until the tension in my body is at breaking point before slowing his movements down and allowing it to subside.

"Mason, please, please." My cries for more are muffled by the pillow still covering my mouth, so I have no idea if he can hear me or not. If he can, he sure doesn't listen. Why am I not surprised?

His fingers thrust deep and he curls them inside me as he goes to town on my clit. I scream and allow myself to fall at his skilled touch.

My back arches, my hips grind against him and my nails dig into my pillow as I ride out wave after wave of pleasure. My fear about the dark forgotten, my anxiety about what tomorrow brings long gone, the only thing I feel right now is what he's done to me. It's an incredible feeling until I start to come down from my high and realization sets in.

What the fuck did I just do?

20

MASON

The second my tongue connects with her clit, I realize something. I'm addicted.

If I thought tasting her off my fingers last night was mind blowing, then I don't even know what this is.

It wasn't my intention to come in here, drag her down the bed and have her basically ride my face as I licked at her, but the second I stepped into the room with the noble intention of making sure she was sleeping soundly in the darkness I came home to and the sounds of her labored breathing hit my ears, I knew there wasn't any chance that she was asleep.

I remember all too well how scared of the dark she is, and I might be an asshole but there was no way I could be on the other side of the wall and try to ignore the fact that she'd be here terrified.

I thought I probably owed it to her to make her feel safe. I stupidly thought that if she was awake maybe she'd just let me sit with her to keep her calm like when we were kids, but it was all shot to shit when I discovered how worked up she was.

Her cry of pleasure is unintelligible, but I like to think it's my name she's screaming into the pillow. Her legs try to close around me, but I press my palms down against them and continue licking at her gently until she's come down from her high.

I think it's safe to say that this is one blackout I'm not going to forget for a very long time.

My cock strains against the fabric of my pants, desperate to find the same relief she has from the fucked up foreplay we've had going on recently.

I know I don't deserve to be here right now, but my need to try to make her feel safe was too much to bear, especially after discovering what Noah's really been up to only last night. She needs this escape more than ever, and if I'm being totally honest, last night wasn't enough for me. I needed this, and fuck if I don't need more.

She slowly stops twitching against me, the pillow falls from the face, and her fingers thread into my hair to drag me up. My heart pounds and my cock aches to find out if she's going to continue this, if she's going to give me everything I've wanted since I was a horny fourteen-year-old boy.

I pull back, a smug smile on my face at what I just got to experience. Lifting my hand, I wipe the back of it across my mouth but it doesn't reach the other side because a click sounds and then we're both blinded as the bright lights of her room come back to life.

Neither of us says anything, but our eyes immediately lock. Embarrassment, and, I hate to say it, regret fill her. Her hands fly up to cover her breasts, and I almost groan in frustration.

"Cami." I fight like hell to keep my eyes on hers and not allowing them to drop to her exposed body like I'm desperate to do. I've had my hands on almost every part of her body, I know exactly how she feels; now all I need is to see her incredibly sexy curves without the cover of clothing.

"Get out," she whispers, her eyes widening even further. She fights to get away, but my hands land on her hip, pinning her in place. Her chest heaves and her breaths race past her lips as her eyes search mine, trying to read me.

"Cami, don't—"

"I said get out." Her voice is stronger this time, and I start to believe that she really means it. My stomach drops with disappointment. "That was probably the biggest mistake I've ever made. Now get the hell out of my bedroom. You're not welcome in here."

"But I—" She pins me with a vicious look and my words falter. Nothing I can say right now is going to change her mind. Camila might be a lot of things, and stubborn is most definitely one of them.

The second I begin crawling from the bed, she reaches out for the sheets and wraps them around her. Only her head pokes out the top.

My cock tents the front of my pants, and when I look over, her eyes are zeroed in on the bulge. *Well, what did she expect after allowing me to taste her?*

I'm pulling the door open when her soft voice fills the room. I don't look back, I don't dare to, because I know all I'll want to do is climb back under those sheets with her and continue.

"Don't get the wrong idea about this. *This* is nothing, and it will not be happening again."

I hear her warning loud and clear, and I can't help that it fires me up to prove her wrong.

Camila Lopez was mine from the first moment I laid eyes on her. It was always inevitable, and it's about time I started proving that she feels the same.

With the weight of the world on my shoulders, and a raging hard-on, I head straight for the bathroom in the hope that jacking off in the shower might at least take the edge off.

It's wishful thinking, because as I stand under the cold stream of water with my length in my hand, the only thing I can think of is how tight she'd be as I slide into her. How she'd feel as she came around me.

Tingles run down my spine and my balls draw up and I spill my seed into the shallow water at my feet. But her taste is still on my tongue, so the second I come, I'm fucking hard again.

I had girls hanging off me at Ethan's the past two nights. I could have easily taken one of them up to a bedroom to help clear my mind, but something stopped me. I hate to admit it, but that someone was *her*. Especially tonight, knowing that she was probably sitting at home still thinking about Noah and how he could betray her like that. I shouldn't have even gone to Ethan's. My heart ached to stay home and make sure she was okay, even if it was from the safety of my bedroom while she was next door.

"Fuck," I roar when I get into my bedroom with only a towel wrapped around my waist. I slam my fist into the solid wood and revel in the mind numbing pain that shoots up my arm.

I don't give a shit if it wakes anyone up. I don't give a shit about anything but trying to get these fucked up thoughts from my head. I've spent the past four years trying to push her away. My life exploded the day her dad exposed the fraud my dad was committing at work. It was wrong, Dad was in the wrong, I'd never dispute that, but he and Clint had been friends for years and he just went behind Dad's back with all the evidence he'd compiled and watched as his best friend was marched from the office, changing his, and all our lives, forever. The only saving grace, I guess, was that it was never reported to the police. I don't know the reason for that. I can only assume that he was understanding and didn't want to ruin our lives any more than necessary. I do know that the money Dad had stolen was paid back, forcing us into even more debt.

Dad lived for his job, and for his family. We were the reason he was doing what he did. Mom was falling apart. She wasn't earning an income, and because of her, we were drowning in debt. He was just trying to support us, and if Clint had bothered to ask his friend what was going on instead of marching straight to the boss with his little secret mission, then things could have turned out very differently.

I was young. I didn't understand, still don't, the finer details of what happened. All I saw was my parents and my family falling apart, and it was all their fault. The family up the road who were meant to be part of our support network. How could they betray us like that?

They watched as Mom began drowning herself in vodka, staying out all hours and leaving Dad to dive headfirst into his own depression while I was forced to bring up my brothers single handedly. I was a child, yet everything fell on my shoulders.

I so desperately needed the support of my best friend,

but every time I looked at her, this uncontrollable hate bubbled up within me. She had a hand in this. Not physically, but she stood beside her parents and watched us fall.

Dad couldn't find a job—he now had a record—Mom was drunk all the time, and I was ripping apart at the seams. If it weren't for Jake, Ethan, and football, I'm not sure I'd have gotten through it all.

As if all that wasn't bad enough, Mom had to bring home one of her drinking buddies. Dad had taken us out to get some food and when we came home, there they were, going at it in the middle of the living room.

They were so drunk, fumbling around each other that they had no idea they'd been caught.

I remember vividly the coldness in my dad's eyes as he turned to me and told me to take my brothers upstairs. I rushed to do as he asked, terrified by the vacant look in his eyes.

I have no idea what was said, but shouting and screaming from below bellowed up as I put some cartoons on the TV in an attempt to cover the noise. Once I knew they were okay, I snuck to the top of the stairs and listened to everything unfold from then on out.

Dad was wild, Mom was manic. There were thuds, grunts, screams, pleading. I could go on. It was exactly what no fourteen-year-old should ever have to endure after everything that had already happened.

Dad left that night. He packed a bag, told me that he'd see me soon, kissed my brothers on their head and he was gone. To this day I've not seen or heard from him.

I had no choice but to try to stay as normal as possible for my brothers while Mom fractured. She was a shell of the woman she used to be, and I was terrified someone would find out and we'd all be split up and shipped off to foster homes around the country. With that thought constantly in the back of my mind, I just kept going.

Even after everything, Gabriella still came around. It seemed that no matter what, she and Mom were still as close as ever. I was grateful for the support; she helped Mom somewhat get herself back together, but I'm pretty sure that to this day, Mom never told her the whole truth. I think that Gabriella still thinks she just fell apart when Dad left, not that she was the catalyst that made it happen.

I hated seeing Gabriella at the house. She and her family represented everything I used to have and everything I craved to have back. A stable home with loving parents, but I feared even back then that neither were something I'd ever have again.

Seeing Camila happy after I turned my back on her hurt. It hurt almost as much as watching my dad leave that day, but what could I do? Her face was a reminder of where it all started. I knew that if I gave her the chance she'd wiggle her way back in and see the ugliness that I was forced to endure on a daily basis, and I couldn't do that to her. One of us deserved to live a good life and to be happy. So I let the hate that had taken up permanent residence under my skin fester and I turned it on her.

I laid awake most of the night, my cock throbbing for some action and my head spinning as thoughts of my fucked up past mix with my equally screwed up present.

Everything I tried to keep hidden was crushed the second I had no choice but to move in here, under their roof. I tried to keep her out of it, to allow her the freedom from getting involved, because I have no doubt it's what she'd have done if she'd have been given the chance.

She'd have helped me babysit. She'd have used her own money to buy us food when we had none, and she'd have ensured I focused on the positives. But fuck the positives. Everything, including myself, was poison, and I wasn't allowing her to be touched by it too.

The last thing I need is a sleepless night, seeing as I've got school and work every day and night this week, but when my alarm goes off and my eyes are still wide open, it seems that I don't have much choice.

Knowing that she's not going to take too kindly to seeing me, I do us both a favor and get the fuck out of the house before I even hear movement from her room. I take my gym bag and hit the machines before anyone one else.

By the time I'm joined by a few other members of the team who all look at me with curiosity, I'm covered in sweat and still trying to outrun my memories of last night. Not sure any amount of fucking miles will help with that one somehow.

I ignore each and every one of their stares as I make my way to the showers to get ready for class.

The moment I step out of the locker rooms, Noah is the first fucker I see. He's walking along with a couple of his computer geek buddies, laughing like he's got no cares in the world. My fingers twitch to feel his neck compressing beneath them as I force him to accept what's coming to him for hurting her. I refuse to do it with a fucking audience though. It's definitely a conversation we need to have with a little privacy.

Your time's coming, you fucking waste of space, I promise as I silently trail behind them.

21

CAMILA

Mom was super sweet to me this morning and made me pancakes for breakfast before school. I know she feels bad about my breakup, but she's equally feeling guilty about leaving me on my birthday weekend for New York. I don't know how many times I've told her that it's fine, but I've given up now because I'm sick of repeating myself. She keeps offering for me to go with them and I've been adamant about staying, but after last night, I can't help being tempted by the offer. Being in a different state might be the only thing that will keep my mind off Mason at this point.

Did I do the right thing by sending him away last night? Yes, I can say with complete certainty that I did. Do I regret it, however? Yes, yes, I fucking do.

The reality check that hit me upside the head when the lights came on and I saw him for the first time between my legs was nothing short of painful. My chest constricted so hard I was worried I might have broken a rib or two. How could I have allowed him in to do that to me? I know it was Mason, but I barely batted an eyelid before I allowed him to strip me half naked and have his way with me.

I pull my cell from the charger I plugged it into sometime after Mason left my room last night and power it up.

One single message comes through.

555-617-9764: Girls like you never win. Enjoy the fall.

What the actual fuck? I throw my cell into my purse, angry at whomever is at the other end of those messages and equally confused and hurt by the fact that Noah seems to be ignoring me. I assume that means he knows he was caught and is hiding. A fucking apology at least would be nice.

The drive to school is silent, and it makes me yearn for the mornings not so long ago when I'd pick up Amalie and we'd shoot the shit together about whatever drama was going on. Now she's spending so much time with Jake, she doesn't need me to pick her up, seeing as she's hardly ever home. That'll be even more true if she goes through with her plans of buying them both a place to live.

Suddenly, a feeling of loneliness washes through me. My parents are about to head off to New York to embark on the next part of their lives, my best friend is busy planning hers, my boyfriend is... well, we all know what he's doing. Where does that leave me? Alone in a house with a guy who appears to be torturing me on an hourly basis. Just hearing the water running in the bathroom last night after he left me was fucking hard work. My imagination was running on overdrive, imagining what his body might look like as the water ran down over his muscles. He was obviously hard as he left my room. Was he in there fixing his situation? Fuck if the thought of that didn't have me on the verge of breaking the door down so I could find out.

I'm later to school than usual. Students are already making their way to their first class of the day, and the hallways are starting to clear out.

I go directly to my locker, keeping my eyes locked on the floor. I have no idea if anything's got out yet, although if the silence of my cell is anything to go by then it's still very much a secret.

I'm just swapping some books when I sense someone behind me. Glancing over my shoulder, I don't find who I was expecting.

Shane looks seriously sheepish as he stands with his hands shoved deep in his pockets while he chews on his bottom lip.

For the first time since Saturday night, I wonder if those messages came from him. He clearly knew what was happening under his roof. He was there waiting for me.

Shaking my head, I push the thought aside. That's crazy. He'd never do something like that.

"How are you doing?"

"I've been better, but glad I'm not walking around with my head in the clouds anymore."

"I'm sorry you had to find out like that."

"How long have you known?"

"Not long. I've suspected something for a while but never had any evidence. Then after Mason kicked his ass, I started to look a little deeper. We were supposed to just be having a guy's night, watch the game, have a few beers, but the second the girls showed up, I knew he had other ideas. Sadly, it didn't take long to watch him lead her upstairs when he thought we were all distracted."

"So you called me there?"

He casts his eyes away. "No. I was just going to talk to you about it. I didn't want you to find out like that. But it was taken out of my hands."

"By whom?"

He shakes his head. "Doesn't matter. What matters is that you know the truth and you can do what needs to be done."

"Does he know I know?"

"Not that I'm aware of. I thought I'd leave that to you."

I'm not sure if I'm grateful or not. The thought of standing in front of Noah after all the time we've spent together and telling him it's over when he has no idea it's coming, even after what he's done, fills me with dread.

As it turns out though, I don't get the chance.

I was so focused on what Shane had to say that I didn't realize that the hallway around us was not completely empty. Well, that is until an almighty crash sounds from just around the corner. A deep grunt follows before a very familiar voice sounds out.

"This isn't even half of what you deserve, you motherfucker."

Shane and I run around the corner, and what we find is exactly what I feared.

Mason has Noah pinned up against the lockers by the throat as he growls like a wild fucking animal in his face.

"This is going to hurt," Shane mutters, sounding way too amused about this situation.

Mason's fist connects with Noah's cheek, and his head snaps to the side. Both of them seem oblivious that they've got company. I can only hope that the words that fall from Mason's mouth wouldn't if he knew others were listening.

"You know, I probably should be thanking you. If it weren't for you fucking up, then I wouldn't have spent most of last night between her legs." Noah visibly pales, while my lips purse in frustration. This is just one big pissing competition to him. Noah screwed up, so he made it his first priority to take something from me that Noah never managed to.

I feel Shane turn to look at me, but I can't take my eyes off the car crash happening in front of me.

"What I can't figure out is why you'd play away with a slut like Tasha when you had her with her sweet, tight little pus—"

"You're lying. I know you're lying, because that frigid bitch won't let anyone touch her. I've been dating her for years, I should fucking know."

Mason turns a strange shade of purple, and I know I need to put an end to this before he kills Noah.

"Enough," I bark, having had enough of listening to this mortifying conversation.

"No. You're a fucking liar." Noah struggles to get out of his hold as I reach them. Neither of them turns to me. They're both locked in their stare off.

"Put him down, Mason. This isn't your issue, or your fight to have. Now back the fuck off."

"Like fuck it isn't. You know—"

"Just shut up. I think you've already said enough, don't you?"

Reluctantly, Mason releases Noah's neck and he falls down with his hands on his knees as he catches his breath.

"You're going to fucking regret ever touching that whore," Mason warns. I sense he's got more to say, but he soon shuts his mouth when I turn my stare on him.

"He's lying. Tell me he's lying, Cam," Noah begs, clearly not able to handle that while he was off getting his rocks off, I was able to give someone else what I never gave him.

I look back to my pathetic excuse for a boyfriend. Does he actually think he has any kind of right asking that question?

"It doesn't matter."

"You're lying," he snaps, looking up to Mason. "You never would have let him touch you. You hate him."

The sound of Mason's quick intake of breath at this statement is hard to miss, but how he can be surprised after the way he's treated me over the past four years I have no idea. Noah's been by my side through all of it and knows as well as I do how Mason's treated me.

"Yeah well, I never thought you'd cheat, but I guess we can all be wrong at times."

He blanches, but he must had been given a clue that his indiscretions were out in the open when Mason flew at him not so long ago.

"Just in case you need it spelled out for you, we're over. The cheerslut can have you. I hope she chews you up and spits you out like they all do."

"Camila, wait."

Ignoring Noah's pleas for me to hear him out, I turn my back on him and start off down the hallway toward my first class. That is, until Mason reaches out. I tug my arm away before he makes contact. I can't deal with him being this close having done what he just did, let alone touching me.

"Don't," I snap.

"What he just said... does that mean—"

"It doesn't mean anything, Mason. Just leave me the fuck alone. You've already done enough damage."

His face drops, and I almost take every word back, but when I recall what he just did and said to Noah, my back straightens and I leave the three of them behind me.

I intend on going straight to class, but instead of turning left toward history, I find myself heading straight for the exit. After a short drive, I order myself a takeout milkshake from Aces and take it down onto the beach.

I find myself a spot on the last bit of dry sand and sit and watch the waves crashing in.

My fingers grip the cup a little too tightly as I replay those horrendous few minutes in the hallway. Mason had no right doing or saying what he did. Noah was my mess to fix, yet he stormed in like a bull in a fucking china shop. What exactly was he trying to achieve? Does he want to be seen as the big man who always gets what he wants so badly that he had to go after Noah to tell him what he spent his night doing before I even got the chance to look at him?

Digging a little hole for my cup, I drop my head into my hands, trying to figure out where I go from here.

Two things are for sure. One, things are over with Noah, and two, I need to stay the hell away from Mason.

I hang around town for the rest of the day, not feeling prepared at all to face the music, but I know that the gossip will have spread around Rosewood like an out of control wildfire by now. My cell's been vibrating almost constantly in my purse, but I've ignored it, preferring the distraction of shopping for a new outfit for my birthday meal on Friday night.

I don't venture home until I know school's out, knowing that the chances of both my parents being home is high seeing as they're busy packing for Dad's move. But when I pull into our driveway, I find that it's not only their car waiting for me but there's also a red little sporty thing parked there. Knowing it can only belong to one person I know, I suck in a deep breath and prepare for the questions that are about to come my way.

"Hey, sweetie. Did you have a good day?" Mom asks the second I walk into the kitchen. She pulls the refrigerator open and hands me two cans of soda.

"Yeah, it was…" I don't get to finish because Mom's sympathetic eyes find mine.

"It'll get easier, I promise." They're the same words she said to me last night. Just like then, they don't fill me with any kind of confidence for what the next few days and weeks might be like. "Amalie's up in your room starting on her homework. Here, I bought you doughnuts to cheer you up." She passes me a box and my mouth waters.

"Thank you."

"You're welcome, baby. If I can do anything, just let me know."

"Will do." I'm not sure that extends to kicking the Paines out, so I take everything she offers and head up to my room.

I pass Mason's brothers' room and poke my head in to find them playing with their cars, so I leave them to it in favor of the one-on-one session that's about to commence.

"Hey," I say, dropping onto my bed when I find Amalie sitting in my desk chair working.

"Ah… here's the little skiver."

"Skiver?"

"Yeah, you skived class." When I raise an eyebrow, she translates it for me. "Ugh, you skipped class. That better?"

"Much. And yeah, well... you would have too in my position."

"Hey, no judgment here. I've done it a time or two if you remember. That was because of a guy as well."

I groan, choosing to focus on the doughnuts as I ask my next question. "Does everyone know?"

"That Noah's been shagging Tasha? Sadly, yeah. I'm so sorry, Cami."

"Yeah, well, it's not like I wasn't warned it was happening."

The bed dips as she joins me. "Don't beat yourself up for wanting to trust him. It fucking stinks what he was getting up to, but at least you know the truth now, I guess. Is it true that you walked in on them?"

"Sadly."

"How'd you know where to find him?"

"I got a message telling me to go to Shane's house."

"Who from?"

I shrug. "I don't know for sure, but it was one of them."

"One of them?" Amalie asks, but I'm fairly sure she knows the answer. She's had enough run-ins with certain members of the squad.

"The cheerleaders. I had a message saying something like 'girls like you never win' or some crap. They're just jealous. You've got Jake, my boyfriend screwed me over with one of theirs. They're probably seeing it all as one big game."

"I bet it'll go down like a lead balloon then that Mason's been on your side of this whole thing."

"That's not the half of it," I mutter, not really expecting it to come out loud.

"Oh? Is there something I should know about?"

"They might have other reasons to be pissed at me."

"Oh my god, oh my god," she squeals, clapping her hands and bouncing on the bed. "Have you and Mason—"

"Not gone all the way." I wince, dropping my head into my hands.

"But you've done... stuff?"

"There might have been stuff, but I really regret it and would rather not talk about it," I say into my hands in a rush, hoping we can drop the subject.

Amalie's fingers wrap around my wrist and she pulls my hands from my face.

"Firstly, stop hiding. Secondly... how was it?" Her eyebrows wiggle in delight and I want to die a thousand deaths as my mortification from last night when the lights came on consumes me once again.

"It was... a mammoth mistake. We had a power outage, I'm terrified of the dark, he claimed he only came in to make sure I was okay but one thing led to another and..."

"And..." Amalie's eyes are wide as she waits to hear more.

"And I let him... do stuff. But it was a mistake," I add in a rush, just in case she missed it the first twenty times I said it.

"Say that it was a mistake one more time and I'll start to think you're only trying to convince yourself. So he let himself in during a blackout and went to town on your body, just like that?"

"Kind of," I admit with a wince.

"So this wasn't the first time something happened?"

I shake my head. "There was a... moment, Saturday night when I came home after finding... *them.*"

"Mason seems like a really good guy to have around in times of trouble, I'll give him that." Her lips curl in an amused smirk and I swat her shoulder for turning this into a joke, but I can't help but allow myself to laugh along with her.

"Well, distraction or not, it shouldn't have happened, and his behavior this morning only served to prove that."

"I heard he confronted Noah."

"It was worse than that. He basically bragged about what happened, rubbed it right in his face."

"And? The guy was shagging Tasha behind your back, why does it matter if Mason shares what you've been up to?"

She's probably right. Why should I care after what he's done to me? But I do. I also care because I don't want to be branded with the same label of 'slag' as the rest of the girls that offer themselves up to the football team without second thought.

"I don't need everyone thinking I bounced straight from one to the other. It really isn't like that, even if it kinda looks that way." I blow out a long breath, wondering how I ended up in this situation.

"I get, Cami. I do. But this is Mason we're talking about. The guys who's been in l—"

"Don't. Don't say it, don't even think it." I narrow my eyes at her but I know it's too late. She's had crazy ideas in her head about the two of us since the day she first met us. "It's not happening. It doesn't matter how good last night felt." Amalie's eyebrow rises in an 'I fucking knew it was good' gesture, but I press on. "He's been nothing but an asshole to me for four years. I doubt that just because he's gone down on me that's going to change. He's set on making my life hell. He'll just use this against me too."

Her eyebrow lifts, and it makes my stomach twist in frustration. Why does she always have to stand up for him? "Do you really believe that?"

I've got to, because I can't allow myself to think about the alternative.

22

MASON

"Motherfucker," I growl, planting my fist firmly in the mirror hanging in the boy's bathroom. Glass shatters, ripping my knuckles to shreds, but I don't give a fuck. I don't feel it. All I can feel is the clenching of my heart and my burning lungs as I fight to drag in the air I need.

"That frigid bitch won't let anyone touch her. I've been dating her for years, I should fucking know."

His words from only a few minutes ago repeat in my head. What he's implying would mean... No. No, she can't be. She wouldn't have allowed me into her room last night to do what I did. She wouldn't have allowed me to slide my hand beneath her panties the night before if she's a virgin. Would she?

"You never would have let him touch you. You hate him."

My chest constricts as I hear those words over and over. They're not news to me. In fact, I've heard them before, directly from her own lips, but having someone else tell me how she feels about me... fuck. I rub at my chest, hoping to ease the ache, but it does little for the organ that's fighting to keep going beneath my ribs.

She should hate me. It's what I was trying to do when I set out on my 'ruin Camila's life' mission. I wanted her to suffer like me. But hearing it, and from him...

I crash back against the wall and slide down to my ass. My head bangs back against the grimy wall behind me, but I don't even feel it.

I'm too lost. Lost to her.

First period is almost over when I eventually emerge from the bathroom with my knuckles cleaned up as best as I can.

"Mase, what the fuck, man?" Jake calls down the hallway. Fuck only knows why he's not in class where he should be.

"I'm good. I'm just...uh..."

His eyes scan my face. Fuck knows what he sees staring back at him, but the second they drop they find my busted up hand. "Who was on the other end of this?"

"No one. Well, not the time that caused this."

His eyes narrow. "So who was it before that?"

"Noah." I admit quietly.

"Again?"

"Can you just leave it?"

"Not likely. Especially when you're bleeding out on the floor. Wanna get a burger?"

"It's barely ten."

"And? You know Bill will cook us what the fuck ever we want the second we stroll in."

I can't really argue with that, so with a small nod in his direction we head out.

"Pull over here."

"What are you—" I stop asking when the pharmacy comes into view.

"Just shut the fuck up, yeah?" Jake says with a laugh, jumping from my car and running toward the entrance.

In only a few minutes he reappears. "Hand," he demands.

"This is very domesticated."

"Yeah well, maybe Amalie's rubbing off on me." I raise an eyebrow. "Oh yeah, she's definitely rubbing me that way." I want to punch the smug motherfucker in the face with the hand he's nursing. He must sense it because he holds tighter, making it sting. "Oh stop being a pussy. You punched a fucking mirror, I'm just making sure there's no glass in it."

"What happened to Jake Thorn, the guy who didn't give a shit about anything or anyone?"

"He fell in love, man, and she cracked his heart wide open."

"I think I like this new version of you better."

"Yeah?"

"Yeah. Just... keep the touchy feely shit to this though. I don't want you turning into a hugger."

"Fuck off am I hugging you. You need a shoulder to cry on, you call my girl. She's good at that shit. Actually, on second thoughts, call your own."

"I don't—"

"Oh that's right. You don't need to call her, you live with her. Just smash her door in and take what you need."

Staring out the windshield, I swallow as the memories from last night hit me. The feeling of her thighs pinning my head in place, the sound of her cries, her taste.

"Mason?" Jake asks, reading me correctly. I don't need

to turn to look at him to know he's got a smile on his face right now.

He's probably the only person who knows how I felt about her all those years ago. We were young, I didn't really understand my feelings for her, but he did. He always has, and I hate how fucking perceptive he is. He's given me so much shit for what I've done to her, but I know it's only been his way to attempt to make me admit that I still have feelings for her.

I've shot him down every single time, but I'm not so sure if that's because I was trying to convince him that he was wrong or myself. It's becoming more and more obvious that I've never forgotten how I felt at only fourteen every time I so much as glanced Camila's way, and I fear it's only been getting worse, not better.

"What did you do?" He finishes whatever the fuck he's doing with my hand and allows me to pull it back to the wheel. I slam my foot down on the accelerator and speed down the street in the direction of Aces.

He allows me the silence, but I know he's only going to let me get away with it for so long.

Seeing as we should be at school, our booth at the back is empty and Bill's eyes widen in shock when we walk in.

"Your Monday going that well?" he asks with a laugh, coming over to serve us himself.

"Something like that," I mutter, then groan at Jake's response.

"Mase has girl problems."

"Ah, I see. Well, if you need any advice, I've had plenty of experience."

We both smile at him before ordering. He turns to leave and I fall back against the bench with a sigh. My hand is fucking throbbing, I flex my fingers, wincing when it only gets worse.

I picture Noah's panic as I pinned him up against the lockers this morning and I know without a doubt that I'd do it again. Even now knowing what I learned soon after.

"So..." Jake encourages once our sodas have been delivered and we're left alone once again.

"I took something that didn't belong to me."

His brows pull together as he studies me.

"You're gonna need to give me more than that."

"Camila caught Noah fucking Tash at a party."

"Shit." Jake winces. "She okay?"

"What do you think?"

"So what's this got to do with you punching a mirror?"

"I might have... distracted her. Twice." A smug smile twitches at his lips and I look away, not wanting to witness him being so happy about the situation. "But it seems that the reason that Noah was banging someone else was because he wasn't her..." I trail off, hoping he'll put two and two together. The last thing I need to do right now is spill any more of her secrets.

He's silent for a few seconds and I look back up at him. I see the second the penny drops. "No fucking way. They've been together for like..."

"Two years," I helpfully add. "That doesn't excuse his cheating though."

"I'm not saying it does, I'm just shocked is all. They've always seemed so... close."

"I know. I didn't even think. I just barged in and..."

"And..." He wiggles his eyebrows, wanting to drag the dirty details from me.

"Distracted her."

"So what? You took her V card. It was always meant to be yours anyway, even you can't deny that."

"It didn't get that far. She kicked me out."

"So what's the fucking issue then?"

I'm silent as I consider his question. I pushed her further than she's comfortable with without a second thought. I might have been horrible to her, but that shit's not me. I don't take without knowing my partner is with me one hundred percent.

"Ohhh... you're pissed you didn't get all the way."

"What? No. I'm pissed because she didn't want it and I did it anyway. What the fuck, man? I thought you were here to help." I push from the bench and go to leave.

"Sit your ass back down, dickhead."

Without instruction, my legs bend and I hit the seat.

"I know Camila, and I can assure you that if she wasn't into it, she'd have kicked you out long before you touched her."

We're both silent as Bill approaches with our food and places two huge plates of burgers and fries in front of us. We thank him and he leaves us to it. All the while, Jake's words spin around in my head. He's right, I know he is. Camila is headstrong. She hasn't backed down to any of the shit I've given her, and she's not likely to just roll over now. But it doesn't change the fact that she's clearly been denying Noah any action but quite happily allowed me what I thought she needed.

I poke my pile of fries as my head races.

"This is so fucked up," I mutter. I don't even really mean for Jake to hear it, but he does.

"Is it? As far as I can tell, you're on the cusp of getting everything you've ever wanted. It just depends on what you do next and if you fuck it up."

I look up at my best friend, my jaw dropped in surprise. When the fuck did he become so wise?

———

We don't return to school. Instead we head to his trailer and hide out in his little makeshift gym. My muscles scream at me to stop after my workout this morning, but I welcome the pain. Anything in an attempt to keep my mind from Camila and what's going through her head after what happened this morning.

Once we've both run out of energy, we collapse on Jake's sofa. He lights up while I make do with a bottle of water from his lukewarm fridge.

"Amalie's talking about buying a house for us to live in," he blurts.

I splutter with the water I was attempting to swallow. "Shit, man. That's like... serious."

"You're telling me." He pulls himself so he's sitting up straight.

"What's the problem? You love her, right? Want to be with her always?"

"Yeah, I don't even need to think about that. It's just..."

"Just?"

"She's got all this money just burning a hole in her bank account, and what do I have to offer?"

"Besides your outstanding personality and sharp wit?"

"I'm serious. She's, well... everything, and this is all I have." He gestures to his old trailer.

"She doesn't care, Jake. She wants you, not what or what doesn't come with you. She loves you, what's in there." I nod down to his chest and he blows out a long breath.

"I know. It's just so huge."

"Agreed. But there are no rules. Trust her to know what's right for her and trust yourself to make the right decision. If moving in together feels right, then do it. You've both experienced enough shit over the years to be able to make a serious decision about this. Just do what feels right."

"You know, I could say the same thing to you."

"We're not talking about me."

He shakes his head but thankfully keeps his mouth shut. We hang out at his place for the rest of the afternoon before Jake has to head back to school for practice.

"When are you coming back?"

I shrug, bending down to pull on my shoes. "Whenever Mom pulls her finger out of her ass and gets a real job."

"Never, then?" he says sadly. "We need you if we stand any chance in our next few games."

"I'm doing my best, man."

"I know. It just fucking sucks."

I drop Jake back at school before heading to work. I change in my car before pulling my cell out of my pocket. I've got a few messages, most from Ethan asking where the fuck I am, and a few are from the other guys on the team, but there's nothing from Camila. Not that I really expected there to be.

Should I have left her to deal with the fallout of what I did this morning? No, probably not. But I couldn't hang around and be forced to look at Noah after what he admitted. I equally couldn't look at Camila, knowing the truth. Seeing the regret in her eyes would kill me. It's most definitely something I can live without.

With a sigh, I climb from the car. This is my life now. I'd better man up and deal with it.

————

Every day that follows is just a repeat of the one before. I somehow drag my body from bed just in time to get to school before the final bell. I spend all day with my head down, ignoring Camila in the few classes we share. I've already done enough damage. If she wants to bring up what happened then she's going to have to come to me, not the other way around. I'm still undecided if I actually regret going to her that night or not. On one hand, I still remember how she reacted to my touch, but on the other, I remember Noah's face as I filled him in on what we'd been up to, and guilt consumes me that she might not have been as into it as I remember.

The second I walk out of the school building after class, I head straight for work. Each night is the same, even down to some of the same customers buying the same items every day. It's monotonous, but it's exactly what I need.

By the time Friday rolls around, I want to give up. When I head downstairs before leaving for school, there are birthday balloons and banners everywhere and a pile of gifts the size of a small mountain on the dining table.

Rolling my eyes at the sight. I grab a cereal bar from the cupboard and leave before any of the celebrations start. They're definitely something I don't want to be a part of. As if living here as it is isn't a constant reminder of the stable family life I don't have, I don't need to see them spoil Camila on her special day.

23

CAMILA

"Happy birthday, baby!" Mom calls the second my foot hits the bottom step. She comes rushing over and wraps me in a hug. A ball of emotion clogs my throat as I embrace her back. It's exactly what I need.

This week's been... weird. She and Dad have either been out or packing getting ready to head to New York tomorrow, and I've either been in the house with Mason's brothers or at school being ignored by the guy himself. I was expecting him to corner me after he tried to talk to me in the hallway but nothing. I lie awake every night after he gets home from work, expecting him to let himself in so he can ask me about what Noah said, but again, nothing. Whenever I see him at school, he just looks down as if I don't exist. I don't fucking get it and it's frustrating the hell out of me.

I thought it would be worse with him moving in, but this week I've seen him less than ever. I should be relieved after everything, but I'm far from it.

"I can't believe my baby is eighteen." Mom pulls back,

her eyes swimming with tears. "Come on, I made you waffles."

I take her hand and allow her to lead me toward the kitchen where Dad, Nic, Ollie, and Charlie are waiting.

"Happy birthday," they all sing in unison. I thank them, looking around, wondering if I'm the only one who notices the person who's markedly absent.

Shouldn't he be here for this too?

I don't want to ask. I want to ignore him as much as he has been me, but I find the words tumbling out nonetheless.

"Where's Mason?"

"He'd already left when I knocked. Probably got practice or something."

My chin drops at his mom's excuse. "He's not on the team anymore, so why would he be at practice?"

"He's... what?" She's totally taken aback, and it ignites a fire in my belly. Does she really have no fucking clue what he's doing for her? For his family?

"He quit," I spit, taking a step toward her, my fingers curling into a fist. "He quit to pick up more hours so he could look after his family."

She swallows and breaks our eye contact. At least she has the decency to look guilty about it.

"But—"

"But what? Are you going to find a job so he doesn't have to work so hard, or are you going to continue fucking around?"

"Camila," Dad snaps, but I ignore him.

"Bringing money into the house shouldn't be his responsibility. It should be yours," I seethe. "He's risking everything for you. College. His future. All because you can't be bothered to do your job and support your kids."

I'm only assuming the bit about college is true. The guy I used to know used to spend all his time talking about playing college football, so I can only assume that hasn't changed, and him not being on the team at the most vital time of the year is not going to help. They've got three games left before the playoffs. Three games he should be playing in.

"I'll fix it, I promise," she whispers.

"Really. When is that going to happen? His team needs him on the field tonight. The season is almost over already. I'm afraid it's going to be too little too late."

"He'll play the last two games. I'll make sure of it." She puts more conviction into those words than I've heard from her in years, so I can only hope they're true. "Tell him to sort his hours so he can play."

"Do your own dirty work," I snap, finding my chair and ignoring the atmosphere I've created around the breakfast table.

The second I've forced down my waffles, I run for my car, desperate to not have to look at Nicky any longer. I'm starting to understand why Mason suddenly changed. His mom was never like that when we were kids. Maybe things were worse than he allowed any of us to see.

I'm met at school by Amalie and Alyssa, who are holding out a tray full of doughnuts with candles poked into them.

"Happy birthday to you, happy birthday to you," they sing, but the fact that now both Shane and Noah are missing doesn't pass me by. First I lost Mason, then Shane, and now Noah. I know the reasons for each absence, but it doesn't mean it hurts any less. Okay, so after everything, maybe I'm not all that bothered about Noah.

"Thank you." I plaster on a smile that I don't feel. So

much is already changing, and we're not even that close to the end of the year and the end of our school careers. As always, that thought makes me think of what I'm going to do next. Everyone tells me that I'll figure it out and not to worry, but how can I when everyone seems to know exactly what they want to do and I'm like a lost little sheep running around the field, trying to figure out which way is up.

I take a pink-striped doughnut from the box and cram it into my mouth in the hope it covers how I'm really feeling. I'm eighteen today. An adult at last. I should be celebrating, but my uncertain future along with everything has me feeling nothing like doing so. It makes me glad I decided on a quiet evening with my parents tonight and a day with my girls tomorrow. I don't have it in me to party.

I'm gutted to miss tonight's away game, but it's a little too far to travel and I knew my parents wouldn't have any of it if I tried demanding to go. It's the first and hopefully the last game of the season I'll miss. I know that I'll go to college next year and have a new team to support, but the Bears have been my team for as long as I can remember, and to be able to see them succeed this year under Jake's leadership would be everything.

"I'm so excited for tomorrow," Alyssa says, bouncing toward our lockers. "A day to chill, no boys."

"Something you need to tell us, Alyssa?" Amalie asks before I get the chance. As far as I'm aware, she's still free and single—but things can change fast, as I'm beginning to learn.

"Nah, I'm still working on the basketball team. Any day now, one of them will figure out that their life is not complete without me."

Amalie and I laugh at her serious expression.

I pull my locker open the second I get there to pull some books out, but when the door opens, a squeal rips from my lips as something flies out at me.

"Fucking hell," I say, my heart racing as an 'Eighteen Today' balloon rises into the hallway. "Was this really necessary?" I ask, turning to look at the girls.

They glance at each other, questions filling their eyes.

"I wish it was us, but we just brought the doughnuts," Amalie admits.

"So who?" I mutter, pulling out the weight, hoping there might be a note, but there's nothing. "Weird."

"I bet it was him," Amalie whispers in my ear.

Tingles run down my spine at her suggestion, and I know he's looking at me. I close my eyes for a moment, not wanting anyone to see the water that fills them. His absence has hurt this week. I know I was the one who sent him away, but is it wrong to have expected him to fight? He's never been one to go down easily; that's what makes all this worse. He's not himself, and I fear all this might have hurt him more than he'd ever let on.

When I turn and look over my shoulder, Jake and the team are at their usual benches, but Mason's not with them. I quickly glance around, but I see no sign of him. I do, however, spot Shane, who's hovering a little down the corridor, looking like he wants to come over but is unsure because of Amalie's presence. My heart aches for him once again that he feels he needs to keep his distance for something he didn't do.

I wave him over. He hesitates, but when Amalie notices who's holding my attention she smiles at him.

"Happy birthday," he says, giving me a hug.

"Thank you."

"Hey," he says to both Amalie and Alyssa. I hate the uncertainty in his eyes, and as he looks up to where Jake is, I realize that he's more scared of him than anything else.

Following his line of sight, Amalie turns back to Shane. "Just ignore him." She reaches out and places her hand on his forearm encouragingly. Jake immediately jumps from the bench and starts making his way over.

"Watch out, caveman incoming."

Amalie rolls her eyes but doesn't make any effort to put space between her and Shane, and why should she? They're not doing anything wrong.

"Let me walk you to class," Shane says, turning my way.

"You don't need to be afraid of him."

"I'm not, I'd just rather not be in his way."

I grab what I need and step into Shane's side, saying a quick goodbye to both Amalie and Alyssa. "Everyone knows it wasn't you," I say, looking up to Shane. It's not the first time I've said the words, and I'm sure it won't be the last.

"People will believe what they like." He shrugs.

"But you're giving them the power to make you hide, make you run away."

"I'm not doing anything I don't want to do, Cam. I never have wanted to spend time with Jake, and I still don't. Nothing's changed."

"But the parties."

"Meh... my brothers have held parties most weekends since I was a kid. They're nothing new."

I look up to him, trying to read if he's telling the truth or not.

As we close in on the math department, almost all the cheer squad seems to emerge from the girls' bathroom.

"You should have seen her face," one of their high-pitched voices screeches over the rest.

"She so had it coming to her," someone else adds.

Shaking my head, I go to side step them, but sadly I'm noticed before I get to escape.

"And people call us the sluts," Chelsea says, rolling her eyes at me. "I know it's only Shane, but seriously, how many guys do you intend on getting your claws into this week? Noah was doing the right thing, if you ask me. Do you know how long it was going on for?"

The blood drains from my face. It's a question I've tried not to think about, knowing the answer could only make the whole situation a hell of a lot worse.

Shane's stance changes beside me before he steps up to Chelsea. "That's enough," he barks. I can't deny my opinion on Shane changes in that one instant.

He's always been the quiet one who does anything he can to stay out of trouble. Unfortunately, who he is and the life he's been born into means he's often dragged right into the middle of it all.

Chelsea's eyes widen in shock, her chin dropping. Is she... is she lost for words?

"Camila's not in the wrong here. *They* are." He flicks his eyes to Tasha, who's cowering behind her leader. "I don't care if she's a cheerleader or the fucking President, she shouldn't have gone after someone else's boyfriend. End of."

Shane holds Chelsea's eyes captive as he stares down at her. It's as if he's willing her to bite back. His chest heaves, his fists clenching at his sides as his frustration gets the better of him.

I wait, hardly breathing to see what's going to happen next, but after a silent, and tense, few seconds, Shane releases her and turns to me.

"Shall we continue?" It's almost painful to drag my eyes away from a shell-shocked Chelsea and over to him, but when I do, it's worth it because his eyes are glittering with accomplishment, and so they should. He just silenced the queen bitch, and in front of her team.

"That was fucking awesome." I practically bounce all the way to my math class. "Did you see her face? She was so fucking shocked. Man, if people stood up to her more it would knock her down a peg or two." Shane remains silent beside me. Noticing the tense set of his shoulders, I slow our pace and come to a stop in a quiet part of the hallway. "Are you okay?"

"Yeah, I'm good." He doesn't look down at me, just stares off over my shoulder. When I turn to see what has his attention, I find an empty hallway.

"I know things are weird now Noah and I aren't..." I trail off, not wanting to think about all that. "But I'm here, if you need to chat or anything, you know that right?"

His eyes finally find mine and I breathe a sigh of relief when I find his usual green happy-go-lucky ones looking back at me.

"Come on, we're going to be late."

Both Noah and Mason are in my second class of the day, so just as things start to settle down in math, I know I've got a potential storm brewing. We should have all had a class together on Monday, but I skipped and since found out that I wasn't the only one.

I slip down in my chair, hoping it makes me invisible as Noah walks in. My stomach twists and my heart aches. There's so much familiarity there. I could so easily get up and go and sit on his lap. It would be second nature. I've spent so much time with him by my side, in my corner, or so I thought. But then his betrayal hits me like a bat, and I have to fight to keep my waffles down.

It's weird. Not even a week's passed since I found them, but already, I don't think I hate him. I'll never forgive him, I know that much, but I just can't find it in me to give him the time or energy it takes to hate him.

With a sigh, I pick up my pen and start doodling in my book in an attempt to look busy. I don't think he'll try to talk to me—he hasn't all week, so I can't imagine he will today even if it is my birthday.

To my utter shock, as he passes my desk, he drops a white envelope down, but he doesn't stop.

I should stuff it in my bag, or the trash, and forget it exists, but only after a few seconds my curiosity gets the better of me.

Pulling the lip open, I slide out the birthday card. On the front is a vintage typewriter with happy birthday typed on the paper sitting in it. It's pretty but nothing special. It's not until I open it that my breath catches.

I'm so sorry.

A silent sob rumbles up my throat. The fuck load of emotions I'd been managing to keep shoved down threaten to bubble up and spill over.

Sucking in a long, slow breath, I attempt to calm myself down. I'm in the middle of class, and I'm not the kind of girl who just cries during a school day, I'm stronger than that.

I close my eyes and will myself to pull it together when the atmosphere in the room presses down on my shoulders. I don't need to look to know why, but I do, nonetheless.

Mason's hard and cold eyes are locked on Noah, who squirms in his seat. He's not a fighter, so I'd imagine being pinned against the lockers and punched in the face the other day terrified him.

As Mason steps farther into the room, he seems to suck all the air out. I fight to drag in the breaths I need, but as he passes my desk all I get is a lungful of his scent. My body betrays me and sends me back to being laid out on my bed with him between my thighs. I squirm in my seat but it's for a very different reason than with Noah, although both involve Mason's hands.

When I was with Noah, the idea of going further was always on my mind, but that was mainly because I knew he wanted it, although I was a little curious. But now, after experiencing just a taste with Mason, it's all I can think about. And I'm pretty sure it's not just the act or the pleasure, but the person who delivered it.

I'm fucked.

He doesn't stop. His steps don't even falter as he passes me. I turn my head away from him to ensure he can't see the emotion swimming in my eyes.

He doesn't walk much farther, seeing as he sits directly behind me. The scratch of his chair against the floor makes my teeth grind.

It's another five seconds before I hear anything else from him. The rest of the class have gone back to their previous conversations, so they're probably totally unaware he even says anything to me.

"Please don't tell me one pathetic I'm sorry card will send you running back."

My spine stiffens. I didn't even realize I'd dropped the card on the desk in front of me. Quickly reaching out, I close it and shove it into my notebook.

"I thought now that you'd been shown what it could really be like, you'd realize that you can do better than that—"

"Enough," I snap, turning to face him. A satisfied smirk plays on his lips as my eyes narrow at him. The rest of the room silences and turns toward us to watch the show. They're all well aware that there's no love lost between the two of us. This isn't the first time we've had a standoff in school in the past four years, so they're probably waiting for their next installment of the Camila and Mason show.

"What time shall I stop by later for your special birthday surprise?" His words drip with sex, and I wouldn't be surprised if all the girls within a ten-foot radius aren't wet right now from the deep rumbling of his voice and the promise in his tone.

"Fuck you." My voice is low and angry, but he doesn't miss it. His smile curls up wider.

"What's that? You want to go all night this time?"

I swear steam nearly blows from my ears. My teeth grind as my fingers twitch to lash out at him. If it weren't for the fact that the rest of our class are all staring at us, waiting for something to kick off, then I might just do it.

Something crackles between us as our stare holds. I want to say it's hate, but even I'm not blind enough to recognize that it's laced with desire, a need that I'm not sure either of us is going to be able to deny forever.

I open my mouth to say something, fuck knows what, when our teacher slams the classroom door. Rustling fills my ears as everyone turns to look to the front of the room.

"Miss Lopez, Mr. Paine, do we have a problem here? I'm sure it could all be sorted out in detention."

I blow out a frustrated breath and turn toward Mr.

Lawrence, who's standing with his hands on his hips waiting none too patiently to begin his lesson.

"N-No, sir. We're good."

I take my seat, but Mason's stare burns into the back of my head, and the second Mr. Lawrence turns to write on the board, I look over my shoulder to find that he is indeed staring daggers into me. His eyes might be narrowed and hard, but I see more within them. I see the twinkle of delight, the promise, the lust that sends tingles headed straight between my thighs.

The second the bell goes, I scoop up everything from my desk and run. I don't know if I'm running more from Noah or Mason—not that it really matters. I don't want to talk to either of them.

Thankfully, the rest of the day is uneventful. Well, unless you count the huge chocolate cake that Amalie appears with in the cafeteria at lunchtime with eighteen candles lit and ready to be blown out by the birthday girl.

With the majority of the school making the trip to Eden Falls for the game tonight, it means that Aces is pretty dead after school when I walk in with Amalie and Alyssa flanking my sides.

"You know you could have gone tonight, right?" I say to Amalie, who's missing the game to have a milkshake with me.

"We can be apart sometimes, you know."

"Really?" I ask, my eyebrows almost hitting my hairline.

"Anyway, I'm having dinner with Gran tonight. Going to broach the subject of me moving out."

"That sounds like fun."

"I'm pretty sure she knows it's coming. I'm hardly ever

there and living in Jake's trailer. She knows how much money I inherited, so I'd be crazy not to use it."

"You found a place yet?" Her face transforms at my question. "You have?"

She pulls her cell from her pocket, swipes the screen and then turns it to me. I look down at the small but perfectly formed newly-built duplex on the outskirts of town, and my heart drops. I feel selfish that it's my first reaction. It's not all that far away, but it will put the final nail in the coffin for any more morning trips to school together. Not that they'd been happening recently. It's just another thing that's changing, and I don't like it.

"It's cute."

"You could sound a little more enthusiastic."

"I'm sorry. It really is nice. I can totally see you living there." That perks her up a little.

"Really?"

"Yeah. Have you viewed it?"

"We're going Sunday. I'm so excited. A place of our own, no worrying about damp or my gran walking in on us."

"As if everyone at school didn't envy you enough already," Alyssa helpfully adds.

"Yeah, the girl with dead parents who had to move halfway around the world. All they see is the good stuff, they ignore the pain it took to get there."

"I-I know that. I was just saying."

An awkward silence settles over us.

"So you think they're going to do it tonight?"

"Of course they are. Jake was confident they were ready. Still pissed Mas—sorry," she cuts herself off when she sees the grimace on my face.

"What's up with that anyway? He suddenly gives up

the team and starts fighting your battles for you. Has he had another personality transplant?" Alyssa asks, and I feel guilty that we're not as close as we were when Mason changed the first time. She experienced it all with me back then, knew every little thing he did to me, but now she's barely on the sidelines of what's going on.

"He's got some family stuff going on. He's had to stop playing, but it's only temporary. He'll be back before the end of the season." I want to believe what Nicky said to me this morning but honestly, I'm having a hard time doing so.

Our conversation turns to another of my favorite topics right now: college applications. I just about manage to hold in my groan as Amalie explains that she's managed to get Jake to a meeting with Miss French and he's finally beginning to accept that college could be an option. It makes me realize that I'm not the only one dealing with everything changing in my life and that I should suck it up and get on with it like everyone else around me seems to be doing.

Once our milkshakes are empty and we've exhausted our college chat, they both agree to meet at mine tomorrow morning before our date at the spa. I just hope that our conversations tomorrow while being pampered can stay on the lighter end of the scale. We're supposed to be relaxing, not stressing about our futures.

My parents are both in their bedroom getting ready for our meal when I get in, but I find Nicky, Ollie, and Charlie playing in the living room. The second I see she's alone I turn to escape, not wanting a rerun of this morning at breakfast.

"Camila, please wait."

I pause halfway to the stairs, but I don't turn around.

"I wanted to apologize. I was out of order this morning. You were right, everything you said about me as a mom. You're right. I've failed. I've failed Mason, and if I'm not careful, I'm going to ruin those two in there too. I'm going to fix it though."

"How?" I ask, spinning on the balls of my feet and pinning her with a look I hope comes across as threatening.

"I-I... uh... I've got a job."

"Just like that? How convenient."

"I had been looking, just not putting as much effort in as possible." I raise an eyebrow, not believing a word of it. "It's a bar over in East. I start after the boys' bedtime and will be home to make them breakfast and take them to school. The wages are so much more than my last job, so hopefully we'll be able to get back on our feet sometime soon and out of your hair. I know life's not been easy for you with us all—Mason—living so close."

"It's—"

"Don't try to pretend that it's anything other than it is, Camila. I've leaned on your mom too much, relied on her to help me, but she's my best friend, not my keeper. I start tomorrow night and I've arranged for the boys to have a sleepover, so the house is yours if you wanted to celebrate your birthday without any adults around." The reminder that my parents leave in the morning doesn't fill me with joy. I'm also not sure how I feel about the prospect of Mason and me having the house to ourselves. Anything could happen. I fight to keep the wicked smile from my lips that threatens to break free at the prospect. "I won't take up any more of your time. Go and get ready, I just needed to tell you that you're right and I'm sorry."

With a nod, I turn back to the stairs, but before I lift a

foot, I say over my shoulder, "I'm not the only one you need to be telling this to."

"I know. I'll speak to him, I promise."

The only thing I can do is take her word for it, so I continue up to my room. Before pulling out the dress I bought for tonight, I grab my cell and send both Amalie and Alyssa a text.

Me: Got the house to myself tomorrow night. Want a girls' night in?

I avoid adding *to keep me away from Mason if he's here,* but I'm pretty sure Amalie will be able to read between the lines. And I'm proved right ten minutes later when I get a reply.

Amalie: Sounds like fun but if you want him, go get him!

Groaning, I throw my cell on my bed and take my outfit with me to the bathroom.

24

MASON

"Get your ass over here now. I had this party for you," Ethan complains when I answer his sixth call after finishing work and replying to his message that I'm not coming to his house to get wasted.

"Fuck off. That's bullshit and you know it."

"But we won," he whines like a little bitch. "You know how horny I get when we win."

"Fucking hell, if I agree, will you stop talking?"

"Yes! I've got a row of shots waiting for me and a gaggle of girls all wanting a piece. You might not even find me when you arrive."

"A gaggle?" I ask, although really, I don't need any more detail than that.

Ethan seems to be diving headfirst into whatever bottle and willing girl he can find recently. He claims to be having fun, but there are shadows in his eyes that tell a different story. He's friends with the wrong two guys if he thinks that Jake and I can't see that it's all a cover for something. For what though? We have no idea.

"Yes, now get your ass here. There's plenty to go around."

The idea of touching another girl besides the one I can't get out of my head is anything but appealing, but knowing Ethan needs me has me putting my car in drive and heading to his place. I know Camila was going out with her parents tonight, so I can only hope she won't be there so we won't have a repeat of last week.

The music's pounding when I step through Ethan's front door, and, as usual, there are people everywhere, quite a few of whom I don't even recognize. Making my way to the kitchen, I try to find Jake. I'm sure he wants to celebrate as much as Ethan does after another win. I try to push aside that it's another win that they managed without me.

"Mase, my man. Get over here," Ethan calls the second he spots me. "Here." He hands me two shots of something dark. I hesitate in knocking them back, unlike him. "Live a little," he says, having another before leaning in and whispering, "She's not here. No rescue mission needed tonight. Kick back."

Without a second thought, I tip the small glass to my lips and allow the liquid to burn down my throat before warming my belly. It feels good. But not as good as the haze that begins after the third... or fourth one. Damn, it's been too long since I felt this free.

I hang around with Ethan for a bit before a couple of girls come over and drag us to the living room to dance. I have no clue who they are, but as I watch Ethan shove his tongue down one of their throats, I guess he does, or he just really doesn't care.

I drink, I dance, I fight off multiple advances from different girls. I must admit that by the end of the night when people are either starting to leave or pass out, the temptation of those who are still interested is high. I haven't had sex for-fucking-ever, and the thought of sliding balls deep into a willing girl has my cock thickening in my pants. But then the image of Camila with her fingers gripping onto my hair so tightly I thought she was going to pull it out hits me, and the temptation to drag one of them upstairs wanes a bit.

I'd gotten a text from Mom when I'd left work to tell me that she'd organized for the boys to have a sleepover tomorrow night and that she'd be out, so I know I don't need to worry about my responsibilities tonight. Knowing that is such a weight lifted from my shoulders, but my desire to go home to her only gets stronger the more alcohol I have.

"I need to go home," I slur to whomever's listening.

"Nah, man. You've had too much." I squint my eyes at the face which has just said that. I vaguely recognize him. A member of the team? Who the hell knows.

"I need... I need her."

"I'm sure I can find you someone suitable." As he says that, someone I do recognize comes hopping around the corner. "Hey, Chels. Mason needs a girl."

She licks her lips and eyes the length of me. Any desire that was coursing through my veins instantly vanishes. She hobbles over and attempts to look sexy as she falls onto the sofa.

"What can I do for you?" She winks, and it makes me want to bring up the drink I've consumed.

"I think I'm good."

"Here, have a drink with me."

I oblige because there's nothing else I want to do with her, even if she does suck good cock.

———

A sharp pain to my shin wakes me up. My eyes fly open in shock as it radiates up my thigh.

What the fuck?

Rubbing at my leg, I look around a room I recognize as being one of Ethan's guestrooms before dropping my eyes to the bed beside me.

Oh no, no, no.

My heart starts to pound and blood rushes past my ears in panic as I stare down at a sleeping Chelsea.

No, no, no, no.

I slide from my bed on still drunk, wobbly legs and back away. Did I drink that much? Looking down at myself, I'm relieved to find that I'm still wearing my jeans and boxers, although my fly is undone.

I look around the room, hoping to find my shirt, but I come up empty. *Fuck.*

Chelsea stirs and I panic. Rushing from the room, I don't look where I'm going and stub my toe on the corner of the dresser.

"Motherfucker," I cry, grabbing my toe in agony as my eyes water.

"What's wrong, baby?" Her sweet, sickly voice has bile racing up my throat.

Please tell me I didn't. Please, dear fucking god, tell me I didn't.

"Come back to bed. I'll make it all better."

Glancing over my shoulder, I find her sitting up in bed with the covers pooled at her waist.

"Put them away, Chelsea. I'm not interested."

"Not what you said last night."

"You're lying," I state, reaching for the door handle to

get the fuck away from her. There might be a pair of tits ready for the taking, but knowing who they're attached to doesn't make the risk worth it by a long shot.

"Am I?"

Not being able to stand her voice any longer, I close the door behind me and go in search of my shirt and some painkillers.

"Yo, sick night, man," Ethan says, stumbling into the kitchen while I'm rummaging through his cupboards with a bottle of whiskey in his hand.

"Please tell me you're not having that for breakfast."

"What?" he asks, lifting it to his lips and downing a generous shot. "Hair of the dog."

"What the fuck's going on with you?"

"Enjoying life, just like you should be."

"Who says I'm not?"

"Your face." He looks up over my shoulder, his eyes lighting up. "Wait a minute, is there something you want to share?"

Before I get a chance to ask or even look around, arms slip around my waist and Chelsea appears at my side wearing... my fucking shirt.

"Give it back," I demand, removing her from my body.

"Aw, I thought you left it for me, baby."

"Un-fucking-likely. Give it back."

"Okay," she says with a shrug and a salacious smile. She props her crutch against the counter and curls her fingers around the bottom of the fabric. "If you insist."

As she peels it up her body, Ethan's eyes go wide as saucers.

"Damn, girl. What were you wasting your time on him for?"

"Fucking have her," I spit, pulling the fabric of my

shirt over my head and cringing when I realize it smells like her pretentious perfume.

"Come here, baby. Let me show you how a real man does it."

Chelsea takes Ethan's outstretched hand, not giving two shits about the fact that she's standing there stark naked. Girl's got no shame or morals, and the further away I am from her, the better.

Reaching into my pocket for my car keys, I find something else first. I pull the foil free from the fabric to find an empty condom wrapper.

Anger bubbles up inside me. Storming back over, I wrap my fingers around Chelsea's arm and pull her from Ethan's grasp.

"I don't know what game you're playing, but it needs to stop." I flick the wrapper in her face. "You might be a bitch, Chelsea, but this isn't you. I know I didn't fuck you last night. I wasn't even capable of getting up the stairs, so cut the shit and stop pretending. You're only trying to convince yourself."

She opens her mouth, but I've had enough of her bullshit and storm from the house.

Why the fuck did I come here last night? I should have just gone home to bed, or even better, the bed next door.

The house is in silence when I arrive home. Camila's parents have left for New York, she's at her birthday spa trip with Amalie and Alyssa, and Mom's pawned the boys off on a friend, presumably so she can have a night out. I roll my eyes. Taking myself straight to the bathroom, I strip out of my Chelsea scented shirt and throw it at the wall like this whole mess is its fault. Turning the water up as hot as it goes, I step underneath. I'm fairly certain nothing happened between us last night and she's just playing her usual game, probably trying to make some poor guy jealous by making it look like everyone else wants her. I'd like to have hoped she'd grown up enough to realize that that shit don't work, but apparently not. The water burns but I ignore it, wanting to wash away every second of last night. The less I remember the better.

Once I get back to my room, I fall onto my bed with the intention of getting some more sleep but I end up just lying there staring at the ceiling, wondering what time Camila's coming back.

I eventually get fed up of just wasting time and pull some homework from my bag and attempt to catch up a little after another week of working late. The sooner Mom sorts her shit out and I can cut down, the better.

I get lost in what I'm doing, and whoever it is at the front door ends up ringing incessantly before I give up and climb from the bed to find out who it is.

"Wassup, man!" Ethan booms, stepping into the house with a crate, followed by Jake and the rest of the team.

"What the hell are you doing?"

"Bringing the party to you, what's it look like?"

"I said no to this," I call over my shoulder, but he ignores me. Racing after him, I stop him in the kitchen just before he starts raiding the cupboards. "This isn't my house. You can't party here."

"Camila won't care. I have it on good authority that you two have it to yourselves for the weekend so... here we are. Got things to celebrate, man."

I blow out a breath. "I don't want all the guys knowing I had to move in here," I admit quietly.

"Don't sweat it. We told them it's Camila's thing. Wanting a blow out after Noah and all that shit. We got your back, man."

Music comes on as the sound of the guys' banter from the living room filters down to us.

"Okay fine. We'll order pizza," I say, slapping his thieving hands away from the cupboards. "But just the guys, okay?"

"Yeah, whatever you want." He winks at me and my stomach twists. He's so not telling the truth, but I roll with it—for now, at least.

Beers and pizza with the guys soon turns into shots and beer pong, and beer pong soon turns into body shots with the cheer squad and a few other girls Ethan managed to drag here from fuck knows where. I can't help but notice Chelsea's absence though. I'd have thought she'd have been first here after last night.

"Hey, handsome. Ethan said I should come over here and show you a good time," a soft voice whispers in my ear. I turn to look over my shoulder and the room spins at my movement.

She's pretty and her voice isn't like nails down a chalkboard like Chelsea's. She walks around me and makes herself at home on my lap.

"Nice house you've got here."

"Thanks. Can't say I pay much attention."

Her hands run up my chest and over my shoulders. Leaning in, her nose brushes against my neck. "Hmmm... you smell so good. I bet you taste even better." Her lips hit my skin and the world vanishes around me as I focus on her attention. Fuck if it doesn't feel good.

25

CAMILA

Seeing as both Alyssa and Amalie are coming back to my house for the night, we make the most of the spa's restaurant before heading home. We've had an incredible day. We've been scrubbed, buffed and tanned, and I haven't felt this relaxed in ages. A day with my girls to talk about mindless crap and gossip (that didn't involve me) from school was exactly what I needed today. It also helped take my mind off the fact that we're going home to a house without my parents. They're probably living it up in New York without me. My happiness wanes a little, but I try to cover it. I'm so proud of my dad. He deserves this after all his hard work, but it's going to be weird with them being in a different state most weeks. At least when they've been absent in the past I know they've only been a phone call away.

"That was incredible," Alyssa says, pushing her dessert plate away from her and rubbing her belly. "I don't think we did enough exercise today."

The two of us laugh with her. I can't help but agree. The food here has been almost non-stop all day; my belly feels a little bloated and my eyes are getting heavy with my need to curl up and sleep it all off.

"Ready to head back?" I ask them both.

"I'm not sure I ever want to leave here," Amalie complains. "It's pretty incredible."

"Aren't you used to this kind of thing from before?" Alyssa asks. Amalie's still quite tight-lipped about her past life, and I must say that I assumed this would have been a weekly event in her glamorous life.

"Mom and I used to go to a spa maybe once a month. It was our thing."

I immediately feel awful when her eyes water a little. "Shit, you should have said. We could have done something else."

"No, don't be silly. I'm not going to stop doing something I enjoy just because it's something I used to do with them." I frown at her when a tear escapes.

"Really?"

"Really. This is good. I don't want to spend my life hiding from my past. I need to push myself. This is now, that was then. I'm good."

I'm still skeptical as we emerge from the hotel entrance to find Amalie's little red car. She insisted on driving, seeing as I've been her taxi almost since she arrived. I wasn't going to argue about sitting back and enjoying the ride.

I don't think I even make it five minutes into the journey before my eyes fall closed and I drift off into my food coma.

"Camila. Cami." A hand shaking my shoulder is what eventually drags me from my slumber.

"Yeah, I'm awake."

"Cami, I think you might have an issue."

"What's that?" I ask, opening my eyes and seeing we're parked out front of my house but we're surrounded by other cars and... "Motherfucker." Movement from inside proves that my assumption is correct. That fuck wit is having a party. In my house. Without my permission. "I'm going to fucking kill him."

"Camila, wait, don't you think that—"

I don't hang around long enough to hear the end of her sentence. I push the front door open with such force it slams back against the wall and knocks a vase full of flowers in the hallway over, but I don't so much as flinch as the anger that's descended over me forces me forward.

I storm past a couple of guys from school until I spot Ethan fondling a girl in my kitchen.

"Where is he?" I seethe, my lips pursed, my hands on my hips.

"Calm down, baby girl. He's allowed to celebrate too, you know." At no point does he remove his hand from the girl's top. I want to scream at her to get some morals, but she looks too drunk to care right now.

"Where the fuck is he?" I spit out. He casually looks around, feigning making an effort to find him and pushing me right to my limit. "Ethan?"

Slowly his eyes come back to me. Amusement plays on his lips, making me want to punch him in the face.

"Ah... now I remember. I last saw him dragging a girl upstairs." My stomach turns over at the suggestion, my fancy dinner threatening to make a reappearance at the thought of him being with someone else. Although, that's not enough to stop me from turning on my heels and running for the stairs.

"Camila, what's—" I don't stop to allow Amalie to finish her question. Instead I storm up the stairs, ensuring my angry footsteps can be heard. I might not bat an eyelid about going after him, but I will give him some warning that a storm's brewing.

Wrapping my fingers around the cool metal of his door handle, I don't even wait long enough to think.

"Mason, what the fuck do you—" My words falter when I find him sitting on the edge of his bed with his bare back to me. At the intrusion, a female head pokes around him. She's sitting on the floor. I can only imagine what I'm interrupting right now, but I don't give a fuck. I'm too angry that he thinks this is okay.

"Get out," he growls, but he doesn't turn to me. Not giving in to his demands that easily, I take a step further into his room. "I said get out." His voice is low and rough as he repeats his demand, but I hold my ground. I'm not going to be bossed around in my own home by this asshole.

I soon realize that I wasn't the one being demanded to leave when the girl makes a show of getting to her feet and storming from the room. At least she was fully clothed.

Mason stands and I swallow, a ball of dread forming in my stomach.

"What do I think I'm doing?" he asks, turning his dark, angry stare on me.

"Yeah. This is my house, you can't just—"

"You think I don't know that?" His voice echoes off the walls of his small bedroom. "I'm reminded every single fucking day that I'm not in my own house. That I don't have a fucking home." He steps right in front of me. His scent fills my nose and the heat coming from his bare chest seeps into me. "Trust me, I don't need you of all people pointing this shit out to me."

"You have no right to have a party here."

"So everyone has to do what you want because it's your fucking birthday? What the fuck about mine? Don't I get to fucking celebrate too?"

My body sags. Of course I knew today was his birthday. For years we had joint birthday parties, every single year until, he abandoned me.

He shrugs when I don't come back with an answer, and it really fires me up. "Don't fucking shrug at me."

"Why, what would you rather I did?" He steps closer. "You want me to touch you again? Do things to you that no other has? Make you scream my motherfucking name?" My back hits the wall in my attempt to keep distance between us.

"Fuck you."

"Didn't get the chance, Cami-bear."

Before I know what's going on, Mason's fingers tangle in my hair and his lips descend on mine. He's still for a second, I guess waiting to see what I'm going to do. I intend to fight, on pushing him away and causing him some physical harm for touching me, but then his tongue runs along my bottom lip and mine part to allow him entry without instruction from my brain.

His tongue sweeps into my mouth, teasing mine until it begins dancing with his. The taste of alcohol mixes with him and makes my muscles relax. He steps into me, one of his thighs coming between mine and pressing against my core. My need to grind down on his is all-consuming, especially when the solid length of his cock pushes against my hip.

My shirt is lifted and the rough skin of his hands lightly scratches as he explores. He moans and grinds his hips into me, but the noise has reality hitting me full force.

"No," I shout, slamming my hands down on his chest until he backs up and away from me.

We stare at each other for a few seconds, our chests heaving, his cock straining against his pants.

Words elude me, so instead of coming at him with some smart remark, I just push from the wall and walk away.

"That's it. Run. Run away like there's nothing going on here. Clearly he was right—you are a frigid bitch."

I gasp in shock, turn and run toward him. He doesn't see it coming this time, and my palm connects with his cheek. The sound of skin hitting skin echoes around us. His eyes darken and my stomach clenches in fear. The muscles in his neck pull as he holds himself back. From what, I have no idea, and I don't intend on hanging around long enough to find out, because I run.

I practically fly down the stairs before pulling the plug on the sound system and sending the house into almost silence. The few people I can see turn and stare, looking slightly shocked before I make an even bigger spectacle of myself.

"Get the fuck out of my house," I scream as loud as my lungs will allow.

People start moving, but not as quickly as I expect.

"Get out. Get out. Get out," I shout, racing through the house, repeating myself until everyone gets the hint that I'm not fucking joking.

It feels like forever before Ethan eventually gets his ass dragged out by an apologetic Jake. I give him a thankful smile just before he kisses Amalie and closes the front door behind him.

With a large sigh, I fall down on the sofa. Amalie and Alyssa drop down beside me and each take one of my hands.

"Are you okay?"

I'm silent for a few moments as I consider what just happened. "I'm sorry. I think I kinda freaked out a little bit."

"What happened upstairs?"

"I... uh..." I'm not sure how much I want to share, but when I turn and find Amalie's kind eyes, I find it all spilling from my lips. "I walked in on Mason with a girl. Shouted at him. Kissed him and then slapped him."

"Whoa. Rewind," Alyssa demands. "You kissed him."

I shrug. "He was obviously horny, I was mad, it just kinda happened."

"You said he was with a girl."

"Well, I assumed he was. She was on the floor by his feet and he was sitting on the edge and she was—"

"Not giving me a blow job," a deep voice finished for me. "If you're going to give them the gossip they might as well get the whole truth."

I refuse to turn around. I refuse to even acknowledge him with an answer. Both Amalie and Alyssa turn around but the silence is deafening.

"Cami." Amalie elbows me in the ribs, but I ignore her. I'm not dealing with him, not when I'm still so angry. "Fine. I'll be back in a minute."

We listen to her soft footsteps before hearing the low mumbling of their voices from the kitchen.

"You know, I didn't believe the gossip at school that started going around about you two. After everything that he's done to you, I really didn't think you'd ever go there. But I see I was wrong."

"It's nothing, Alyssa."

"You just kicked everyone out of your house because you found him with a girl."

I fume, turning to look at her. "No," I snap. "I kicked everyone out because he had no right inviting them all here without so much as asking."

"I know that he takes the piss, a lot actually. But shit, Cam. It's his birthday weekend too. Doesn't he deserve to have a little fun too after everything?" Alyssa doesn't know the whole story when it comes to Mason's life. Hell, even I don't know the whole story, but I can't deny she doesn't have a point, much like he did upstairs.

I blow out a long breath as the sound of Mason's feet thundering up the stairs fills the space around us before Amalie returns with drinks.

"Mojito? They're strong."

"Yes," I say, jumping up so fast I almost knock the tray from her hands. I pour myself a glassful before downing the glass in one swallow.

"Whoa, slow down, I don't need to get Mason to carry you to bed again."

I pause for a second, then swallow what's in my mouth and look up at her.

"What?"

"That night you passed out at Ethan's. You do know it was Mason who got you home, right? Not Noah."

I mumble some kind of agreement. My memories from that night are still hazy at best, but I never believed he would have looked after me like that.

"You've really got under his skin. That's if you ever really left. I think you should go and apologize for tonight."

"I will," I agree, pouring myself another drink. "Later."

The first jug soon turns into the third as the three of us trawl through Netflix, watching all the chick-flicks that have been released recently. No one says a word about the guy hiding upstairs, but every time I hear a creak from his movement, my stomach knots knowing that I really should do as Amalie suggested and apologize for ruining his night.

The problem is, I'm scared. Not of him. I could never be scared of him. I'm scared of being alone in a room with him. He's going to be as angry, if not more so, than he was earlier, and look how that ended.

What comes next?

26

CAMILA

We head up to bed before we're drunk enough not to be able to set about getting beds made up. I let Amalie and Alyssa use the bathroom while I find something to watch on the TV and grab a clean pair of pajamas.

I take a very quick shower to freshen up, seeing as I can still smell a whiff of chlorine from the jacuzzi earlier, then I let my hair down and brush it and my teeth before pulling the door open.

I expect the hallway to be empty, but when I lift my eyes I find that it's very much not.

"Shit," I mutter under my breath as he just stands there, taking up all the space with his wide frame and sucking all the air out. "Excuse me."

"Why?" he taunts. "Want to finish what we started?" His scent hits my nose and my mind takes me back to earlier. I remember how it felt when he put his hands, his lips, on me. My knees weaken, and I fight the urge to lean toward him to do as he just suggested.

"Get out of my way. I've got friends waiting." I duck

under his arm, and surprisingly he allows me to escape. That is, until he opens his mouth.

"Ah, that's right. Birthday girl Camila is celebrating the big one eight. What fun that must be to be able to have a good time."

My muscles lock as guilt overwhelms me. I shouldn't have flown off the handle earlier. He's right, it's not fair that I get to do whatever I want for my birthday and ruin the only thing he had. I haven't even seen any presents around the house pointing to the fact that his mom remembered.

I reach out and grab the doorframe, suddenly feeling very sick at the realization that no one's done a thing for him.

"I hope you all have fun," he spits before disappearing into the bathroom where I just was.

I blow out a long, slow breath. I feel awful. It doesn't matter how horrible he's been to me or what he's done, the truth of the matter is that the boy I knew and loved is still buried in there somewhere, and he's crying out for something special today. My eyes burn with emotion as I rack my brain for something I can do to make his day not a complete waste, but it's so late. I guess I could get in touch with Ethan and restart the party, but something tells me he wouldn't want that now anyway.

With a huge sigh, I push my door open and crawl onto my bed.

"Hey, you okay?" Amalie asks, dragging her eyes away from what's on the TV.

"Yeah, I'm good. Just tired."

"You want us to turn this off?"

"No, no, it's okay."

I cuddle down under my sheets with the lights from

the flashing around me and the noise barely registering. The sound I do hear loud and clear though is that of Mason leaving the bathroom and shutting himself back in his room.

I have no idea how long I lie there, tossing and turning with the weight of what I did today pressing down on me, but eventually the TV gets turned off and the sound of the girls sleeping around me fills the room.

There's still a low beat coming from Mason's music next door. It's not loud enough to keep me awake, but as I lie here, it's all I can focus on.

He's in there. Alone on his birthday. It's wrong. So wrong.

Making a snap decision, I throw the sheets back and let my feet drop to the carpet. I'm silent as I make my way to the door and ever so slowly crack it open. The glow from the light out here fills the room, but no one stirs and I slip out into the hallway.

My heart's hammering to get out of my chest before I get anywhere near his door. My temperature rises as I consider what I'm about to do, but I don't let it stop me.

My hand shakes as I wrap my fingers around his door handle. The click of the lock seems like the loudest thing I've ever heard and I still, thinking it might have woken the girls. When I hear nothing, I push on. I twist more. The door moves, and my time for backing out vanishes as the soft light from the room beyond appears.

One inch. Two. Three. My eyes drift across the carpet until they hit the base of his bed. Then, sucking in a huge breath of confidence, I look up.

I find him immediately, sitting in the middle of his bed with school books around him. My heart physically aches to see him doing his homework on a night he should be celebrating.

His hair's falling over his face and he looks up at me through it, waiting for me to announce what the hell I'm doing if the hard set of his muscles are anything to go by.

"Y-You were right. I'm sorry."

His head tilts to the side to show he's listening and I take a step forward, pushing the door closed behind me, halting a quick escape.

"Go on," he encourages.

"I-I...I was wrong. Today is your day and I freaked out and ruined it. If you wanted a party, then you had every right to one."

He's silent for a beat. His intense eyes bore into mine as he digests what I've just said.

"I didn't want a party."

"Then why—"

"Ethan." He rolls his eyes at his friend's antics.

"Oh. Okay, well still. I ruined your night. I stormed in and sent the girl—"

"There was nothing going on with the girl."

"But she was—" His eyes narrow. "Doesn't matter. Not my business," I say, feeling ridiculous for thinking this could even be a good idea.

"Why are you here, Camila?"

"Because... Because it's your birthday, and you're in here alone when you should be celebrating."

"And what exactly are you going to do about it?" he taunts, his eyebrow lifting as he waits for my next move.

I take another step toward the bed, and then another until I'm over halfway across the room.

Mason drops his pen to the bed, and, pushing the

books away, he rests back on his hands as if he's about to enjoy a show.

For the first time since I entered, his eyes drop from mine. A trail burns down my body as they run over my breasts, my nipples pebbling as if he's touching them. My stomach clenches with lust as he drops lower down my satin covered body until he finds my bare legs.

He makes his way back up, an amused smirk playing on his lips, but the heat in his eyes is unmistakable.

"You just come here to tease me? To remind me of what's usually right on the other side of the wall that I can't have." He nods his head toward the wall that separates us from each other every night.

I shake my head, my nerves getting the better of me.

"So what then, Cami-bear?" He sits forward and scoots to the edge of the bed. He could touch me if he reached out, but he doesn't. "You must have come in here with a plan. I know you remember. I know how you think."

Isn't that the fucking truth. Four years of not being friends, but he can still read me as well as he did back then. It's how he's managed to hurt me. He knows my weaknesses, my fears like the back of my hand, and he's used them against me so many times. Yet, despite all that, here I am basically offering myself to him. No... to the boy I know that's hiding inside. The little boy who's scared he's lost his family and has no one to turn to. The little boy who thought the best way to deal with everything was alone. Well, I want to prove tonight that that isn't the case. I once loved that little boy with all my heart. I'd have done anything for him, but I'm realizing that when times got hard and he backed away from me, I allowed it. I didn't fight for him like I should have done. I didn't drag him kicking and screaming out of the pit he'd fallen into so that we could fight it together. Well... now's the time to make all that right.

With a new sense of determination, I lift my hands and curl my fingers around the lace trim on my cami, and, with a deep breath of air, I lift it up. As it leaves my body, cool air replaces it. My hair falls down onto my back and I drop the fabric to the floor.

His eyes hold mine, pride swelling in them as he waits me out.

With my heart trying to beat out of my chest, I take a hesitant step forward. His knees part so I can stand between them. His chest heaves beneath his shirt, and the muscles in his neck ripple when he swallows.

"Fuck."

He stands, his chest crashing into mine as his hand grips the back of my neck and his lips find mine. His part almost instantly, and I find myself following his movements. Our tongues duel and tease as we devour each other. It's a kiss that's been a long time coming, eighteen years to be exact, and right now, standing crushed up against his body, I don't ever want it to end.

His fingers grip my hip. It's bordering on painful, but I don't care. I need more. I need everything.

My hands find their way up and under his shirt, and his muscles bunch as I make contact and I smile into his kiss, knowing that he's as affected by this as I am.

His hand drops lower and slips inside my shorts and panties so he can grip onto my ass. The move pulls our bodies closer together, and the feeling of his cock pressing into my stomach has a wave of heat racing through me.

Ripping his lips from mine, he trails kisses along my jaw before descending my neck. He sucks on the sensitive skin beneath my ear that makes my entire body shudder with pleasure before he stills.

He breathes me in with his lips still pressed to my skin, but he doesn't do anything and I start to panic. Doesn't he want this? Me?

His fingers tighten against the back of my neck before he blows out a breath and whispers in my ear.

"If this continues, I won't be able to stop. I need you to tell me now if you don't want this."

The only sounds that can be heard are our heaving breaths as I fight to find the right words to answer him with.

"Mason." He groans as I say his name, his grip on me tightening once again. "I want you."

"Fuck."

He stays where he is with his face tucked into my neck for a beat before he pulls back and looks deep into my eyes. All I see is him. The boy I remember with his silly jokes, supportive, kind nature, and insecurities. He really is still in here.

His large hands wrap around my waist and he moves up until it's my legs against the edge of his bed. With one hand on my back, he slowly lowers me down, never once taking his eyes from mine. It's like he's trying to tell me something that he's too afraid to admit with words.

With his knee on the mattress next to my hip, he reaches behind his head and pulls off his shirt. My eyes drop in favor of enjoying the inches of toned skin he's just revealed. Apparently, I don't have the restraint that he does.

Once he's dropped the fabric, his palm connects with my stomach before brushing upward until he finds my breast. He squeezes gently, and it's like a direct line to my clit. It throbs as a wave of heat hits me, practically melting my panties right off me.

His lips find mine again as his fingers continue to drive me crazy, moving from one side to the other, pinching and palming my breasts until my hips start lifting from the bed in search of more.

"Mason," I moan when he pulls his lips from mine in favor of my neck.

"Never thought I'd hear you moan my name," he admits quietly as he descends over my collarbone. "Never thought... fuck." His eyes fly up to mine. The heat in their depths has me squirming, but I can still see his hesitation. He's still not convinced I'm in this fully with him. It's like he's thinking it's a joke or something, and I'm going to run at any moment. Little does he know that I'm deadly serious about this.

Taking his moment of hesitation. I place my hands on his shoulders and flip us over so I'm straddling his waist. I sit up straight and throw my hair back over my shoulders, giving him a full view of everything. On the inside I want to curl up and die with embarrassment, but Mason's always had this way of making me feel brave.

"Happy birthday, Mase."

I trail my fingertips down his chest and over the deep ridges of his abdomen until they hit his waistband. His muscles twitch with my contact and I can't help but smile. If possible, his cock grows even harder beneath me. I lick my lips and glance up at him. He doesn't miss the move, his own lips parting in anticipation

My fingers make quick work of undoing the tie around his waist, and in seconds he's lifting his hips from the bed to help me pull them and his boxers down his thighs.

His cock springs back and rests up onto his stomach.

My eyes widen slightly before the corner of my mouth curls up. Maybe he does have a reason to be such a cocky asshole if he's rocking junk like this.

Dropping to my knees, I pull the fabric free of his feet until he's bare before me. It's not the first time over the years I've seen him naked but fuck, he was a boy then. Now, he's most definitely all man.

Excitement bubbles up in my stomach as I settle myself between his thighs and he props himself up on his elbows to watch the show.

"Ready for your present?" I ask in what I really fucking hope is a seductive voice.

His chest heaves and he bites down on his bottom lip, but at no point do any words leave his mouth. He never was a chatterbox like me, and I guess that extends to situations like this.

Knowing that his lack of response doesn't match his interest level, I reach forward and take his steel length in my hand. My fingers wrap tightly around, causing him to suck in a breath through his teeth.

His eyes are locked on where we're connected as I start to move. His teeth grind and his jaw pops, and I feel more powerful than I ever have in my life.

His eyes start to shut as the feelings take over. Leaning forward, I lick the tip of him. His eyes fly open as he stares at me with disbelief. With my confidence growing, I wrap my lips around his head and suck him into my mouth.

He groans and sits up. His hand finds my head and his fingers dig into my hair to hold me in place. He guides me slowly until his cock's swelling even more.

"Cami," he warns, wrapping his other hand around my forearm. I look up at him. His pupils are blown, his cheeks flushed and his lips parted. It's the most erotic sight I've ever seen, and it pushes me forward.

I suck him deeper, almost gagging when he hits the back of my throat.

"Cam, I'm... I'm gonna—" I lick around the head and suck him deeper. His words falter as his cock twitches. His roar that follows makes my chest swell with pride and my panties even wetter.

"Fuck, Cami-bear," he says between his heavy breaths.

Helping me up from the floor, he immediately seeks out my lips and captures them in another earth-shattering kiss.

I'm not aware I'm moving until my back hits the bed and my shorts and panties are pulled down my thighs. My muscles clench as I remember how incredible he made me feel last time he touched me. I'm not waiting long for a reminder because his hands land on my inner thighs and they're spread wide, exposing every inch of me to him.

"You're so fucking beautiful. So much more than I ever imagined."

"You've thought about this?" I ask, my voice coming out stronger than I was expecting.

"Only every fucking night before I fall asleep." I'm not expecting that, and words fail me to respond. Although it soon becomes apparent that he wasn't expecting one, because he dips his head and rubs his tongue up my seam.

"Oh shit."

"You can't tell me you've not thought about getting a repeat."

"Every second since you walked out." He stops and looks up at me, and I immediately regret my words.

He opens his mouth but no words form. Instead he

goes back to the job at hand. He parts me, finds my clit and licks and sucks until I'm chanting his name.

"Come on, Cami-bear. Let me feel you coming." His words rumble through me, setting off the first sparks of my release. His fingers push higher into me and touch a part of me that has stars flashing behind my eyes. "That's it. Let go. Show me how good it feels." He licks faster, circling around my most sensitive spot as he thrusts deeper, and it's only seconds later when my body quakes and I come with his face between my legs.

"Holy fucking shit," I pant, one arm thrown over my face as I try to catch my breath.

"Good?" I don't need to look at him to know he's got a shit-eating grin on his face.

27

MASON

Standing up, I wipe my mouth with the back of my hand and stare down at her laid out naked on my bed.

Fuck knows what made her decide to walk in here tonight, but fuck if I'm going to put too much thought into it.

It was obvious she turned up with a mission in mind. Her eyes we set and her body ready, despite the obvious nerves that were racing through her. She might think she can hide it from me, but I can read her like a book. I always could.

My eyes run up from her feet, which are placed on the end of my bed, over her bent legs to her swollen pussy. My cock weeps for more despite being inside her hot little mouth only moments ago. I skim up over the curve of her waist, pause at her breasts for a few seconds taking in her tight, rosebud nipples which taste like fucking candy, until I find her face. As if she knows where my attention is, she lifts her arm.

Her breath catches when she finds me staring down at her.

"Hey," she squeaks, suddenly looking unsure of herself.

"Hey."

She lifts herself up on her elbows and I panic that she's about to run. I warned her what would happen if she allowed this to continue. We're not done. Not by a long shot.

I kneel on the bed, caging her legs in, and land with my hands beside hers, bringing our lips almost within touching distance. My eyes flit down to them. I desperately want to take them again, but I need to know she wants this.

"You sure?" I don't want to ask, I just want to do it, but I know this is a big deal and I need to know she's serious and not going to regret it once it's over. She only gets one shot at her first time, and whenever she thinks of it, she'll be forced to think of me. My chest swells at the thought.

Her hand wraps around the back of my neck and she pulls me down. She lies back and I follow, my weight pressing her into the mattress.

I kiss her like I should have years ago. I pour everything I've ever felt for her into it and pray that she can feel my desperation, my regret, my love.

"It's okay, Mase." She pulls back and looks into my eyes. "It's okay." She thinks I'm doing this to ensure she's ready, but she has no idea that all I'm doing is making up for lost time, replacing all the kisses she gave that motherfucker with my own because we both know that her lips should have only ever touched mine.

"Aren't I allowed to take my time with you?"

Biting down on her bottom lip, she shakes her head. "I need to feel you. *All* of you."

"Fuck." There's no fucking way I can deny her that.

Reaching over, I pull open my top drawer and feel around for a condom. I pull out a box and tip the contents on the bed beside her.

Her eyes widen in horror. "I didn't agree to needing that many."

"We'll just stick with the one for now. These can be for tomorrow," I add with a laugh.

Just like when we were kids, when I'm with her, everything seems that little bit easier, that little bit more possible. My reality washes away. The fact that I was sitting in my bedroom alone doing my homework on the night of my eighteenth birthday has vanished, because all that matters right now is her.

She watches intently as I roll the condom down my length.

"Lift up and lie back against the pillows," I instruct, pulling the sheets from beneath her when she follows orders. I flip them back with a little too much enthusiasm and they fall to the floor, my school books disappearing inside. I ignore them, it's not like I have any intention of needing them anytime soon. I've got a naked Camila in my bed, the one good thing I've allowed myself to fantasize about over the years. It's actually happening, right now, and I intend on making the most of it.

Her dark hair fans out on my pillow and as she gets comfortable, I find myself exactly where I've always wanted to be. Between her legs. I push them wider to allow me the space I'm going to need before taking myself in my hand and rubbing the head of my cock through her wetness. She's soaked from her previous orgasm, so I have no question as to whether she's ready for this or not.

Her body trembles beneath me with a mix of lust and fear, and her eyes never leave mine, as if she's finding the strength she needs within them.

"I'll take it slow, I promise."

I've never taken anyone's virginity before—well, not that anyone admitted to—and I'm just as terrified as she is of hurting her.

Dropping lower, I push inside her. Her eyes widen, but she doesn't do anything to stop me.

Leaning over her, I grip onto the back of her neck and crash my lips to hers. Pushing into her a little more, I kiss her harder, hoping that I'll be able to mask any pain. I know it's wishful thinking, but I do it nonetheless.

"Just do it," she mumbles against my mouth, and I do exactly as I'm told.

I thrust forward and all the way inside her. My muscles lock tight as her walls ripple around me, trying to accommodate my sudden invasion. I'm fucking desperate to move, to feel more, but her little whimper beneath me puts an end to my selfishness.

When I pull my eyes open that I didn't realize had slammed shut, I find hers staring at me with tears pooling at the edges.

There are so many things I want to say to her, to reassure her that it'll get better, but I push all of those aside in favor of showing her. My tongue delves back into her mouth as my fingers go in search of her clit. The pain's going to fade, or so I've heard, and hopefully it'll soon turn into pleasure. I fucking hope so, because if I don't get to move soon, I might fucking explode.

I play her body the only way I know how, and soon she

starts to relax under me. I test the waters by flexing my hips slightly, and she gasps.

"Sorry, I'm so sorry," I whisper into her neck.

"No. It was... it was good, I think."

"You think?" I ask with a smile.

"Do it again and we'll find out."

So I do, and she makes this incredible little noise that I want to hear for the rest of my fucking life.

Sitting up so I can see her, see where we're connected, I stare down at the vision below me. She reaches for my hands and our fingers intertwine as I start to rock into her faster.

"Mason," she moans, her eyes getting heavy with pleasure.

Letting go of one of her hands, I go back to her clit. Pressing down with the pad of my thumb, I gently start to circle. Her hips lift, her back arching as she cries out. Her muscles clamp around me and tingles shoot up my spine.

I continue what I'm doing, increasing the pace with each thrust, and before long, she's chanting my name.

Just before she falls, I take her lips once again to muffle her cries. Her fingers grip onto my sides, and, as she finds her release, her nails dig in. That little shock of pain along with the tightening of her pussy pushes me over the edge with her, and I roar my release.

I fall down beside her, our chests heaving with exertion. I remove the condom, dropping it over the side, and I pull her into my body and hold her tight.

"That was some fucking birthday present." She laughs, her body jolting in my arms with her amusement. "Are you okay?" I drop a kiss to her shoulder as she thinks.

"I don't know," she admits quietly. Rolling her over, I give her no choice but to have to look at me.

She reaches out and tries to tuck a bit of my hair behind my ear, but like always, it just falls forward once again.

"Was I totally crazy coming in here tonight? Have I just made the biggest mistake of my life?"

"Why would you say that?" My thumb gently caresses her cheek as I try to hide the fact that her questioning what just happened between us cuts.

"Things haven't exactly been easy sailing between us, have they?"

"Nope. But no one said love was easy."

Her lips part to respond, but she must decide better of it. "I should probably go."

"Go, like run back to your room?"

"I was thinking more the bathroom, but yeah, I should probably do that too."

Dropping my head, I whisper in her ear, "Don't make me your dirty little secret, Cami."

I know it's probably what I deserve, but I'm not ready to give her up and I'm certainly not ready for other guys to now think she's single. Our history is common knowledge around Rosewood, and I have no doubt I've pissed off enough guys who would willingly go after her if they got the chance just to piss me off.

She doesn't respond, just drops a quick kiss to my lips before climbing from my bed. She looks around at the floor before quickly finding her discarded pajamas and pulling them on. Every inch of me wants to demand that she gets back into bed, but I need to allow her some space if that's what she needs. She'll come to me when she's ready. At least I hope she will.

The second she closes the door behind her, I roll onto my back and throw my arm over my eyes.

I just fucked Camila. I just took her fucking virginity.

A smile twitches at my lips. I always thought it would be the two of us. We kind of went a long way around to get here, but it happened. I now just have to hope she doesn't regret every second of it and hate me more than she should.

The silent seconds stretch out into long minutes, and I start to think that she's snuck back into her room and I'm going to have to spend the night in my bed alone. The thought doesn't thrill me.

I've given up hope and I'm just drifting off when the sound of a door opening brings me back around. I've turned the light off so I can only see her shadow with the sliver of moonlight shining through the curtains.

The sheets lift and she climbs in next to me, immediately tucking herself into my body.

"Do you need me to turn the light on?" I whisper, knowing how much she hates the dark.

"I'm good as long as I'm with you."

My heart damn near explodes in my chest. I remember her saying the same words when we were kids, but I didn't expect her to still feel the same all these years later.

I kiss the top of her head and hold her a little bit tighter, because in the cold light of day, this could all just be a memory.

28

CAMILA

I wake up hot with my legs stuck to something.

What the—

And then it hits me. I'm not stuck to a thing, I'm stuck to a person, and that person just so happens to be Mason.

Memories play out in my mind like a fucking movie. Me walking in here bold as brass and telling him in not so many words that I was his birthday present and whipping my top off. My cheeks flame and my temperature increases as embarrassment at my forwardness hits me full force.

My personal movie continues, me with his cock as deep in my mouth as I could get it, the taste of him on my tongue. Me writhing in his bed as he pushed me toward my release with his tongue and fingers. The biting pain as he pushed all the way inside me. My muscles clench at that memory. I knew it was going to hurt, but I wasn't disappointed with what came next. Fuck, that was mind blowing. The way he felt moving inside me, stretching me.

Jesus. I need to get out of here.

With him snoring lightly beside me, I somehow manage to unattach myself from him and slide from the bed. He doesn't so much as stir, just proving that the hours he's been putting in to support his family really are taking their toll.

After using the bathroom, I sneak back into my room and slide between my cold sheets. It's only then that I wonder if I just made a very bad decision. He's going to wake and find I've left. Is he going to hate me?

I don't get to dwell on my decision, because fabric rustling fills my ears before my mattress dips and someone climbs in beside me.

"If you even think about lying to me, then I'm going to drag you next door and demand answers from the man himself," Amalie whispers, her eyes twinkling in the morning sun.

"I wasn't going to lie," I whisper back.

"So you didn't just do a very short walk of shame in the hope I didn't know you slipped out last night and rocked Mason's world?"

"Shush, Alyssa might hear you!"

"Are you kidding me? She snores louder than a fucking rhino. If she can sleep through that and you screaming last night, then she certainly can through our whispering."

"You heard me screaming?" I cover my face with my hands, mortified that my best friend heard everything. "Oh my god. Oh my god."

"No, I didn't actually. The bed banged against the wall a bit, but that was it. You shouldn't need to worry about your parents knowing what's going on under their roof when they return."

I peek through my fingers at her.

"So how was it? I'm assuming you gave him a fine birthday treat."

"It was..." I trail off, trying to find the words to describe what my time with Mason last night was. "What I'd always hoped it would be."

A wide smile breaks across Amalie's face. "I always knew you two were meant to be together."

"Whoa, hold your horses. Just because we..."

"Fucked," Amalie helpfully adds.

"Yeah, that. It doesn't mean we're together."

"Really? You're going to lie there and try telling me that you've not been secretly yearning for him for the past four years."

"I was mostly hating him."

"Yeah, trust me when I tell you that I understand how quickly that can change."

I open my mouth to tell her that she's not all that far from the mark, although I'm only just starting to understand how I've been feeling myself when another voice pops up.

"What are you two whispering about? It sounds juicy." Alyssa's head pops up over the mattress.

Amalie looks to me. I widen my eyes and shake my head slightly. I'm not ready for the world to know about this yet.

"Just talking about Jake."

"Ugh, of course you are. You know those guys don't need their egos boosting any more, right?"

Amalie laughs. "I'm aware."

"Come on, I want pancakes," I announce, sitting up and putting an end to any more of Alyssa's questions.

I throw a hoodie over my pajamas and leave them both to get washed and dressed.

Pausing at Mason's door, I press my ear to the wood and listen, but only silence greets me, so I assume he's still sleeping.

I make my way to the kitchen, opening the curtains we'd shut on our way up last night and turning the radio on as I pass.

With all the ingredients I need out on the counter, I get started making my batter just like my granny taught me. She made the best pancakes. I smile as I think of the lady who taught me to bake as a kid and fire up the stove.

By the time the girls join me I'm dancing around the kitchen and have a stack of pancakes that almost hits the counter above.

Amalie immediately reaches for the jug of orange I'd pulled from the refrigerator and downs half a glass.

"If I didn't know any better, I'd think you got some last night," Alyssa says, watching my hips wiggle in time to the music.

Amalie snorts mid swallow and sprays the kitchen in juice as she starts coughing and spluttering.

"Oh my god. I'm so sorry. It... uh... went down the wrong pipe?" Thankfully Alyssa buys the lie. I, on the other hand, can't help laughing as she begins cleaning up.

Once the counter is clear of juice, Alyssa and Amalie grab the items I've got lined up and take them to the table. I'm just about to join them with the pancakes when the atmosphere in the air changes. It's suddenly hard to breathe, and I don't need to turn around to know the reason why.

"I must have missed my invite for pancakes." His voice rumbles through me and hits me right between the legs. I can't deny that I'm not feeling a little sore down there this morning, but I like the reminder of what happened last night. Looking over my shoulder, I watch him stalk toward me and I stiffen. "I didn't like waking up alone."

His hand slips around my waist and I jump away, grabbing the plate of pancakes and holding them in front of me like a shield. His entire face drops at my reaction to him, and it breaks my heart. I didn't mean to hurt him.

"Oh, I see." Without saying another word or picking up anything from the kitchen, he disappears and storms back up the stairs.

A lump forms in my throat and my eyes burn with unshed tears. That wasn't how I intended our first meeting the morning after to go.

"Cami, come on, we're starving to death in here," Alyssa shouts, and I shake my head to get it together. I'll give them breakfast, point them in the direction of the front door and then go and sort Mason out.

Amalie gives me a sympathetic look when I appear, probably looking a little worse for wear. She'd have seen Mason storm past this room on his way back to the stairs. She knows that something is off between us.

"Thank god. I'm dying for one of your pancakes—or five."

They both eat more than their body weight in syrup and fruit covered pancakes while I push one around my plate, my mind repeating that short interaction with Mason in the kitchen. The second I jumped away from him, I regretted it, but I didn't want Alyssa walking in. It's stupid, I know. If I told her not to say anything, she wouldn't. I trust her, but this is all so new, so scary and potentially serious that I don't know which way is up.

Alyssa sits back, downing the last of her juice, and lets out the most unladylike burp before announcing that she needs to get home because she's got a family meal this afternoon for her grandparents' wedding anniversary.

The three of us take all the plates to the kitchen and they help me fill the dishwasher and clean up before we head upstairs to get the girls packed.

Alyssa shoves all her stuff in her bag, says her goodbyes and is gone before I even blink. Amalie hangs around a little longer. Once she's sorted, she sits on the edge of my bed with me and takes one of my hands in hers.

"Just go and talk to him. Explain how you're feeling. He'll understand. Chances are, he's feeling the same."

I nod. "I will, if he'll listen."

"Of course he will. That boy's been in love with you forever. It was in his eyes the first time I saw him look at you."

I give her a smile but I don't share her enthusiasm. Things between Mason and me are more complicated than anyone else understands. "I'll do my best."

"I'm at the other end of the phone if you need me. And he might be his best friend, but if I promise sexual favors, I'm sure Jake would knock him out for you, should you need that option."

"Thank you," I say with a laugh, smiling for what feels like the first time all morning.

Amalie gives me a hug and assures me that she can see herself out. I stand at my window after she walks out and watch as she climbs into her car and drives off.

The house is still empty besides the two of us. I have no idea what time Nicky and the boys are due back, but I know that we need to make the most of the peace. With the number of people living under this roof right now, times without threat of interruption are going to be hard to come by.

Thinking against knocking and walking into his room, much like I did last night, I decide on trying a different tact.

Grabbing a fresh set of clothes, I carry them down to the bathroom. I turn the shower on and strip down before dropping a bottle into the shower tray, ensuring it's loud enough that he'd have heard before I grab my phone and send him a message.

Me: Any chance you could help me please?

29

MASON

Waking up alone kinda hurt, but in the end I tell myself that she just woke up earlier than me and got bored. Why she wouldn't wake me to keep her entertained plays on my mind, but I rationalize that she's got friends sleeping over in her bedroom so I guess she needs to be social. It still pisses me off though.

But that was nothing compared to the way she jumped away from me when I touched her in the kitchen. It was like my touch physically burned her and she couldn't get away fast enough. I thought last night was the beginning of something, something that should have happened a long time ago, but it seems that I might be the only one who feels that way.

Pushing aside the books I'm trying to focus on, I throw myself back on the bed. The need to work out my frustration pulls at my muscles, and I tug my cell from my pocket to see if either Ethan or Jake, or both, are free to work out. I'm missing out on my daily practice with the guys and I'm desperate not to ruin the hours of work I've put in. I might not be on the team right now, but that doesn't mean my dream of college football has died.

I let out a sigh. I sent my applications in as early as possible. I know it's still way too early to hear anything back, but the radio silence makes me feel a little sick nonetheless. My stomach twists that college might not even be an option at all if I don't get a scholarship. Getting a roof over my brothers' heads is more important right now. This place isn't exactly a long-term home for them.

The sound of Amalie's car backing out of the drive sounds out over my music before Camila's small feet move down the hallway. I hold my breath, thinking she might come storming in, but she walks straight past my door. My heart drops but I refuse to go chasing after her. If what happened between us last night meant nothing to her, then so be it. I'm not being one of those pathetic guys who goes begging to the girl. No fucking way.

The bathroom door bangs shut before the shower turns on. *Fucking tease.* My imagination gets the better of me as I picture what her sinful curves might look like covered in white fluffy bubbles. My cock swells and I fight to stop my need for her getting the better of me. It's something I've become a fucking master at, so it shouldn't be all that hard.

But you've made her yours now, a little voice says in my head, but it's forgotten when a loud crash comes from the bathroom. I sit bolt upright, trying to hear if she's okay.

Chastising myself for caring so much when she clearly doesn't, I open my messages but before I find the chat, a new message pops up.

Cami-bear: Any chance you could help me please?

I stare down at my cell, blinking a couple of times just to make sure I'm not hallucinating. A wicked smile turns up the corner of my lip. This is karma kicking her ass for this morning.

Running my hand through my hair, I climb from my bed and head toward the bathroom, hoping like hell I'm about to walk into something that can go straight into my wank bank.

My smirk still firmly in place as I walk into the bathroom, half expecting her to be curled up in a ball on the floor having tripped over the toilet or something stupid, but what I actually find makes my eyes widen and my jaw drop.

Camila's standing under the torrent of water, her hair soaked and sticking to her shoulders and down onto her chest. Rivers run over her breasts, down her stomach and over her hips. I'm instantly hard, my cock tenting my sweats.

"What are you waiting for?" Her voice is like pure sex, and I don't waste a second. Pulling my shirt over my head, I drop my pants and step into the shower. But I don't touch her. I keep an inch between us and just stare into her eyes, my need to know what the hell she's playing at only marginally more important than her body right now.

"I'm so sorry," she whispers over the sound of the running water. "I just... I didn't want Alyssa finding out something before we even know what's happening here. She was in the other room and—"

"What about Amalie?"

"She... uh... she knows everything. I can't hide anything from her, she's too damn percept—ah." Her back hits the cold tiles behind her and I sweep the hair away that's sticking to her cheek. My lips slam down on hers and she instantly opens for me.

All my panic and frustration from this morning instantly settles. I skim my hand up from her hip, over her waist until the weight of her breast sits in my palm. I pinch her nipple between my fingers and she gasps, pulling my body closer so I'm pressing her against the wall.

I kiss along her jaw and nip at her earlobe as she shudders beneath me.

"Show me how sorry you are," I growl in her ear.

Her head pulls back in shock and hits the wall, but she doesn't do anything about it. She stares into my eyes, hers narrowing as she tries to figure out if I'm serious or not. I don't respond to her silent question. I don't need to, because a sly smile turns the corners of her lips up before she leans forward and presses them to my chest. She kisses a line down the center of my torso before dropping to her knees. The sight is exactly as I pictured it in my head.

Her delicate fingers wrap around my solid length and my skin erupts in goosebumps as she slowly starts pumping. My knees threaten to buckle. Resting one hand against the tiles and threading the other into her hair, I stare down as she wraps her lips around my cock. Best fucking sight in the fucking world.

It's all too soon when my balls start to draw up, but it's not ending this way. Slipping from her mouth, I lift her to her feet and push her back against the wall. The cold makes her breath catch again, and I make the most of her shock by plunging my tongue into her mouth.

Lifting her leg up around my waist, I tease her with my fingers.

"So fucking wet," I murmur against the sensitive skin of her neck, making her shiver.

She moans, flexing her hips forward, seeking more.

"Tell me you're on birth control."

"I... I am."

"I've never gone bare before, I fucking swear to you."

"O-Okay."

I pull back and look at her, unable to keep the wide smile off my face.

"Yeah?"

"Mason, please." Her lids are heavy with desire, her usual rich chocolate eyes almost black with need.

"I could never say no to you."

Hiking her leg higher, I pull her hips from the wall and find her entrance. I slide in slowly, assuming that she's probably still sore from yesterday—not that she's said anything if she is. I push in an inch at a time, studying her face for any kind of discomfort, but there's none. Instead her head drops back and her eyelids flicker shut as she absorbs the sensation.

I drop my head into the crook of her neck once I'm fully seated. The feeling of her, skin against skin, is fucking mind-blowing, making me so fucking glad I've never been stupid enough to go bareback with anyone else. There was never supposed to be anything between us, but I allowed life to break us apart. Well no more. Camila is mine, and there won't be a fucking thing separating us ever again.

I roll my hips and she starts to moan, her nails digging into the skin over my shoulders, but I don't let up. I increase my tempo, gripping her tighter as she begins to clamp around me.

"Fuck, Cami. Fuck. You feel so fucking good."

Her cheeks flush at my compliment, and it makes me smile that she can be embarrassed by my words while she's full of my cock.

Her body starts to tremble in my hands, and I drop one of mine to find her clit. I barely touch her and she cries out my name, her pussy clenching me so fucking tight that it sends me over the edge with her. My orgasm slams into me and I empty myself inside her, making her mine from this day forward.

"Well, that was unexpected," I say into her sopping wet hair after I've lowered her leg and pulled her into my embrace.

"I really am sorry," she mumbles into my chest.

"I know. I wouldn't be here otherwise." My fingers thread into her hair and I gently tug until I can take her lips.

By the time we step from the shower, I'm hard again and ready to be inside her. I pass her a towel and then wrap another around my waist.

"Already?" she asks, staring down at the tented fabric.

Taking her hand in mine, I pull her up against my chest. If this is happening, then I intend on going all in with the honesty. "The second I learned what sex was, there was only one person I wanted to be doing it with. I've had to wait a fucking long time for that to happen, and I intend on making up for it now."

She looks up at me, and the emotion in her eyes hits me right in the chest. It's exactly how I've wanted her to look at me for the past four years while I was on self-destruct mode.

Slipping one arm around her back and the other under her knees, I sweep her up into my arms and carry her toward her bedroom.

I lay her down on her bed before pulling the towel from around her body and setting about making her chant my name once again. I always feared this girl would be the death of me, and I'm finally discovering why.

I have no idea how much time passes, and while I've got my lips and hands on Camila's body, I really don't give a fuck. But eventually the sound of the front door closing filters up to us along with the excited chatter of my brothers.

"Looks like our peace is over," I say, pulling back from her lips and propping myself up on my elbow so I can stare down at her beautiful face.

Her wide, awe-filled eyes stare up at me. She studies me like she hasn't looked at me a million times before with a soft, satisfied smile on her lips.

Lifting her hand, she cups my cheeks. "What happens next, Mase?"

"Well, I'm kinda hungry, seeing as I didn't get any pancakes this morning."

"That's not what I mean. I meant with us. What happens from here?"

"Anything you want," I say.

"Anything?"

I nod, wondering what she could possibly be thinking. "What do you want?"

"Me? I want more of you, any chance I can get," she says.

"So this is just a sex thing for you?" I ask.

"What? No, not at all. Why, are you just using me for my body?"

"I might just be." I wink and move over her.

"Hmmm... I think I can handle that. Should I warn the

others?" Her eyebrows nearly hit her hairline. "I'm joking, baby. There's only you. There's only ever been you."

"You're serious, aren't you?"

"Deadly."

"But what about the last four years, the—"

"The way I've treated you? I was a dick, Cam. My life went to shit, and I saw you in this house playing the perfect family. You had everything I wanted, you were everything I wanted, but I couldn't handle it. So I made myself hate you. It was easier to hate than it was to allow you to see what was festering inside me. I mean, it's still not pretty, but I think I'm finally understanding that I can't continue like this, hiding from who I am and what I really want."

"And what do you really want?" she asks, and I realize that she really needs me to spell it out for her.

"I want you, Cami-bear. I've only ever wanted you." I lift her hand and rest it over my heart. "You were in here long before I even realized what it meant." She gasps, her eyes filling with tears. "I'm sorry for all the bullshit. I'm sorry for all the pain I caused you. I was lashing out at my bullshit life, and I targeted it at the person I loved the most."

"You... you love me?"

"I've loved you since the first moment I saw you, Cami. It was always meant to be us."

A sob rumbles up her throat, but her hand drops from me.

"If this is a game... If you're playing me right now, I swear to fucking god that I'll hurt you."

I can't help but laugh at her. She looks too cute, trying to threaten me.

"The only thing you can do to hurt me is to walk away.

I need you, Cami-bear, and I'm fed up with trying to convince myself of anything else."

Her eyes bounce between mine as she tries to decide if she can trust me. I hate that she has to hesitate, but I can hardly blame her. I see the moment she decides. I feel the change in her even before the words leave her lips. "I love you too, Mason. Always have, always will."

"Fuck." Her words make my chest constrict to the point of pain. Dropping my weight on top of her, I kiss her like I should have been doing for the past four years instead of trying to send her life into the pits of hell like mine was.

I have every intention of taking her again, but that's all shot to shit when Mom calls my name up the stairs.

"Fuck." Dropping my head to Camila's shoulder, I drag in a few deep breaths.

Mom calls again, and this time I shout back that I'm coming, much to Camila's amusement. "Are you?" she asks with a raised brow.

"Don't tempt me."

"Up you get. You need to hear what she's got to say, and I've got homework to do."

"I can think of better things to do than homework."

She climbs from the bed and walks over to her drawers to find some clothes. "I'd like to still be able to walk tomorrow if possible."

"Walking's overrated."

"Go and get dressed, your mom wants you." She throws a pair of panties at me and I catch them and bring them to my nose.

"I know they're clean, but really?"

"Yep. In fact, I think I'll keep these."

"Weirdo."

"I'll be whatever you want me to be."

"Right now that would be dressed so you can hear your mom out."

"Do you know something I don't?"

"I might, but if you want to know for sure then you need to get some clothes on and find out."

Reluctantly, I leave her in her room getting dressed to find some clothes of my own. I don't waste any time, and the second she steps out into the hallway, I join her.

"Ready?" I ask, holding my hand out for her.

"Have you even washed them?" She nods at my hands, that have spent a significant amount of time inside her in the last hour or so, with her nose screwed up.

I wink at her and she flushes bright red. "Ah, Cami-bear, we're going to have so much fun." Despite my potentially dirty hands, she threads her fingers through mine and together we descend the stairs.

"Do you have to call me that?"

"Sure do, sweet cheeks."

"Ugh, that's worse. Maybe Cami-bear isn't so bad after all."

We're both laughing as we walk into the kitchen. There are a couple of presents sitting on the counter beside a football cake. My brothers are sitting at the breakfast bar while Mom leans against the worktop with a coffee in her hands.

Her eyes lift from our joined hands and a wide smile spreads across her face. "Have you two... are you two...?"

"We are," Camila announces happily as a shit-eating grin spreads across my face. This incredible girl by my side is fucking mine. How did my life go from one big disaster to, well... this?

"Oh my god, I'm so excited. You might get to be my

daughter-in-law after all." I swear Mom's eyes get a little wet at the prospect.

"One thing at a time, yeah? She's only just started talking to me again."

Mom laughs, pushing one of the presents toward me. "Happy birthday, baby. I'm sorry I wasn't here to celebrate yesterday, but I thought you'd want to spend it with friends over me. Plus, I worked an extra long shift."

"It's fine, I—wait, you worked?"

"Yep, I've got a job. A well paying job that means you don't need one. I was looking, I swear, but it wasn't until your girl here had a few choice words for me that I really started taking it seriously."

I squeeze her hand in mine for fighting for me.

"It's still nights, so I'll need a little help with the boys but I'll be back for the school run and I start after their bedtime. Hopefully in a couple of months, I'll have saved enough to get us our own place again and we can restart our lives.

"I can't possibly thank you enough for everything you'd done for me, for us. I'll never be able to repay you for everything you've done to keep our family going, but I need you to call your boss and tell them that you need your life back. Friday night, I expect you to be out on the football field where you belong."

Emotion clogs my throat. "You serious?"

"Yep. Being here, it's been a bit of an eye opener. I haven't had a drink in... well I can't remember, and Gabbi convinced me to start taking the pills the doctor gave me months ago. I should have done it years ago. I finally feel like I can be the mom the three of you deserve."

"That's awesome, Mom. I'm proud of you."

"New starts from here on out for all of us." She lifts her coffee in the air in a toast we all agree to.

I open the gifts—a new bottle of my favorite cologne, some boxers, and some chocolates. To most people it wouldn't be anything, but to me, it's everything. Mom's been so lost over the past few years that she's barely realized my birthday had happened, so these few gifts are just proof that the speech she just made could be true. I really fucking hope it is.

30

CAMILA

The next morning, hand in hand, Mason and I walk into school. The second we approach, everyone turns our way. Most people are shocked to see us walking side by side, but when their eyes drop to find our fingers connected, their eyes almost bug out of their heads. Our four-year feud hadn't been private after Mason made every attempt to humiliate me as possible in front of the people we'd grown up with. They knew us as the untouchable two-some, but suddenly, almost in the blink of an eye, he turned on me and everyone was witness to my misery.

The few people who know us better look much less surprised and way happier for us. Amalie and Jake are the first to greet us as we head for the main doors.

"About time, man," Jake says, slapping Mason on the back while Amalie smiles and winks at me.

"Well, fuck me if Mason Paine hasn't handed his balls to Camila at last," Ethan announces as we descend on Mason's locker. His voice booms down the hallway, but there's an unmistakable slur to it which has all our brows drawing together. "I guess there's only me now to serve all these wonderful ladies of Rosewood High."

"Ethan, are you drunk?" Mason asks, bringing us to a stop in front of him. The answer is obvious the second we're close. He stinks of alcohol.

"Just enjoying my senior year."

"It's Monday morning."

"And who are you? My mom?" A bitter laugh falls from his lips.

"What the hell?" Jake asks, releasing Amalie and getting in Ethan's face. "Do not tell me you fucking drove here in that state."

Ethan shrugs, and every muscle in Jake's body tenses while Mason's grip on my hand becomes painful.

"Come with me," Jake demands, wrapping his hand around Ethan's forearm and pulling him away from the lockers.

"Or fucking what, asshole?"

"Don't you fucking question me right now." Jake's jaw tics as he goes nose to nose with Ethan. "You wanna stand here and get caught, get suspended and miss the rest of the season?"

Ethan pales slightly but doesn't back down. "So what if I do? Not like you two would care. Too fucking busy getting your dicks wet to notice what the hell I'm doing."

"Yeah, and that's why we're standing here now trying to make you see fucking sense, because we don't fucking care. Now. Let's. Fucking. Go."

Ethan allows Jake to move him this time.

"I'll be back," Mason says, dropping a kiss to my temple.

"It's fine. Stay with your girl. I'm just gonna get him

sobered up," Jake says, already making his way down the hallway.

"You sure?"

"Yeah, man. I got this."

"What the fuck's going on?" Amalie asks like she's been left out of the secret.

"Fuck knows. Something's been going on a while though. He's been partying more than usual, getting drunker..." Mason trails off as he watches his two best friends make their way down the hall. "He's not said fuck all, though."

"Jake will get it out of him. Plus, he's drunk, so I'm sure his tongue will be a little loose."

Mason turns his attention back to me, pushing me up against his locker. "I know he said not to, but I'm going to go and find them. But first, they need showing exactly who you belong to."

"Mase, I think—" My words are cut off as his lips find mine.

There are a few hollers of excitement behind us, but I block them out. How could I focus on anything else other than his lips when they're consuming in a way only he can?

"About fucking time," a familiar voice says when Mason pulls back.

"I'll see you later." He kisses my knuckles and I practically melt into a puddle on the floor. I watch as he walks away, my eyes fixated on his body and the rippling muscles of his back.

It's not until he's out of view that I turn to Alyssa, a wide smile on my face.

"Ugh, do you have to look so fucking happy?"

"Sorry, can't help it. I had one hell of a wake up this morning." I wiggle my eyebrows and she rolls her eyes.

Movement behind her catches my eyes, and when I look up, I find Chelsea standing in the entrance, staring daggers at me.

Making a snap decision, I push away from the lockers and stalk toward her. She doesn't move as I approach, not that it would really matter if she did. She might have lost one crutch, but she's still got a boot thing on her foot.

"Looks like you were wrong," I say once I'm confident she can hear me. I don't stop moving until I'm right in her personal space. Leaning into her ear, I whisper my final words. "Girls like me do win, after all."

She gasps as if it's a shock that I knew it was her who sent me after Noah. Who else did she really think I'd think it was?

"Only Ethan left now, but even he has standards." I stand back and run my eyes down the length of her. "Have a great day." My smile is wide and fake, but fucking hell, I've never felt better.

Flicking my hair over my shoulder, I turn and walk away from her with my head held high. That won't be the last we hear from her, of that I'm sure, but right now, I feel on top of the world.

Amalie and Alyssa smile at me as I stalk past them and toward my English class to get the day started.

Miss Phillips sets us up with a task before sitting behind her desk and calling us all up one by one to give feedback on our "Against All Odds" paper.

"Camila," she calls halfway through the class.

Pushing my chair out behind me, I make my way to the front of the class. A few sets of eyes burn into me. Apparently, I'm much more interesting since Mason's public claiming of me this morning, but I ignore them and take a seat.

"I really enjoyed this, Camila. Your writing was engaging, creative, descriptive. I was really impressed."

My smile grows as pride swells in my chest. "Can I ask what you're thinking about majoring in at college?"

"Honestly, I have no idea. English has always been my strength, but I don't really know what I want to do, or if I have a career in it."

"Have you considered journalism? After reading this, I think it could really suit you."

I pause for a few minutes, letting her suggestion roll around in my mind.

"Obviously, this paper was based on football, but I'm confident you could turn your hand to a different subject quite easily—unless, of course, sports is your thing." I'm not sure if she takes my silence as me ignoring her. Possibly, but that's far from the truth. In reality I've got tingles of excitement that have so far eluded me whenever I've thought about college.

"Okay, well... I've made a few suggestions but really nothing much. I was really impressed, Camila. Think about what I said, okay?"

"I will. Thank you so much." I walk back to my desk with a wide smile on my face and hope bubbling up inside me. Things are starting to turn around. Hopefully, I can stop focusing on everything that's changing but embrace all the new things. Mason, college, our future.

By the time lunch rolls around, I'm desperate to see Mason and tell him about what Miss Phillips said. The more I've thought about it, the more excited I've gotten at the prospect of a journalism major. I spend most of my last class looking up colleges—well, that was until I realized that I have no clue what Mason's plans are and that I don't want to set my heart on anything until we've at least had a conversation about it. For all I know, he wants to move halfway across the country, although if I know Mason at all, then I'm pretty sure he'll want to stay fairly close for his brothers.

His usual table is still empty when I get into the cafeteria, so I grab some food and take a seat at our spot. It's only a few minutes before Shane joins me, shortly followed by Alyssa. As expected, they both grill me about Mason. They look at me skeptically when I don't have all that much to tell, but it's only been a few days and I'm still trying to get my head around it all, if I'm being honest. I went from slapping him when I was so angry on Saturday night to walking into school as his girlfriend this morning. It sounds crazy even thinking it, but it's my reality.

I know the moment he and the rest of the team walk in because a brief silence falls over the students and they all turn their way. It's easy to see Jake, Mason, and Ethan as normal guys when you hang out with them outside of school, but to everyone else, they own this school. Realizing that I'm now a part of that is a sobering thought.

Looking over my shoulder, I find him immediately. His dark eyes lock on mine and he moves away from his crowd and directly over to me.

"Come sit with me?" I look over to Shane, seeing as Alyssa already excused herself to hit on the basketball team when they arrived. Mason watches my movement before coming a little closer. "It's okay, we can stay here. How's it going?" he asks Shane, dropping to the seat beside me and wrapping his arm around my shoulders. His lips land on my temple and a wave of heat washes through me.

"I'm good. Congrats, man."

Mason nods at Shane.

"I called my boss earlier," Mason says so only I can hear. "She's allowing me to start later so I can do practice, but until she gets a replacement, she still needs me Monday and Tuesday night."

My heart drops. "That sucks."

"It's okay. I didn't want to just quit. Who knows how long Mom's new job could last. We need a fall back. Plus, I like earning my own money."

"So I won't see you after school?"

"No, but I was hoping for a sleepover maybe."

A smile twitches my tips. "I would say that's a sure thing."

"On that note," Shane says, grabbing his tray and standing from our table, "see you later, Cam. Mason." He nods at Mason before disappearing.

"He's all right, you know."

"I know."

"And he didn't drug Amalie, that's not his style."

"Never said it was. I didn't think he had it in him either, to be honest, but with no other suspects what's everyone supposed to think?"

"I know, it just sucks. He's basically gone into hiding." A silence descends around us but I soon remember what I was so excited to tell him about. "So, Miss Phillips thinks I should consider journalism."

"That's awesome. Where have you applied?"

"UFC, Maddison, a couple out of state, but I'm not sure I really want to move away. You?"

"I want Maddison. Their team's awesome, plus they have a fantastic teaching department."

A soft smile finds its way to my lips. "You want to teach?"

"I think so. My brothers have shown me how awesome kids are and how rewarding it is watching them learn. Why are you looking at me like that?"

"Because I equally hate that I didn't know this but at the same time love that I get to know you all over again."

"I feel the same, Cami-bear. But deep down, you were the only one who ever really knew me, and I haven't changed, not really. I might be a little tougher skinned now, some might say an asshole, but I'm still the boy you used to play hide and seek with in the woods."

I swoon at his words and tuck myself into his side.

"I still see him," I admit quietly.

A couple of seconds pass as I enjoy being in the warmth of his arms before he speaks. "I'm taking you out Wednesday night after practice."

"Out. Like a date?"

"Exactly like a date. Be ready at six."

Excitement blooms on my belly before the sight of Chelsea and her gang of bitches catch my eyes as they arrive in the cafeteria.

"Ugh," I complain when she locks eyes with me.

"What's wrong?"

"Chelsea's not thrilled about us."

"Chelsea can fuck off. She acts like she and the rest of the squad own us. She needs to realize that the guys only keep them around because they're so easy."

"Nice. So tell me, boyfriend. How many of the squad have you been easy with?"

"Can I have a pass on that question?" I lift a brow at him. "I can say that I've never fucked Chelsea though. I always drew the line there."

"Good to know you had some standards." I laugh, because it's easier than being pissed off that he didn't answer my question. Not that I'm really sure I wanted the answer. There's a lot to be said about ignorant bliss at times.

31

CAMILA

I don't see Mason for the rest of the day as we're in different classes, and then he heads straight to the locker room after school so he can talk to Coach and hopefully grovel for his place back on the team. I get a brief message saying everything's fine and that he'll see me later, but that's it, and I hate it. I know it's greedy and selfish, but now I've got him back I want him all to myself. I want to continue learning all the new things about him, the things I've missed out on in the last four years.

"You're thinking about him, aren't you?" Amalie asks, dropping in the booth in front of me and pulling what's left of her milkshake back in front of her.

"N-No, I was thinking about the homework," I argue.

"Fuck off, were you. You've got this soppy, heated look on your face. You're so imagining what you'll do to him when he gets home from work tonight."

My cheeks burn. "I'm so not," I try to argue but Amalie has none of it.

"So, Wednesday night date? Did he say what you were doing?"

"Nope, just that I had to be ready at six."

"Mysterious. I like it."

I laugh at her and finish my milkshake.

I spend the rest of the evening doing homework and then keeping an eye on Mason's brothers once Nicky heads to work. I can't wait for him to get his hours sorted, not just so he has to work less but so he can lose some of the worry in his eyes. He hates not being here for his brothers when his mom can't be. It's not his job, but he feels that it is. I just hope Nicky manages to stick with her new attitude and she finds a way to work and support her kids that allows Mason to live the life he deserves.

Thankfully, both boys stay in bed and asleep, so I'm not really needed. They know me well enough now, but I'm not sure I'm who they'd want if they woke up with an issue.

I climb into bed ten minutes before Mason is due home, wearing my sexiest nightwear. It's a black lace slip that's almost see-through. I bought it a few months ago when I thought I was going to go all the way with Noah. I shudder at the thought now, but I'm so glad I stuck to my guns and held back. I know that I'd have always regretted doing it with him, especially knowing that it could have been Mason.

My heart pounds in my toes and fingertips as I wait. He never said he'd come to me, but I can't imagine he wants to get into his own bed alone. I'm just wondering if I should have waited in his bed instead when his car pulls up outside. By the time his feet thunder up the stairs, I'm trembling with anticipation.

His footsteps pause at his room, and my heart drops. But then the floorboard creaks and my door is slowly pushed open.

I've got my nightlight on so I can clearly see him slip into the room. He glances over but must assume I'm asleep. Turning away from me, he toes his shoes off before pulling his work uniform from his body. His back muscles ripple and pull as he undresses, and heat floods me knowing that body is going to be pressed up against mine at any moment.

He's still got his back to me when I sit up, allowing the sheets to pool at my waist. And I wait.

He turns, takes a step forward and then looks up. "Oh shit." A wicked smile curls up his lips as his eyes drop from my face in favor of my barely covered breasts. The slip is cut down low, revealing almost everything—not that the sheer lace hides much.

He stalks toward me, my panties getting wetter with each step he takes.

"Maybe working late and missing you was worth it." He steps up to the bed then drops his last item of clothing, revealing his hard length to me. If I wasn't sure enough already then it most definitely confirms that he likes what he sees.

He crawls up my body, taking one of my breasts in his hand before finding my lips.

"Missed you tonight, Cami-bear," he mumbles when he kisses down my neck. "My night was long as fuck. If I knew this was waiting for me then it would have dragged even more."

His lips trail over my chest and down the valley of my breasts before slipping the fabric aside and sucking my nipples into his mouth, alternating between the two.

"Oh god," I whimper, my hips grinding, desperately trying to find some friction.

He pulls the covers from the bottom half of my body

and throws them off the bed in his desperation. Before I know what's happened, he's the one lying on his back and I'm sitting across his thighs.

"Now that's what I'm fucking talking about." He links our hands and tugs me so I fall forward against his chest. My nipples brush against his skin and sparks of lust shoot straight for my core. My hips flex without any instruction from my brain, and Mason groans when the heat of my pussy rubs his length.

"Need you, Cami-bear. Ride me."

My eyes fly open at the demand and nerves hit me out of nowhere. I've not had a moment's hesitation with him so far, but that's because he's been in charge, he's been the one calling the shots. But he's just given me the power, and the realization that he's been with others who are more experienced than me hits me full force.

I look away from him and close my eyes.

"Hey, what's wrong?" His hot palm rests on my cheek and I'm forced to look at him. "Get out of your head, Cami. The only place in the world I want to be right now is here, inside you. Forget about the past and just go with it." His fingers slip inside my panties and he moans when he finds me ready for him.

"How long have you been lying here, waiting for me?"

"Long enough," I whisper, enjoying the feeling of his fingers teasing my entrance too much to hold a conversation about this.

"Lift up."

I do as I'm told, and in only seconds, Mason has the lace of my panties pushed aside and he's impaling me on his cock.

My muscles clench as I slowly lower myself down on him.

He hisses as I get lower, his teeth grinding and his jaw popping as he tries to restrain himself.

"Don't hold back. I want everything you've got." His eyes flash with heat.

With his fingers gripping onto my hips, he thrusts himself up until I'm so full of him, I swear I'm going to split in two.

"Oh, fuck."

"You okay?"

"Yeah, yessss," I squeal when he thrusts again.

I move with him and begin to meet his movements like for like until the sound of our skin connecting and our heavy breathing is the only thing that can be heard as we both chase our releases.

"Cam, I'm gonna—"

"Let go."

His hips get even faster, his face tensing and the muscles in his neck straining. It's fucking fascinating to watch. I'm totally lost to him, but the second I feel the first twitch of his release, my own hits me. My upper body sags as I'm consumed by my orgasm and the incredible guy who delivered it.

At some point, I end up on top of his chest with his arms wrapped tightly around me. His cock still twitches inside me, reigniting my own pleasure each time.

"Did you have a good night at work?"

Mason smiles and tucks a lock of my hair behind my ear. "Not really, but coming home to you certainly makes up for it."

We lie locked in each other's embrace, a comfortable silence falling around us. The events of the day run around my head when a thought strikes me. "Is Ethan okay?"

Mason lets out a long, pained breath. "I have no idea. Coach ended up taking him home after ripping him a new one for showing up to school in that state, but we never got to the bottom of why."

"He'll talk when he's ready." It's the only thing I can think to say. I don't know Ethan well enough to know how he deals with stuff, aside from getting drunk it seems.

"I've never seen him like that this morning. Yeah, he likes to party, he likes to drink, none of that is news to anyone, but he's been going to the extremes recently. I'm worried about him."

"Do you want me to try talking to him?" I offer.

"Yes. No. I don't know. I think you're right. We'll only get to the bottom of it when he's ready to talk."

Eventually we drift off to sleep in each other's arms, and we're exactly the same when we wake to the sun streaming in the next morning.

As promised, Nicky is there to get Charlie and Ollie up. She actually makes us all breakfast. I'm surprised, but Mason is astounded if the look on his face is anything to go by.

"I like this look on her," he says to me while she goes to refill the coffee pot. "I hope it continues."

"It will," I say, hoping to keep up the positivity. Things are turning a corner for all of us. We need to start embracing it, not fearing things changing.

Ethan doesn't show his face, and I can see the concern on Mason's and Jake's when they try calling him and get no answer. Something serious is going on and it's bothering them so much, two guys who like the world to think they care about nothing, that it's really starting to worry me. But short of showing up at his house, I have no idea what I can do to help.

———

I'm desperate for our date to start by the time Wednesday evening rolls around. I'd fallen asleep when Mason go home from work last night after our eventful night previously, and we haven't had any classes together today.

I stand in the hallway waiting for his car to pull up to find out what he's planned. I had no idea what to wear, and after standing in front of my closet for the longest time I went with a black denim skirt, a plain white shirt and a pair of boots. I didn't want to dress up and look like an idiot. Equally, I didn't want him to think I hadn't made an effort.

I pull my blazer on, hoping it's enough to dress up my outfit should I need it. My stomach clenches when I look out the window and still find it missing Mason's car. I blow out a slow breath. He'll be here.

When a car does pull onto the driveway, it's not the one I was expecting. Pulling the front door open, I walk toward the little red car and lean down to talk to the driver.

"Get in."

"I can't, I'm waiting for Mason."

"I know. I'm your taxi. Get in."

"Ooookay." I do as I'm told and drop down into Amalie's passenger seat. "Where are we going?"

"My lips are sealed."

Sticking my tongue out at her, I sit back and wait to see where she takes us. "So, I'm assuming you helped plan this, whatever this is?"

"Nope. It was totally him. I just agreed to pick you up."

I start to tick things off as we drive through town as I attempt to guess what he's been up to. We pass the cinema and bowling alley, so they're out. We continue past Aces and a couple of other restaurants I thought could have been possibilities. When Amalie pulls into a deserted beach parking lot, I start to wonder if she's made a wrong turn.

"Okay, out you get," she says, dismissing me with a flick of her hand like she's bored of me.

"Here?"

"Yep."

"But there's nothing he—" Just as I say that, a figure appears over the dune. "Mason," I breathe. The sun's just set and the horizon is still a dark orange hue that makes him appear larger than he really is.

"So are you going to get out now?"

Without taking my eyes from him, I unbuckle myself, thank Amalie and climb from the car. My feet eat up the space between us in only seconds, but still it feels too long. Amalie's tires crunch against the gravel as she leaves us.

"Surprised?" Mason asks, grabbing my hand and leading me toward the beach.

We're right at the end, the same place Dash was all those weeks ago. I think back to that night briefly as we walk. I was flying on the excitement of starting senior year with my boyfriend by my side and making sure Amalie took hold of her new life with both hands. I really had no idea that the next time I'd be here Noah and I would no longer be together, and that I'd be holding on to Mason's hand like I need it to survive. I truly believed our relationship was dead. He sure made it seem that way. How things seem is a funny thing. Jake seemed like he was an asshole who had the world at his feet. Wrong. Mason seemed like he was going to forever hate me. Wrong.

Ethan? Well, we all know he's a party boy, but what's he hiding right now while everyone's assumed he's just enjoying himself? I guess only time will tell.

"Oh my god," I gasp when we hit the top of the dune and I get a look at the beach beyond. A bonfire sits in the middle of the sand. Tiki torches mark a path toward it and a blanket and picnic basket that sit in the warmth of the fire.

"You like it?" The hesitation in his voice has me turning toward him.

"It's incredible. Thank you."

"Anything," he says, reaching for my cheek and resting his forehead against mine. "Anything to make you smile."

My heart damn near shatters in my chest. I'm just about to tell him that the feeling is mutual when he takes my hand and leads me toward his bonfire, telling me that he's starving.

I take a seat on the blanket while Mason unpacks the basket, showing me everything he's brought for us to eat.

"Wow, were you planning for others to join us?" I ask with a laugh but soon realize that I'll be gutted if he says yes.

"No, I just wasn't sure what you'd want."

I look down at all the food before glancing back up at him from under my lashes. "How about you?"

He reaches forward and runs his knuckles down my cheek. "All in good time, Cami-bear."

Desire that was already sitting heavy in my belly races through my veins. "Here?" I ask skeptically, looking around at all the open space.

"Anywhere you want."

I sit up straight and glance over my shoulder. The

excitement of getting dirty down here where anyone could find us has me more excited than I'm willing to admit.

"Food first. We'll see what happens later."

With all the food laid out between us, Mason passes me a plastic cup before popping the top of a bottle of pink champagne and filling mine up. "This is fancy."

"It didn't cost much more than juice. It probably tastes like crap."

"It's only the company I care about." He smiles at me before chucking a chunk of cheese into his mouth. I focus on his lips as he chews and realize that I'm really not interested in food at all right now.

"Eat," he demands, and I'm powerless but to reach out and take something. "How was your day?" he asks, distracting me from my need for him as I run through my classes and the gossip I'd heard.

"Any more issues with Chelsea?" he asks begrudgingly.

"Nah, she's steered clear since I ambushed her."

"Good. If she knows what's good for her, it'll stay that way."

32

MASON

My beach date was everything I hoped it would be. When I told Camila that I wanted to take her out, I didn't have a fucking clue where we were going to go. As I ran through the normal options, I soon realized that none of them were good enough for her. The little effort that goes into arranging dinner and a movie just wouldn't cut it. I can tell by the way she looks at me that she's still a little dubious about my intentions with her, and it guts me every single time. I deserve it. No, I deserve worse than that. She should still hate me, not be agreeing to dates with me, let alone allowing me to spend every night in her bed, but that's just who Camila is. It's why I fell for her all those years ago and why I was never truly able to rid myself of her.

I breathe a sigh of relief when I walk out of the locker room on Thursday afternoon. My work hours might not be quite back to normal, but I'm already feeling the benefit of cutting back. I told Camila to be at home waiting for me when I finished; I have no idea what she's expecting when I show up, but I plan on spending the evening with my girl in my arms, pretending to watch shit movies on TV while we make out. Knowing that Mom will sort out dinner for my brothers is a huge relief, although if I'm honest, it has left me feeling a little lost. I used to operate on a such a strict regime in order to function and not crack that I don't know what to do with my sudden free time.

As I drive past my old house, movement around the back catches my eye. Pulling up in the driveway like I've done a million times before, I get out and walk around to make sure everything's okay.

What I'm not expecting when I get to the back of the house is to find a woman, probably Mom's age, staring in through the window with her hands blocking out the light in the hope of actually seeing something.

"Can I help you?" I ask, my voice booming across the space between us.

"Oh shit. Fuck." She jumps back like I've just shot her, her eyes wide, her hand covering what's probably her racing heart. "I'm-I'm so sorry. I'm not going to break in or anything. I just... I came looking for you."

"For me?"

"Yeah. You're Mason," she states, her eyes softening. "You look exactly as I was expecting."

My eyes narrow in curiosity and suspicion. "Who are you?"

"I think we should probably sit down." She nods toward our old swing bench and I reluctantly follow her lead.

I sit but she hesitates despite this being her idea. Eventually, she blows out a shaky breath and lowers beside me. She stares ahead at our old overgrown garden that my dad would hate if he ever saw it.

"I'm... um... I guess I'm your stepmom."

My jaw drops as I turn to stare at her.

Her blonde hair is in tight curls and hangs just above her shoulders. She's got light makeup on, but to be fair, she doesn't really need it. She's pretty. If what she's saying is true, then I could understand why my dad would be interested. I notice that her looks aren't all that different from Mom's. It's a slightly unsettling thought.

"How's that?" Dumb question, and I almost regret asking it, but I'm going to need more information than her 'guessing she's my stepmom.'

"I first met your dad about three and a half years ago at a rehab group. We chatted a bit, but due to both our reasons for being there, it was never more than that. Then two years ago we quite literally bumped into each other in the store. We started meeting up regularly—dating, I guess."

I'm silent as I listen to her tale, trying my best to read her expression to figure out if she's telling the truth or not, but I can't help but believe her.

"Six months later I discovered I was pregnant. Your dad asked me to marry him and we had a city hall wedding a few weeks later."

I've got another brother or sister? "Boy or girl?" The question is out before I realize. I need to know, but equally I don't want to fall into her trap by being distracted. This could all be bullshit. "This little trip down memory lane is nice and all, but why are you here telling me about it? If you're married to my dad then you'll know that he's had no contact with me or my brothers since he walked away."

"Sister," she says, her eyes softening as she thinks of her. "I promise you that is something he battled with every single day."

"Because that fixes everything. Why are you here?"

"He..." She pauses, her chin trembling, her eyes filling with tears. Dread twists my stomach. "He died."

Those two words are like a baseball bat to the chest. "No. No, you're lying. How do I even know you know him? You could be making all this up."

"W-Why?" She sniffles. "Why would I do that?"

"I don't fucking know. People do all sorts of crazy shit."

"I-It's true. Look." She rummages in her purse and pulls her wallet out. She opens it and turns it toward me. My world crumbles in on itself as I stare at the man I used to idolize standing with a new family.

"Fuck." I stand, looking out at the jungle of a garden, unable to stare at that picture any longer, although when I close my eyes, it's right there, burned into my memory.

"I'm so sorry to spring this on you like this."

"Really? If you were that sorry then you wouldn't have bothered," I snap.

"He wanted to come and see you himself. He'd been putting it off for years. But then he got ill and—"

"This is bullshit. It's so easy to try to convince me of all this crap now he's gone."

"It's true, Mason. Not a day passed when he wouldn't talk about you or your brothers. I've never met you before but I feel as though I know you, know this place," she says, waving back toward the house. "Things weren't supposed to end as they did, but your mom broke him. He loved her so much, Mason. When he discovered..." She trails off, not that I need her to fill in the gaps. "It broke his heart. When we first met, we were in a group session trying to find our self-worth once again after being in a relationship that almost ended us. I may not know everything that happened between your parents, Mason, but trust me when I tell you that I know how he felt about leaving you, how much it gutted him."

"Then he should have come back."

"I know, and I can't argue. I tried to get him to do it, but he was scared. Scared you'd hate him."

"Well, he should have been. Are we done here? I've got shit to be doing."

Her mouth opens but she doesn't say anything. I take two steps before her words make my legs stop working. "He's left you and your brothers everything." I turn and pin her to the spot with my stare. "H-his parents died last year. He got all of their estate. Now it's yours." Anger swells within me. He never spoke to his parents. I've never even met them. Why would I want their money?

"I don't want anything from him. He left us. He found a new family. He. Chose. You."

"He didn't. He found himself with us. His heart never left this place. He yearned to be back here, and I prayed every day that he'd love me like he did her. He loved me, in his own way, but it wasn't like it was with your mom. He loved Megan, but she could never make him forget you. If anything, it made him worse." She digs into her purse and pulls out an envelope. "Here. It's from him. Please, take it. He was planning on seeing you, he got tickets to your final game. He wanted to watch you play, tell you how proud he was of you but... he didn't make it."

My heart pounds in my chest so hard that I start to feel a little lightheaded. Is she telling the truth? Was he really going to come?

"What killed him?"

"Brain tumor. He'd been complaining of headaches for weeks, months even, but refused to go and see a doctor. By the time I convinced him to go, it was too late.

They gave him six months at best. That was only six weeks ago." She sobs, her hand coming up to cover her mouth. "I'm sorry, I just had to see you. To explain to you that he never forgot you, or your brothers. Take it, please."

My hand trembles as I raise it to take the envelope. I stare down at it the second she releases it.

Mason.

Seeing his handwriting makes my knees buckle, but I force them to hold my weight, taking a step back instead. She doesn't say anything as I walk away from her.

Yanking my car door open so hard I'm surprised it doesn't come off its hinges, I rev the engine and gun it onto the street. I have no idea where the fuck I'm going, but I need to get the hell away from here—from her.

I have no idea how long I drive around town for, trying to make sense of all the bullshit that's running around my head, but at some point, my need to drown it all out has me pulling up to Ethan's house.

I don't bother knocking, we never have in the past, and it's only his car sitting in the driveway. I make my way past all the empty yet perfectly presented rooms before climbing the stairs and walking toward the end of the hallway.

I knock on his door but only in the hope it'll alert him to a visitor and stop me from walking in on something I'd rather not see if he's got a girl in here.

To my shock, when I open the door I find Ethan alone, sitting on his bed and resting back against his headboard. He's got a cigarette in one hand and a bottle of whiskey in the other. The room is in darkness aside from the glow from the light in the en suite at the other side of the room. There's no music, no TV, just Ethan.

"What the fuck do you want?" he barks without even looking at me.

"I get it, you don't want to talk, nor the fuck do I." Walking into the room, I fall down onto his sofa and rest my head back. It still spins with everything she told me, and the photo she showed me is still front and center. "What are you waiting for? Chuck me the bottle, asshole."

He doesn't move, and when I eventually pull my head up to find out what the fuck his problem is, he's staring right at me, deep frown lines between his brows.

"You fuck things up with Camila already?"

"I said I don't want to fucking talk. Drink. Now."

He complies with my demand this time and I reach out to grab it as he throws it at me. Twisting the top, I lift the glass to my lips and swallow, one, two, three shots. By the fourth I don't feel the burn and my head slowly starts to swim. Exactly what I need.

33

CAMILA

All fucking night I sat there waiting for him, but he never showed. He never answered his phone, and when I spoke to anyone else who I thought might know where he was, they hadn't seen him either.

By the time he doesn't show up to school Friday morning, I'm starting to go out of my mind.

"Where the fuck is he?" I ask Jake, coming to stand toe to toe with him. It wasn't so long ago that I was terrified of being anywhere near him, but now I don't bat an eyelid at confronting him.

He swallows, and it tells me everything I need to know.

"What do I need to make Amalie withhold from you to get the answer?"

"Hey, don't drag me into this," she complains.

Ignoring her, I continue to stare into his mesmerizing blue eyes. "Tell me."

"Ugh, fine. He's with the other idiot who's skipped all week. Happy?"

"Not at all." I storm off down the corridor.

"Camila, please don't do something stupid," Amalie calls, but I know for a fact that if it were Jake hiding that, she'd be there demanding he speak to her.

I'm at Ethan's in no time, feeling stupid for not thinking he'd be here before. I pull up next to his car and jump out of mine, leaving the door wide open in my haste to find him.

I slam my fists on the door but I know it's pointless. The music inside is so loud that there's no chance either of them will hear me.

With my frustration growing, I march around the back of the house, but finding those doors also locked, I growl in frustration.

What the fuck happened for him to go from messaging me about waiting at home for him to locking himself in Ethan's house?

Some movement catches my eyes and my heart jumps into my throat that he's about to walk into the kitchen, but when someone appears, it makes my stomach falls to my feet.

A girl, dressed in only a guy's white shirt, pulls the fridge open and grabs a six-pack before disappearing the way she came.

"You're a fucking asshole, Mason Paine," I scream, tears streaming down my face as I try to tell myself that everything between us this week wasn't one big joke to him. I told him I loved him, for fuck's sake.

I don't remember the drive home, but when I get there to find my parents' car parked outside, I almost reverse back out. The last thing I need is them digging into what's wrong with me and why I'm not at school where I should be.

Wiping at my face, I pull my visor down and attempt to clean my face up, but my red-rimmed eyes practically shine like a fucking homing beacon.

Blowing out a long breath, I wrap my fingers around the door handle and prepare for what's to come.

The house is silent when I step inside. I go to the kitchen but find no one. It's not until I walk toward the stairs that I spot my parents' heads out on the love seat in the garden. They're laughing together and the sight makes my heart ache. Is that kind of happiness so hard to find? I've been screwed over by two guys in less than two weeks. Can things get any worse?

Shutting myself in my room, I crawl under my sheets fully dressed and hating that I can smell his presence. With the sheets over my head, I allow myself to cry for everything I've lost in the past two weeks.

Mason was right: I am a fucking idiot. I didn't see what Noah was doing right under my nose, and now I've opened myself up to him, the guy who's spent the last four years making my life misery. So. Fucking. Stupid.

At some point I must cry myself to sleep, because the next thing I know I'm being gently shaken awake by a hand on my shoulder.

"Camila, Cami. Come on, I'm worried about you," a familiar British accent says from the other side of the sheets.

"Go away," I mutter. I'm not ready to deal with the situation. I'm happier just hiding under here and locking it all out.

"Not a chance." Slowly, the sheet is peeled away from me. The light makes me wince. I scoot up so I'm sitting with my arms wrapped around my knees. "What happened?"

"He's having lock-in with Ethan and a barely dressed girl." My voice shakes with every word. "I thought he was telling the truth about how he felt about me. How could he do that to me?" I sob.

"You don't know he's done anything, Cami. That girl could have been there for Ethan."

"Why else would he be there?"

She shrugs, and I hate that she doesn't have an argument. She's usually so quick to defend Mason, and right now I need her to make me think I'm wrong. I need to be wrong. I need to know the boy I fell in love with really is the man I see now. I can't cope thinking it was all an act to play me.

"It might not be how it looks. I know it's hard, but you need to reserve judgment until you've spoken to him." I look to her and narrow my eyes in frustration. She reaches out and smooths my hair down. "Are you going to get changed?"

"For what?"

"Uh... the game, silly."

"I'm not going." I reach for the covers, but Amalie's quicker.

"There are two games left. I'm not allowing you to miss one of them."

"I don't care. I don't want to see—"

"Him?"

"Anyone. I'm fed up with everyone judging me. I'm the poor girl Noah cheated on, then I was the girl everyone hated because I turned straight to Mason, and now I'm the idiot again."

"No one's judging, Cami. Hold your head high and show the world you're stronger than that."

Amalie gets up from the bed and I start to think I've

won and that she's going to leave. Unfortunately, she just goes to my wardrobe and pulls my Bears shirt from inside.

"Now go to the bathroom, freshen up, put some makeup on and let's go. I refuse for you to make me late so I miss seeing Jake in action."

Rolling my eyes at my best friend, I let out a sigh and climb off the bed. After everything she's done for me, attending this game is the least I can do for her. Then the second it's over, I'm coming right back here and not leaving.

The atmosphere at school is electric. We've never had such a successful season, and if it were any other night I'd be shouting and screaming with the best of them. Unfortunately, my heart's just not in it.

"They've so got this in the bag tonight," Amalie says beside me, bouncing up onto her toes.

"Even if Ethan and Mason turn up drunk?"

"They wouldn't do that to Jake, or Coach, for that matter. They also know it would get them benched for the final game and none of them want that, Mason especially after missing the last couple." I try to share her enthusiasm, I really do, but her words fall flat.

It's only a few minutes later when the roar of the crowd makes me wince and everyone is suddenly on their feet as the Bears run onto the field. My eyes zero in on our players, trying to find number eleven. I shouldn't be surprised when he's last out along with number eighty-nine, Ethan, after what I saw earlier but I am, and I'm even more surprised they both turned up.

"See, I told you it would all be fine. Maybe Ethan was just having a meltdown or something."

"You say that like you don't know already." Jake knew

exactly where Mason was earlier, so am I really supposed to believe that Amalie is clueless in all of this?

"I don't know anything. Jake doesn't tell me all his friends' secrets, just like I don't tell him all yours." I want to argue with her, but I know she's right. "Now, try to relax and enjoy the game."

It's a good game. We dominate for most of it and manage an easy win, thanks to our opponents losing their quarterback to injury only a few minutes in. But there's something different about our team, and it's all because of two players. Mason and Ethan. It's obvious to everyone, especially Coach and Jake who are constantly shouting at them to focus, that there's something wrong with them. Mason especially as he slams into the opponent's players with as much strength as he has. He's not usually rough player, but tonight he's on the verge of being sent off more than once.

"See, I told you something's wrong," I say to Amalie when Coach gives Mason another ear bashing. "That's not how he usually plays."

"I know. You need to find him after and talk to him. You're coming to Ethan's, right?"

"No, I'm really, really not."

"Camila," she sighs. "Rip the plaster off. Talk to him and get it over and done with. Find out the truth before you drive yourself crazy."

"Fine. I'll talk to him and then I'm leaving."

"Fine," she says, mimicking me.

———

"Come on, I told Jake we'd meet them at Ethan's," Amalie says, walking past the entrance to the locker room and toward her car. I kind of hoped I'd be able to see Mason before getting to party central to save me from having to step foot inside.

We're one of the first ones there, so the house is still quiet when we walk through the front door.

"Something's different here," I say as we make our way to the kitchen for a drink.

"In what way?"

"All the family photos are gone." I look around the room, making sure I'm not going crazy and they've just moved. Previously there were pictures of Ethan and his mom and dad everywhere over the years, but now, every single one is gone.

"Weird. Although family issues would explain how he's been acting recently."

We find bottles laid out in the kitchen and Amalie helps herself to one before the sound of everyone else arriving fills the house. Dread sits heavy in my stomach. I shouldn't have come here. I should have gone home and hidden.

I've barely lifted the drink Amalie made me to my lips when Jake sweeps across the room and pulls Amalie into his body for a celebration kiss. She eagerly returns it and I turn away, not wanting to intrude on their moment. Most of the rest of the team head our way to find drinks while others put the music on and start chatting and dancing around us.

With the intention of slipping out the back, finding my car and disappearing, I head down the hallway. I've got the exit in my sights when a hand reaches out from one of the rooms and grabs my forearm. My heart slams against my ribs as I prepare to look into Mason's eyes, only when I look up, I don't find his dark ones boring down on me. Instead, I look into Noah's.

"What do you want?" I spit. "I was leaving."

"Trouble in paradise already?"

"Fuck you, Noah. You don't get to judge or have any opinion on what I'm doing anymore."

"You're right, I'm sorry."

"So what did you actually want? I'm assuming you dragged me in here for a reason."

He takes a step forward and I take one back. Unfortunately I bump into the wall, stopping me putting any more space between us.

He reaches out and takes a lock of my hair between his fingers. The move is so familiar, but unlike every other time he's done it, I want to slap his hand away from me. He has no right touching me after everything he's done.

"I just wanted to apologize properly. I never got the chance to tell you that I never meant to hurt you."

"Really? So you fucking a cheerleader behind my back wasn't meant to hurt?"

"No, that's not what I meant." He leans a little closer. The smell of alcohol on his breath is obvious.

I glance to the side, thinking that I could side-step him and still get out of here when movement by the door catches my eye. There's a flash of blonde hair, but it's all I need to know that it was Mason.

Fuck.

As I turn back to Noah, it registers to me how this must look to an outsider. Pushing my palms against Noah's chest, I force him to back up.

"I don't want to hear it. Go and find your cheerslut if you want to talk to someone."

I'm walking away when my cell pings in my purse. Pausing for a moment, I pull it out hoping that it's Mason, but when I find *that* number staring back at me, my heart picks up pace. Nothing good ever comes out of that number.

My hands shake as I swipe to unlock it. I could be about to read anything, but what I find shocks me even more than I was expecting.

Photo after photo flashes up on my screen of Mason and... Chelsea. My stomach turns over, my hand automatically lifting to my mouth.

His promises that he'd never slept with her ring through my mind and fire me up, and when my feet move, it's not in the direction of the exit. I storm through the house looking for him. Or her. I don't really care if I should happen to find her first and show her what I really think of this little stunt.

It seems I'm in luck because when I do find them, they're together. Red hot anger fills my veins as I watch from the doorway as Chelsea walks over to Mason with two drinks. He already looks pretty out of it, but he accepts the cup and tips it straight to his mouth. He watches her as she steps into his side. I see red when she places her hand against his stomach and runs it up to his neck.

Marching over, my hand lands on her shoulder and I pull her away from his body.

"What the—oh, Camila's joined the party."

Mason looks between the two of us, his eyes wide, and he places his cup on the table next to him.

"You're a filthy fucking slut, you know that?" My hand goes flying out, and I'm so ready for the satisfying sound of my palm connecting with her cheek, but just as I'm about to swing, fingers wrap around my wrist.

"Whoa, she's not worth it." Jake's deep voice fills my ears and I spin on him.

"You." I narrow my eyes and poke him in the chest. "You need to get out of my way. That bitch needs a fucking lesson. She thinks it's okay to interfere in our lives just because we have what she wants, what she seems to think she deserves."

"Trust me, I know and I agree, but you don't want to do this with an audience."

"Why? Give me one good reason why I shouldn't."

A loud crash from behind us has us all turning around, and when we do, we find Mason in a heap on the floor.

"What the hell?" Jake's on his knees by his side, instantly turning him into the recovery position. I've only been here a few seconds but one image stands out in my mind. Reaching over, I grab Mason's drink and thrust it under Chelsea's nose.

"Drink. It," I demand.

She stares down at the cup before looking up at me. Guilt flashes in her eyes and everything falls into place.

"I said drink it."

"Camila, what are you doing?"

"Finding out the truth."

I can feel everyone's eyes burning into my back, but I don't look away from Chelsea.

"It was you, wasn't it, at Shane's party?" Amalie comes to stand beside me, waiting for an answer. But we don't get one, not yet anyway. "Those photos you just sent me. They're staged, aren't they?"

Chelsea has the gall to actually roll her eyes at me like what I'm suggesting is actually ridiculous.

"Fine," she mutters. "Yes, it was me, and yes they're fake." The attitude on her face doesn't falter, and this time when I move, there's no one behind to stop me.

My palm stings like a bitch as it collides with her face.

"What did you give him?" She continues staring down at the floor, my handprint glowing on her face. I close the space between us. "Tell me what you gave him and we might make it a little easier on you. Not that anyone's going to want anything to do with you after this."

"Ugh, it's nothing much. It'll just knock him out for a bit. No harm done."

"No harm? No fucking harm?" This time Amalie comes to stand between the two of us.

"Get the fuck out of here, and if you're lucky, we won't call the police." Without batting an eyelid, Chelsea turns and runs—well, hobbles.

"She's so fucking done here." My chest heaves and my fingers continue to curl into fists as I stand and watch her.

"We should probably try to get him to bed," Jake says from behind me, reminding me of what's actually going on here.

Running over, I fall to my knees and place my hand on Mason's cheek. "He's going to be okay, right?"

"I'm sure he'll be fine. It shouldn't hit him as hard as it did Amalie."

Ethan walks past at that moment, his arms around some girl I've never seen.

"Savage, a little help here?" Jake barks, catching his attention. He does a double take of us crowded around a passed out Mason before walking over.

"Jesus, how much has he had?"

"Not enough to do this," Jake seethes. He's barely holding himself together, and when I look up to his eyes, I see that they're wild with fury. He's wanted someone's blood for what they did to Amalie that night. He was so convinced he'd got it when he plowed his fists into

Shane's face, but Amalie and I told him that he was wrong. Shane wouldn't do that. As nice as it is to be proved right about my friend, I'm not about to point it out anytime soon. "Help me get him up."

With Jake and Ethan at his sides, we manage to get Mason up to one of the guest rooms.

"Do you want me to stay?" Amalie asks once he's laid out.

"No, it's okay. I'll call you if I need you."

She's hesitant to leave, but after a few seconds she turns and closes the door behind her. I make quick work of pulling Mason's shoes from his feet and then crawl onto the bed beside him.

"What the hell is going on, Mase? Why did you disappear?" I'm staring at the ceiling, not expecting a response, so I almost jump out of my skin when he speaks.

"Cami?" His voice is rough and slurred. It hits me right in the chest despite wanting to hurt him for abandoning me for no reason.

"I'm here. It's okay."

"I'm so—"

"Just sleep, Mase. We'll talk tomorrow when you're more with it." It seems that's all the encouragement he needs because he's out like a light again.

I don't leave his side, and I toss and turn all night. Despite the light being on, I can't settle, too many thoughts racing around my mind trying to come up with why he could have hidden from me.

I eventually drift off when the sun starts to rise, and I'm only woken by footsteps a while later.

When I open my eyes, I find Mason sneaking toward the door.

"You're leaving?" I ask, my voice rough with sleep.

"I've got something I need to do."

"I'll come, just wa—"

"No. I need to do this alone."

"What the hell's going on, Mason?" I demand, swinging my legs over the edge of the bed and standing in front of him.

"It's... it's..."

"Is there someone else?"

"No. Although I could ask the same thing. I seem to remember you getting up close and personal with your ex last night."

"Oh yeah, I'm cheating on you with him. Don't be so ridiculous." I can't help rolling my eyes. "A little trust would be great."

"Yeah, same here. I'll see you later."

"You said that before," I call out as he makes his way down the hallway.

He looks back at me, his eyes haunted and sad. Unease fills me, and it's probably the wrong thing to do seeing as we just talked about trust, but I rush to pull my boots on and follow him out of Ethan's house. There are passed out bodies everywhere downstairs. I quickly step over them and get to my car without being spotted by Mason.

I sit tight while he backs out of the driveway and then I follow. I hate that I'm doing this, but that look in his eyes haunts me.

I follow him to the east side and then out to the next town. When he eventually indicates to turn off the main road, my brows draw together.

It's a cemetery.

I hang back, allowing him to turn around if necessary, but he doesn't come back. Instead, when I drive into the parking lot, I find his car with the engine off and him walking down the path toward the graves.

I fight with myself for long minutes as to what to do. I should just drive home and wait, I do know that, but my need to know he's okay is bigger than my need to do what's right.

I push my door open and follow the path he disappeared down. There are rows and rows of gravestones and a few people are scattered about, placing down flowers or just having a morning chat with a lost loved one.

I keep walking, looking left and right, trying to spot him. Just when I think he's vanished I find a figure sitting on the ground in the distance, facing a gravestone.

I gasp when I see his shoulders shaking and his head lowered in pain. My heart breaks for him and I have no fucking clue what's going on or who's died.

My legs carry me to him without instruction from my brain. My need to comfort him is too strong to deny.

I have no idea if he hears me coming, but when I sit down on the damp ground beside him, he doesn't so much as flinch.

He blows out a long breath, and I wrap my arm around his shoulders in comfort. It's then that I look at the stone in front of him.

David Michael Paine.
Beloved husband and father.

Oh fuck.

"Mason, I'm so sorry."

It's then he lifts his head from his knees and looks at me over his arm. His dark eyes are almost black with grief and full of tears. That sight has my own burning the back of my throat.

A sob rumbles up from his chest and I crawl closer. He uncurls himself and pulls me onto his lap. I wrap my arms around him and hold him as tight as I can as he cries on my shoulder. I rub his back and whisper that I love him in his ear, hoping that it does something to help.

I feel utterly useless, but as he clings to me, I know without a doubt that I did the right thing following him here.

"How did you know?" he eventually whispers in my ear.

"I followed you," I admit. "When you turned and looked at me, I knew something was seriously wrong. I couldn't leave you."

"I'm so sorry. I-I didn't mean to... get lost but fuck—" Some more tears fall and I catch them with my thumbs as I rest my forehead against his.

"It's okay. I wish you'd told me. I could have helped, supported you. I thought... I thought..." I trail off. It doesn't matter what I thought right now. What matters is Mason and how he's feeling. "How did you find out?"

"I had a visit from my stepmom."

"You've got a stepmom?"

"Apparently so. He was going to come and see me, but he didn't make it. He wrote me a letter. She wanted me to have it so..."

"She brought it to you," I finish for him. "Have you opened it?"

He nods. "But I haven't read it. Inside was the address for this place, her address, and his folded letter. I didn't have it in me to read his words, not yet."

"That's understandable."

"But I woke up this morning and I knew I needed to see him. I needed to put everything behind me. I've held onto the past for long enough. It kept me from you for too long. It's time to face up to it and move on."

I nod, allowing him time for his thoughts.

"She said he's left everything to me and Charlie and Ollie."

"Wow," I breathe.

"I mean, *everything* could mean a beat-up old car and a twenty-dollar bill..."

"Or it could be enough to secure your future."

34

MASON

"He could give you everything you need to start your life properly. It might be a little late, but in the end, you'd know he had your best interests at heart."

I didn't know that the only thing I needed after running from my old house the other day was to feel Camila's arms wrapped around me, but the second she appeared at my side my muscles relaxed and everything that woman's appearance disturbed inside me settled instantly.

I woke up this morning with a raging headache and a need so strong to get out of that house that I can't even describe it. I thought I needed to get lost, to drown myself alongside my best friend and forget everything I'd discovered. Turned out I was wrong, because Ethan is hell bent on ruining his life right now whereas I just needed a distraction. What I'd discovered wasn't going to disappear anytime soon. I knew that I'd need to poke my head back into the real world and deal with it all.

The moment I saw Noah leaning into Camila, I knew I needed to pull my head out of my ass and talk to her, but then Chelsea happened and the next thing I knew I was in bed with Camila at my side.

I could have told her everything this morning, but my head was so fucking fuzzy and the last thing I needed was for everyone in his house to start waking up and questioning me on everything.

"So, what now?"

"I think I need to go and see her. I wasn't exactly polite the other day."

"She turned up and told you your dad had died. I'm sure she understands."

"They've got a daughter, Cami. I've got a sister."

"Oh."

"Do you want to come with me?"

"If you want me to."

"Always." I can see the skepticism in her eyes, thinking about the fact I decided that I didn't need her when I first found out all this. But after a second, she takes my hand and together we leave my dad behind and head toward our cars.

Pushing her up against her car, I press my body into hers and stare down into her eyes. Lifting my hand, I tuck a lock of her hair behind her ear, brushing my knuckles down her cheek and onto her neck. I wrap my fingers around the back of her neck and hold her to me, our foreheads together, our breaths mingling.

"I'm so fucking sorry."

She looks away and I hate that she feels the need to. "Mase." She pauses and it makes my heart thunder in my chest. "Do you remember what happened last night?"

"I had a few too many and you guys put me to bed?"

It's the only explanation I have for how I went from Jake ripping me a new one for my behavior on the field to being in bed fully dressed with Camila beside me.

Slipping her hand behind her, she pulls her cell from her back pocket and opens it up.

"Do you recognize these at all?" She turns the screen to me and my eyes almost pop out of my head. Taking it from her hand, I swipe to see more of the same. Chelsea with her hands all over me, her lips pressed against mine and her hand... "What the fuck? This never happened. Cami, I haven't... I didn't..."

She lets me stew for a few seconds before she opens her mouth. "I know. She staged them. She's been going after me since she called me to Shane's the night I discovered Noah. That girl's got some issues."

"You don't fucking say." I scroll up through the other messages she's received.

"Why didn't you tell me about these?"

"Because they're nothing. Just a pathetic girl trying to play games to get her own way."

"True, but you shouldn't have to deal with this." I look back at the photos and my stomach turns over. I know exactly which night these are from. I was so fucking drunk that I passed out. I never thought she'd pull something like this.

She shrugs. "It could be worse. Those could actually be real."

"I don't even remember getting up to the bedroom that night. There's no way I was capable of this."

"I know. She drugged you."

"She fucking what?" I ask, thinking I must have misheard her.

"That night, last night, did you accept a drink from her?"

I think back. "Yeah, but—"

"It was her. She was the one who drugged Amalie at Shane's party."

"Fucking hell." My hands lift to my hair and tug. "What the fuck was she playing at?"

"I don't know, but I'm pretty sure she needs some help. The shit she does isn't normal."

"You're fucking telling me."

Camila's hands run up my chest and I'm dragged from thoughts of Chelsea as I look into her dark eyes. "Her issues aren't our responsibility. Everyone is going to know what she's done after last night. Hopefully it'll be the reality check she needs."

"We'll see." I can't help feeling like she's always going to be the way she is. She's so desperate for attention that it seems she stops at nothing.

"Shall we go then?" Camila asks, reminding me where we were heading.

"Yeah. I'll put her address in my GPS if you want to follow me."

"I'm right behind you."

"Thank you, Cami-bear." I don't know if I mean for chasing me, for believing in me or for giving me a pass after my behavior the past two days, maybe a little of all of it. I drop my lips to hers for a quick kiss. I'm afraid if I allow it to go on for too long that I'll use it as an excuse to get out of here and not do what needs doing.

It's only a short drive to the address I found inside the envelope. It's a cute little duplex home with flower boxes under the windows. I stop the car out front and Camila pulls up behind me. I don't move as I stare at the house my dad had called home for the last years of his life. Regret fills me that I never made the effort to find him. I told myself it wasn't my job, seeing as I was a kid, but if I'd made that effort then maybe I'd have seen him again, maybe we'd have had the chance to rebuild our relationship. All the possibilities of what could have happened swim around in my head until Camila appears at the window beside me.

I open the door and look up at her. Sympathy fills her eyes. "I can't even try to imagine how you're feeling right now, but whatever you need, I'm here. You need to leave, just give me a sign and we're out of there."

After releasing a slow and steadying breath, I climb from the car.

Maybe they're not in, I tell myself as we make our way up the small front garden.

Camila raises her hand to the door and knocks three times. It becomes immediately obvious that someone is inside, because the sound of a young child crying filters through the door.

I suck in a breath when I hear footsteps heading our way. Camila must hear it or sense the tension within me because she reaches for my hand just before the door's pulled open.

"Mason." She's shocked to see me, that much is obvious. "It's so good to see you. Hi," she says, turning to Camila. "I'm Julie, and this munchkin is Megan."

"Hi, I'm Camila. I'm Mason's girlfriend."

"Camila, it's so good to meet you. I've heard so much about you."

"Really?" Camila asks, sounding shocked.

"Of course. David used to tell me what you two used to get up to, how you were both attached at the hip. He

always hoped you'd end up being his daughter-in-law."
Camila's chin drops but no words pass her lips.

"We've just been to see him," I blurt like an idiot.

"Would you like to come in? I was just making us some
lunch."

"Oh... um..."

"That would be lovely," Camila answers for us, and
when Julie moves aside, Camila all but drags me inside.
This is why I needed her here, because I'd have bolted by
now otherwise.

My hand slips from hers as we make our way through
the explosion of toys in the living room in favor of looking
at a photograph that's hanging from the wall.

"That's from our wedding day," Julie says from behind
me, not that it really needed explaining with her in a
white dress and Dad in a suit. "It was just a small thing.
He'd have loved to have had you there."

I nod. Hearing things like that doesn't really make any
of this better, because at the end of the day, no matter how
much he'd have liked me there, he never invited me.

Dragging my eyes away, I look at the other
photographs scattered around her house. Most of them
include my dad, whether it's the two of them together or
him with Megan. My heart aches more with each one I
look at. I was desperate to see him, to ask him why he
never came home, to tell him that I understood why he
left, but here he was only one town over, living a new life
with a new wife and daughter. Why weren't we good
enough?

"It's only cheese sandwiches, I hope that's okay."

"It's perfect, thank you so much," Camila answers as I
trail behind her, trying not to let it show just how much
I'm struggling with all of this. "Just say the word, Mase,

and we can leave," Camila whispers in my ear after Julie's placed Megan in her highchair and turned to the kitchen

"I'm okay." In reality, I'm anything but, but now I'm here I want to find out more.

"Megan's almost nine months old. I never thought I'd have kids, but she was the best thing that ever happened to me. I'm not sure how I'd have got through all this without her."

Julie gives me some more detail about how she met my dad and what their lives were like together. I'm torn as I listen to her happy stories. Of course, I wanted him to be happy and to restart his life after everything that happened, but at the same time while I was drowning at home, trying to keep his family above water, a part of me hoped he was struggling just as much. I guess the fact that they met at rehab means his life wasn't always like this.

I let out a sigh and both Camila and Julie turn to look at me.

"I know this is a lot to take in, Mason. I just... I had to come and find you. That letter and everything he left you deserved to be in the right hands."

"I don't need his money," I say sadly.

"I never said you did. Nor did he. When his parents died, they left quite a big estate behind, and him being an only child meant it all went to him. He never spent a penny of it. He wanted you to have it all. He'd already written it into his will before meeting me. Everything's all ready for you, our lawyer just needs somewhere to send the money. Your brothers' shares have been put into trust ready for when they're eighteen."

I nod, still unsure about how I feel about all of this.

We stay just over an hour before Camila makes our

excuses. She can see I'm struggling and thankfully makes the call for me.

I follow her out to our cars after saying goodbye to Julie and agreeing that I'll consider coming back one day to get to know both her and my sister better. I haven't decided if that will happen or not. My head's spinning too much right now to make any kind of serious decisions. I left my bank details with her so she can forward them to Dad's lawyer, so all I need to do now is wait to see what he wanted me to have.

I hate that Camila and I are about to get into different cars right now to head home. I desperately want her beside me as I try to process everything.

"We'll be back in no time," Camila says, reading my thoughts. "We could order pizza and watch a movie, maybe."

"Sounds perfect. Thank you for this."

"You're more than welcome."

I pull her into my arms and hold her like it might be the last chance I get. "I love you, Cami-bear," I whisper into her hair. I'm really not sure how I'd have handled this today if it wasn't for her.

"I love you too. Come on, let's get back." I nod, dropping my lips to hers for a chaste kiss before allowing her to climb into her car. Once she's strapped in, I close her door and make my way to my own car.

I set the GPS to home. I should be able to navigate my way back, but with the way my head's spinning the last thing I need to do is think about anything else.

In forty-five minutes, we'll be back and I can pull Camila into my arms and never let go. The last few days have been stressful at best, and I need to lose myself in her more than I need my next breath right now.

My head's still back in Julie's house as I stared at the photos of my dad living a life I didn't know existed as I make my way out of town. I'm so focused on getting back that I'm not paying enough attention. I look up and see the red light I should have stopped at and slam my foot down on the brake, but it's too late.

35

CAMILA

Mason's a mess. Every time I looked at him in Julie's house I could see his internal conflict about even being there. He was trying, but it was taking its toll on him. Unable to see him suffer any longer, I make our excuses and get him away.

The drive home should be easy. It's one straight road back to Rosewood. I trail behind Mason, wishing that I was sitting in his passenger seat and holding his hand in support instead of being all the way back here.

The lights change up ahead, but Mason makes no attempt to slow down. He flies toward them and my heart jumps into my throat as his car speeds toward the intersection.

"Brake, Mason. Brake," I shout, but obviously he can't hear me.

My heart thunders in my chest as he continues forward as a car comes into view from the left. It's not slowing down either, but why would it? It's got a green light.

Fuck, fuck, fuck.

I can't drag my eyes away from the inevitable. Mason's brake lights finally shine bright but it's too late. Both cars are going too fast, and I have no choice but to watch as the two collide. The sound of crushing metal echoes around me as I sit frozen, my hands gripping onto the wheel, my foot pressing so hard down on the brake it's hitting the floor, but I stopped long ago.

Get out of the car. Get out of the fucking car, I repeat over and over as I stare at the wreckage, but I know it's wishful thinking. There's no way either driver is walking away from this one.

A few other witnesses go running toward the cars, but I can't make my body move. I can't do anything. My fear for what this means locks my muscles tight. The only thing that seems to still be working is my heart as it pounds against my ribs.

Mason please, come on. Just get out of the car. GET OUT OF THE CAR.

I have no idea how much time passes. All I know is that I'm still in the exact same position in my car and Mason hasn't emerged when the flashing lights of an ambulance race toward the scene.

Knowing that help has come gets me moving. I'm like a robot as I climb from the car and slowly make my way over. I'm not aware of my body moving, but I'm not aware of the distance I've traveled until I'm standing just in front of Mason's car.

I'm not able to see him, but the soft tone of the paramedic fills my ears.

"My name's Devon, I'm a paramedic. Can you hear me? You've been in a accident. We need to get you assessed and get you out of this car." I start to assume he's awake and listening. I begin to relax a little until he speaks again. "If you can hear me, squeeze my finger."

I don't feel anything as my knees hit the concrete, or the stones digging into them.

The sound of a scream hits my ears, but it's not until a policewoman bends down in front of me that I realize it came from me.

This can't be happening. I just got him back. He's got his whole future ahead of him. This cannot be happening.

"Shhh... calm down, sweetheart." The policewoman joins me on the ground and rubs my back, encouraging me to suck in a deep breath and release it through my nose.

"M-My-My boyfriend. He-He's—" I can't get the words out past the giant lump in my throat and the panic crushing my chest.

"He's being looked after by the best. You just need to stay back and give them space to do their job."

"Is he...is he alive?"

"I don't know anything right now, darling. I know it's hard, but you just need to be patient. Those guys are the best, they'll do everything they can for him, I can promise you that. Would you like me to call anyone for you?"

I think for a moment. The only person I need is in that car. A sob erupts from my throat at the thought of losing him like this.

I shake my head. "Okay. It would be really helpful if you could give me his details to pass on."

I nod, because moving my head seems to be the only thing I'm capable of right now. "M-Mason Paine. He's eighteen." I rattle off my address, phone number and his mom's name before she runs over to one of the paramedics.

Two other ambulances arrive along with a fire engine, and I sit frozen on the ground as I watch them begin to cut people from cars. It's the most surreal experience of my life, sitting there waiting to find out if the person I love more than anything in the world is dead or alive.

"Camila, fucking hell," Amalie's scream fills the air but I don't move, I can't rip my eyes away from what's happening in front of me. Her body falls down beside me and her arms wrap around my shoulders, but I still don't move. I vaguely remember texting her with my location, but I did it on autopilot. I have no idea if I even gave her a reason for it. "It's going to be okay. *He'll* be okay."

"You don't know that. He could... he could be—"

"No, you need to think positive. He's going to be fine."

"But what if he's not," I wail, not able to process that thought. "What am I supposed to do then?" She pulls me tighter to her and I soak her shoulder with my tears.

When I eventually pull back, I find Jake looking between the two of us and the wreckage beyond with concern written all over his face. When his eyes don't come back to us, I can't help but see what's caught his attention.

I'm horrified as we watch the firefighters cut the top of Mason's car away before the paramedics rush in to tend to him.

"Oh my god," I whimper, my hand covering my mouth as even more tears pour from my eyes.

What will I do without him?

"Where are you going?" Amalie shouts and I manage to drag my eyes away from where Mason is to see Jake talking to the police.

"They'll be taking him to Rosehill Hospital. Let's go

there so we're ready for him when he wakes up." Jake talks to both of us but I refuse to look at him.

"No. No, he needs us here. I need to be here."

"You can't do anything right now, Cam. You need to allow them to do their jobs and be ready for what Mason's going to need from you when he wakes up." She must see the fear on my face. "He'll wake up, Cami. He'll be fine."

"She's right. He's stronger than this."

I want to scream at them to look at the wreckage in front of us, but I know they're just trying to keep me calm. They see the devastation, they know how bad this is, they just don't want to voice it.

"Look." Jake points over my shoulder. "They've got him on a gurney. They'll be heading to the hospital any minute and they'll be faster than us. We need to get there now."

"What about my car?" I look over to where I abandoned it in the middle of the road.

"I'll go and pull it into the shoulder. You two go and get in the car. Take my cell, call his mom." He hands it to Amalie and runs toward my car.

Amalie does as she's told and pulls me along with her. I'm still trying to process his first statement to know what I should be doing right now.

The blue flashing lights illuminate the interior of Amalie's car. I climb into the back, my nose pressed up against the window as I fight to see him, to see if he's okay, but they all move too quick. One second they're running toward the ambulance and the next they're slamming the door and one of them is jumping in the driver's seat.

"He's leaving, we need to go now."

"Jake's coming. Try to stay calm, we'll be there as soon as possible."

The second Amalie brings the car to a stop, the three of us take off running. There are two ambulances already out front of the building, one of which had Mason inside it.

"We're here for Mason Paine, he was just brought in my ambula—"

"Camila," Nicky cries, and I turn just in time for her to collide with me and wrap her arms around my shoulders.

We hold each other for the longest time. When she eventually releases me, I find myself swept up into my parents' arms, who are also here waiting.

"Any news?" Amalie asks.

"Nothing. Did they say anything at the scene?" I shake my head, although I have no clue if anyone's actually addressing me.

Eventually all of us find seats and we begin the long wait to find out if he's going to survive or if we somehow have to find a way to continue on without him.

When someone eventually walks through the double doors and heads our way, a collective gasp sounds out.

"Family of Mason Paine?" We all stand, and the doctor looks along the line of us. "Immediate family."

Nicky and I stand forward. I don't give a fuck what they consider immediate family. I'll lie through my fucking back teeth if it gets me past those doors and to his side quicker.

Nicky looks to me and takes my hand. "We are."

"Okay, follow me."

Just before we disappear through the doors, I look back. Everyone is still on their feet, desperation on their faces. I feel for them but not enough to stop me walking through and hearing firsthand what's happening.

"Please take a seat." The doctor gestures into the room and we both shuffle inside and drop on to the edge of the chairs. "Mason has been very lucky—"

I don't hear any more. Those five words repeat through my mind long after the doctor has finished explaining whatever might be wrong with him, because right now I don't care about any of that. He's alive and that's all that matters. We can work through anything else as long as he's still here.

I drop my head into my hands and sob tears of relief.

"When can we see him?" I eventually ask when the doctor finishes.

"Not yet, but it won't be long. Someone will come and get you when he's ready."

I nod, although I'm far from happy with the answer. I need to see with my own two eyes that he's going to be okay.

Silence descends around us after the doctor closes the door to give us some privacy.

"What did he actually say?" I ask Nicky after long minutes when I realize I heard nothing.

"Um... broken ribs, collapsed lung, concussion, b-broken something else... I think." She breaks down, unable to say any more as her emotions get the better of her. Wrapping my arms around her, I hold her while she shatters. If she thought she had a wakeup call when I gave her a few home truths not so long ago, then this should really open her eyes to what's happening around her.

"I should go and let the others know he's going to be okay."

She nods at me and releases my hands that she was holding for support.

The second I push the doors open, everyone runs at

me. At some point they were joined by Ethan, who looks equally as distressed.

"He's going to be okay." I go on to explain what I can remember Nicky told me about his injuries.

Amalie and my parents hug me and I fight to keep my tears in. I need to start getting myself together and so I can be strong for him when we're allowed to see him.

It's another two hours before Nicky and I are allowed into his room. We follow a nurse down toward him, but my feet stop moving when I get to the door. We've already been warned that he's under sedation because of his head injury and that his face has been cut up from the glass that shattered around him. I can't cope with the images that have been filling my mind, let alone see the real evidence of what this has done to him.

"Camila, are you okay?" Nicky asks, turning to see where I've gone.

"I-I don't know if I can do this," I admit quietly. Watching the crash and him getting pulled from the car from a distance was one thing. But having to sit next to him while he's unable to do anything, seeing him so vulnerable... I'm not sure I can hack it.

"Of course you can. Mason needs you right now. He needs you to be strong, he needs you to hold his hand and help him get through this."

My chin trembles as I picture sitting vigil at his bedside for however long it is until he wakes up. The doctor said they'll reduce his sedation tomorrow if things are moving in the right direction, but there's no guarantee he'll wake up that quickly.

Nicky looks between me and the door behind which her son lies, and I feel like the worst person in the world for keeping her from him.

"It's okay, you go. I just need to catch my breath."

"I'm not going in there without you."

I blow out a breath. I can't keep her from him.

Sucking in a deep breath, I take a step forward. Her arms wrap around my shoulders and she pushes the door open. She releases me the second we're in the room and races over to Mason's side, a sob ripping from her throat.

I'm frozen in the doorway, watching as if this is just one big nightmare and that my boyfriend, the boy I've loved since I was old enough to know he made my heart race, isn't lying in a hospital bed with wires and tubes coming out of him and attached to some really scary machines.

"I know it looks scary, sweetheart, but it's all okay. It's just helping him. Mason is still Mason," a nurse says softly, her eyes full of compassion. "He might be able to hear you if you talk to him. He'd love to know you're here."

I nod slowly and take a step toward him. My eyes stare at his sheet covered feet and slowly I make my way up his body. The sheet stops mid chest and then his body is hidden by his hospital gown. His body just looks like he's sleeping, but then I get to his face. A small cry passes my lips as I take in the cuts, the dried blood, the stitches.

"Oh my god." Racing toward him, I find his hand and lift it to my lips. I manage to push aside the hospital smell, and when I breathe in, it's all Mason. He's here. He's going to be okay.

Dropping down to the chair behind me that the nurse pushes forward, I keep his hand clutched in mine as I drop my lips to the back, staring at his battered face.

When the doctor came back after his initial visit, the panic of not knowing if he was dead or alive had alleviated and I was able to focus when he repeated Mason's injuries. He's broken two ribs which had caused a punctured lung. He has a concussion from his head injury. But other than that, it was just cuts and bruises. He was very, very lucky because with the speed both of the cars were going, it could have been much worse. Hopefully if all is well, he'll wake up once they reduce his sedation and he could be home in a week. God, I really fucking hope so. We've only been here a few hours and I'm already ready to get him out of here.

36

CAMILA

It's been two days. Two days since I watched that car plow into the side of Mason's. Two days since I watched him get cut from the wreckage. Two whole fucking days since I looked into his eyes, since I heard his voice, and I feel like I'm fucking dying. Every breath is a fight to drag in. Every movement is heavy, not that I've moved far from his side. People keep bringing me food and trying to force me to eat, but I can't stomach it.

The doctors said he should wake up once they reduced the meds, but other than a few movements, he's yet to do so and it's scaring the shit out of me.

Crazy thoughts keep running through my head like, what if they got it wrong and he's not okay? What if his concussion is worse than they think and he's not going to remember anything, not going to remember me? The thoughts have my heart racing and the room around me starting to blur.

Everyone keeps telling me to stay positive. To trust the doctors. But as each hour passes, I find it harder and harder to do so.

"Camila, you really need to come home, baby," Mom says softly from her spot by the window.

"I've already told you that I'm not leaving him."

"Please, just let us look after you. You need a shower, you need sleep and you need a decent meal inside you."

"I'm not leaving." This isn't the first conversation like this I have had with my parents, and I'm sure it won't be the last.

"Nicky is here. If anything happens, she'll call right away, won't you, Nic?"

"Of course. But your mom's right, Cam. Mason needs a better version of you than you are right now."

Something unpleasant stirs in my stomach that I'm not what Mason needs right now. I always want to be what he needs.

With a sigh, I allow my mom to pull me from the chair I've turned into my home. I don't take my eyes from Mason as she gently pulls me toward the door. I don't want to leave him. If he wakes and I'm not here, I'll never forgive myself.

The car ride home is in silence. I just stare out of the window, regretting that I allowed them to take me away from him. He needs me there. He needs me by his side.

"How about I run you a bath and then I'll make your favorite dinner, sound good?"

I don't respond, because how could anything sound good right now? Selfishly, I don't even want to hear the words 'he's awake,' because it would mean I'm not there by his side.

I robotically follow her up the stairs and sit on the edge of my bed while I listen to her run the bath. The last thing I want to do is sit in there alone with only the images of the crash and Mason's broken body filling my mind, but I also don't have it in me to argue right now either.

She comes back in to tell me it's ready before pulling some clean clothes out of my closet and some underwear from my drawer. I'm grateful she's not expecting me to think for myself and thankful to get some fresh clothes. I might not be totally with it right now, but I know I'm still in the same clothes I was wearing Friday night, and they most definitely do not smell good.

She leaves the folded-up clothes on the counter, kisses my forehead and then leaves me to it.

With a sigh, I strip down and climb into the tub. The hot water surrounds me, and where I'd usually enjoy the feeling of the soothing water relaxing me, I feel nothing. I'm numb. It's like I left a part of myself on that road where I abandoned my car. I fear that without him waking up, I'm never going to find it again.

The silence around me is deafening, and it only makes the questions in my head louder. I'd put music on but have no idea where my phone is—not that I really want to listen to anything.

I allow myself to slide down until I'm fully submerged. I don't resurface until my lungs burn for air, and when I do, I make quick work of washing my hair and body. When he does wake up, he deserves for me to at least look like I've tried.

"Camila," my mom's panicked shout fills the room, and I jump from the bath. Something about her tone has me moving and flicking a towel around me as fast as I can. "We need to go, Nicky just called. He's waking up."

Fuck, fuck, fuck. I'm not there. I told them not to make me leave. I knew it was wrong.

My legs tremble as I try to pull on a pair of leggings.

My skin's still damp and I end up crashing to the ground in a heap in my haste to get back to the hospital.

"Are you okay?"

"Yeah, I'm coming. Get the car started."

Thankfully I manage to pull the rest of my clothes on slightly more efficiently, and, with sopping wet hair that's dripping down my back and soaking my hoodie, I run to the car.

My heart threatens to pound out of my chest and my nails dig into the leather beneath me. My legs bounce with my need to make my dad go faster, but there's no point in me demanding him to do so. He's the world's most cautious driver, even in these kinds of situations. According to my mom, he even drove like Miss Daisy when she was in labor with me, a story that I've always found amusing until this very moment.

I'm out of the car before he's even brought it to a stop. I hear them shouting behind me, but I don't stop. My only focus is getting up to his room as fast as I can.

I stumble up the stairs, my legs moving faster than my body can cope with, and by the time I crash through into the ward, my muscles are burning with exertion. There's a reason I don't make an effort to do sports, and this is why.

The nurses look up from their station as the door crashes back against the wall, but they all stay put when they see it's me. I've become part of the furniture the past two days, so they all know who I am at this point.

I race down the corridor, almost overshooting the door when I get to it. Swinging around the door frame, I come to an abrupt stop at the end of Mason's bed.

But he's not looking at me. His eyes are still shut.

"What happened? Mom said he woke up." I can barely get the words out between my heaving breaths.

"He was. He moved, he squeezed my hand, he moaned. I thought it was it, it was more than we've got from him so far, but then he just fell back to sleep."

"Fuck," I bark, the realization that our wait is going to continue for longer slamming into me. I fall down into the chair at the opposite side of Mason's bed to Nicky and take his hand in mine. "Come on, baby. Wake up for me, please," I beg, more tears slipping down onto my cheeks. I'd have thought I'd have run out by now, but it doesn't seem to be the case.

"I'm just going to grab a coffee," Nicky says, dropping a kiss to Mason's head and leaving me alone with him.

"It's time to wake up, Mase." I rub my thumb over his rough jaw, being careful of his cuts and bruises.

The machines have been taken away now. There's no beeping, nothing apart from the sound of his shallow breathing as he heals.

I stare at him, praying that he'll do something to show me he's coming back to me. I'm so focused on the stillness of his face that when his eyelids flicker, it actually scares me.

"Oh my god, Mason. Can you hear me? I'm here, baby. I'm right here. Everything's going to be okay."

There's nothing for long seconds and I start to wonder if I imagined it. But then, right as I'm starting to believe I hallucinated, he does it again, only this time they open. Not a lot, but they open nonetheless.

I move closer, taking both his hands in mine. "Can you hear me? Squeeze my hand if you can."

Then the most incredible thing happens. His fingers tighten in mine. "Oh my god, Mase." A sob rips from my throat and I carefully prop myself on the edge of his bed, being careful of the tubes he still has coming from his chest.

"They made me go home. Can you believe that? I've been here since the moment you arrived, and when they make me go, it's when you start waking up. Are you trying to tell me something with that?" I ask with a laugh, because I'm fully aware that he has no control over what his body does right now.

"Everyone's been here. Jake and Amalie, Ethan and his whiskey bottle, your mom, my parents. We're all here for you, Mase." I sigh when there are no other signs of him waking up.

"What the hell were you playing at?" I ask. "Do you have any idea how fucking scary it was to watch you run that light and a car impale itself in the side of yours? I thought you'd fucking died, Mase. I thought that was it. I already lost you for four years. I only just got you back and I thought you'd fucking died on me." My tears make my vision blurry, but when I look up from our joined hands, it's not enough to hide the pair of eyes that are staring back at me.

"Mason, fuck. Oh my god." I wipe my eyes with the backs of my hands and wait to see if he's going to do anything. The second I connect our hands once again, he squeezes them tightly.

His lips part, his tongue sneaking out to wet his dry lips.

"Wait, hang on." I reach over for the cup and straw that's been sitting unused for the past two days and fill it with some water. Lifting it to his mouth, he sips a little before I pull it away again and place it down.

I look into his dark eyes, my heart thundering in my chest as I read everything he wants to say to me. I see his fear, his confusion but also relief, and I hope that's there because I'm here with him right now.

When his lips part again, one single word manages to break free.

"Sorry."

The small amount of control I had on my emotions snaps and I cry. I'm desperate to crawl in beside him and feel his arms around me, proof that he's here and that he's awake, but I know I can't and it kills me.

"It's okay, baby. You're here and you're going to be fine. I love you. I love you so much."

His own eyes fill with tears, and when one trickles from the corner, I reach out and catch it with my thumb, cradling his cheek in my hand.

"Everything's going to be okay," I repeat, sensing that he needs to hear it again.

We're still staring at each other when Nicky comes back in, cradling her coffee in her hands.

"Mason? You're awake."

A small smile twitches at the corner of his lips when he sees her, but his eyes are starting to get heavy, and after another few seconds he's drifted back off to sleep.

37

MASON

I was aware that everyone had been here. I'd heard their voices, I'd felt their touch, I just wasn't able to open my eyes. It freaked me the fuck out the first time it happened, but hearing everyone around me talk and a few hazy memories, I quickly figured out what had happened and where I was.

No sooner had I got frustrated with the situation than I'd fall back to sleep and forget all about it, until the next time I woke again.

I knew Camila was here. I'd heard her voice many times and I could feel her tiny hand in mine. She was all I needed, and every time I heard her say that everything was going to be okay, I believed her. But it was one thing she said that gave me the strength to finally open my eyes and see her.

"I already lost you for four years. I only just got you back and I thought you'd fucking died on me."

The guilt that hit me hearing that statement had my eyes flying open. How could I be so fucking selfish? I should have been paying attention to where I was going, not busy thinking about the past, my dad, but instead, I once again caused Camila pain. Pain that I'm not going to be able to do anything about, other than to apologize, and that is nowhere near what she deserves after witnessing what she did and sitting beside me all this time.

Over the next few days, I manage to stay awake longer and longer. Every single time I open my eyes, she's there, sitting in the same chair, wearing the same clothes, looking equally as beautiful as she does exhausted, and I wish she'd take some time to look after herself.

"Hey, you're awake," she says, pulling her chair closer before standing and dropping a kiss to my lips.

"Hey," I say, my voice rough and croaky after being asleep for fuck knows how long.

"How are you feeling?"

"Better actually. I feel like I can breathe again. My head kills though."

"I'll call the nurse. Get you some more painkillers."

I want to say no, to keep it just the two of us, but I know she's doing the right thing. If I want to get out of this place anytime soon, then for once I need to learn to listen to those around me and do as I'm told.

I have no idea how many days might have passed. Sometimes I wake up and it's dark out, other times it's light. I have no sense of anything, and it's seriously disorientating.

"What day is it?" I ask Camila when I wake up once again to find her sitting in the chair beside me on her tablet.

"Friday."

I think for a few minutes.

"The game." Tonight's the final game of the season and the one to seal our fate. We've already secured our place in the state playoffs, but if we win tonight, then we finish as district champions, something none of us thought was even a possibility when Coach started getting us excited for it all those months ago.

Jake's aim was the playoffs. He said he didn't care if that meant we came first or fourth, as long as we placed, but we all knew that he was desperate for that top spot. And he deserves it after the work he's put in. He deserves to be able to celebrate something.

"What do you think I'm doing? Amalie is sending me updates. It's a tight game by the sounds of it."

She turns the screen to me and hits play on a video that she's sent through. Every muscle in my body aches to be out on that field with them. After missing those games because I had to work, I'd hoped that we'd be able to finish the season as a team, but it seems fate had other ideas for me.

"You've still got the playoffs. There's still a chance you'll be okay to play."

"I know. It just sucks that I can't even be there."

"You've got loads of games ahead of you yet, Mase. Just think of all the college games to come."

"If I get in."

"You'll get in. Stop worrying. Your grades are good, and you're shit hot on the field. Maddison would be crazy not to accept you."

I let out a sigh, hoping that she's right. From as early as I can remember, Dad and I talked about me playing for the Panthers and that dream is now in touching distance and the risk of fucking it all up is getting higher and higher.

"I need that fucking scholarship." I've got no hope without it.

"You'll get it, but you might not need it after all. We still have no idea what your dad's left you."

The memory of sitting in Julia's house slams into me, I gave her my bank details. I wonder if she's already passed them on?

A more pressing thought takes over. "Have you told my mom?"

She nods. "I have. I hope that's okay. They wanted to know why we were where we were and in separate cars. I didn't have it in me to make something up."

"No, it's fine. How'd she take it?"

"She was upset. Shocked. She hasn't said so, but I'm pretty sure she's been out to his grave."

I nod, wondering how she's really taking it. She's been managing to get her life back on track since moving in with the Lopezes. I fear hearing about Dad might send her spiraling back down again.

"She's doing okay though. Work gave her this week off to be with you and the boys, but she hasn't touched a drop of alcohol. She's good, Mase. Just worry about yourself, yeah?"

I can't help it. After spending the past four years basically doing her job for her when she was unable to look after herself, let alone her kids, I'm scared of going backward. We might be living under someone else's roof right now, but my life is better than it's been in a really, really long time, and I don't want that to change.

Sucking in a deep breath, I prepare to ask a question I'm not sure I want an answer to. "Cami?" She turns her eyes on me and my chest aches that I've put her through this after everything else. "W-what happened to the other car— the people in the other car?"

She reaches for my hand, and I panic. "She's fine,

Mason." Relief bubbles up to the point I think I might actually burst into tears. "Your mom has seen her and spoken to her. Everything's going to be okay."

I nod, images of how different things could have been playing out in my mind.

My thoughts are put on hold as Camila suddenly jumps up from the chair. "They did it. They fucking did it."

A smile breaks across my face.

"They won?"

"They did. *You* did. You're a champ."

"I didn't—"

"Don't you fucking dare. You've given your all to that team, don't you dare downplay this right now."

———

Two hours later, we hear them before we see them. But seconds after there's a commotion out in the corridor, Jake, Ethan, and the rest of the team come crashing into my hospital room. Their excitement is infectious, and for the first time since Camila told me, a sense of pride and achievement races through me.

"We fucking did it," Jake cheers, coming over to my side and pulling me to him, albeit carefully. "We're fucking champions, bro. We did it."

I might hate that they were forced to do it without me, but Camila was right, I am a part of this, and as the excitement reaches a whole new level inside my tiny hospital room, I can't help but get carried away with it. Even Ethan seems to have left his issues at the door as he laughs and jokes with the rest of the team.

"Not that I don't want you guys here, but aren't you supposed to be celebrating your win right now?"

Everyone but Jake, Ethan, Amalie and Camila have left, and I've been waiting for them to make their excuses to leave as well.

"We are," Jake says, pulling Amalie down onto his lap.

"No, you're hanging out in a shitty hospital room when you should be fucking shit up."

"It can wait," Ethan says, shocking the hell out of me.

"You're telling me your place isn't party central right now?"

"Nope, not without you, man."

"Don't stop enjoying yourself because I'm stuck in here. You guys deserve it."

"Yeah, well, we'll still deserve it when you're out of here and can celebrate with us." I smile at my two best friends. They might be their own brand of fucked up in certain ways, but fuck, I couldn't ask for two better boys to have my back.

"I appreciate that, but I really don't want to stop you."

"It's all good. Plus, I think we can probably all agree that I need to slow down at bit."

"Yeah, about that."

All eyes turn on Ethan as he lets out a huge breath. "I'm sorry I've been a bit of a fuck-up recently." Jake goes to say something, but Ethan doesn't give him the chance. "My dad's been cheating on my mom. She left a few weeks ago."

"Oh fuck. I'm so sorry."

Amalie reaches over and places her hand on his shoulder in support when he drops his head into his hands, and I don't miss the look that passes between her and my girl. It makes me wonder if they'd already figured this out.

"Where's she gone?"

"To my grandparents in Connecticut. She wanted me to go but..." He blows out a breath. "My home's here. I couldn't leave but—fuck."

Silence falls around us.

"I just needed to get it off my chest. I know I've been acting like a dick and I'm sorry, I just—"

"It's okay, Ethan. We get it. Families are hard fucking work. Parents are hard fucking work. All of us in this room know that. Whatever you need. We're here."

"I appreciate that. Anyone want a drink? I just need to get some air." The girls ask for a coffee, but Jake and I go without.

"Fuck."

"Well I guess that explains the missing photographs." My brows draw together at Camila's words. "You locked yourself in his house for two days. Don't tell me you didn't notice all their family photos had gone." When my face stays blank, she rolls her eyes at me.

"What? My dad had died, I needed a release."

Seeing as no one looks shocked, I assume that Camila has filled everyone in on what's happened in my life and excuses my lack of attention. Not that I ever really gave Ethan's family photos a second glance. I do feel for him though, a family breakup can be seriously fucking tough.

"I wish he'd have said something sooner," Amalie muses.

"Explains a lot though. He idolizes his dad for the success he's had, so knowing he's betrayed his mom must be a serious kick in the teeth."

"I wonder who the woman is," Camila adds.

"I'm sure he'll tell us when he's ready," I say, knowing exactly how he's feeling right now.

"Well, that seriously soured the mood, huh?" Jake says with a laugh, seeing as we're supposed to be celebrating.

"We're in a hospital, it's not exactly the best place for a party."

"We'll make up for it once you're back on your feet."

Ethan reappears about twenty minutes later. His shoulders seem wider than when he walked out, and I can't help but wonder if having the weight of his secret lifted was exactly what he needed.

They stay for another hour, the guys filling me in on every play in tonight's game and how they managed to turn things around at the last minute to take the lead and the title.

"Playoffs, here we fucking come!" Jake announces, slamming his closed fist to his heart.

"We've got this. Well, you guys have. Only time will tell for me."

"You'll be there. I won't have it any other way."

When they see me starting to fade, they make their excuses and leave us to it. I feel bad that they're only heading to Aces for a burger and not to a party, but I can't exactly make them.

"Can I?" Camila asks, nodding to the space on the bed next to me.

I shift over the best I can, the pain from my ribs taking my breath for a few seconds, but we just manage to squeeze on. Having her in my arms feels so damn good, and I never want to let her go.

EPILOGUE
CAMILA

Mason ended up staying in the hospital for eight days in all. After the fourth day, my parents demanded that I leave each night so I could get some sleep. I argued, of course, but in the end, they won and I can't deny that I felt a hell of a lot better after a full night's sleep in a bed and not just a series of catnaps in a hard hospital chair.

I did put my foot down, however, when my parents and Nicky started talking about getting Mason's room ready for him. The three of them looked horrified when I announced that he would be moving in with me, but to be fair to them, they didn't argue. They must have known it wasn't one they were ever going to win.

They told me that they'd allow it for now, while he recovers, but that it would need to be readdressed in the near future. I fought hard to hide my eye roll. I have no clue what's going to happen when Nicky decides to move out, but until then, I have no intention of allowing Mason to sleep anywhere but my bed.

My dad had to go back to New York. Mom was

planning on going with him again, but with everything that happened, she insisted on staying home and helping Nicky out with Mason and the boys. We both told her it wasn't necessary, but she wouldn't have it.

So the following Monday morning, the three of us escorted Mason home and up to my bedroom. I hadn't told him about his sudden bedroom move, but the smile that curled at his lips as we moved slowly to my room told me that he was happy about it.

I refused to go back to school, much to my mom's horror, but I'd already missed one week. What was another really going to do? I emailed our teachers and got schoolwork so neither of us fell behind, and we spent the afternoons working.

Spending time together was incredible. We were able to make up for our lost time and talk about everything that happened during our years apart, and Mason totally opened up about what happened after his dad left.

My heart bled for him, and I so wished he could have just talked to me at the time instead of building his walls up so high that I had no choice but to be pushed out. I might understand why he did it, but that doesn't mean I'll ever be happy about the years we lost.

True to his word, Ethan held off the celebration party until Mason was able to attend, and that's where we're headed tonight. Mason's still in pain, mostly with his ribs, but he's insistent that he's well enough to go. As much as I want to demand he stays in bed until he's fully recovered, I also know that being stuck inside the house is driving him crazy. I can't really argue with him that sitting on Ethan's sofa won't really be that much different from sitting at home.

He's not able to drink due to the pain meds that he's

still on, but he's not all that bothered about drinking anyway. Something tells me that's a side effect of Chelsea taking advantage of him the last two times.

Without being at school, we've missed the gossip firsthand, but Amalie was very quick to tell me that Chelsea never reappeared the Monday after Ethan's party. No one knows where she's gone—not that anyone really cares. I can't help but feel sad for her. Yes, she's a bitch, but there's a reason she does what she does, and I get the feeling that her life could be very different to what we all assume it is. She's all designer labels and caring what everyone thinks, but underneath that, I think there's a girl who's just desperate to be liked and fit in. One day we might get the chance to know the real Chelsea. I guess that all depends if she decides to show her face again.

Stepping out of the shower, I dry myself off, slather my body in my favorite moisturizer and slide my new dress up my body. Mom and I went shopping the other afternoon to give Mason and Nicky a little time together. The moment I saw it, I knew I needed it. It's nothing special, just a short little black dress with a lace overlay. It's simple, fits me perfectly and makes me feel like a million dollars. I also have a sneaking suspicion that Mason will like it too.

After blow drying my hair and applying my makeup, I make my way back to my bedroom to see what he thinks.

Pushing the door open, I find him sitting on the edge of the bed dressed in real clothes for the first time since his accident. After ditching the hospital gown, he's lived in joggers, not that you'll hear me complaining because they certainly look good on him when they're riding low and giving me a hint of what he's got hiding beneath.

His eyes lift as I step inside the room and they widen as they take me in.

"Fucking hell, Cami-bear. Are you trying to kill me?"

"You like?"

"I more than fucking like. Come here." He stands from the bed. It's awkward and I can tell by the frown that mars his forehead that it hurts, but he doesn't complain. Instead, he holds his hand out for me and I slide mine into it. I take a step toward him before he lifts his arm, encouraging me to spin for him. I do it because I'll do pretty much anything he asks of me.

"Do you have any idea how badly I want to bend you over and fuck you in this dress?" I bite down on my bottom lip and look up at him through my lashes. "Don't fucking do that," he growls, reaching down to rearrange himself in his pants. "How long did the doctors say until these ribs will be healed?"

"A while yet," I say with a laugh. "We'll just have to be creative."

"Hmmm..." He drops his head into the crook of my neck, breathing me in. "I like the sound of that." His hand slips around my waist and down to my ass. He pulls me up against him until he hisses with pain, but the unmistakable length of his cock presses into my stomach.

"We do not have time for that. Amalie will be here any minute to pick us up."

"I'm sure it would be quick. It's been over two weeks since you touched me."

"Even more reason to make it even more memorable by waiting a little longer."

He groans as I step away from him and slide my feet into my shoes. "I'll make it worth your while," I say with a wink.

"How's that?"

I move to leave the room, but I stop to whisper in his ear on the way out. "I may not be wearing any underwear." I am, but he doesn't need to know that right now.

"Fucking hell." He bites down on his knuckle, a pained look in his eyes. "Come on. I think I just heard her car."

He mutters something behind me, but I don't make the words out as I start to descend the stairs.

"Whoa, Ethan really pulled out all the stops for this one," I say as we attempt to get near his house. There are cars lining the road leading toward it, and when we walk up the driveway, we find it full. The music booms from inside and there are people everywhere who've come to celebrate the team's win, or to just make the most of the free alcohol courtesy of Ethan's dad who's been even more free with his credit card since the truth about what he's been up to has come out.

Turns out he's been seeing a woman from Michigan for months. His mom had known for a while before she handed him divorce papers and announced she was leaving. Ethan was totally blindsided by it all. According to Ethan, his dad's still seeing the woman. He's tried to convince Ethan to meet her, but he's point-blank refused, although Ethan's worried he's not going to have much choice in the matter soon because his dad has been talking about moving her in. He's angry, understandably so, and he has no idea how to release it other than to get fucked up and fuck anything that moves. He's trying to rein it in, but he's struggling and none of us really know how to help him other than to listen when he is willing to talk.

We make our way through the house and we head out to the kitchen. "I see what you mean about the photographs. I have no idea how I didn't notice before."

"You had other things on your mind."

A few days after Mason got home, he logged onto his internet banking to find out if Julie had organized for whatever his dad had left him to be transferred. His eyes nearly popped out of his head when he saw the figure staring back at him. He got on the phone immediately to her to find out if there had been some kind of mistake, but Julie assured him it was correct. I literally watched the weight of worrying about paying for college and having to support his family leave him. It was incredible. Since then, he's been smiling just like I remember from before his dad left and his life spiraled out of control. He's truly been the Mason I remembered and always hoped was still in there somewhere, even if he is a little battered and bruised right now.

"Are you okay? Do you need to sit down?"

"I'm fine. Stop worrying. Let's get you a drink, you need to relax."

"I'm just—"

"Trust me, if I need to sit down then I will, but right now, I just want to try to be normal."

I nod, continuing beside him and following Jake and Amalie to the kitchen where we find Ethan.

"The party's really starting now, ladies and gentlemen. The captain is in da house!" He lifts his drink in salute to Jake before downing it. The rest of the team who are all huddled in the kitchen cheer while Jake laughs at Ethan's antics. It's nice to see him being his usual crazy self.

I have a drink with Amalie while Mason catches up with the guys before he turns to me. "Dance with me."

"Are you sure—"

"Stop it." His fingers press against my lips. "I just want a normal night with my incredible girlfriend to thank her for being by my side through all of this."

My heart swells at his words. "I'd love to dance with you."

He slips his hand into mine and he pulls me toward the living room turned dance floor. He twists me into his body and wraps his arms around my waist. We don't really dance. I can tell by the slight narrowing of his eyes that he's in too much pain, but he refuses to let it stop him. I'll humor him for a song or two, and then I'm going to make him sit his ass down to rest.

Goosebumps prick my skin as he runs his hands up my waist until he threads his fingers into my hair and tilts my head so he can capture my lips. We stand in the middle of the dance floor and kiss like we're the only ones in the room. I pour everything I've always felt for him into it. It was always meant to be Mason and me. We may have had a few bumps in the road, but we finally found where we're meant to be.

Pulling away from my lips, he tucks his face into my neck. His breath races over my sensitive skin, and I shiver in his arms.

"Cami-bear?" he whispers into my ear.

"Yeah?"

"You're going to be my wife one day. I hope you know that." A wide smile curls my lips and my heart sings. I thought I'd lost my best friend, the one who made my heart beat a little faster and every second of my days better, but it seems our time apart might just have been to prove one thing. We were always meant to be together.

———

I eventually manage to get Mason to sit on one of Ethan's giant sofas. The others join us along with some girl that's attached herself to Ethan like a fucking rash. She's not Chelsea, so I guess we can't really complain.

I'm busy watching everyone around us when a girl catches my eye. She doesn't look like a typical Rosewood student, and she's definitely not someone I've seen here before. She's dressed head to toe in black with leather cuffs around her wrists and fishnet tights with giant holes on her legs, finished off with a pair of biker boots.

Her eyes run over our group before she stalks over. I knock my knee against Mason's to get his attention, and he soon spots who I'm pointing out and watches her approach.

"So, these must be your dumb jock friends. Jesus, you're so cliché it actually hurts to fucking look at you," she says, glaring at Ethan.

Whoa, who the fuck is this chick?

Ethan's eyes turn hard, the muscle ticking in his neck as he stares up at her. Jake tenses beside Amalie, who looks as shocked as I feel.

"And you are?" Jake asks, his chest swelling as he stands and stares her down. She's short, probably shorter than me, and she has to tip her head back to look him in the eyes, but she doesn't cower one bit.

She laughs in his face, proving that she has no idea who he is. Well, that or she really doesn't give a shit.

Ethan shifts the girl on his lap to the other side. "This..." He points up to the biker chick with a snarl on his face. "This is Raelynn, my darling never-to-be fucking stepsister."

"Your what?" Mason asks, his mouth gaping open.

"Don't get too used to her being around. She's not staying. Not if I have anything to do with it."

They stare at each other and something crackles between them. Ethan was already struggling enough; she's surely the last thing he needs. Only time will tell.

Ethan's story is NOW AVAILABLE!

ACKNOWLEDGMENTS

It's no secret that I fell in love with Jake the moment he smacked me upside the head last summer but Mason... swoon. I love him so hard.

This book has been the longest I've written for a very long time. It wasn't meant to be this long but man, Camila and Mason just kept it coming and I was powerless but to keep writing.

I hope their story has touched you like it did me. I'm so excited now to be working on Savage, the third book in the series.

As always, there are so many people I need to thank for supporting me with this book and helping to bring it to fruition. Michelle, as always, thank you for alpha reading and giving me your honesty. Sam D, well what can I say, you've already claimed Mason as yours, you fell in love with him so hard. Thank you for putting up with all my editing errors and falling in love with him anyway.

Deanna, Lindsay, Suzanne and Tracy, thank you so much once again for beta reading, for dropping everything and losing yourself in everything Paine.

Sam B, I already know that Thorn's release wouldn't have been so awesome if it wasn't for all the hard work you did in the background. THANK TOU for everything you do, I literally don't know how I did all this without you.

Ellie, at My Brother's Editor, once again, thank you for editing this over the holidays and putting up with all my Britishisms.

Evelyn, thank you for being awesome and proofreading Paine to make it as perfect as possible.

I can't let this pass without a huge shout out to Michelle Lancaster and her incredible photograhy skills, and of course the gorgeous Lockie for being the most awesome Mason I could have imagined.

A HUGE THANK YOU to you for giving Thorn a chance and for following the Rosewood boys' story through to now. If you're still reading then I hope you're looking forward to Ethan's story. And who knows, it might be the last, or it might not. Is there anyone you'd love to read more about? Let me know.

And finally, as always, a huge thank you to my husband and daughter for putting up with me having my head stuck in my laptop all the time so I can continue on this crazy journey.

Until next time.

Tracy xo

ABOUT THE AUTHOR

Tracy Lorraine is a new adult and contemporary romance author. Tracy has recently-ish turned thirty and lives in a cute Cotswold village in England with her husband, baby girl and lovable but slightly crazy dog. Having always been a bookaholic with her head stuck in her Kindle Tracy decided to try her hand at a story idea she dreamt up and hasn't looked back since.

Be the first to find out about new releases and offers. Sign up to my newsletter here.

If you want to know what I'm up to and see teasers and snippets of what I'm working on, then you need to be in my Facebook group Tracy's Angels.

Keep up to date with Tracy's books at
www.tracylorraine.com

ALSO BY TRACY LORRAINE

Falling Series

Falling for Ryan: Part One #1

Falling for Ryan: Part Two #2

Falling for Jax #3

Falling for Daniel (An Falling Series Novella)

Falling for Ruben #4

Falling for Fin #5

Falling for Lucas #6

Falling for Caleb #7

Falling for Declan #8

Falling For Liam #9

Forbidden Series

Falling for the Forbidden #1

Losing the Forbidden #2

Fighting for the Forbidden #3

Craving Redemption #4

Demanding Redemption #5

Avoiding Temptation #6

Chasing Temptation #7

Rebel Ink Series

Hate You #1

Trick You #2

Defy You #3

Play You #4

Inked (A Rebel Ink/Driven Crossover)

Rosewood High Series

Thorn #1

Paine #2

Savage #3

Fierce #4

Hunter #5

Faze (#6 Prequel)

Fury #6

Legend #7

Maddison Kings University Series

TMYM: Prequel

TRYS #1

TDYW #2

TBYS #3

TVYC #4

TDYD #5

Ruined Series

Ruined Plans #1

Ruined by Lies #2

Ruined Promises #3

Never Forget Series

Never Forget Him #1

Never Forget Us #2

Everywhere & Nowhere #3

Chasing Series

Chasing Logan

The Cocktail Girls

His Manhattan

Her Kensington

SAVAGE SNEAK PEEK
CHAPTER ONE

Ethan

The sound of his car pulling up in the driveway fills me with dread. I've avoided spending any time with my father since his secrets were exposed a few weeks ago, and, being the spineless prick that he is, he's allowed me the space. Any decent dad would force me to sit down to hear him out, but no... he ran. Ran back to *her,* no doubt.

My parents have been even more absent than usual recently—not that I'm complaining. It meant I had the place to myself and was able to do what the fuck I wanted whenever I wanted, just the way I liked it. But I had no idea that they weren't just on another one of Dad's work trips. The reality of it was that Mom had moved back in with her parents in Connecticut, and my dad was banging his assistant in Washington.

I shake my head, still refusing to fully accept what

he's done. I'm not ashamed to admit that he is my idol, and the fact that he's just screwed my mom over in the worst possible way shakes me to my core. The man I've always looked up to, who I thought was a god, just pissed all over everything I ever believed. I thought he was honest, trustworthy, honorable. But it seems that all of that was an act, a lie. All it took was a woman in a short skirt with an easy smile, and he ruined everything we had.

My fists curl as the sound of the front door slamming shut echoes through the empty house.

"Ethan?" My name booms up to me. I want to pretend I'm out, but he's just parked next to my car. There's no chance I'm going to get away with this. "Ethan?" he shouts again, his feet pounding on the stairs as he makes his way to my room.

His knock on the door is strong and assertive, and it makes me want to slam my fist into his ribs just to show him how fucking strong he really is.

When he still doesn't get a response from me, he pushes the door open anyway and walks inside.

"There you are, son. Didn't you hear me calling?"

Keeping my head down for a beat, I then turn toward him. He's wearing his standard suit and tie duo, the one I thought always made him look so powerful and successful, but now, I just roll my eyes. He's a joke.

I don't respond. He knows full well I heard but that I have no intention of talking to him. He didn't just betray my mom when he stuck his dick in that whore, he betrayed our whole family. Our name. Everything we stand for.

Ignoring the fact that I clearly have no interest in what he's got to say to me, he continues nonetheless. "I've got tickets to today's game. Thought it would be good for us to spend some time together."

Although the thought of the game is appealing, especially knowing that he'll have fucking epic seats, if it means sitting next to him and pretending everything is perfectly fine, then no thank you very much. "I'm good, thanks. I'm busy." I turn back to stare out the window. In reality, I'm doing fuck all, and the fact that I'm sitting on my bed with nothing turned on or even my cell in my hand should clue him in on that.

"Really?" he asks, the amusement in his tone pissing me the fuck off.

"Really."

"Ethan, come on. Don't be like that. I know you're pissed at me, but not everything is as it seems."

"Oh, really so you weren't dipping your pen in the office ink while being married to Mom, then?" He pales. "If I've got it so wrong, please, enlighten me, Father." I stand, stepping right in front of him. I'm taller and wider than him now, and I know how much he hates it. His neck ripples as he swallows. It's not with fear. This motherfucker's not scared of anything, especially not me.

"You wouldn't understand."

My teeth grind, and my chest swells with anger. "I'm not a fucking child," I seethe. Relationships are complicated, I get that. Things happen, I get that. But what I don't get is why he couldn't be a fucking adult about it and talk about it instead of fucking the first woman who crossed his path.

He stares me down, daring me to say exactly what's on my mind, but I refuse to acknowledge his behavior with that kind of attention.

"I had to pull some serious strings to get these. Are

you coming, or what? It's supposed to be an outstanding game." He waves the tickets in front of my face.

I haven't been to an NFL game in forever with him out of town, and the temptation of the roar of the crowd, the shared excitement, the knowledge that I can forget about my own bullshit life for sixty minutes is enough to have me agreeing, although I'm not happy about it.

A smile of achievement curls at Dad's lip, and I regret it instantly.

"I'll meet you downstairs in twenty. We'll go for steak after, too." Damn him, he knows I can't refuse the offer of steak.

With a nod of his head, he ducks out of my room, leaving me to stew in my anger some more.

Pulling my shirt over my head, I drop my joggers and step into my en suite. It might have been different if I'd have seen it coming, but my parents have always seemed so happy, so solid. While I watched my friends at school fall apart over the years when their families were ripped in two, I always felt grateful knowing that that would never happen to me. I was that confident in the love my parents had. So the day I got a tearful phone call from my mom, it wrecked me in a way I could never imagine.

"I'm so sorry, baby, b-but I'm not coming home. T-Things are over between your father and me."

I've watched people break when their girlfriends have split up with them, when their teams have lost, when they've failed the test they spent weeks studying for, but I never thought it would feel quite like it did in that moment.

She begged me to leave and move to Connecticut with her, pleaded with me that she couldn't lose me as well, but my life is here. Everything I have—besides her—is here. I can't just up and leave everything I've worked so hard for, or my friends who I know have my back no matter what.

As much as it gutted me to do it, I had to tell her that I was staying put. I had plans for my future, none of which included moving in with my grandparents. Although, now thinking about it, following my dad's footsteps to study business at UFC isn't all that appealing. I always wanted to be just like him, but now, I'm thinking being the opposite might not be so bad.

The drive to the stadium is in silence. Only the sound of Dad's V8 engine could be heard as I kept my eyes on the world passing by outside the window. I might have agreed to this, but I don't want him under any illusion that there's been any kind of truce between us. There's a very good chance I might never forgive him for this.

The game is exactly as I hoped. The excitement and roar of the crowd seeped into me the second we stepped foot inside the colossal stadium. My buzz as the cheerleaders shook their pom poms filled my stomach with the kind of tingles I only get when a football is involved. I live for this. Shutting the world out and focusing on one goal. I love the cheer of the crowd, knowing, whether playing or spectating, that I'm part of something bigger than just my little life.

I'm sure everyone around me thinks it's the attention of being a Bears player that I love, and yes that's part of it, but it's not all of it. Being beside my brothers, taking on the world together, means everything to me.

My focus is solely on the game and putting myself in the players' shoes. Playing in front of the Rosewood High crowd is a serious buzz; I can only imagine how those guys feel when they run out to this exuberant crowd.

It's a tight game, and it keeps us all on our toes

throughout. My heart's racing when the whistle blows for the final play, not knowing which way it's going to go.

I fall down onto my seat, the high from the game making me want to celebrate. It might not be my win, but fuck if I don't have the same response. There's nothing like a good party and a fuck after a successful game.

I glance around to see if there are any options for the latter, but when I look to my left, I find my dad looking back at me with a smile on his face and my excitement immediately vanishes. My mom has told me stories from what he was like in high school. They didn't get together until years after, partly due to his reputation. Am I just as bad as him? Am I destined to make the same mistakes when it comes to women?

"Ready to eat?" he asks as everyone starts to leave.

I'm not. The last thing I want is food right now, but I doubt I've got a chance of getting out of it. "Let's go." There's no enthusiasm in my voice, and the way my dad's eyes narrow, I know he doesn't miss it. It doesn't stop him from taking me to the most expensive steak house in the district though.

The atmosphere is heavy, the tension between us becoming seriously uncomfortable as he orders us both a fillet steak and sits back with his beer, practically waving it in my face after refusing to order one for me, claiming that I'm underage—which of course is true, but it doesn't stop him filling the house every weekend for me, or leaving his credit card for me to stock up with more should we run out.

"I know you're angry, Ethan. I understand that this was a shock, but things haven't been right between your mother and me for a very long time. We—"

"I don't care, Dad. You didn't need to cheat. There are a

million ways to deal with a failing relationship, and fucking your assistant isn't one of them."

He rears back slightly at my blunt tone.

"It's not like that with Ash." I raise a brow, not missing the fact he's talking about her in the present tense, like she's still very much a part of his life. "She was there for me as a friend long before anything happened."

"Spare me the details of your sordid little affair."

"Keep your voice down, Ethan. The whole town doesn't need to know our business."

A spiteful laugh falls from my lips. "And you don't think the gossip is going to be rife when they realize Mom's not coming back?"

He opens his mouth to respond but nothing comes out. "Listen, son," he says eventually, and my stomach drops. I should have known he had a hidden agenda with this spur of the moment daddy/son bonding day. "I know you're not going to be happy about this but—"

I blow out a slow breath as I prepare for the next bit of information that's going to rock my world.

"Ash is going to be moving in with us."

"She's fucking what?"

"Look, I know this isn't ideal. I hadn't planned on asking her yet, but things are tough for her in Washington right now. She's lost her apartment and—"

"I don't give a fuck, Dad. We're not a fucking homeless shelter for women you randomly pick up."

His face turns beet red with anger. His eyes narrow and his lips twitch. I recognize it as the look he gets when he's trying to keep his shit together. "It's my house, Ethan. If I want her there, then she'll be there."

Well, isn't that just fucking great.

"It might be your house, but you're never there. Are

you expecting me to play house with this woman, or is she going to disappear with you for weeks at a time?"

"She'll be with me, but—"

Fuck my life, there's another but. I stare at him, my expression blank as I wait for the next blow.

"Her daughter will be coming with her and enrolling at Rosewood. I'm going to need you to take care of her while she settles in." I wait for him to tell me that he's joking, but at no point do his lips twitch into a smile. "She's a lovely girl. I think you'll like her."

FALLING FOR THE FORBIDDEN SNEAK PEEK

CHAPTER ONE

Falling down on my bed, I blow out a long breath and tell myself that everything will be okay.

I had plans for this summer—a few weeks of fun before uni starts. The girls and I had been looking at last-minute holiday deals, and we had tickets for a music festival...but then my dad swooped in, in that way that he does, and ruined everything.

I knew it was coming.

I just wasn't expecting it quite yet.

I'd hoped agreeing to study what he wanted me to and working for him was enough—apparently not.

I decided a few years ago that I wasn't going to move away to study. I mostly love my life in London, and I loved living with Mum. I'm not ashamed to admit that she's one of my best friends. It was only as I started looking at universities that my dad piped up and told me that I would be studying accountancy and finance at The London School of Economics. He'd done his research and decided it was the best place for me to learn my trade so I could enter the family business.

I just about managed to contain my laughter when he emphasised the word *family*.

I've no idea how long I lie on my bed trying to convince myself that moving into his house with his new wife and her son isn't the worst thing to ever happen to me, but eventually my stomach rumbling has me moving. I sit on the edge of the bed and take in all my half-unpacked boxes. A large sigh falls from my lips. If I don't find everything a home, maybe I won't have to stay. I know it's wishful thinking. This is it for me now.

Disappointment floods me as I make my way through the silent house. It's not that I was expecting a welcome party or anything, but someone being here would have been nice. Someone to help me carry everything up to my room would have been even nicer. Since Dad moved in with Jenny a few years ago, I've been told to treat this place like my home.

It will never be.

It's just a house, a show home, a shell in which I'm scared to touch anything for fear of making a mess. Home is a place with character, with mess from day-to-day living, with people who love and care for you.

My dad isn't a bad man, per se, but he's not exactly what you'd describe as a doting father. Everything he does is for his own gain—if it happens to help others in the process, that's just a bonus.

My step mum, Jenny, is lovely. She really is, but I can't help feeling like she's just a little bit...broken. She makes all the right comments and does all the right things. She's a great mum. But there's such sadness in her eyes.

The fridge is full, as usual. It's strange, because I've never witnessed anyone eating more than a slice of toast or an apple in this kitchen.

I fix myself a salad with the unopened packets of fruit and vegetables, but it doesn't really have the effect I needed it to have. Being here makes me feel kind of empty, and no amount of lettuce leaves is going to fill the void after moving out of the flat Mum and I shared for the past few years.

Rummaging through the cupboards, I can't help smiling when I find a stash of naughty stuff hiding at the back.

Pulling my hair back into a messy bun, I put my thoughts to the side and set about making something that will make me feel just a little bit better.

The sun's just about to set, casting an orange glow throughout the kitchen. It almost makes it feel warm and inviting—almost. My mouth waters as I pour melted chocolate over the crushed biscuits and marshmallows I've managed not to eat already. Standing in only a vest and a small pair of hot pants, I decide to make myself a hot chocolate, grab a blanket, and enjoy my bowl of goodness out on the deck with a magazine. Chocolate makes everything that little bit better. If I eat enough, it might make me forget what this summer's actually going to be like for me.

I'm just waiting for the kettle to boil when a shiver runs down my spine. I'm sure it's just the size of the house that freaks me out. I've seen enough horror films to know there are plenty of hiding places in a place this big.

I'm still for a second, but when I don't hear anything, I continue with what I was doing. That is, until a deep rumbling voice has every nerve in my body on alert.

"Wow, step daddy sure is attracting the young ones these days." His voice is slurred, his anger palpable. It makes goosebumps prick my skin and a giant lump form in my throat. "You look too pure. Too innocent to be with that prick," he spits.

There's no love lost between my dad and my stepbrother, that's not news to me, but the viciousness of his voice right now makes me wonder what their relationship is really like. My dad might be many things, but he wouldn't cheat on Jenny—he loves her too much.

I can't remember the last time I saw him, but there's no way he can't know it's me. Who the hell else would be cooking in his kitchen? Deciding he's just trying to rile me up, I go to collect my stuff and get out of his way. Unfortunately, he seems to have other ideas.

His breath tickles up my neck moments before the heat of his body warms my back.

"You came here for the wrong man. I can put that right, though." The alcohol on his breath surrounds me. It's a reminder that there's a good chance he has no idea what he's doing right now.

The softness of his nose running up the length of my neck has tingles racing through my traitorous body. I don't realise he's smelling me until he blows out a long breath and the scent of alcohol hits me once again. I turn to leave, but his hands slam on the counter behind me and cage me in.

"Look at me," he demands.

"Let me go, Ben."

If he's surprised to discover it's me, he doesn't show it. If anything, his eyes shine with delight as he takes in every inch of my face before focusing on my lips. My stomach flips, knowing where his thoughts are.

Something passes over his face but it's gone too quickly to be able to identify. He pushes himself from the counter and away from me. No more words are said, but when he gets to the door, he looks back over his shoulder and runs his eyes over my body. They hold a warning I don't really understand.

Once he's disappeared from sight, I sag back against the counter. What the hell was that?

After putting half of the rocky road on a tray in the fridge, I forgo sitting outside and instead take my spoils to my room to hide. There's stuff everywhere in my room and, unlike the rest of this house, it makes me feel a little more relaxed.

Since the day Ben and I were introduced by our parents, we've not really had any kind of relationship. He's pretty much stayed out of my way and, in turn, I've done the same. It's not all that much of a task. When I'm here, he spends almost every minute somewhere else. When he's home, he's moody, arrogant, and generally a prick, so I'm more than happy to stay out of his way.

It's just a shame he's so damn pretty to look at. As the years have passed, he's only become more attractive, too. I've no idea if it's just his job or if he works out as well because every inch of him seems to be toned to perfection.

Jenny spends most of her time apologising for his attitude and trying to explain that he's got a lot going on. I'm yet to discover what that is. As far as I can tell, he seems to be your average twenty-year-old guy who'd rather be off his arse drunk or with a woman than spending time at home with his parents.

By the time I've dug my way to the bottom of the bowl, I feel pretty sick. There's still no sign of my dad or Jenny, but the music pounding from Ben's room across the hallway leaves no doubt as to what kind of mood he's in.

DOWNLOAD NOW to continue Lauren and Ben's story.

Printed in Great Britain
by Amazon